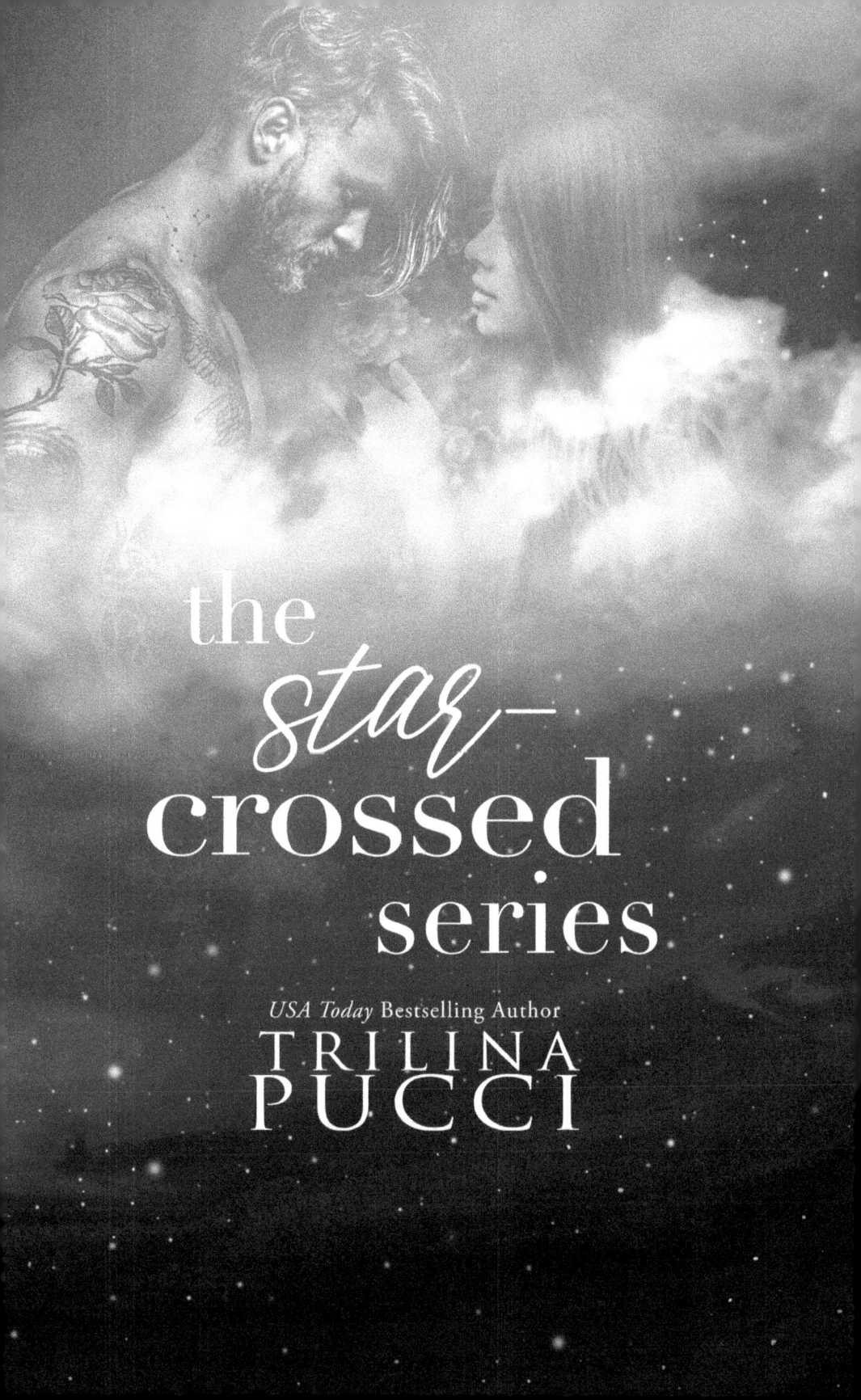

the *star-* crossed series

USA Today Bestselling Author

TRILINA PUCCI

just like heaven

USA Today Bestselling Author

TRILINA PUCCI

Sutton—April, end of junior year

"Hey, guys," Aubrey calls, looking over at Piper and me. I glance over my shoulder, realizing I've lost myself in a bunch of vintage magazines displayed neatly in a cart outside of a quaint little boutique bookstore.

"Check this out."

She holds up a piece of paper that looks like some kind of advertisement. Piper walks over, resting her chin on Aubrey's shoulder, reading whatever's in her hand. But before I can peek at what they're staring at, Aubs looks up at me, smiling brightly.

"We have to do this."

I shake my head, holding out my hand for the paper, wondering what the hell she's talking about. Instead of showing me, Aubrey grabs my outstretched palm.

"Just keep an open mind, Sut."

She wags her brows, opening the french door to the tea shop behind her, making a bell chime above the door.

"What does the paper say, Aubs? Hand it over."

I roll my eyes, already knowing this has "*dumb idea*" written all over it, but that doesn't diminish the grin on my face.

She passes it to me just as she lets my hand go, turning toward Piper, who's already lifting the top of a metal container to smell what's inside. I gaze around the dimly lit shop, past black walls and Turkish rugs to a gold-painted Victorian buffet. It's stocked with dried herbs and leaves, all in glass apothecary jars.

My eyes drop down at the creased white paper.

Tea leaf readings. Today only. $10.

I glance up as Piper says, "Aubs, just give me your ten, and I'll be happy to tell you that you're about to meet the love of your life and win the lottery."

We giggle, but we're silenced as someone behind us clears their throat. The three of us swing around simultaneously to deep-set dark brown eyes staring back at us, so dark they almost look black.

The old woman smirks, pointing her finger at Piper, all her metal bracelets jingling as she does.

"No lottery. But maybe true love."

Piper nudges me as I reach for my hair, fidgeting. Aubrey pushes through us, bold as ever, her ten-dollar bill readied in her hand.

"Ten, right? I'm so in."

The woman accepts the money, then motions to the small table near the bay window. Streams of light filter in, blocked only by the shade from the trees outside. She points to a seat, saying, "Sit," before walking around to the other side of the table, sweeping her long skirt up before seating herself.

Aubrey plops down onto the chair as Piper and I stand behind her with piqued curiosity, glancing at each other and trying not to smile. The woman flips over a gold-rimmed porcelain teacup, pouring in water and adding some herbs. My nose scrunches up at the smell, but she looks up, making me dart my head down.

Whoops.

Aubrey takes a whiff and laughs, "Gnarly," but the woman says nothing as she places a deck of tarot cards on the table.

Piper furrows her brow. "I thought it was a tea reading?"

Those dark eyes flick up, the hint of a smile on her lips. "It is."

Piper's eyes swing to mine, both of us still trying not to smile, watching as she shuffles the cards before looking at Aubrey and saying, "Drink. All of it at once. Then turn the cup over."

I'm staring, fascinated, as Aubrey gulps the tea back, doing what she's told.

The woman lifts the cup, staring down at the broken pieces of herbs strewn over the table. An indent forms between her eyes as she flips over a card. She stares at it, a heart with three swords stabbed into it.

That can't be good.

She goes back to the leaves and then flips another card, her hand immediately covering it before she shakes her head.

"What does it say?" Aubrey blurts out. "Is my future that dismal? Great. There goes my hope for Chase."

"Don't make her state the obvious," Piper chuckles under her breath, but the woman's head lifts, eyes locked on mine.

"This card." She holds up the heart with the swords. "It means heartbreak." I dart my eyes to Piper, slightly freaked-out that the woman is staring at me so intensely. "And this one—" She holds up the one she'd covered. A grim reaper dressed as a knight riding a horse. "—this means death, endings."

"But I didn't drink the tea," I whisper, not knowing what to say, drawing my arms behind me.

"Mon amie, the stars and moon are already in motion." She drops the card in her hand next to the other, my eyes following. "Your love will end tragically—he won't save you."

I lift my gaze, words stuck in my throat as she looks deeply into my eyes.

"But *you* will save him."

Chills explode over my body, eyes searching hers, almost feeling like I want to cry. Like I can feel the end of a story I've never read.

Piper grabs my hand, giggling, "Oh my God," before covering her mouth as she pulls me out of the store. I glance back at the woman, who's watching me the whole way out. Aubrey joins, laughing hysterically.

They're both speaking at the same time as I blink, trying to make sense of what just happened.

"What was that?" ... "She was so weird. Your love will end tragically... um, okay, freak."

Piper wipes a tear from her eye from laughing so hard as we hurry down the street before our feet slow, and their amusement tapers off.

Aubrey smiles, holding up the ten-dollar bill that she apparently took back, shaking it. "Let's get cupcakes since I didn't get my fucking leaves read by the witch."

Piper claps her hands with a gleeful "Yes. Sugar is life" as I smile, turning toward the store, still weirded out. I shift my face to Aubrey's to say something, but my words are cut off.

"Holy fuckballs, who's that?" Aubrey snaps, grabbing my hand and pointing toward the street. My head follows, goose bumps blooming over my fair skin before my eyes land on a car full of guys passing in a matte-black Mustang.

Whoa. They do *not* belong here.

It's like one of those movie moments—the car rolling by slowly, my breath held as I lick my lips—locked in a moment I'm trying to memorize and live at the same time.

The sandy-haired driver has a cigarette dangling from his full lips. He lifts his chin, showing off a jawline that looks like it could take a punch or makes you want to run your tongue over it all the way to the tattoo on his neck.

Jesus, he's the definition of bad ideas with one hand on the steering wheel as the other hangs lazily out of the window. His fingers, adorned with thick black rings, tap to the beat of the music filtering from the window.

But if the music isn't enough to draw scowls as they come to a stop at the crosswalk, his foul mouth does the job.

"It's rude to point," Piper offers, lowering Aubrey's finger. "But damn. When did *Sons of Anarchy* move in? That's hot."

Hot isn't the word. That's too tame for them. I don't even need to completely see them to know that.

The engine growls, idling, making me blink rapidly from my trance. I tug my hand from Aubrey, stepping forward, and loop my arm around a black lamppost, my curiosity urging me on for a better look.

With my mouth slightly agape, I let the tip of my sneaker hang over the edge of the sidewalk. I look stupid, but I don't care. It's not every day that a bunch of tattooed outsiders find themselves in a place like St. Simeon.

"Holy shit. St. Simeon just became interesting." Aubrey laughs behind me, pulling me backward.

I'm nodding, captivated by the tattoo on the driver's hand, trying to make out what it is, as two women make their way across the crosswalk. The Miss Manners duo all but clutch their pearls as they stare at Main Street's newest fascinations through the windshield.

From where I stand, I can only see the driver's profile.

"Ugh. I can't see his whole face."

Aubrey clutches my hand, settling shoulder to shoulder with me as the car's engine revs—making me jump, Aubrey laugh, and the women move faster.

"Animals," she snarks, shaking her head.

The driver flicks his cigarette toward the street, laughing as one of the women gasps.

He's an asshole, not an animal. But that laugh—so deep and carnal. Piper comes up on the other side of me, staring up at my face with a grin.

"I smell the need for a confession coming on. No hate. That jawline alone puts him in my dream rotation."

I giggle as Aubrey exhales, "Jesus," and fans herself.

"It's a good thing we go to Catholic school—because those dudes' vibes were immaculate, and staring at them definitely got me pregnant."

Piper reaches behind me, shoving Aubrey's shoulder. "You have to be a virgin for that..."

"Shut your blasphemous mouth. I am still a virgin because anal counts in the tally too, bitch."

They start playfully sparring back and forth, but I'm not paying attention. My eyes are on the set of taillights turning the corner. Until the feeling of someone watching me has my head shifting to look over my shoulder.

The woman with those dark eyes and even darker words makes the sign of the cross before walking back inside the shop.

"Dad?" The door slams behind me as I walk inside my house. "Mom? Hello? Anyone?"

"Sutton," I hear my mom call from her office off the entryway. "In here."

Peeking my head inside the door, I see her sitting at her desk, papers littered across the surface. Her sleek blonde tresses shine like she's in one of those hair commercials as her blue eyes affix to mine.

"How was your day, kid? Aubrey and Piper exhaust you too much with all the shopping? I still don't understand why you need to shop for clothes this much when you wear a uniform most days."

I shrug with a smile. "What about all the free-dress days and the dances? And don't forget the wild parties and secret trips into the city we take and never tell you about. And the most obvious is summer. I can't just wear a bathing suit every day. That's indecent—so say the nuns."

She piles a manila folder on top of the impossibly high stack next to her.

"And yet, you own enough to do so. Just make sure everything is front page appropriate."

I roll my eyes, walking inside as she gestures for me to sit down.

"Back to your day."

Plopping down on the chenille armchair in front of her glass desk, I relax back, doing what we always do. She pretends to listen as I speak, and I only give her the headlines. It's almost like a real family.

"Well, in order, it was boring. Boring. Boring. Then way less boring."

Her perfectly shaped brows raise. "Oh yeah? Definitely start with the less boring part, please."

I wrap my hand around the ends of my long copper hair and pull my legs up to sit crisscross as she takes another file from the stack, looking it over.

"Well...you'll never believe what I saw downtown today. There were these boys—well, not really boys—and also this super-strange lady giving like tarot slash tea leaf readings. It was weird—"

Before I can finish, my father bursts through the doorway, tossing a newspaper onto the desk as he stalks toward it.

"Did you see this?"

My mother scrambles for the paper as my head shifts between them. My father's face grows crimson as his voice gets louder, making me jump.

"Read it."

I stare at my mother's surprised face before I look over at the fury scrawled over my father's. The words on the tip of my tongue are swallowed because I'm too scared to draw his attention.

She shakes her head.

"This is a commercial real estate announcement, Baron." Confusion mars her brow. "I don't under—"

"Look at the goddamn name, Elizabeth," he barks, cutting her off. "Look at who bought up all those properties across the tracks."

My father slaps the paper from her hand back to the desk, stabbing his finger on it, and I quickly cover the shriek that shoots from my mouth, drawing their attention.

My father straightens, motioning toward the door dismissively. "A moment, Sutton."

I stand quickly, nodding as I walk toward the door, hearing, "That scum takes my town over my dead body."

Chapter two

Sutton

Golden sunrays bathe my cheeks as I lift my face toward the sky. Eyes closed. Mind quiet.

My Doc Marten–adorned heels bounce off the cement wall I'm perched on as the chatter from my friends becomes muffled.

I take a deep breath, drawing in the ocean air, and feel my shoulders relax. A smile begins to bloom on my lips as tiny birds chirp their songs and the leaves on the nearest tree rustle.

May's always warm on St. Simeon, but this year it's as if summer's come early.

I can almost smell the scent of the coconut oil that'll replace all the musty library books and taste the cherry Popsicles that'll become my only communion—no more nuns, homework, or mass on the first Friday instead of pep rallies.

One more week and goodbye, junior year.

"Sutton, are you listening to me?"

A faint breeze carries a stray copper tendril over my lip, getting it stuck on my gloss as I soak up the moment. I brush the strand away as Aubrey's voice cracks through my daydream.

"Hello?"

Shh, I think, but my smile gives away that I've heard her.

Piper tsks. "No. She isn't. Her head is in the clouds, as usual. A penny for your thoughts, Sut. Although, I bet I can guess."

I don't move from my sun worship as I answer.

"If you must know, I'm thinking about how this is always my favorite time of the year. There's something kind of sexy about it. You know?" My hands grip the cement as I tip my chin a bit higher. "It sounds weird, but it's like all of a sudden, the sun comes out, and everything comes to life. Like the world becomes more vivid. Even the stars shine brighter."

There's silence, and then they both laugh.

"Oh my God, you dreamy bitch." Aubrey gently pinches my arm. "Open your eyes. I need you on planet Earth. Stat."

She's only half-joking. My friends are used to me. They should be, considering our whole lives have been intertwined since birth. We're the three musketeers, minus the swords and the unknown fourth member. *Why do people even say "three" musketeers? It's so misleading.*

"Hello. Eyes. Open."

Knowing I got lost in thought again, I grin as a contented sigh drifts from between my lips. My chin lowers, emerald eyes reopening, ready to join the conversation with a laughed, "What?"

Aubrey holds her phone to my face, showing me her Instagram feed. *Ah, that's what.* There's a photo of a senior she likes named Chase. His arm is wrapped around a girl she despises, named Chloe.

The caption reads: **All my sunsets belong to you.**

"Gross," I answer like a good friend. "And ironic, since that photo was taken in the middle of the day. Sunset?"

"Exactly," Piper adds. "You dodged a 'dumbass' bullet. He's totally the kind of guy that doesn't know the diff between *your* and *you're*."

We're nodding as a hint of a smile graces Aubrey's face before disappearing just as quickly. I frown down, sticking out my bottom lip, but she rolls her eyes, acting like she doesn't care—even though she's still scrolling.

Boys are dubious creatures. They always assure you that they mean what they say but never seem to do what they mean. Aubrey looks up, attempting to mask her feelings.

"Whatever. He's a shitty lacrosse player anyway. And a terrible kisser. He basically tried to french my tonsils."

Piper lies over my lap, propping her chin on her hand as we both watch Aubrey pull shades from her bag and squint into the sun before putting them on.

"Aubs—" Piper offers, extending her other hand, but Aubrey ignores the gesture, changing the subject.

"I'm fine. I'm so ready for a tan *and* for all the families that come to summer. I wonder if we'll see those Hillcrest boys again? Which one did I think was cute?"

Piper glances up at me with a smile but answers Aubrey. "Um...both."

Aubrey smirks. "That's right. Choices are the key ingredient to a happy life. You can write that down."

"Whore," Piper mouths, eliciting a chuckle from me.

"I saw that. And speaking of whores." Aubrey closes in on me, motioning with her chin over my shoulder and whispering, "Hunter's here."

Piper stands, looking behind me, but I don't dare do the same. I can't.

I know my cheeks are already red.

Hunter is *that guy* at St. Simeon-Burr Catholic Prep, Burr for short. He plays every sport and wins. Excels academically. He's the one everyone listens to and wants to emulate.

And to add insult to injury, Hunter has flawless hair, a perfectly tanned six-pack, and is blessed with eyes almost as seductive as his pedigree.

He's the All-American golden-boy type.

And last week, that golden boy called me Freckles.

It was a two-second interaction, but enough to be kind of memorable. I was on the field taking some last-minute makeup photos for the yearbook. One minute I'm hidden behind my camera, and then the next, he's right there next to me.

"Want to take my photo?"

I keep my eye against the viewer, heart racing, trying to play it cool.

"I didn't realize you were in Band too."

He laughs, and I sneak a quick glance, still pretending to take photos.

His thumbs are tucked under the straps of his backpack. And—Oh. My. God —he's shirtless. I'd shake his parents' hands if I could. Well done, Kellys.

"I'm not. I was at swim practice."

Lacrosse, crew, swim—he really does do everything.

I don't answer, clicking at nothing because what else am I going to do? Hunter doesn't move or offer anything else as he stands next to me, making the butterflies in my stomach flutter like a tornado.

We may have known each other our whole lives, but I've never been on his radar, like ever. And I'm starting to feel grateful because I feel too nervous to speak.

"So?" *he laughs, bumping my shoulder.* "Are you going to talk to me or what?"

Swinging my camera lens toward his face, I click without warning, grinning when he jumps.

"Hey. No fair. You didn't tell me to say cheese."

I lower my camera and shrug, chewing the inside of my cheek. His smile grows, gleaming white teeth on display. Hunter steps in closer, crowding my space, but I don't back away, feet rooted to the turf, lump in my throat.

He bends forward, his face so close that I stop breathing.

"Well, whaddya know? I like 'em. A lot."

He straightens as he presses his thumb to his bottom lip and sweeps it across. My eyes obediently watch.

Hunter's feet carry him backward a few steps before he turns to leave. When he does, my body finally unfreezes, heat burning my cheeks as I call out.

"Wait. What does that mean—you like 'em?"

Hunter looks over his shoulder, giving me a wink. "See you around, Freckles."

Laughter from under a sprawling oak tree draws my attention, quieting the memory. A group of freshman boys in khakis are huddled together, playfully shoving each other while taking quick glances at some girls in tartan plaid school skirts like mine.

"Sut." Aubrey nudges me. "Hunter's so hot. You need to secure that boy."

"Leave her alone. Maybe she's not into him, Aubs. Not everyone wants to date a god."

"Zip it," I hiss, watching her wink.

Aubrey spins around quickly. "Oh my God. He's totally looking over here. Smile at him or something, Sutton. Go. Do it now."

I shake my head quickly. "No. Nooo. No way. That's dumb."

Piper speaks to my profile, keeping her lips together to pretend she isn't talking.

"Just, like, look over your shoulder. Like in a movie, all slow and hair flippy. Give him a tiny smile. Trust me, it works in every Netflix movie."

I take a breath, trying not to laugh. "Oh sure, if it's good enough for Netflix. Because that's real life. I mean, maybe if he were Jacob Elordi—"

"Get in the car, Elle!" Piper growls, quoting *The Kissing Booth* and making us laugh before adding, "Just do it, chicken."

Aubrey pokes me. "Do it, ya dirty virgin."

Ugh, she had to go there. It's the equivalent of a double-dog dare.

A groan rattles my chest. "I hate you two so much. Like a tremendous amount of despising is happening inside of my body right now."

"Yeah, but our hymens aren't begging, pleading, to be broken."

Piper laughs as Aubrey sticks her tongue out at me while I attempt to hide my smile.

I seriously dislike being the only one of the three of us with absolutely zero experience. Maybe not zero. Fingers, sure. Kissing, yes. Even a good dry hump has happened. But I'm sans all the rest of the goodies in the sex department. And it sucks. Times are starting to feel a bit desperate over here because, at this rate, I'll be a forty-year-old virgin.

Then again, that almost seems like a better idea than flirting back with Hunter. Because Piper's right. I am too chicken. Especially with Hunter— because, Jesus...he's Hunter.

Rubbing my lips together, I hope for the bravery I need before steeling my spine. Another giggle escapes. *This is so dumb.*

My forefinger picks at the Tiffany blue polish on my thumbnail as I swallow and casually glance over my shoulder, trying to ignore Aubrey moaning, "Oh, Hunter. Yes. Right there. It's so big. Put it in my butt."

I scream and turn back, laughing, shoving Aubrey's shoulder.

"Would you stop? You're a child. I hate you. Do you want me to be a virgin forever?"

Piper's still grinning as she makes a "zip the lips" motion to a more subdued Aubrey, who just winks at me. I take another deep breath and sweep my hair over my shoulder, going in for the kill, but as my cheek touches my shoulder, it's not Hunter I see.

My bottom lip draws between my teeth as everything around me goes silent. It's like two hands are holding the sides of my face, locking me into place—right onto the boys from the wrong side of everything.

I haven't seen them around since that first day, but I also haven't forgotten any detail either. I bet everyone that was there remembers. It's impossible to forget. It was the most exciting thing to happen in St. Simeon since forever.

Those boys driving on Main Street were a greasy smudge on a high tea white dress. A Wednesday tainted by inconvenience in the elitist eyes that followed them down our fancy tree-lined streets.

Streets chock-full of French bakeries like St. Honoré Boulangerie and picture-perfect window displays. All worthy of a magazine spread. All unwelcome to them.

But here they are, thirty-six days since they made their debut driving down that street, standing on the basketball court on our side of town.

"He's smiling, Sutton," Aubrey whispers.

I swallow, eyes ticking toward Hunter, because I know that's who she's talking about, before slingshotting right back to where they shouldn't be.

They don't look like any boys I've ever seen. Not even the ones from the side of town I'm not allowed to visit—their side. Two of them look older, but one seems about my age. Are they brothers? No. There's zero family resemblance.

My eyes roam over them, their backs to me, wondering if any of the boys I know could ever grow up to look like that.

The one that's hot in a "street" kind of way—lean with an angular jaw and black shaved hair—like a guy that would be in a fight club, laughs loudly while taking a practice shot. My eyes follow him as he jogs toward the ball, laughing as he easily fights off the one who looks my age.

That guy seems easy in charm, armed with a dimple that would make you drop your panties on the first date, and long cross earrings. Nothing about him screams religion, so that's definitely for looks. He lifts his cap, exposing tousled honey-brown, curly hair before twisting it backward. The motion makes his bicep flex as he snugs it back onto his head.

Damn. Hello Vinnie Hacker look-alike.

I'm mesmerized, caught in the moment, staring at them until Baseball Cap calls, "Calder," toward the sideline. My eyes shoot to the profile I haven't stopped thinking about—the driver. He turns, giving me his whole face. Dark lashes imprison stormy blue eyes laid out for adoration on smooth tan skin.

Suddenly, my throat is dry, like dying in the desert kind of dry.

Even from here, I feel the same thing I felt standing on that sidewalk—tingles up my spine. My heart rate picks up when my eyes lock on Calder, my lips quietly forming the word, cementing *that* name to *that* face.

I bite my lip as Calder swipes a water bottle from the asphalt, high-lighting the veins in his forearm. His head swings sideways toward Hunter's group as he twists the lid, and I can't help but shift my focus to Hunter, wondering how he's reacting.

Oh. He's pissed, arms crossed, facing Calder with a look that can only be described as *wrong neighborhood.*

It is the wrong neighborhood. There are courts over the tracks. But Calder commands attention like he's entitled to it, and I guarantee he doesn't give a fuck about who's watching or from where they're doing it. That much is obvious.

This should be interesting.

Calder winks at him, tipping the water bottle back, dismissing Hunter like he doesn't matter. *Don't laugh, Sutton*—not that I would...well, maybe a little—but I'm too busy watching Calder's Adam's apple dip as he gulps, making me do a slow blink. *Jesus. H. Christ.*

My gaze stays locked on him as he tosses the empty bottle in the trash before dragging his black T-shirt over his head. My thighs squeeze together, watching his muscles ripple as he exposes the black band of his boxer briefs that peek out from under his basketball shorts.

"Skins," he bellows, tossing the shirt to the ground.

Calder's painted shoulders are broad but not bulky, more like defined. He looks built for aggression, not gentleness. Even his hands seem as if the softest touch would leave a mark.

That thought makes me shiver, but also, something about it makes me want to stare longer.

"Sutton," I hear Piper say.

Before I can answer, the sound of sneakers squeaking against the pavement invades my ears. The basketball beats against the pavement with a thunderous force, sounding a lot like my heart right now.

"Sutton," she presses, but I'm lost to watching them play.

No. Watching Calder play.

The longer I stare, the more time begins moving in slow motion. I can hear my blood pumping through my veins as all the thoughts in my head die.

Calder's glistening, sweat-beaded body penetrates my focus. He jogs backward, his long fingers flicking at the bottom of his black Nike basketball shorts, tugging them up to his muscular thighs as he crouches, ready to defend his side of the court.

My tongue darts out to wet my dry lips, and I swallow, rocking forward on the wall, fingers digging into the concrete. He's—So. Fucking. Hot.

My entire body feels tense and achy as Calder steals the ball. He runs it down between the guys for a lay-up, landing back on his feet and combing his hand through the top of his sandy undercut.

What would it feel like between my thighs? I bet it would tickle my—

"Oh my God, Sutton," Aubrey cackles. "You are so horny for the town criminal."

I blink quickly and turn my head, embarrassed. "Do you ever shut up?"

Aubrey's eyes grow wide, amused that she's right, as Piper links her arm to mine, looking in the guys' direction.

"Sutton," Piper teases, making me grin, "the only thing you're getting from boys like that is a felony record and an unwanted pregnancy."

"Mmhmm—" I answer absentmindedly. "You guys are snobs."

I feel a harmless pinch to my arm from Aubrey. "Sutton...Piper. Seriously. Stop staring. People will see. Plus, Hunter'll think you're uninterested."

I linger one last glance at Calder dunking the basketball before settling back on Aubrey's annoyed face, tossing her words from earlier back at her for fun.

"I thought choices were the key ingredient to a happy life?"

She laughs and sticks her tongue out at me, reaching up to tug a piece of my hair.

"Very funny. But I meant good, excellent, non-'possibly' criminal choices." I roll my eyes as she bends down for her bag, saying, "Ooh, that reminds me."

I shrug, looking out at the trees.

"Don't you wonder about them? They've lived here for a month, and they're such a mystery—what does anyone even know?"

Piper shrugs. "Other than they make you want to make bad decisions? Nothing, I guess. But they're Eastsiders. What do we know about anyone that lives over there?"

Aubrey huffs, squatting and almost falling onto her butt. "Umm, exactly. I don't sit around thinking about those thugs just like I don't ponder all about herpes, and neither should you, bitch."

We laugh at her, Piper rolling gloss over her lips as she looks down at Aubrey, who's still rummaging around in her bag.

"Oh my God. You said thugs? Really? You sound like an eighty-year-old woman." Piper bumps her polo-covered shoulder to my arm. "And who are you kidding, Aubs? You told me you'd let them do bad things to your body after we saw them."

"Oh really?" I beam, eyes jumping to Aubrey, whose own are now narrowed on Piper as she stands.

"Never happened," Aubrey offers, almost sincerely.

Piper raises her brows. "Liar. Liar. Pants not even on fire because you're slutty."

A laugh cracks in my chest, even though I try and hold it back. Aubrey joins in before saying, "I hate you," making us all laugh even more before my head sweeps back over my shoulder to steal another peek.

The ball bounces off the backboard and bounds over toward where Hunter and his friends are. Baseball Cap jogs up, motioning for it back, but Shephard, Hunter's best friend, holds it in his hand, staring them down.

"The ball," he requests, only barely friendly, but nobody moves.

Whoa.

Piper and I exchange a nervous glance, her whispering, "Are they going to fight?"

All eyes in the park are fixed on them. Piper grabs my knee as Fight Club cracks his neck, stalking toward Hunter's crew. Everyone in the park is buzzing with the anticipation of a battle. Even me, seeing as my mouth refuses to close as I watch with eyes open wide.

"Roman."

Calder's command shakes my chest and halts Fight Club's—now known as Roman—steps. I didn't even realize I was holding my breath until Aubrey laughs, and I suck one in.

"Oh yeah. Not thugs at all. Come on, horndogs. Let the animals entertain the masses. I have a surprise."

Aubrey grabs my wrist, tugging me off the wall, and I nab Piper's wrist, making us a little chain gang as Aubrey hauls us away. But I glance back, only to see Calder staring down Hunter until the sound of the ball bouncing on asphalt becomes a waved white flag.

Damn. That was intense.

Chapter three

Sutton

Piper and I follow quickly behind Aubrey now that the almost throw-down is over. We disappear behind the bathrooms before coming to a stop.

"What are we doing, Aubrey?" Piper laughs before blanching. "Eww, it smells like pee back here."

I smile, saying, "Boys' side," before dropping her wrist.

Aubrey looks over her shoulder, then puts her finger to her lip, telling us to be quiet, before holding her hand up. She wags her perfectly arched black eyebrows while shaking a small white-and-red square box.

"Look."

I slap a hand over my mouth, laughing as Piper stares between us.

"Oh my God. You stole cigarettes." Piper smacks my arm. "She stole cigarettes."

Aubrey opens the box, and I lift my chin, trying to peer past her hands. She hands a long white stick to each of us before digging around her purse again.

It's so dumb, but we made a pact a couple of weeks ago during a sleep-over that quickly became a joint breakdown over how shitty and uneventful high school has been. I came up with the idea of a list of ridiculous stuff we wanted to check off our high school experiences before we graduate.

This is Aubrey's because she's obsessed with Audrey Hepburn and thinks channeling her through smoking will improve her luck with boys.

Piper's is to sneak into Manhattan for a whole night because if there were ever anyone who wanted out of this town and into the real world more than me, it's Piper.

Mine is to lose my dumb virginity. I'm done with the idea of falling hopelessly in love and sharing some magical experience. It's not happening for me.

So, now I kind of just want to get fucked and move on. Just rip the Band-Aid off so that when my real life starts, I'll be ready for it.

"Dammit. Dumb lighter—" Aubrey mutters to herself.

"Are we really doing this?" Piper questions, looking around nervously.

I get her nerves. But we're doing this. Aubrey lifts her head for a moment, letting out a frustrated breath.

"We're in high school, Piper, and the worst thing we've done is nothing."

"You've done plenty," Piper counters, rolling her eyes, making me laugh again.

"Regardless." Aubrey huffs. "I need a life. We need a life. Junior year's been a wasted experience with boys that don't like me back."

She lowers her voice to sound like my dad. "And lame 'you may only attend parentally supervised parties,' thanks to Sutton's overprotective dad. We finally all got cute at the same time—braces off, boobs on. We can't chance another gap year."

I internally cringe because she's right. The fact that they've lived my miserable party existence with me and never complained makes them the truest ride or dies. And she's right—freshman and sophomore year was like RIP to love. I can't even think about it. I may have PTSD over my hair alone.

"Don't worry, Piper," Aubrey continues. "God will forgive us. And if the extra Hail Mary those witches made me say counts today—then my soul is safe." She gives us a wink. "At least until next week."

I bump a hip to Piper's, who smiles back, giving in. Aubrey looks inside her bag again before holding up the lighter victoriously.

"Got it."

She steps in closer, the click sounding around us as I lean forward. I'm trying to act like a natural, even though I don't know what I'm doing.

Piper's watching me, pointing a finger toward the butt.

"I think you have to, like, inhale really big to make it stay lit."

The burn filters into my mouth as I take quick draws like I've seen my father do with his cigars, but it doesn't stay lit.

Aubrey smirks, clicking the lighter again to relight mine.

"I bet your criminal shares these with the girls he sleeps with, like after doing the deed—they lie there naked and share a cigarette, letting the high they feel fade away as they smoke."

"No, like a deep inhale," Piper instructs, taking hers and pretending to inhale dramatically to show me.

So I suck in, hollowing my cheeks as the tip glows red, just before my chest heaves, rejecting my stupid idea and leaving me in a coughing fit.

Piper starts smacking my back. "Oh my God, Sutton. Are you okay?"

Aubrey cackles as I open my mouth to speak, only to heave out another cough just as footsteps accompanied by a husky voice turns the corner.

"Oh fuck," Aubrey whispers, still laughing, shoving the pack back into her bag and hiding the evidence of our stupidity. We're like stooges, turning in circles and bumping into each other as I keep coughing.

"You good?" The rough baritone makes us freeze. Aubrey's laughter murdered.

Rich chocolate-brown eyes stare back at me—Roman.

He's focused on me. And what was so hot about him from far away feels intimidating now. Especially since his question might've seemed friendly, but *he* definitely isn't.

Roman's glare shifts to Piper, making her shrink back, and then to Aubrey as if he's working out everything that just happened. I push into Aubrey, taking her hand in a vise grip, forcing us to take a step backward, when my attention's stolen by a chuckle.

The other guy, Ball cap, strides up, propping his elbow on Roman's shoulder, his thumbnail finding his teeth as he stares at us, a smirk on his face. He leans into Roman, saying something in his ear—something that faintly sounded like "Dibs on, Red" before Roman says, "Chill, West," under his breath as he looks back, drawing his bottom lip between his teeth and letting it out slowly.

My heart is racing, not because I'm scared, but I'm also not stupid—they feel unrestrained under the guise of civility. I swallow, looking between them, feeling overwhelmed by the intensity of their stare.

Hold on—West, and Roman. That means... *Shit.*

Goose bumps explode over my body because my eyes know just where to go as Calder rounds the corner. The bluest pools I've ever seen fix on me, arresting my lungs like my heart, making the cough that wants out burn worse.

Calder looks at his friends, giving nothing away before turning back to *me*—not *us*—his blue eyes never drifting from mine. The black T-shirt he took off earlier is draped over his shoulder. All of his smooth olive-colored skin is on display underneath the intricate details of the raven on his chest.

"Sut, we need to go," Aubrey whispers in my ear, but I don't know what's wrong with me. My eyes refuse to look away from his.

I'm slowly tugged backward, my feet begrudgingly moving. Aubrey's hand tightens around my wrist, her nails accidentally digging into my skin, and I wince.

Calder's jaw tenses, eyes dropped to where she's holding me before he brings them back.

I swear to God, I almost twist from Aubrey, but another step has me exhaling and then another forcing me to spin around. I blink, rubbing my lips together, feeling my heart begin to slow, just as a rough hand wraps heavily around my other wrist, turning me to stone.

My head swivels in time with my hand being lifted, a faint *"Oh shit"* heard in the background.

Calder bends forward, close to my face, eyes level to mine, as he brings my palm toward his face.

My lips part, watching him bring his mouth to the cigarette held between my fingers.

I'm still holding the cigarette. How the hell did I miss that?

The light blond stubble under his bottom lip shines in the sunlight as he nabs the end between his teeth, drawing my eyes to his lips that have the faintest glisten as if he just licked them.

His brows draw together as he stares at me, making him look like some kind of fallen angel. Like the ones from the Catholic Church's stained glass windows—the angels with blood on their swords and anger in their eyes as they fight for the heavens.

Seconds that feel like minutes tick by as Calder says nothing, eyes locked on mine, stealing all my rational thought.

Because he has that same storm behind his eyes.

And as strange as it sounds, it makes him beautiful, like an exquisitely broken soul at war with himself and everyone else around him.

He gives a slight tug for me to release the smoke. But I'm liquified—a total waste. Completely lost to him. His fingertips snake up my palm, making me draw in a breath before he weaves his thick digits between mine, forcing my fingers to spread and release the cigarette.

My chest rises and falls too fast—way too fast. But I can't control it.

As he lets go of my hand, Calder's lips drag slowly up my fingers, and my eyes almost roll into the back of my head.

If he saw, I'd never know because Calder is unreadable, staring down at me at his full height, with *my* Marlboro Red between his lips.

He sucks in the tobacco, releasing a plume without so much as touching the damn thing, eyes still on mine, unwavering.

Oh. My. God.

Calder pulls the cigarette from his lips between pinched fingers, letting his eyes drift down my body, giving me a once-over. Then he turns, leaving me in a puddle, and walks into the men's bathroom.

Not one of them looks back even once. Even as laughter erupts behind me, accompanied by "Did that just happen?" and "What the fuck?" pelting down simultaneously.

But I don't have any answers. I'm dumbstruck because Calder just lived up to every fantasy I've had of him since the first day I saw him.

Sutton

Sutton

"Whoa. Where's the fire?"

My feet skid to a stop, and my hair swings across my face, but I smile brightly, hoping to avoid a lecture about rushing. My father's standing in the marbled entry of our home, arms crossed over his chest, dressed in one of his signature black suits.

I knew he was flying in from DC today. I just didn't think he'd be home right now.

"Sorry, Dad. I wish I could stay, but Piper's qualifying meet is about to start. Aubrey and I promised we wouldn't miss it. She needs her cheering section so she can kill it and level up next year. Mom said it was okay."

He's nodding, but there's worry on his face. His eyes dart to the already opened front door, then back.

"You can take the town car. My driver's still here."

I look over my shoulder to see the driver carrying his bags inside.

"It's okay. I'm good to drive myself."

He holds up a hand. "Sutton. Hold on. While I was away, I heard there was some trouble at the park on Thursday. Some boys from Eastside."

I shake my head and shrug as if I don't know what he's talking about. *Snitches get stiches, Dad.*

And technically, there wasn't any trouble. Nobody actually fought, so I'm not lying.

He checks his phone, ignoring a text before walking toward me.

"Three brothers. You're sure you didn't see anything?"

So they are brothers.

My head shakes again.

"I'm surprised. Those Wolfe boys caused quite a ruckus at the park you kids like to hang out at. I know there had to be some talk."

His last name's Wolfe...it suits him.

"Nope. No talk."

More like a morbid fascination dipped in obsession from the amount of conversation that's happened at school.

I shrug, keeping my eyes up so he doesn't catch on to my little white lie. Lying isn't something I often do with my father, but yesterday is on a *need-to-know* basis. He definitely does not need to know why I left and didn't see everything. The lecture on smoking from the man on the Senate Health Committee would be one of epic proportions.

"Sutton. I'm sure someone said something. Did you see them at the park?"

I nod, shifting my stance and drawing an arm behind my back, trying to think of a clever subject change as I answer.

"I think so. Maybe. I don't remember. I was busy hating on a boy that Aubrey likes while we scrolled Insta. Hey, speaking of social media, Mom said you made huge waves on the Hill this week, even made the cut for Trevor Noah's Twitter."

A rare grin graces his face. "My task force to combat organized crime was approved. We're set to go after the lowest forms of humanity—starting with the O'Bannions and their Italian counterpart, the Sovranos."

"Wow, that's great." *Mission accomplished.* "And now the press can stop hammering you about meeting your campaign promises."

He steps in front of me, staring down, dismay on his brow. "So, I take it from all this bait-and-switch that you *did* see the ruckus. Nice try though."

Shoot.

"Define ruckus—because if you mean Hunter Kelly and his band of merry preppies marking their territory, then fine, yes, I saw. But boys will be boys, right?"

He chuckles, saying, "Good," looking pleased. Of course he does, because there's nothing more appealing to a walking legacy than misogyny. My father is a good man, but elitists will be elitists.

"But if you mean anything else, then sorry, Senator, I know about as much as you." I hook a thumb over my shoulder. "As much as I'm enjoying this inquisition, I seriously have to jet."

He's already waving me off. "All right, smart-ass. Get lost. But stay out of trouble. I will not tolerate poor press."

"Okay," I answer, only half-heartedly rolling my eyes, but he gives me that look. The one that says he's serious.

I nod, knowing he means what he says.

"Okay, Dad." When he narrows his eyes at me, I smile, adding, "I promise," and crisscross a finger over my heart.

Aubrey swings her jet-black hair over her shoulder. "Dude. Piper smoked everyone. I'm so proud."

I smile, agreeing, "She did amazing. I don't even know why she was worried."

The smell of chlorine infiltrates my nose as we stand in the walkway between the bleachers and the pool, waiting for her to dry off and get dressed.

Aubrey looks around the pool, rolling her eyes as she spots Chloe before turning her attention back to me.

"Do you think she's cuter than me?"

"No. Not at all. She's cute. You're gorgeous. There's no comparison, Aubs."

It's a good pep talk, but I'm also not lying. Aubrey's beautiful, armed with delicate features, an aristocratic nose, and soulful brown eyes—all bestowed on her by her Brazilian and Japanese descent. Sometimes I'm jealous of how effortless her beauty seems.

Too bad for her she doesn't feel the way she looks—superior.

"Hey," she says, mischief in her eyes, "there's a party tonight. And it's at Hunter's. Tag's throwing it. Now that he's on probation from Yale, he has too much free time on his hands. Yay us."

My head's already shaking as I sidestep water droplets launched off a swim cap as some girl removes it. Tag is a notorious douchebag slash former god at St. Simeon. He's also Hunter's older brother.

"A Tag party is out of our league, Aubrey. Like, way out."

She grabs my elbow, hauling me over to the bleachers to sit, whispering, "Sutton. This is a once-in-a-lifetime opportunity. Tag's parties are legendary."

"No way. First off, the senator would never let me go. In case you've forgotten, he'd be saying no because everyone remembers what happened at Tag's parties. Sex, drugs, and more drugs. Again I say—out of our league."

"Oh my God." Her voice rises. "Can you please think outside of the box and stop being such a perfect daughter. I swear, if I left our social existence up to you and Piper, we'd be fucking doomed."

A throat clearing makes us sit up straighter. Aubrey gives a tight smile, looking over my shoulder.

"Sorry, Sister."

Three nuns in full habit, cloth sweeping the wet ground, pass by. Their glares issue a silent judgment, no doubt having just heard Aubrey's foul mouth. But she doesn't care, giggling as they walk out of earshot.

I smile but narrow my eyes at her.

She waves me off.

"Come on, Sutton. We don't have to do meth, dude. And as for your 'rents, tell the senator you're sleeping over at my place. My parents are gone for the weekend, and our new housesitter will cover so long as I line her pockets. Piper can say the same. Nobody will know. You promised."

God, I did. I promised to make our party life happen, but I was tipsy after we'd snuck vodka shots back to Piper's room during our sleepover.

One day I'm positive Aubrey will become an evil genius, master-minding the world like her PR exec mother. But today, she's just a pain in the ass.

"This is a terrible idea. And, might I add, how every unsolved murder begins. Girl lies to parents. Girl goes to a party, only to never be seen again."

She slaps her hand on my leg. "First off, shave your legs. Second, that shit only happens in like the Bahamas."

That makes me laugh as she continues.

"Third, we need a social life, you little weirdo. And *you* need to go and fucking—" she shoots her head over her shoulder to make sure the sisters are still gone, opting to whisper anyway. "—and fucking play tonsil hockey with Hunter. There's no man left behind, Sutton. It's your turn to pop that cherry. And with the hottest guy at fucking Burr. We decided."

I blow out air, making my lips flap.

"Who says Hunter wants to even do *that* with me?"

Her grin is evil because she knows she's got me on board. Of course she does.

"I say. Hunter's fucking DNA says. Man up—we're getting you laid tonight. He's absolutely perfect, and you know he collects virginities the way that nerdy-ass dude you liked freshman year collected Pokémon cards."

I'm frowning, trying to hold back my smile as Piper slides up next to me, staring down.

"So? Are we partying tonight and watching Sut ho out with Hunter?"

My mouth pops open as I look between them, unsurprised but still shocked. I groan unconvincingly because they roll their eyes.

"One of these days, I'm getting new friends. Mark my words, bitches."

I stand at the same time Aubrey does, and Piper links her arm through mine.

"Lies. You'd die without us. Plus, we love you too much to let you go. Now, let's talk strategy."

Sutton

"I can't believe you two talked me into this. If we get caught, I am fully blaming you. Fully. I'll say you drugged me and brought me here."

"Noted." Piper smiles, brushing my hair over my shoulders. "Now, remember the plan. We get drinks. Mingle. Ignore Hunter, and then talk to whatever boy is the closest to him."

Suddenly, panic sets in, and I scrunch my nose.

"And we know this will work because?"

She puts her hands on my bare shoulders. I was feeling brave earlier when I chose to wear a strapless top and high-waisted jeans. But now I feel exposed.

Aubrey looks over her shoulder as she pushes the front door open, letting all the noise spill out.

"Boys are like dogs, Sutton—they hate it when someone else plays with their toys. That's how we know it'll work. Trust us. Plus, you look like a fucking goddess."

My face shoots to Piper's, who's grinning, her lips folded between her teeth.

"Fantastic. I'm a beautiful chew toy," I mutter, but Piper looks thoughtful.

"Beautiful chew toy sounds like a Billie Eilish song."

We laugh as we walk inside. People are scattered around in small groups, holding red Solo cups, talking and hanging out, music subdued in the background. Eyes land on us and leave just as fast as we make our way through the entry, only adding to how awkward I feel.

None of this should be a big deal, but it is for me. I've been complaining about being left behind. But sleeping with someone, in theory, is totally different than doing this shit in real life. *Do I really picture myself all sweaty on some random bed with a bunch of people downstairs? Do I even imagine doing it with Hunter?*

At first, I thought I'd just find some random guy, but then Hunter came out of nowhere. I didn't really see him coming. I mean, it's not as if I'm socially unacceptable. I'm not. I'm a catch, but guys like Hunter run in a faster crowd than I do, which is both a pro and a con.

A pro for him is that he's managed quite the reputation for taking virginities. In the same breath, he seems to leave the girl feeling grateful rather than discarded. It's so weird. But there's never been a complaint lodged, so when he started talking to me, I figured—why not.

A con is that I'll be relegated to the basic bitches of the world that all lost it to Hunter Kelly. That's not really a club I want to join.

But eye on the prize and a means to an end and all.

The other con is how all my bravado is beginning to taste like bile.

Come on, loser, get it together.

Piper's head swings back to me, all smiles before returning to the front.

I got this. It's fine. There's no right way to do it, and if I keep trying to plan it, senior year will suck. College will suck. And then I'll be on my deathbed, just me and my virginity, together forever. BFFs.

No. Hunter's a perfect choice, and if the rumors are true...he's hung. That's a plus, or so I hear. *Ooo, but maybe it would be better the first time with something more midsize. Like something I could have a better handle on.*

Oh my God. What is wrong with me?

"You holding up okay, Sut?" Aubrey laughs, intuitively knowing I'm in my head, as she takes my hand to pull me farther into the house.

I nod in answer, half a smile on my face as we snake through some people. The crack of a cue ball makes my shoulders jump as my eyes swing to a room with an arched entryway, watching some college guys tease the girl they're with. Shifting my head to the other side, I take in a large living room with more people that look way older than us, and worry starts to grow.

"I don't see any other people from our class. You think they'll let us stay?" I whisper into Aubrey's ear.

She points, making me turn my head toward a glass accordion door that's opened to the backyard.

"Whoa."

Kids are everywhere, flanking the rectangular pool that's illuminated by red lights. Past them, stairs lead out to the beach where a bonfire's raging and even more people are partying.

"Jesus, all of Burr is here. Probably Eastside Public too."

Eastside? *Maybe West goes there since he looked younger. Or maybe they all do.*

My dad's voice pushes to the forefront of my mind. *"If they come anywhere near you, I want to know."* No way would they come to a party like this. Then again, they did come to our courts.

Piper smiles at me. "This is a rager. You still think this was a bad idea, Sutton?"

Definitely not now. *Not that I'm hoping to see them.*

"Time to party," Aubrey interjects, stopping us in front of a big silver keg.

Our eyes collectively land on a guy I recognize as a senior named Phillip.

"Ladies." He grins. "Thirsty?"

"Absolutely," Aubrey answers way too seductively, making me and Piper laugh.

"Well, ask and you shall receive, gorgeous."

He hands us each a cup, eyes lingering on Aubrey before Piper pulls her a few feet away, closer to the back doors, with me in tow.

"Pace yourself. He's a skeeze, and everyone knows it," Piper snarks. "I'm only taking the drink because I watched him pour it."

The honey-colored liquid sloshes as I bring it to my nose to sniff, half-joking.

"Um...mine smells like shoe. Is that normal?"

Piper sticks her tongue out at me.

"You drink it. You don't wear it," Aubrey jokes, taking a big gulp, and then she looks at us. "Well? Am I doing this alone? We're here. Finally. All in, sluts."

Piper giggles before holding up her cup, saying, "All in," and takes a drink. She looks at me when she finishes, having chugged the whole thing. So I lift the beer and wink because there's no way I'm doing what I came for without a little liquid courage.

"Bottoms up, and cherries popped."

They both squeal, but as the rim touches my lips, I'm rammed from behind and sent flying. My knees buckle, hands hitting the ground as the cup goes flying but not before I'm drenched in cheap beer.

"What the fuck, dude!" Aubrey yells, shoving some guy.

Piper's at my side in a split second, helping me to stand, darting her glare back behind me as she says, "Are you okay, Sut?"

A slightly slurred, deeper voice behind her cuts in. "Hey, sorry, chick. That was my bad."

"It's fine," I mumble, looking down at my ruined and partially see-through top as I wipe my cheeks.

"Do you want another drink?" the idiot says, making me blow out a frustrated breath.

Piper snaps her fingers. "Dude, get the hell out of here before I—oh."

The change in her tone has my head jerking around to see perfectly tousled hair and an awfully familiar smirk.

Hunter's smile grows, and I turn bright red as I pat the back of my hand over my mouth. His eyes dart to my outfit, then back to my face.

"You look wet."

I smile. I can't help it.

"I feel wet."

Oh God—put the words back in my mouth. My embarrassment isn't helped by my shitty friends that laugh.

"Come on. I can help."

I raise my brows as he takes my hand.

"You can borrow a shirt, Freckles."

Duh. You horny weirdo—he wasn't going to fuck you right here.

"Oh. Yeah. Okay. Cool. Thanks."

"Yeah, you go get that shirt, Sutton." Piper smiles, and Aubrey joins in. "Yeah, take your time choosing the right one. We got all night."

I'll kill them.

Hunter turns, joining both his hands behind his back, holding mine in between them, as he leads me away. *Oh my God* begins running consecutively through my head, as if I'm hyperventilating.

I glance back over my shoulder at Piper and Aubrey, who are doing different versions of hip thrusts.

A giggle escapes before I turn back, knowing they haven't stopped but still trying to play it cool.

Hunter says hello to everyone as we make our way through his massive living room decorated in white—all white. It's sterile. But I bet his parents boast about the clean lines and minimalism. It's something I've heard my mother say, and it seems to fit.

As we walk, I begin to notice the number of curious faces each time they see whose hand he's holding. *Are they surprised he's into me or that I'm into him?*

Or maybe they're all hearing the soundtrack of my life right now —*Another One Bites The Dust.* I have to bite my lip to stop the laugh that wants to shoot out over that thought.

Hunter takes me up the stairs and down a long hallway until everyone from downstairs disappears and we get to what I assume is his bedroom door. He grabs the brushed-gold doorknob, pausing to look over his shoulder at me.

"Have you ever been in a guy's room?"

I chew the inside of my cheek before I tease, "Yes. But the door had to stay open."

He laughs, and I bite the tip of my tongue before I add, "Then again, I don't plan on spending time in yours either. So you can shut it since I'm just here for the free shirt."

Lies. Throw me on the bed and do me.

He nods, eyes dropping to my lips before he opens the door, leading me inside. It's exactly what I expected. Trophy shelves line the wall, and posters of the Olympic crew team hang like collages. There's even a Yale banner.

He really is a perfectly packaged St. Simeon heartbreaker.

Whole Pinterest boards could be made from this room, and they'd all be called "hot guy aesthetic."

The thought makes me chuckle, causing Hunter to look over from where he's standing, next to his bed. He jumps onto the mattress, lying back with his hands behind his head.

"Closet's over there," he offers, motioning with his chin.

Wait. What? Seriously?

"Cool. Thanks."

I wrap my long copper hair around my hand, crossing my legs before I turn around and close the distance to his walk-in. Every few steps, I glance back over my shoulder, watching him watch me and wondering if I'm really only getting a shirt.

"Hey, Sutton."

My eyes swing back to his.

"You can have anything you want. I hope you know that."

And we're back. I lick my lips and nod. Heat blooms on my cheeks as Hunter runs his hand over his stomach, so I walk inside the closet to hide. Oh my God, I'm such a nerd. That was the moment to say, *"Great, I'd love the assistance of your dick. Thanks so much."* But instead, I'm hiding.

I'm like one of those yappy little dogs—all bark and no bite.

But this is so weird. *What am I doing?* Maybe I should just date him and see where it goes. Like, let it all unfold naturally like a normal person. Ordinary people don't put their virginity on a to-do list.

I smile to myself, wallowing in the ridiculousness of this moment as my fingers brush over his perfectly arranged T-shirts, all hung by color. *Okay, Hunter, a little anal but not a deal-breaker.*

He laughs from inside the room, so I lean sideways, peeking out of the doorway. Hunter waves from the bed, remote in hand, and I pull back, kind of embarrassed.

He's so cute. Like so fucking cute.

I'm out of my depth here. The last guy I did anything with quoted Star Trek when he fingered me. I can't even hear anyone say "Beam me up" anymore. This is why girls should never read. I've been stuck in all the smart classes, limiting my damn dating pool. *Supermodel tastes, MIT budget.*

Focus, Sutton. I pull my phone from my back pocket, shooting off a text to the group chat.

> Me: Spiral in effect. How do I do this? I'm failing. Thumbs up, I take off my clothes and walk out of his closet naked. Thumbs down, I pretend to have a seizure and sneak out when he goes for help. Vote now.

I don't bother to read the responses because I know it'll be two thumbs up—they're assholes. Then, taking a deep breath, I exhale, feeling my chest grow cold.

Shoot. The cold, damp shirt sticking to my skin reminds me that I need to change. I work quickly, untucking it from my jeans and peeling it off as I give myself a mental pep talk. My nude strapless bra is relatively dry, but I use the least wet part of my top to pat my damp chest.

"So gross," I say to myself, lifting my head to inspect Hunter's shirts when I hear footsteps.

"Hey, I have some smaller T-shirts on the top shelf—"

Oh my God. Hunter's voice is too close. I turn back and forth, panicking, reaching for anything just as he walks into the closet, making us both freeze.

His mouth opens, then closes as I cling to my bundled shirt in front of me, eyes popping out of their sockets.

"Oh my God. Turn around."

He exhales as he spins around quickly, bringing his palms to the back of his head. "Oh, wow. I'm sorry."

I jerk a plaid flannel from a hanger, shrug it on, and work quickly to button it up. I'm swimming in it because Hunter is much bigger than I am, but it's better than him seeing way more of me than he should until I've talked myself into it.

"Okay," I breathe out, tucking the front into the top of my jeans. "You can turn around now."

When he does, all he does is smile. I sweep my hair over my shoulder and wrap it around my hand, feeling awkward and nervous.

"What? Why are you looking at me like that?"

"You look different, Sutton."

My brows draw together, head diving to the front of me to inspect myself.

"What does that mean?"

"It means you don't look like the other girls." He cracks a small laugh. "No. I don't mean that...wait. I do, but not how it sounds. Damn."

If *what the hell* was a face, it would be mine. He takes a step closer, shoving his hands into his pockets.

"You've always been pretty, Sutton." I must call bullshit on my face because he adds, "Yeah, I've noticed. Our whole lives, actually. But there's just something new—"

I'm smiling again.

"New?"

His fingers fall between strands of my hair before he cups my head.

"Something different. Something special, Freckles. You're not like the other girls."

I'm staring up at him, bated breath, eyes closing as he leans in torturously slow. *It's happening.* Hunter Kelly is going to kiss the girl—me.

The sound of a door banging open paired with the music filtering in has my eyelids fluttering open and Hunter freezing centimeters from my lips.

"Shit," he exhales, and he's so close to me that his minty breath feathers my face.

I keep my eyes on him, willing us to happen. *Just kiss me. Come on, you got this, champ.* He licks his lips, saying, "Goddamn, that mouth is tempting," before barely brushing them against mine.

"Hey, dick. I don't care if you're jerking off or fucking that chick you brought up here. Quit. Now. Basement."

Fuck you, Tag—or Cockblock, as I will unaffectionately always remember him—I think as he bangs on the wall. Hunter touches his forehead to mine, groaning as he cradles both sides of my face.

"Favor?"

My head's already nodding.

"Go find your friends and check in, then meet me in the last cabana before the dunes. You can't miss it. It's at the very end of the deck. Give me fifteen minutes, maybe twenty. I want you all to myself tonight, and every night after that, Freckles."

What?

He brings his lips to mine, giving me a chaste kiss, so I close my eyes, but he pulls back just as fast when Tag yells again, "Hunter. Now, you pussy. It's business."

All I hear is, "We're happening, Sutton. Those lips are mine," before he's gone.

I can't speak. My mouth won't move. The only thing I can do is burn red as I stand inside Hunter's closet. The moment his door shuts, I break out into a little dance.

I can't believe this is happening. *Holy hell. This is actually going to happen.* Freaking out, I reach for my phone.

My fingers fly over the keys until I realize that neither of them responded to my other message. There's not even a Read receipt. Crap, I must not get service in here.

Walking out of the closet, I give myself a once-over in the standing mirror before heading out of Hunter's room. I make my way back the way we came, taking the stairs slowly, using the height to scour the open spaces for my friends. But I don't see them.

As I reach the bottom, I bump shoulders with a girl, offering a passing

"*Sorry*" as I keep searching the crowd for Aubrey and Piper. But the girl I recognize as Tiffany Astor huffs while glaring at me, so I stare back.

She doesn't even go to St. Simeon. Guess the parties at Madison are no fun—but no surprise there. All-girls schools aren't known for their party atmosphere.

Tiffany's friend whispers into her ear, and Tiffany grins, but something about it makes me feel momentarily self-conscious.

Only briefly because it's obvious they're talking shit about me. And frankly, that's none of my business. I adjust the baggy shirt on my shoulders, and they laugh, glancing over at me again. Yep, over it.

I push past, hearing, "Nice souvenir," making lines form between my eyes before I turn around and smile because I realize that she thinks I fucked Hunter. *Not yet, Tiff.*

"Thanks. I really earned it. My knees are a wreck."

They stare at me, shocked and probably a little surprised, so I add, "I know. This isn't how the mean girl dynamics are supposed to work. But I'm a smart girl. So that bullshit doesn't work on me. In the meantime, don't worry, Tiff. I'm sure Hunter will let you know when you get called up to the big leagues. But...it'll be when I'm done with him."

I hear a familiar laugh, making me smile, so I turn and walk away.

Piper sounds like a hyena. It's unmistakable. But her blonde pixie cut and perfectly winged eyeliner paired with a waifish stature give her a Natalie Portman look, so no boy could ever hold her laugh against her.

I work my way toward the front, where I saw the pool tables earlier. I'm looking down, rolling up my sleeves, as a pool stick drops in front of me, blocking the way, making me jerk back.

"Excuse me?" I frown before lifting my face.

Piper grins, reaching her hand out for me. "Shephard, quit. Stop being a dick."

He lifts the stick and turns, smacking her ass and making her jump as she yelps. My eyes pop open as I dramatically blink.

"Um, I've been gone for like, what? Twenty minutes. How did this happen? When? Where's Aubrey?"

She shakes her shoulder and lifts a shot. "I forgot how to pace myself. And Shep's so cute."

Her cough is muffled by the back of her hand before she blows out, smiling at me again. Oh, man. Piper's tipsy.

"But Shephard? Really?"

My nose scrunches. It's not that Shephard isn't hot. He completely is. But he's just so frat boy to Piper's indie rock. Then again, I'm about to do it with the possible future president of Alpha Beat-off Pi.

Aubrey throws her arm over my shoulder, coming out of nowhere, and presses a kiss to my cheek. "So? Spill it. Was it the best five seconds of your life?"

I look between them, my smile already beaming. "We're meeting in a cabana. Hunter said he wanted me all to himself, tonight and every night after." They quietly squeal. "But—"

Aubrey's finger comes to my lips, quieting me. "No."

Piper covers Aubrey's finger on my mouth with hers, shaking her head. "Absolutely no. No matter what you're going to say, the answer is no."

I nod, and they narrow their eyes but take their hands away, glaring at me, so I shrug as I'm handed a shot by Shephard.

"Okay. Fine. No buts. I'm nervous though." Piper pushes the shot glass toward my mouth, so I throw the liquid back, feeling the burn in my throat.

Shephard comes up behind me, putting his arms around us. "Can I join? We can braid each other's hair, practice kissing...you know, *wherever* you want me to french you."

"Eww," we groan simultaneously, all shrugging him off as I add, "Get off...alone."

"Sorry." He laughs, tickling Piper. "I forgot you've been claimed. And Aubrey's just a bitch."

"True," she answers, putting her hands on my shoulders. "Are you ready?"

Piper comes up behind me, wrapping her arms around my waist, her head on my shoulder.

"This is your choice, Sut. No means no, even to us, and to our dumb list."

"Shot me," I say to Aubrey. Her eyebrows rise as she hands me another. "I'll see you in a bit. I have plans in a cabana."

Aubrey reaches across and gives Piper a high five as I let the liquid slide down my throat with ease.

"'Kay, I'm going before I lose my nerve."

They're nodding, smoothing my shirt and my hair. I let out a harsh breath and smile goofily before spinning around and heading directly to the last place my virginity will ever be a reality again.

Sutton

A shaky breath leaves my lips as my feet hit the steps outside and pad down slowly toward the cabanas.

Three white tents, drowning in the shadows, sit between the edge of the deck and the bonfire that's illuminating the debauchery happening on the beach.

The crowd is way bigger out here. There's a mix of faces I recognize and others that I don't. The lit rectangular lap pool also seems to have attracted a following. Because while it was empty when we first got here, there are now people playfully splashing around in makeshift bathing suits.

And, oh, even some couples making out.

"Electric Love" by BØRNS beats in the background, setting the mood under conversation and laughter as I slip between people, trying to keep my eye on the cabana prize.

Despite my bravery, my eyes flick over each person I pass, wondering if anyone can tell what's about to happen to me. But nope. Of course they can't.

I'm carrying the secret of all secrets while hiding in plain sight. It's kind of exciting. Like I'm getting away with something I shouldn't. My fingers find the ends of my hair as I walk, playing with it as I hide my smile, but the closer I get, the more the butterflies erupt in my stomach.

Sliding around a group of cute college-age guys—*they must be Tag's friends*—I offer a quiet "Excuse me." Their eyes roam over me as one of them raises his beer, giving me a small, appreciative salute. It makes the smirk I'm hiding harder to keep hidden.

I really have been missing out by not coming to more parties.

A few more feet and a few more people navigated, and I'm standing at the top of the three cedar stairs that lead to the sand—and out to the cabanas.

Wait. Which one did Hunter say to go to? Shit. I forgot.

I toe off my checkered pink Vans, bending down to hold them in my hand before walking toward the nearest one. There are only three, so if I have to Goldilocks it, I will.

My bubble-gum-pink-painted toes sink into the ground, causing my steps to drag and forcing me to sashay so I don't kick up sand. It's cool on my bare feet but not cold. With each step, I make my way deeper into the dark, only pausing to look over my shoulder once.

It's strange how lives intersect and collide. Something monumental is about to happen to me, but it's just a regular Saturday night to someone else. It almost makes what I'm about to do seem insignificant, and I guess, in a way, it is. Millions of people do it with strangers every day. It's not anything transcendent.

It's just sex, no big deal—a physical transaction. *A regular Saturday night.* But a tiny piece of me still kind of wishes that it was magical or even earth-shattering. Just like a part of me wishes Hogwarts was real or that lying in the sun would turn my ginger skin tan and not into cancer.

I blame movies. The ideas about the "sexiness of sex" being sold are so false. I know because my dumbasses made me watch way too much porn over the last two weeks. Piper called it a CliffsNote for my "snack"—the grossest name for my vag.

And even the stories I've heard, once they both started having sex last year, cemented the facts. Sex is awkward, sometimes uneventful, and not like the second installment of the movie *After...*there is no Hero Fiennes Tiffin in real life.

There's only a Hunter—hot AF, doesn't read, but wants to eat my snack.

I shake my head with a chuckle, pulling myself out of the kind of thoughts I lose myself in way too often, and shift my head back to the darkness.

Circling around to the front of the tent, the heavy canvas fabric that's usually tied off is closed for privacy. Crap. He beat me here. I stare at the front, rolling my shoulders, hopping up and down like I'm prepping for a fight. *Be casual. Be cool. Don't be yourself.*

Am I ready? Yes. *Am I really?* Yes.

Okay. Game time.

The waves crash, mixing with the music from the party as I slide my hand between the draped material, pulling the front back just enough to duck inside.

My voice is barely above a whisper. "Hunter?"

It's pitch-black, only a beam of moonlight coming in from a slit at the top, turning a shadowed figure from black to dark gray.

"Hunt—"

Faint noise slowly seeps into my ears, growing louder, crawling underneath my skin, spreading heat through my body. It's wet and sloppy like— *Oh my God.*

My entire body freezes, eyes wide, and panic sets in. The scene on display in front of me slaps me square in the face.

A guy's hand is dug into some girl's hair, gripped so hard that his knuckles are white. The front of his jeans hangs open, the silver buckle on his belt making a clicking sound each time he shoves his hips forward.

I blink a thousand times, feeling stuck, fixed on what's happening as he groans, making my body tense as I press my lips together.

He slows her movements, groaning, "Fuck, yes. Suck it," boring into her like the world has disappeared. But I see and hear everything. All the filthy sounds of arousal dripping and slapping from her mouth with each thrust.

He shoves deep inside her mouth, rhythmically, breath ragged.

"Take it. Fuck, yes. That's it. Gimme that fucking throat."

The command in his voice pulls a whimper from the girl on her knees, triggering him to move faster, grunting, rutting into her, making her take it deeper without any gentleness or remorse. God, he looks like an animal.

That's the only way to describe it because I've never seen anything like this. This isn't a blow job. He's fucking her mouth.

My eyes won't budge. And my feet won't move. Not even when she gags. His breath becomes ragged as she bobs her head faster and faster.

"Yeah, baby. Hollow those cheeks. Suck that cock, slut."

Another moan has her hands gripping his hips, mine doing the same to my jeans.

"Yeah, you're a dirty bitch. You like to gag like a little whore, don't you."

His head drops, and I imagine his eyes growing heavy, jaw slack as I lick my lips, lost to the sexual carnage.

The muscles in his forearm strain with ferocity as he presses himself forward, swaying, lost to the feeling. My teeth find my bottom lip, watching as he lifts his chin, displaying his angular jaw.

Aggression oozes off him as he grips her hair harder, using her to get off without restraint.

My chest rises and falls as stars begin speckling my vision. His other hand grabs the chair in front of him, making it rattle just as a raw, animalistic growl erupts from his throat and the face hidden by shadows leans into that damn moonlight.

West.

Dropping my shoes, my hands slap over my mouth as I stumble backward out of the tent. A string of "*I'm sorrys*" leaving my lips.

Holy shit. My mind can't catch up as I make a hasty escape, stumbling over myself, traveling further into the dark toward a group of rocks on the beach.

I whisper to myself, head swinging around, only half looking to see if anyone is witnessing my spiral. "Jesus Christ. What am I doing? Oh my God, Sutton. What the fuck?"

Did that just happen?

My body's still flush, warm in places it shouldn't be. I can't see Hunter like this. For fuck's sake. I'm so out of my depth.

The thoughts in my head refuse to calm down as I rake my hand through my hair, the other reaching for my cell phone, pulling it from my back pocket. My breath is moving too fast, keeping my chest from slowing down. Fuck. Am I going to hyperventilate?

A huffed laugh leaves me as I talk to myself again. "Oh my God. Get it together, hypochondriac weirdo." But humor swings back to panic just as quickly. My hand comes to my chest, rubbing a tight spot in the middle as I put my other hand down on my knee, bending over to take deep breaths.

The cell I've brought to my eyes spotlights my face as I blink, beginning to calm as I scroll the messages looking for my group chat. I let out a deep exhale before I stand.

Holy hell. I'm going to need a Snuggie, eight bags of chips, and three days of true crime shows to counteract this train wreck of a night.

Impatient thumbs hover over the keyboard as I wander around in a circle, trying to figure out what to text Piper and Aubrey, still saying shit under my breath. "Oh yeah. Let me lose my virginity in a tent. Sure. Who cares? It's not a big deal. Gah, you fucking loser."

How am I supposed to be ready for sex in a cabana with Hunter when I'm about to have a fucking heart attack over a blow job I wasn't even giving?

> Me: Code Blue. Plan B. I don't care what. But get me out of here. Burn the house down if you have to. This is a Liam Neeson Taken kind of situation. Help. Me. Hos.

I'm staring at the screen as laugh emojis fill it.
"Assholes." I groan.

> Me: I just watched West get a blow job...

Nope. Delete. That dies with me.
The cell in my hand drops to my side as I tip my head toward the sky littered with tiny, bright explosions. The white dots twinkling down mock me with their perfect existence.

I wanted to see those—just not like this. Fuck my life.

Closing my eyes, I take one last deep breath and open them to stare at the moon. That globed, elegant, bold full moon is nothing but a curse. Nothing good happens when a moon like that is out because it's the only thing allowed to be beautiful, so it curses all the moments that could be.

First Tag cockblocks, now West's actual cock is blocking me. Cursed. And cursed.

A whoosh of air breezes past my lips. "I hate you, moon."

Calder

She's staring at the moon—berating it. Who does that? It's weird. But I haven't stopped watching her since she began because it's equally as mesmerizing.

From the rock I'm seated at, I watch her dramatic little moment unfold, lifting my cigarette to my lips, readied to light it as she whispers.

"I hate you, moon."

My chest shakes, a laugh trying to break free as the lighter clicks. All that wild red hair swings in my direction as I give an exhaled, "Don't stop on my account."

Her eyes grow wide. She's frozen in place but only for a millisecond until a bloodcurdling scream explodes from between her lips.

"Whoa," I rumble, launching from my rock, tossing my smoke to the ground as I do. "What the fuck are you screaming for?"

She's moving backward, obviously scared. So I nab the belt loop of her jeans as she shrieks, swatting at my hands, and yank her flush to my body, wrapping her in one arm, the other slapping over her mouth.

"Chill out."

Her squeal is muffled under my palm as she tries to squirm, eyes squeezed shut. But she can't move. I'm three times her size, and I've got at least a hundred pounds on her. There's no escaping.

"Open your eyes. It's okay."

I shake my head as she does, feeling her chest rising and falling against me. Those big green doe eyes pierce into mine. She's looking at me the same way she did the other day. It's unnerving, like I can almost feel her thoughts. Because they feel like mine.

Who are you?

Her breathing slows as I blink, following the brown speckled pattern over her nose. There's just enough light for me to see them.

Waves crash onto the shore, bringing a breeze with it, making a few strands of her hair blow over my hand, replacing the smell of my cigarette with something I can't place—*grapefruit, maybe?*

She clears her throat, and my brows draw together. Fuck. My hand's still over her mouth.

"I'm not going to hurt you. I'm gonna let you go. But no more screaming. All right? I have no interest in fucking up a bunch of preppy assholes attempting to protect you from nothing. Cool?"

I feel her smile against my palm.

"Nod if you understand."

She does, slowly, then picks up speed. My hand peels away, and I watch as she licks her lips and takes a deep breath. Lips that look like—fuck me, her mouth is built for kissing. She draws in her bottom lip between her teeth, letting her gorgeous eyes peek up at me from under the blackest lashes.

Goddamn.

I brush away the hair that got caught up on her face, still staring down, our breaths matching in rhythm.

"Sorry," she whispers, "You scared me."

"It's my fault. But you and the moon were having a deep one-on-one, so I was trying not to interrupt."

She blushes, and my chest hollows, lips parting. That's a good color on her. Absentmindedly, she begins playing with the strings on my hoodie, staring at my chest.

"Oh my God. It's so embarrassing."

I swallow hard, fingertips curling into her back, suddenly realizing that

I've still got my arm around her.

"Uh…it's not." I let her go, stepping back but only a small step. "What are you doing out here anyway? Cuz I know it's not to smoke."

Her cheeks stain red again, and this time I want to reach out to see if her skin is hot too.

"Weren't you listening?" She laughs, playing with the ends of her long locks, looking up at me from between those long-ass lashes.

I lick my lips, trying to hide my smirk. "I was, but I wasn't going to say anything."

"Oh my God, stop. You were giving me my dignity." Her eyes roll with a grin. "Joke's on you. I have none anymore."

She's teasing, so I do too.

"All right, then tell me who you're meeting out here so I can bury him befo—"

She cuts me off with her fingers against my lips. "Shh." She shakes her head.

The smile on her face makes me do the same. We're locked on each other, underneath a blanket of stars, nestled in the darkest sky. Her hand stays against my lips as I exhale, warmth enveloping her fingers. Fuck, I can't stop looking at her. It's like every piece of her calls to me. Like magnets.

I want to tug her closer—die in that fucking grapefruit scent as I run my nose up her neck. My eyes drift down her body. One I know is innocent, but looks are deceiving because the way that she weaponizes shyness should be illegal.

I almost feel guilty over the defiling thoughts that are doing their worst inside my head.

Before I think twice, not that I've ever been guilty of that, my tongue slowly runs up the pad of her finger. And she fucking shivers, making me feel drunk on her.

Her hand draws back, lips parted by a quiet gasp. But I encircle her wrist, a half-smile pointed in her direction.

"Tell me your name."

Chapter eight

Sutton

My entire body's short-circuiting, still feeling the slickness of his tongue over my fingertips.

"Huh?"

Calder's grin peeks out as I open my mouth, realizing what he's asked, but nothing comes out. *Hmm, do I give you my name? On this night...with this moon?*

I whip around, before glancing over my shoulder as I start walking away. There's amusement in Calder's make-me-quiver kind of deep voice as he follows behind.

"Hey. Hold up. Tell me your name. Don't do me dirty like that..." He chuckles. "What would the moon think?"

I laugh, looking back at him again, as we near the porn tent, before spinning to face him.

"The moon is a wicked bitch. She curses everything."

He stops in front of me, biting his lip, making butterflies lose their minds in my belly. My hand comes to my stomach, hoping to calm them as I feel a strand of my hair being gently tugged.

My smile matches his. Or his matches mine. I can't tell. It's like we're feeling everything at the same time, in this exact moment, with identical depth.

He bends down, catching my eyes that start to drop as I lose myself to that thought.

"Then I guess I'll have to ask you again in the daylight. Wouldn't want us cursed."

God, he has the smoothest lips. They look soft, as if they'd glide over mine like satin. Why doesn't anyone have lips like this at Burr? My question jumps out before I can stop it.

"Do you go to Eastside?"

"No."

His head tilts left as he raises his hand to the base of my neck, weaving his fingers through my hair, massaging while he watches.

"So, you're older, then?"

Oh my God. Am I panting?

He nods, his grip becoming firmer as he forces my chin up. My breath is useless because it's barely there anymore.

"How much older?"

Calder's tongue drags over his lips as he stares at mine. *Oh, sweet Jesus, I want that in my mouth.*

"Nineteen."

Calder gives me a tug, forcing my feet closer, the heat of his body devouring me.

"My turn."

The heart that I think is still in my chest starts beating out of control. He swallows, and my back arches ever so delicately toward him, repeating his words.

"Your turn."

He smirks. "How old are you?"

"I'm a senior."

Going to be... Same difference.

His face lowers as my eyes close. But instead of his lips pressing to mine, Calder runs his nose up my jaw. He inhales, leaving the barest touch of his lips against my earlobe. "Do you really believe in curses?"

I can't move because my whole fucking body wants to shake. "Maybe."

"I don't." He pulls back, locking eyes with me. "Tell me your name."

I'm about to surrender in this little game we're playing, feeling lost in Calder's magic, when his attention's stolen by the sound of someone snapping their fingers behind me.

I'm released, my body suddenly cold.

Looking over my shoulder, my eyes land on Hunter as he rounds the corner, and my heart stops.

He stops dead in his tracks, looking between us.

Oh shit. My head swings back and forth, feeling the air change, tension sweeping over us.

Hunter extends his arm, calling me over. "What's going on here?"

I shake my head because the words aren't coming out. They can't. They're held hostage by the fact that Calder's still holding a strand of my hair, eyes back on me. Zero fucks given to Hunter.

"Fuck off, little Kelly. She's busy. Go play somewhere else."

Calder lifts my hair to his nose, inhaling, and I blink up at the sincerest blue pools as he grins.

"I like your shampoo."

This time I laugh, sweeping my hair over my shoulder, away from him. Avoiding the growl that leaves his throat as I take a step back, I put distance between us, even when his fingers graze my hand, because this could get ugly fast.

Like he said before, there are more than enough juniors and Roman numerals inside for Hunter to call on. I won't be the catalyst for a throw-down between the two schools here.

Calder stares at me, crossing his arms, but I shrug, turning my attention to Hunter, who's mimicking Calder's pose.

The sound of fabric swishing open draws our collective attention, West chuckling as he walks out. His arm is slung over the girl who was just on her knees, and she's staring at him like he's a god.

West's eyes meet mine immediately, then drop to my bare feet. His smile broadens so much that the shine should sparkle on his teeth.

"Hey, Cinderella. You left something in the tent."

He holds up my pink Vans, giving them a shake. Jesus. I reach out, snatching my shoes, the whole tragic night hitting me in the gut again.

"Thank you." I point at the tent, **my cheeks** turning scarlet. "And sorry about the plus-one—"

I shift toward Calder, walking **backward as** he starts following me, pointing to myself. "Sutton. And I **promise no more** screaming."

He laughs, but I spin to Hunter, **who looks** like he's got plenty to say to me. I hold up the sleeve of his **flannel that** my hand's folded over. "Thanks for the shirt and the offer. **But I've had** a weird night. I'm just going to go."

I take four or five quick skips on **the balls of** my feet over the sand before I look back. The expressions **on their faces** pull a burst of laughter from my chest. *The thoughts they must be thinking.* I can almost tell what each is thinking—one with a smirk, **the other a scowl**, and West looking at that girl's boobs.

As I turn, Hunter calls my name, **but it's Calder's** eyes I lock with.

"See you in the daylight."

"I cannot get over that you saw that **dude get a blow** job."

Aubrey shimmies her sweats over **her hips before** reaching up to put her hair in a messy bun. I shake my **head, trying** not to laugh, falling back onto the bed.

"It was so embarrassing. And loud. Eww. I'm still cringing all over again at what a perv I was."

Piper throws a pillow at me. "Yeah. **I mean, I** was super pissed when you made us leave, but this story is so **worth it.**"

Aubrey snuggles up in her bamboo **chair swing,** grabbing her water. "So what happened after the criminal let **you go?**"

I roll my eyes. "Don't call him that. **He's nice.**"

Their heads turn to stare at each **other before** they begin taunting me. "Oh, sorry. Are we offending your **boyfriend?**" Piper puts a hand to her chest. "Oh no, Aubrey, don't talk about **her true love** that way."

I scream-laugh, flipping them off. "**Fuck off,** please, and thank you. And for your information, nothing happened. Hunter walked around the corner, and I left. It was embarrassing. I died. And now we're here."

It's a lie. And I meant to tell it. Guilt blooms, growing and compounding because I just lied as if I do it every day—with a smile on my lips, never skipping a beat. But I don't want to share him.

Aubrey wags her brows.

"What are you going to say to Hunter now? Like how will you explain? We need a plan."

Piper inserts a terrible idea, and they start bickering back and forth about what I should do. And I'm happy to let them because my thoughts are elsewhere.

I may have said nothing happened with Calder, but the truth is it feels as if *everything* happened with him. Like I woke up for the first time in my life. But how do I tell them that I have a hard-core crush on someone they so lovingly refer to as the town criminal?

They'll just tell me it was lust—that I was horny. And yeah, of course I was. Calder's insanely hot. The lips, the eyes...the damn tattoos. He's the inspiration for ruined panties everywhere. But there was more, an attraction I've never felt before him.

I let my teeth find my bottom lip.

He felt epic.

My phone dings from across the room, and I push up to my elbows, staring at it.

Calder doesn't have my number, but everything else tonight has been bizarre—what's one more thing? The girls stop talking as my phone begins dinging over and over, turning their attention to my face before they both scramble to get it.

Piper nabs it first, tossing it to me and laughing as Aubrey jumps on her back.

"Piper! We can't trust her to make her own decisions. What are you thinking?"

I'm giggling, opening my texts, offering, "It's Hunter," as I scroll to the top of the chain.

"Duh," Aubrey mocks, jumping off Piper's back.

They walk over toward the bed, but my smile begins to fade with each step.

"What's he texting?" Piper nudges as I sit silently.

> Hunter: I'm drunk, and you're not here.
>
> Hunter: Why aren't you here, Freckles?
>
> Hunter: Is it because you're slumming it across the tracks?
>
> Hunter: Whatever. Fuck it. Do you. I like my toys brand new anyway.
>
> Hunter: Tiffany says hi.

I drop the phone on my lap, looking up at my friends. They read the messages from over my shoulder, so I don't have to say anything.

"Can I really be pissed? We aren't anything to each other."

I don't say that he kind of lost his opportunity to bang me the minute Calder asked me for my name. Yet still, what a douchebag.

Aubrey shakes her head. "Yes, you will be mad. Fuck him. He's so gross. Tiffany Astor is not a flex. Monday morning, I'm telling everyone he had mold on his cock, and you didn't want to touch it."

Piper's nodding. "Mold allergies are a real thing. I've heard of that. We hate him. For life."

I start to laugh before I grab a pillow, covering my face, and groan, falling back.

Fuck. This. Night.

Calder

"**K**eys," Roman calls, holding his hand up as I toss them, a smile permanently planted on my face.

Like the fucking puppy he is, West pushes past me, calling dibs on the front seat, but I ignore him, pulling back the black leather bucket seat and motioning for him to get in.

"Bro, I called it."

My eyes shift to his.

"Come on, dude. I'm always in the back."

"Get the fuck in, West. It's where the kids sit. It's safer."

Roman chuckles as West flips me off, climbing into the back. I push the seat back, settling in at the same time Roman does.

The Mustang growls, engine revving as I hang an arm out the window, looking back at the house before we pull out of the driveway.

See ya later, Sutton.

We pull out onto the main road as Roman keeps glancing at me.

"What the fuck has you acting like you took a hit of the shit we were just selling?"

I don't answer, looking in the side mirror, then out the window. West leans forward from the middle of the back, propping his arms on the seats.

"There's a girl. The redhead from the park."

My palm comes to his face, pushing him back as he keeps fucking talking, shoving my hand away.

"And she's kinky. She was watching—"

I turn in my seat, bumping Roman's arm and making us swerve as I reach back, slapping West's face before he can finish.

"Shut the fuck up, or you walk home."

West doubles over, having avoided most of my hand as I point to him before falling back into my seat.

"Oh shit," Roman bellows. "Is our Romeo in love?"

"Gimme a break. She was hot. That's it. That asshole was busy," I chuckle, pointing back to West. "I wanted to be too."

I shift my face toward the blurred houses to hide any evidence of my lie. Because it was more than that. I've never felt that kind of attraction. I wanted to bust that little fuck Hunter in the mouth when he called her over. Maybe I will the next time I see him.

West lifts his face to the sky, sounding feminine. "Ah, Calder. Yeah, do me."

I lean down, turning the music up to offensive, drowning out the torment. Roman breaks out into laughter, shoving my shoulder and hitting the gas as we wind around the cliff—guided only by headlights and the moon *she* hates shining down on the ocean.

West howls, standing up in the back, gripping the headrests as we whip around corners, my hand slapping the side of the car.

This is life. Wild, free, and filled with the possibility of Sutton.

West drops back on his ass, and I lay my head back, wind whipping my face as my eyes close.

The first day I saw her wasn't at the park. It was earlier. The guys and I were coming back from a run my Pops sent us on. We were parked at a red light talking about playing some ball later. Sutton was walking into the church next to her school, Immaculate whatever. She was with those friends of hers, laughing as her wild red hair flew around her face.

They were in those ugly fucking skirts that are too long and plaid. But unlike her friends, who'd rolled those shitty things up short enough to show the goods, hers hit her knees.

She was all buttoned up in her white shirt and virtue.

Just a good girl—only willing to get on her knees to pray. And the most dominant part of me wanted to make her dirty.

What the fuck is it with men? We see something clean and want to run a smudge down the middle.

Sutton is pristine.

And the whole time we stood out on that beach, all I wanted to do was run my grease-stained finger down her body. Through her folds, pressing inside her warmest places until she forgot that *good girls* exist because all she craved was my dirty fucking mouth.

I can almost picture it.

I'm pulled from my thoughts as the sound of tires over the train tracks mark our re-entry back onto our side of town. The side where white picket fences need repainting and people cut their own lawns.

My eyes lower to the mirror, watching her side grow smaller.

A town like St. Simeon is an illusion—a mirage. It doesn't really fucking exist. Their side is the same as ours—corrupt, cruel, greedy. We just don't have the luxury of hiding it all behind five-hundred-dollar sunglasses and afternoon polo matches.

Not that I ever would.

It's better to be the wolf than the bitch that hides in sheep's clothing.

But are you hiding, Sutton? Will I find out that you're exactly what I hate—just some rich girl trying to slum it.

Something deep inside of me, something I refuse as fast as it brims, tells me that we're already cursed if she's from that side.

We don't need the moon.

Roman lifts his chin toward a liquor store, and I nod, suddenly feeling like liquor would be a perfect idea.

"Calder."

My father's voice carries through the garage walls, so the guys and I separate as we walk through the yard with a nod. I walk inside the ample space, looking past all the cars he likes to collect.

There are six in here, and the 1970 Plymouth Hemi 'Cuda is up on a custom lift. My eyes drift over the sleek body as I walk the row of cars toward where my old man is seated.

"What's up, Pops?"

He's wiping his greasy hands on a rag as he looks up at me with a sun-worn face behind dark eyes.

"Any trouble at the Kellys' tonight?"

I shake my head. "No, Pops, we made sure they were stocked with product and happy."

"Good. Good. Keep those boys happy. I don't need to remind you how important this arrangement is."

"No, Pops. You don't."

"Okay, you boys get a good night's sleep. We have church in the mornin'. It's time we met the town and I said hello to that goddamn thorn in our side, Senator Prescott. And your souls would do well with a little prayer."

Every once in a while, my Pops' Irish lilt leaks out in his speech. He hates it. It reminds him that he doesn't belong. And for a man like my father, knowing your place in this world is of the utmost importance.

It's one of the reasons Roman and West have the Wolfe name.

Roman's mom was a drug addict, who overdosed, and his dad was a deadbeat. At three, he was left alone eating spoiled leftovers and sitting in his own shit. So a woman brought him to our house—not child protective services or the cops.

To us.

Our way of life is different than most. Loyalty is up there with God. Roman lived on our block, which meant that he already belonged to our family in a way. It meant that he had a place in this fucked-up world.

On the other hand, West tried to pick-pocket my dad four years ago on a Boston subway. It amused my Pops so much that he gave him a place with us because there's always honor among thieves.

"I expect you three ready tomorrow. Bright-eyed and goddamned bushy-tailed. No fucking around, Calder. Tomorrow's business. God first—then business."

I give him a nod. "All right, Pops."

He turns away, standing and popping the hood of the Camaro he's working on, dismissing me. So I turn, making my way out to the yard, toward the small house in the back.

When we moved, none of us wanted to. Boston's home. We know it like the back of our hands, raising hell, dodging cops, and running those streets. But our lives are not our own.

Family means more than the people you're related to. It's loyalty and allegiance.

Roman and West declared theirs years ago. But for me, I was born into it. Baptized in blood as my mother was gunned down—me in her belly.

This life was chosen for me, and I'll die never knowing anything else.

West looks up from the couch as I open the front door.

"Everything good?"

I nod. "We have a curfew. Business in the a.m.—church."

"Shit." He jumps up. "I'll get the shot glasses. That way, we get lit faster."

Roman shakes his head, tossing me a beer, but I crack it open as I head toward my bedroom.

"I'm wiped. I'm gonna pass out."

West grabs the counter, pretending to jack off. "Sweet dreams, bitch."

My middle finger is all I give as I walk into my room, shutting the door behind me before dropping to the mattress on the floor and downing my beer.

I lean over, grabbing a leather-bound notebook from the floor, and toss the now empty can down. My back hits the bed, and I open to the place I wrote my last thoughts.

The cigarette was nice, but she's the only thing I wanted to inhale.

Fuck. I toss the journal, kicking off my shoes as I reach over my shoulder and drag my hoodie off, remembering how she played with the strings. And the look on her face, tempting me to give her the kiss her lips prayed for.

"I should have," I breathe out, lying back to shove my pants off, eyes dropping to my dick.

It's hard, bobbing against my stomach, wanting me to strangle it as I picture her pert tits bouncing in my face or that perfect ass bent over the hood of my car. I dig into the pocket of my discarded jeans and pull out my phone, tapping the very first playlist. I lift my palm to my face and spit into it before wrapping it around my cock.

Air hisses between my teeth as I wind my palm down over the veiny shaft, chin tilting up toward the ceiling. My muscular thighs separate, one knee bent as I close my eyes, pushing into my hand.

Goddamn, I want this girl bad.

I want my hand in her hair, holding her over the hood of my car for anyone to see just to prove they can't fucking have her. She's my wild beauty.

Mine to ruin, to fuck, to have.

My jaw drops open as my breathing gets heavier, each tug turning my exhales more ragged. The side of my ass indents with her pulse as I jack off to the vision of her.

I can see her—legs open, that sweet cunt glistening, begging me to give it pleasure.

"Oh fuck. Spread those legs for me."

I push inside of her, enveloped by her warm pussy. It hugs my cock, quivering as I stroke the soft walls.

"Yes. Take it deep."

Moans fall out of her mouth as she's controlled, my hand gripping her soft mane. I fuck her like an animal, thrusting inside, over and over, listening to her scream my name, begging God to make me let her come.

With each thrust, her silky-smooth ass bounces, screaming to be marked as her pleasure soaks my cock.

"Say my name."

I'm jerking my cock harder, lost in the fantasy of fucking Sutton. Knowing just a taste of her would send me over the edge. A lick of that sweet pussy coming all over my tongue as I ate her from behind.

"Oh fuck," I grunt as my body contracts, warm beads of cum spurting onto my stomach and cascading onto my hand.

My eyes stay closed as my breathing slows, not ready to give up my fantasy. The memory of her walking away tonight pushes to the forefront of my mind as I let out a rough breath and open my eyes.

"See you in the daylight."

Chapter
ten

Sutton

"**S**utton, honey, we're going to be late to mass."
I'm nodding even though my mother can't see me as I text Piper back from the hallway upstairs.

> Me: I don't care if Hunter wants to apologize. He was a dick. What happened to we'll hate him forever?

> Piper: Nothing. Don't kill the messenger. Shephard told me to tell you.

> Me: I see. Shephard told you...mmhmm. Someone wants to get flocked.

> Piper: Don't start. That's a terrible pun. I'm just saying—be prepared because Shephard said Hunter's on a "land Sutton" mission.

> Piper: You should've just texted him back—boys always want the ones that get away.

> Me: (*eye roll emoji) See you soon.

I shove my cell in my purse, hearing my father call this time with his *I'm irritated* voice, so I hustle.

"Sorry," I answer, bounding down the stairs. "I was just grabbing my purse."

My mother's brushing over my father's lapels before he turns toward the door with an annoyed glance at me and heads out to the waiting limo. She offers me a smile as I follow, wishing I'd overslept at Aubrey's so that I could've skipped today.

The idea of asking for forgiveness rather than permission is beginning to grow on me. I need to try it out more because this scene is the same every week.

We dress in our Sunday bests, sit on a hard wooden pew, and deal with my father's mood until we're back home. Then we all complain about going, only to be reminded by the guy who put everyone in a bad mood that the constituency demands it.

I'm not sure either of my parents are particularly religious. Still, according to Baron Prescott, God serves the highest purpose—he helps elections.

"So," My mother pats my knee as we settle into the back of the limo. "How was the sleepover at Aubrey's last night? Anything I need to know?"

"Uneventful." I half-smile, turning my head toward the window.

That lie's going to cost you half a rosary of prayers.

My parents begin talking about some fundraiser they're organizing for the town. I swear my mother does it on purpose to relax my father as I stare out the window.

Life is so weird. Last night was supposed to change the trajectory of my life. I was supposed to be different today—defiled and happy.

I mean, I am different, but it's not because I slept with Hunter. A smile drifts over my lips, thinking about the way Calder played with my hair. My mother says something about Marianne Kelly, Hunter's mother, so I stay zoned out, hating to be reminded of him again.

Such a jerk.

"Sutton, darling?"

My eyes lift to my mother's as I come back from my errant thoughts.

"Sorry, I was—"

"Deep in thought," she interjects.

I nod.

"I was saying that Marianne Kelly called me this morning to tell me all about how smitten her son is with you. Apparently, he messaged her while she and Mr. Kelly are in London. Why haven't I heard anything about this from you?"

My face scrunches up. *Low blow, Hunter—getting the parents on board.*

"Which boy?" my father interrupts. "Because a college dropout isn't someone I want my daughter entertaining."

My mother waves him off, and I wipe my hands over my cornflower-blue knee-length baby doll dress.

"Doesn't matter which one. The feeling isn't mutual. And most specifically, for Hunter."

"Now, wait a minute," my father counters. "Hunter's a star athlete. Wants to go into politics and has the name for doing it. I vote to give the boy a chance."

My head swings between my mother and father. *Since when did my love life become a democracy?*

"We aren't voting. Hunter's a whore. I'm uninterested."

Stern consternation—that's the look he gives me. But I hold my ground. My father may be a professional bully on the Hill, but I have zero interest in a group decision here.

Can it, Senator. It's what I wish I could say but never would.

"You should save that kind of speak for your friends, Sutton. And a word of advice—boys don't like to be caged in. Bide your time, let him fly, and he'll remember you when it matters. Hunter Kelly comes from the kind of family who's worth your while."

Oh. My. God. I should open the car door and jump—my future is bleaker than death. *Let him fly? When it matters?* I'm going to puke. I have to physically force my eyes from rolling back into my head. It's not often I get these lectures, but when I do, I become convinced that I'll be victim to a modern-day arranged marriage—a politically advantageous one.

There has to be a Netflix show documenting how I can escape.

"Geez, Dad." Sarcasm drips from my mouth. "I'd hoped this kind of matchmaking would start in college. You know, our families would summer together, forcing us to be around each other, planting the seed until we cave. Only to realize we don't even like each other. The only thing we have in common is that our families are maniacal institutions powered by greed. So we make the ultimate sacrifice and join the ranks of loveless marriages throughout history, having two-point-three kids and a golden retriever named Chardonnay."

The snort from my mother tells me she enjoyed my little speech, but the unappreciative eyes sitting across from me—they do not share the same sentiment.

His phone chimes, and he looks down, finally losing the scowl. "I like to get the ball rolling early. Sue me. Elizabeth, let's have the Kellys over for dinner next week."

This time, I do roll my eyes.

The car slows in the parking lot, pulling to a stop at the curb. The three of us sit in uncomfortable silence before my father nods at me.

"Try and be pleasant today, Sutton. It is a house of God, after all."

My father is let out first, leaving my mother to raise her brows at me.

"What?" I shrug. "He started it. And do not invite the Kellys over."

She grins, patting my cheek. "Give him a break? Between re-elections coming up and this whole town thing, he's hitting the ceiling. More than ever, you need to be a team player."

My hand falls over hers, stopping her from exiting.

"What town thing?"

The smile I'm given is the one she reserves for the press. "Nothing you need to bother yourself with. If it's pertinent, you'll know. Until then, be the daughter we know you are and make friends with Hunter Kelly. You don't have to marry the kid, but his family's name is an ally I'd like your father to have. I'd hoped you'd want that too."

And just like that, I'm effectively schooled by one Elizabeth Prescott, senator's wife and bloodthirsty attorney-at-law.

"Yep," I whisper under my breath, following her out and joining my father's side.

Friendly waves from my father and gleaming white smiles from my mother flank me as we walk the long wide cement path toward the mini Gothic cathedral modeled after Westminster Abbey. But unlike the abbey, the entry for the cathedral isn't ground level.

Three sets of dark wood doors flanked by arches stand at the top of a grand stone staircase. It's a statement, just like the manicured lawn on either side of me that stretches out along the width of the building.

"Remind me," my father whispers as we walk the pathway toward the front. "The new priest is..."

"Father Paul," I answer discreetly, letting my eyes travel past the archways where families are entering under the stained glass.

There are those angels.

My mother whispers something catty about someone's dress to me as Piper waves from the front lawn, and I smile back.

My nerves grow with each step forward because I just want to make it through the morning without seeing Hunter. It's clear our friendship is out of my hands, but I can at least hold out for today. Especially if he plans on making a big deal about last night. I can't believe he got his mother to call mine. Ugh, I should castrate him for that.

I'm searching the crowd, hoping to spot Hunter so I know where to avoid, when "Hey, Freckles" fills my ear from behind.

"Oh shit," I gasp, spinning around as Hunter takes a step back.

My mother's face shoots to mine. "Excuse me? What did you just say?"

Hunter's grin gets my narrowed eyes as I cover for myself.

"O...ceans of people..." I motion around as my cheeks turn red because I'm positive she knows exactly what just came out of my mouth, but I lie anyway.

"Doesn't it seem like a bigger turnout than normal? I bet Jesus is so happy."

My father stares down at me before giving a nod toward Hunter.

"Nice to see you, Hunter."

"Sir. Mrs. Prescott." He smiles like a portrait of charm.

I hate him.

"What do you want, Hunter?" I huff, pointing toward the church. "Confession is that way."

My father clears his throat, drawing my eyes.

"We seem to have the local press here today. So, stop being yourself and smile. And for God's sake, Hunter, apologize for whatever you did to this girl—because she holds grudges. She still hates me for telling her she was allergic to dogs so that she'd stop asking for one. It happened when she was three."

My mouth drops open as my father's name is called. "Senator Prescott. Sir. Could we have a photo?"

"Absolutely." He beams, escorting my mother toward the front steps of the church, where Father Paul is standing.

Hunter stares at me, reaching for my hand, but I link it behind my back with the other.

"Freckles."

"It's Sutton. Or do you call all your toys that so you don't have to remember our names? Although, you seemed to know Tiffany's last night."

He lets out a deep breath. "Jesus Christ. Can we just start again?"

I draw my brows together in question because I'm not really sure I want to. But as he starts, I don't stop him because far be it from me to rob him of begging for forgiveness.

"Listen, I was a dick because I got jealous." His eyes lock with mine. "Not an excuse, just an explanation. But I thought you liked that asshole, and I got mad and tried to hurt your feelings. My ego is fragile. It's a '*my bad*' kind of thing, and I swear I won't do it again. But you have to give me one more chance to let me prove it."

My teeth find the inside of my cheek because that was unexpected honesty. A lot of it. He steps in closer to me.

"I know the truth probably makes me look worse than the shit I pulled last night, but I'm fucking scared that you've decided to pass on me. Because I like you, Sutton. Like more than any other girls I've dated."

"You've dated people?"

I say it teasingly, but it's the truth. Hunter doesn't date.

He tugs my hands from behind my back, holding them at my side. "See, it's because of stuff like that. You give me shit. Call me out. I like it."

A smile peeks out, even though I try like hell to keep it away. Now he's laying it on thick.

"Nuh-uh. Nice try, but you've officially dipped a toe into '*that guy*' status with 'you call me on my shit.' I mean, we've spoken like, what? Three times? And now you're in love with me? You want me because I turned you down."

He smiles, not even ashamed to admit that I'm right.

"Maybe. But that's not the only reason. I also think you're funny. Pretty. Smart. Unexpected. And hard to get just makes winning your heart that much sweeter. I like you, Sutton. And not that you care, but I didn't touch that girl last night. Because I couldn't stop thinking about you."

I shrug, but he bends down slowly until his mouth is almost touching mine.

"Forgive me? Let me win you over?"

An exhale leaves my lips as I step back. "I'll think about it."

His grip tightens around my hands as I start to tug them away, and he locks eyes with me.

"You can like him. It's fine. Just like me more."

As he lets me go, my heart picks up its pace because I *do* like Calder, and Hunter knows it. And that fact makes me feel a lot less high-and-mighty—because who was the player first? Me.

I lick my lips, hand wrapping around my hair. "Like I said, I'll think about it."

His jaw tenses, a glint of mischief in his eyes as he groans.

"Fuck. You're killing me, Freckles."

The church bells ring, signaling the start of mass. So, I look back over my shoulder toward the steps as Hunter chuckles and says, "I should probably watch my language. We are in front of a church."

As my head swings back to him with a grin on my face, I pause, seeing my father standing close to another man, his hands fisted at his sides. He looks angry, and that's unlike him.

What the hell? My father never cracks. Ever.

"I don't think it counts until you're inside the building," I murmur, my focus fixed on the scene.

The photographers are nowhere to be seen, and more and more, the steps to the church are becoming empty as people filter inside. But my father and the stranger both stand their ground.

Whatever's happening isn't good.

"I'll see you later, Hunter," I offer as I make my way over toward my mother. I feel him following, but I don't care because my focus is on my mom. She's standing at the bottom of the church steps, a few feet away from my father, with a look of concern marring her face.

What the hell is going on?

The closer I get, the more I can feel the tension hanging thick in the air. I'm staring, taking the stranger in because he's familiar, although I've never met him.

He's the same build as my father and looks around the same age just not aged as gracefully. His hands are covered in tattoos, probably attached to more, hidden under his expensive suit.

He looks like...

Harsh words spitting from my father make me bristle and pay attention.

"This is no place for you. St. Simeon will not fall to your drugs and filth."

"Senator, you don't have a say here. And you know it. This town is as much ours now as it is yours. The sooner you accept that, the better it'll be for everyone."

"You piece of shit. St. Simeon is my advantage. You and Connor O'Bannion would be smart to remember that this isn't the only hill I run."

O'Bannion? How do I know that name? The memory of my father talking about a bill targeting organized crime flitters through as I come to stand next to my mother. *They're talking about the Irish mafia.*

"Mom, what's happening?" I whisper, glancing over to see Hunter walk past us, eyes darting to mine before he heads up the stairs.

As if sensing me, my father looks over his shoulder. "Elizabeth. Take Sutton inside."

She takes my hand, patting it as she turns me to take us away. But I tug back, not wanting to leave my father alone.

"We should stay with him," I rush out, but she drags me up the steps, her words harshly whispered into my ear.

"That man is scum. He and his sons will infest our community with drugs and crime and happily ruin everything your father's built. He's an enemy of this state and your father."

"Who is he?" I breathe out, stumbling a bit as I'm forced to take the stairs too quickly.

"A terrible man, in the O'Bannion crime family...Tyler Wolfe."

Wolfe? As in...

My head shoots back over my shoulder as we reach the landing, mind swirling as the pit in my stomach grows so big that all the butterflies that were once there are sucked down, dying in the darkness.

Honey-blond hair and broad shoulders stand above the rest, calling my eyes as Calder comes to stand right next to his father.

No.

My mother's arm wraps around my waist just as Calder's eyes—ones that match the color of my dress—stare up at me with the same tragic recognition.

"Come, darling. There is nothing but trouble down there." I shift my head to look at her. "I forbid you from ever being around them, Sutton. Tyler Wolfe and his boys will be ruined and run out of this town. Your father will see to it. Promise me you'll stay away."

I nod, glancing back at the boy with a storm behind his angel eyes and the devil in his soul, watching him watch me. Feeling just as lost in him as I was last night.

"Then I guess I'll have to ask you again in the daylight. Wouldn't want us cursed."

But we are.

"Why does it have to be you," I whisper to myself, watching Calder's face grow dark as a hand weaves through mine.

I lift my eyes to Hunter, who's looking down at me, and I pull my hand back.

"Come on, Freckles. Sit with me?"

I nod, not really knowing what to do, as we turn and walk inside, but Calder never stops watching me. I know because the goose bumps don't go away until the church doors close.

Chapter eleven

Calder

Her last name's Prescott. What the fuck.

The heavy church doors slam shut, cutting me off from Sutton and throwing me back into reality. Goddammit. If I didn't know any better, I would think I'd been set up.

Baron Prescott is not only my father's enemy but the loathed opponent of the Irish mob. He's a goddamn dead man walking, and I was almost in bed with his daughter. At least I was hoping to be.

That girl's a siren's call—fiery red hair, with eyes greener than envy luring me right off a fucking cliff. Although by the look in her eyes, that wasn't her intention. The regret she hurled in my direction hit me square in the chest as she stared me down.

It felt a lot like Sutton wished she'd never met me, but I'd do last night over again a thousand more times if it meant I could have another chance to kiss her.

I should've fucking kissed her.

West leans in, nudging me. "Dude, Red is Senator Prescott's daughter."

I shake my head discreetly, letting him know to shut the fuck up. This isn't the time or the fucking place to clue my Pops in. Not that there ever will be. Last night goes to my goddamn grave because if Pops finds out, there are only two outcomes: I become a liability or an advantage. I don't like either.

My father snaps his fingers, and Roman, West, and I turn, following him back toward the black SUV waiting at the curb. The guys that work for my father jump out, opening the doors for us, but I hang back, gripping my neck with one hand, a singular thought on repeat.

"Pops, you mind if I stay back?"

What the fuck am I doing?

Roman and West look at me and then at each other as our dad walks toward me, searching my eyes.

"Everything okay, boy?"

Fuck, this is stupid and reckless. There's no way in hell either of us could ever cross this line. But I have to see her. One more time.

I nod, letting my hand drop from my neck. "Yeah. I just want some time to think. Church always makes me think about, you know—"

His face grows stern, understanding that I mean my mother.

Using her as my lie is the lowest of the lows, but if anyone would've understood the part of me that's still human, I think it would've been her. It's also the most convincing lie I can tell my Pops because he harbors the same sadness.

My mother was beloved in our community. Spent all her free time at the small parish by our home, volunteering and helping the nun's with their garden. Looking back, I think it was her way of balancing the wickedness of life. When she died, that church and the people in it made sure I always carried her with me.

Forgive me, Ma.

"Go. Take the time you need. Lena was a godly woman, taken too soon." He pats my face. "Men like us don't deserve peace, but we can pray she gets it."

He turns around, walking back to the car as I stare at his back. I stand in my place, watching as the door closes. I don't move until the SUV turns the corner, just to make sure they're gone before I cut across the lawn next to the church, diving in deep to my bad ideas.

My hand glides over the wall as I sneak around the side, stopping at the first door I come to. *Come on, be open.*

It clicks as I twist the knob, the sound of the priest giving the reading filtering out. I slip into the hall next to the main room, shutting the door quietly as I look around, no plan in mind, just fucking winging it.

My head shifts up and down the hall, scoping shit out. *"What's the next move, asshole?"* I walk quickly toward the stairs by the front, looking over my shoulder to make sure nobody's coming. I'll head to the balcony and try to spot her and then figure out what the fuck I'm going to do next.

As I near an archway that connects the hall to the main room, I take a deep breath before darting past, hopefully unseen. I come to the stairs, taking them two at a time until I'm at the top.

The sound of people lowering the benches to fall on their knees to pray rattles the room, echoing against the walls, keeping my footsteps quiet as I enter.

Sun burning through the stained glass touches everything in the room, creating pockets of light that show tiny little specks of dust floating in the air. I walk by two confessionals sitting side by side, along with an organ that shows its neglect.

It's as if nobody comes up here.

The small balcony juts out, overlooking the congregation below. So I duck down, sliding onto the organ's bench, staying somewhat hidden as my arms rest on the gold-leafed wooden rail.

Prayed responses fill the room as I scan it for the girl I shouldn't be looking for when she suddenly stands.

Making me do the same.

Sutton walks toward the altar and takes a wine goblet from the priest. She turns, smiling, taking her place to help with communion, as row after row of people stand, lining up in front of her.

Look up. Come on, Sutton. Look. Up.

Each person steps forward, taking a sip, and she wipes the goblet before handing it over again as I shift my head, trying to keep my eyes on her around all the backs of heads.

Look up.

Some old man pats her shoulder, making her smile bright, and I can't help but get drawn in. It's the way she smiles...with genuine goodness. Goodness I don't possess. This is her world, one where old men say nice things and people at least pretend to have a heart.

What the fuck am I doing? We don't just come from two different worlds. More like parallel universes. What the hell am I going to do? To say?

My eyes drop as I take a step away, feeling something I can't explain. It's like being shown the sun and then imprisoned in darkness.

Our fathers are enemies. Our lives are predestined—doomed from the start.

Except there was this moment.

An amazing fucking moment when she smiled at me with all that same goodness and I forgot who I was.

I've never hated my last name until now.

I turn, shoving my hands into the pockets of my dress pants, feeling the weight of disappointment on my shoulders.

You walk the fuck away. Forget this girl. Because if you do one good thing in your goddamn life, it'll be to leave Sutton Prescott alone.

A heavy exhale leaves my body as I head back toward the stairs, but the sound of footsteps lifts my face just as her green eyes come into view.

She stops at the top, staring at me, blinking. My head shifts to the balcony, pointing to where I just saw her.

"What are you doing here? How'd you get here so fast? I just saw you—"

"I ran," she rushes out, brushing her hair from her face. "I saw you. So I pretended I had to pee. Then I ran here."

My eyes drop to her chest, seeing it rise and fall quickly, then to her hand, the wine goblet still in it.

She ran.

"You're supposed to give that back." I grin, making her smile.

She drops her eyes before coyly looking up through a forest of lashes. "Why are you up here and not down there?"

"We came to the earlier mass. Is that what you're asking?"

She shakes her head. "No. Are you up here for me?"

Yes. I take a step closer, not on purpose, but her body calls me to it.

"I had something to say to you."

Her eyes urge me to speak, hungry for the words on the tip of my tongue. But more footsteps have her spinning around, then back to me. Her fingers press over her lips as she hurries toward me, pushing me backward with one hand, wine sloshing in the other.

"Go. We have to hide."

The petite hand against my chest presses me backward as I smile, taking the wine goblet from her.

"Nobody's coming. It's from the hall downstairs."

She opens the door to the confessional, shoving me inside as she takes the other side, the one where the priest usually sits.

I'm laughing to myself, ready to walk back out as she whispers, "Shh. Shh. Shh. Please. I just want another second."

Another second...with me. That's all it takes to seal my fucking lips.

We sit in silence, each on our own sides of the box, separated by a wooden partition with small clovers carved out, giving me just enough of her face. The footsteps fade, leaving us alone again, and a sigh of relief leaves her lips. My eyes close, gripped by the sweetness of the sound.

Sutton's face comes closer, exorcising all thought from my body as I stare at her delicate profile. What is it with this girl? I don't think straight around her.

I'm sitting in a fucking confessional, hiding, staring at her face through a partition.

My eyes dart to the goblet in my hand, and I bring it to my lips, downing the rest of the wine as she whispers, "What are you thinking right now?"

She's so close that I can see her lick her lips after asking. I wipe over my lips with the back of my hand before I speak.

"That I'm a criminal... What are you thinking?"

She answers without hesitation, touching the partition.

"That I'm a liar... Why are you a criminal?"

I bring my fingers up, almost touching hers, but hover, tracing them in the air instead.

"Because I was born that way... Why are you a liar?"

"Because I promised I'd stay away from you."

Her hand drops away, but I linger, still lost in the memory of how her skin feels.

More silence stretches out until she whispers, "What did you want to say to me?"

Everything. Nothing. Fuck, I don't know.

"Would it matter?"

"No. But do you still want to tell me?"

"Yes."

The answer leaves my lips without permission because I'm no longer in control of my mind or body. I'm possessed by that same goddamn thought from earlier.

"Get out."

My fingers scramble over the door, searching for the handle, swinging it open quickly as I step out.

I'm already reaching for hers as she yanks it open, but before she can exit, I grip the nape of her neck, pulling her flush against me, sealing my mouth over hers.

Her gasp is swallowed by my tongue dipping inside, taking the exact fucking thing I wanted last night—a kiss.

But this one's rough and forceful. Because I'm willing to steal something undeserved and leave her lips swollen from the fucking possession I feel.

I want to burn my mark into the softness of her mouth—more than I've ever needed anything.

My head twists, taking from her as she grips the front of my dress shirt. Her fingertips curl around the fabric, pressing her body as close as possible, melting into me.

She tastes like regret, but I'm happy to suffer through it because I've never felt a bigger high.

We kiss, untamed like we could tear each other apart, until all the sounds become muted and the darkness of our eyelids takes over. Our tongues glide and dance over each other's, slowing, teasing, just until we're on the brink of need before diving in recklessly for more.

Her lips drag over mine, tongues moving in rhythm, breath stolen and given until we're the only goddamn thing that exists.

Fuck. I've kissed her my whole life—it's what it feels like.

Music floats around us, ethereal and angelic, as she runs her hands up my chest, wrapping them around the back of my neck. My head tilts in the other direction, hand rooted in her hair as I deepen our connection again.

The priest begins the benediction, but I'm not paying any attention until she tries to pull away because I'm fucking desperate for her.

As she does, my mouth finds her jaw, forcing her head to the side to give me more room. I lick and suck down her smooth neck, wanting to mark her as I run my tongue to where her shoulders meet. Goose bumps erupt as I growl into her flesh, hearing her sigh my fucking name.

"Calder."

I'm drawn to a complete stop, eyes meeting hers as I swallow hard. Because of the way she just said it. Fuck. Me.

The shit I'm feeling right now scares me. I barely know her. But right now, hearing my fucking name said like a goddamn prayer from those sweet lips—I'll kill any person that tries to take my place. There's no doubt in my mind. That's the power this girl holds over me.

I want to keep what I can't have.

Walk the fuck away before you actually burn it all to the ground.

Even as I think it, I'm so fucking spun that my mouth's hanging open, wanting more of hers, leaning in as she shakes her head.

"We can't."

"I know."

Her mouth meets mine, body arching toward me, hands in my hair before she pushes me away again.

"We really can't."

"I really know."

I yank her forward, wanting more seconds, but her palms cradle my face, forcing me to look at her as she whispers, "Be someone different."

I can't.

"Don't give a shit." I counter, but the look on her face says it all.

She can't.

My brows draw together, and I let my hands fall away as I step back from her.

She doesn't say a word, stepping out of the confessional, tucking her hair behind her ears before walking back toward the stairs and disappearing back to where she came from.

"Hey. Where the fuck did you disappear to today?"

I look up from where I've been hiding out—the passenger seat of the convertible GTO marked with primer—to see Roman walking toward me.

"Nowhere. Just had some shit to deal with."

The journal in my hand snaps shut as he raises his brows, opening the driver's-side door and sliding in.

"That *shit* wouldn't have to do with a certain little redhead, would it?"

I rest my arm on the door, not answering, so he smirks.

"You know Pops will have your ass. She's not worth that."

I chuckle. "You don't have to worry about me. I know my place. There's no pussy in this world that changes that."

"But—" he presses.

I hate that he can always read my mind. When we were kids, people used to always say that we thought with the same brain. Probably because every single one of our ideas was bad. But even then, Roman and I were always on the same page.

"But—" I groan, dropping my head with a grin. "She was—I don't fucking know. It was like for a hot minute I got out of the grime. You know?"

His brows draw together, and he grips the steering wheel as he stares out the front windshield.

"That's a dangerous game, C. Dudes like us need this life because, without it, we don't make sense. You start going around forgetting who the fuck you are, and shit's gonna go south."

He's right, and I know it. But that doesn't mean I don't hate it. My head falls back on the seat, as I begin tapping the leather journal on my knee.

"Like I said, you don't have to worry. I know my place."

Roman half-laughs. "How many more times are you gonna say that shit before it becomes the truth?"

I stare out the window, jaw tense, not answering because the truth is I don't know. I know my place isn't with her, but I also can't shake the feeling that hers is with me. Goddamn. That kiss... For a few precious moments, she made me forget about the blood on my hands and the gun at my back. Because all I felt was her.

But that's what makes Roman so fucking right. This *is* a dangerous game because there is no "out." Not for real. Sutton's a lie—a mirage, just like the world she lives in. Because the only way out of my life is in a body bag.

My head turns to Roman to say just that, but the door to the garage swings open, hitting the wall as West stumbles in, face busted open.

"What the fuck."

Blood drips down his cheek from a gash over his eye as Roman and I jump out, over the doors.

"What the fuck happened?" Roman barks, grabbing a rag from the tool bench and pressing it to West's head as he sits on a chair.

He's mumbling, barely able to speak through his swollen mouth, but I bring my hands to his face anyway, forcing him to look at me.

"Who did this?"

He stutters, trying to speak, palming his ribs as he coughs, before looking at me, ragged breaths between his words. "Some college guys on bikes...down by...down by the wharf."

Motherfuckers.

"Are they still there?"

Roman doesn't wait for the answer, walking toward the racks and pulling a bat down. West nods, and my eyes meet Roman's.

"Help me get him in the car."

He shakes his head. "He can barely walk."

West groans as I pull him to stand, but Roman grabs my forearm before letting go quickly.

"He's all fucked-up, man. Leave him here."

My eyes lock to West's, gritting the words out from between my teeth.

"You wanna stay behind?"

He drops his face to the floor, not answering, but I tug it back up.

"You never let another man fight your goddamn battles. I don't give a fuck how bad it hurts—if there's breath in you, you fight. To the fucking death if it's your time. But you never roll the fuck over. You understand me?"

He nods, stepping out of my grip, lifting his chin before ambling toward the car door like he should. But as I follow, Roman's hand on my shoulder stops me.

"You gonna run this by Pops?"

I shake my head, looking over my shoulder.

"I don't need permission to protect my fucking brothers."

Roman doesn't move, eyes searching mine before a smile breaks out over his face.

"Then let's fuck shit up."

The minute the car skids to a stop, my feet hit the pavement, bat in hand, nothing but violence in my fucking veins. Adrenaline buzzes like an electric shock as we rush toward three assholes in their pussy-ass leather gear standing next to and on some bikes.

"Which one?" I roar, flipping the bat from head to handle, pointing it in front of me.

West motions toward the guy in the middle, wearing a leather jacket with racing stripes. But all three start to square up laughing as we walk toward them.

You're gonna eat this fucking wood.

"You do this to my brother?" I growl as he flips me off like he's going to fucking do something.

He doesn't get a chance to try because the first crack knocks the motherfucker off his bike. The second splits his skull. My chest heaves as I look over the two still standing frozen from fear.

"Who's next?"

Roman rushes the guy to my left just as I'm encased in a bear hug from behind. Fuck. I'm tossed to the ground, feeling the asphalt embed in my arm as all hell breaks loose. It's like everything is on fast-forward. I shoot to my feet, toe to toe with some wannabe fucking biker, lifting my fists before throwing down.

Everyone's swinging, kicking, brawling—trying to kill each other.

Two more guys make their way out of the bar they were squatting in, running up on us as Roman knocks some cocksucker out. Obscenities fill the air as their yells get louder with each blow we deliver. A crack to my jaw makes me spit blood as I grin because I don't feel anything but invincibility.

And the need to kill.

"You'll have to do better than that, pussy."

The dude comes at me again, but I throw my fist into his throat, hearing him immediately gasp for air and fall to his knees. My head turns to see West with the bat I dropped, using it like a fucking meat cleaver on the guy he pointed out.

"Ro," I bellow, pointing to West as Roman brings his boot down on another guy's ribs.

He nods, stalking over to make sure West doesn't kill the guy, as I throw a heavy kick to the guy on all fours, still searching for air. But as I do, a roar comes my way.

I'm charged, picked up off the ground, tumbling down back on the concrete again. Two hard punches land against my cheek, but it's like fuel to the fucking fire. I grab the dude's hair, knocking my skull into his.

"Fuck," he screams.

I push him back, straddling the piece of shit as I hurl punch after devastating punch into his face.

"You think you can touch my family," I roar. "You're a dead man now."

I grab his hair, yanking his head up before smashing it down on the concrete over and over. All the anger inside of me pours out. I'm drowning him in it.

He spits blood to the side, head flopping down as my knuckles come down, splitting open—my blood swirling with his.

But I don't stop because this is who I am.

The person I will never escape. The man I'm meant to be.

There is no goodness. No soul. No gentleness.

I'm an animal.

I throw one more punch before I'm hauled off, Roman yelling in my ear.

"Cops. We gotta get out of here."

I shove off Roman, throwing a boot into the guy's ribs.

"Fuck them. Let 'em come."

"Calder," Roman yells, tugging on me, but I kick the guy again.

Roman grips my shoulder, smacking my face. "Enough, C. We can't risk cops—Tyler would kill us. Or West. We gotta go."

He's walking backward as I stand, breathing hard, mind fighting with emotion until I nod, stumbling into the present, and follow. West is moving slowly as we walk past him, so I throw his arm over my shoulder, hearing him say, "I fought, Calder. I wasn't a pussy," before he drops the bat, spitting up blood.

My words are breathless as we rush toward the car.

"Good job, West. You can rest now."

I swing the car door open, pulling the front seat forward to let West lie down in the back as I look out over the carnage. Preppy assholes are laid out, slowly trying to get to their feet, except the one I was fighting. He might just be knocked the fuck out. Or he might be dead.

I don't give a fuck either way.

This is my place—in the streets, as judge and executioner.

I look down at my hands, trying to remember what she felt like. But all I feel is the sting from my cuts and slickness from blood replacing where her hair lay softly across them.

"Get the fuck in, Calder."

I do, shutting the door as Roman peels out, shifting his face toward mine.

"You good?"

"Never been better."

Sutton

Chapter twelve

Aubrey's staring at Hunter from her desk, deep in thought, which worries me. What is she plotting?

She blinks, pulling out of her thoughts and shifting her head to my questioning face.

"Sorry, I still cannot get over the fact you saw that West dude get a blow job—I know you said you were cringing, but it's kind of hot. And I'm here for it."

Of course that's what she's thinking about. Perv.

I shake my head, trying not to laugh. "I can't get over the fact that you're still thinking about it. Four days later."

"Shh," Piper whispers from her desk.

Aubrey rolls her eyes. "Whatever. It's been in my spank bank reel since Saturday."

Piper glares at Aubrey, making me fold my lips under as she answers the look.

"Oh, calm down. I'm sure Twisted Sister had some fun in her day before she locked it up for Christ."

We start giggling, garnering a slap on the table that forces us to face forward in our seats. Aubrey stares at me, opening her eyes wide and mouthing, "I hate her," as I smile.

My eyes drop to my desk, the moment washing away as I stare at my nails. The sound of a dry-erase marker fills the room. I don't look up, spreading my fingers over the desk and pressing my fingertips into the hard surface, drifting quickly into the memory of Calder's chest.

I haven't thought of much else since Sunday. That kiss left its mark, leaving me burning in all the right places. But I meant what I said. We can't.

Even if I wanted to change my mind, I couldn't. After my mother questioned if I'd ever met Calder and his brothers in the back of the limo, my father was crystal clear with his expectation.

I was scared she saw right through me when I lied, but it wasn't her I needed to worry about. It was my father. He'd erupted, grabbing my arm as he yelled.

"Sutton, you will stay far away from those boys. They're trash. I won't have my daughter mixed up with those lowlifes. This isn't a suggestion. It's a goddamn order. I will not be disobeyed. Am I understood?"

I wanted to protest and tell him Calder was nice, that he was misjudged, but we'd both know that'd be a lie. Calder admitted as much in the confessional. And for the first time in my life, my father scared me.

Think about him just enough but not enough to forget his name or yours, Sutton. It's what I've repeated over and over in my head every single day.

Especially last night. I lay around, letting my hands roam over my body, remembering every single delicious moment. Hoping if I satisfied my urges, I'd exorcise him from my mind.

I imagined his eyes on me, his smile against my skin, hands on my waist, chest pressed to mine...fuck...the way he wove his hand into my hair before kissing me. I thought about him until all I could chant was his damn name.

A wisp of breath breezes past my parted lips as I trace the swirl pattern on the wooden desk with my fingertip.

"Psst. Psst."

I look up, still lost in thought, as I draw my curved pout between my straight teeth, trying to recreate the perfect sting of our first kiss, but my eyes meet Hunter's.

"Psst."

He smiles from a few seats up, so I half-smile back, feeling Piper pinch my back. I ignore her, almost irritated over being interrupted, but I know she won't stop. They've been bugging me all week to talk to him. I suppose Wednesday's the breaking point.

They almost died, swooned to death, when I told them how he apologized before they jumped right back on the Hunter wagon. I can't be mad. Of course they did—he's Hunter Kelly. A week ago, I would've laughed if someone said that dating him would feel like settling.

But it does because it is. Calder's lips made it that way. Which is fucked-up because Calder is a rule I can't break. There wouldn't be any forgiveness afforded me.

In this world, rebellion is quietly ignored so long as it never affects real life.

You don't date the son of a crime boss for the Irish mob when you're the daughter of a senator. *No matter how much you think about him.*

Hunter waves a note at me, quickly putting it behind him on Shephard's desk. Shep looks up, and I see Hunter whispering something to him before their heads shift in my direction. Shephard glances at Sister Christine, and when she turns to write on the board again, he tosses the note on my desk.

"Open it," Piper whispers.

I cover it quickly, sliding it down onto my lap and unfolding it to read.

Ditch with us to the beach. Don't say no, or I'll cry. I promise you the most epic day. And don't say you'll think about it—time's up, beautiful.

I look up at him, and he's feigning puppy dog eyes. Oh my God. I laugh. I can't help it. But I have to cover a hand over my mouth, faking a cough because Sister Christine is glaring at me.

"Sorry, Sister. Tickle in my throat."

When she looks away, I hand the note over my shoulder to Piper, hearing a whispered "Hell yeah" before she passes it to Aubrey, who stands and puts on her sunglasses.

"Can we go now?"

Piper starts to laugh, but before Aubrey's yelled at or expelled, the bell rings. We all stand, gathering our things, and file out, laughing and joking, only me trying to avoid the nun's glare.

The minute we're in the hall, Shephard snags Piper, mauling her with attention as Aubrey shoots her attention to Hunter.

"Where to, fearless leader?"

He grins, throwing his arm over my shoulder, but I shrug it off. He gives me a slight pout but answers Aubrey.

"Cross Point Beach. Everyone drops what they don't need and meets at the park in ten minutes before the next bell. I'm driving."

"What about bathing suits?" Piper cuts in. "And regular clothes for later. Girls don't carry an extra pair of basketball shorts and a hoodie in the back of our cars."

The guys laugh, but Aubrey waves her off. "My house is on the way. We can stop there, and you two can take whatever from my closet."

"Perfect." Hunter smiles.

The girls link hands as they walk away, Shephard by Piper's side. But I'm still playing catch-up.

My teeth find the inside of my cheek, gnawing as I think. Nobody else has parents that will care or be home to get an absence call, so they can do this stuff. If I ditch, the school will call my father. And he won't care that it's the last week.

Hunter tugs on the bottom of my polo.

"Hey. Freckles. Stop worrying. Just tell your dad you're hanging with me. Trust me, he'll be fine with it. I'll even talk to him if you want."

My head draws back as we walk to my locker.

"Wow, such an inflated ego. Also, how'd you know that's what I was thinking?"

He nudges my shoulder. "Not inflated. Great-grandson of a former president, but it's not a competition, so—"

I giggle, but he shrugs.

"He's hoping for a future nomination, right? A chance at the top seat in politics? Who better for his daughter to get cozy with than a Kelly?"

Hunter's fingers weave between mine as he nods a hello to someone passing by. "Trying to have fun under a microscope is fucking hard. Trust me, I get it. Of all people, I get you."

I push him sideways, tugging my hand away. "I'll think about it."

He groans as we stop in front of the row of metal doors, and I spin my lock open.

"Don't think. Just call. Give me a chance to win you over. I've got epic plans for today." He puts his head on my shoulder. "Have you ever been kissed underwater? We can make out with the fishies."

I swing my bag to the side, shoving everything in except my purse.

"Is this your big offer? Making out underwater?"

Hunter licks his lips, pushing my shoulder so I'm forced to turn my back against the locker as he stares down at me.

"I'll make you any offer you want, Freckles. I haven't stopped thinking about you, and the silent treatment this week is killing me."

"I've been preoccupied." I shrug, feeling his hand on my waist.

Hunter bends down to my ear, speaking quietly. "If you're not thinking about me, then I hate— Every. Single. Other. Thought."

He reaches into my bag, pulling out my cell.

"Call your dad, Sutton. I'm not waiting any longer for you to decide about us—I'm going to make it so you can't say no."

I'm staring back at him, eyes searching his as he places the phone into my hand. *Oh, Hunter, what am I going to do about you?* There's no real reason for me not to take him up on the offer. Absolutely none. What's the alternative? That I sit around and obsess over someone I'll never see again?

I did that in sixth grade over Harry Styles, and obviously, that worked out well.

Hunter grins as I hit my dad's number. He answers immediately.

"Sutton. I have a meeting in ten minutes."

My hand comes to Hunter's muscular chest, forcing him back so that I can have some space.

"Sorry, Dad. It's just..." I fold my lips between my teeth then decide to just say it. "Hunter invited me to a ditch day—everyone's going. But if you—"

"Hunter's going?"

Are you kidding? Wait, why am I mad...I want to ditch, right?

"Yep. Hunter's going. His friends, my friends. Probably the whole junior class. Actually, that's a lie, but it's still a thing. I didn't want to go without asking." I lower my voice, glancing over my shoulder at Hunter. "I know you and Mom prefer me not to go to these kinds of things. But it is the last week of school, so maybe give me some credit for waiting and calling?"

My father cuts me off. "Everyone needs to cut loose sometimes. And I can definitely get behind a few sanctioned outings. Is Hunter with you, Sutton?"

I blink, wondering who the hell I'm speaking with because this is not my father. My head swings over my shoulder, nodding before I answer hesitantly.

"Yes. He. Is."

"Let me speak to him, please."

"No," I draw out. "Please tell me that you're joking. Are you okay?"

He laughs louder this time, and I feel like I'm having an out-of-body experience. I can count the number of times on one hand that I've heard my father laugh.

"Sutton, if you want to go, I get to speak with the boy that will name your future dog Chardonnay."

Oh my God. Let me die. He has to be drunk.

"Dad," I whisper. "What is going on with you? Do not embarrass me. And for the record, we're just friends."

I turn just as the bell rings, holding the phone out to Hunter's smug face. I don't have to say anything. His arrogant *I told you so* look is enough. He takes the phone, motioning for me to head toward the exit as he brings it to his ear.

"Sir."

I can't hear what's said, but Hunter's answering, "Absolutely" ... "You have my word" ... "Will never happen" and "I look forward to it."

He hangs up, taking my hand and shoving my phone into his back pocket.

"What did he say?" I breathe out as we rush across the quad.

Hunter looks over his shoulder with a panty-melting smirk and a wink.

"He said I should knock you up. And then he invited me to dinner this weekend."

"Sutton. Come on. Get in. Right now."

Hunter's yelling from the water, splashing at me even though I'm too far away. Aubrey rolls to her side, looking out at the water and then back to me.

"That boy is so hot for you. I'm glad we gave him a second chance because I'm manifesting prom queen for your future."

I give a half-laugh, propped up on my elbows and staring out at the bluest ocean while white, foamy waves glisten against the shore.

Piper holds her boobs, looking at me and saying, "Do me?" as she rolls up to sitting. I lean over, tying her top for her, giggling again as the guys goof off in the water.

The day is amazing despite the war in my mind.

It's actually been one of those perfectly laid plans. The ones that you know will become a memory that you'll keep tucked inside to pull out when you need to remember a moment in time when you were exquisitely happy.

Piper runs her fingers through her blonde pixie cut and shrugs. "So let's get back to this past weekend. Are you still letting Hunter pillage your treasure?"

Aubrey sits up, tugging down her sunglasses. "Yeah? Because that hymen is still *seriously* intact. Inquiring minds want to know, ho."

I groan, motioning for the sunscreen. Piper hands it over, and I begin applying as I speak.

"I don't know. I'm thinking about it. But I'm leaning toward holding off for a while."

Piper wrinkles her forehead, sitting up further. "Bullshit."

Aubrey, whose mouth is hanging open, laughs.

"Piper. Is our girl about to become a legend?"

She snaps her fingers along with the first few words before adding, "To be the first person—and I say person because everyone wants Hunty's dick —to turn down a god and make him wait?"

Piper's eyes get wide, the grin on her face growing. "That's legend status, bish. Making him fall in love with you and having to wait for the nonny."

Aubrey shakes my shoulders, making me giggle. "Fuck you, Sutton Tensley Prescott. Who knew you had the long con down?"

I roll my eyes as Piper starts laughing, making Aubrey and I do the same because her laugh is atrocious. Only a tiny piece of me wants to tell them all about the kiss with Calder and explain why I really don't want to fuck Hunter. But I can't.

Sometimes when you say stuff out loud, it makes it too real, and I'm not ready to give up the fantasy. Even if I have to give up hope. And I don't care how dumb that is. Right now, Calder's still mine, and I like it that way.

The guys start making their way up the beach to our towels, shoving each other playfully. Shephard descends on Piper, getting her all wet, as she squeals, but Hunter looks between Aubrey and me.

"One of you walks. The other is going over my shoulder. You choose."

Aubrey and I look at each other, grinning before she says, "Stick that bitch over your shoulder. I'm walking."

I scream as I'm hauled to my feet. But it's drowned out by a crackle in the sky. We all look up to the bright orange fire streak climbing toward the clouds.

"Oh shit. Tag must be here. They're over at the cliffs."

Shephard says it like we know what he's talking about.

"He sends up a flare," Hunter offers, grabbing his T-shirt off the towel, "to let everyone around know to come party. The cliffs are gnarly, but Tag and his friends have been jumping off them for years."

He reaches for my hand. "Throw on some shorts. There's a private cove with access. It's close and guaranteed fun."

Aubrey wraps a sarong around her hips as Piper shimmies up her jean cut-offs. But I opt for my knotted T-shirt and shorts before we walk back to Hunter's truck. We toss everything into the bed before Aubrey scoots inside the car next to Piper and Shephard as I take the front seat.

Hunter pulls out as Shep begins talking about all the near-death experiences he's seen when people jump, so I turn to Hunter, raising my brows.

"You guys are jumping?"

"Hell no," Shep barks from the back. "My face is too pretty for a casket. But his ugly mug can."

Hunter smirks but keeps looking at the road. "Don't trip. Although I'm happy to see you care."

I roll my eyes with a grin on my face as he continues.

"There are three levels. I jump from the middle one, and the bottom one is for the girls, mostly. Nobody does the top—it's too dangerous, and only people with a death wish try that shit. It's fine. You'll see."

My eyes are still on him, unconvinced as he pulls onto the small side road that winds down to a private cove. I hear Shephard say, "There's my place, way over there, babe," to Piper.

Babe? Well then. Time to start grilling her for a change.

Hunter parks at the dead end, and I spot Tag's Corvette because his name is on the plate—*douche*—along with a few other cars I don't recognize.

We get out. Hunter comes around to take my hand as we walk down some wooden steps onto the sand. This time I let him, not pulling away. Because would it be so bad if Hunter was the one?

The music gets louder as more people come into view, about thirty feet away around a fire pit, cutting off my thoughts and drawing a smile on my face.

"How does he have this many friends to hang out with? Don't they have classes?"

Hunter smirks. "The semester's over for them, Sutton. Duh."

"Oh."

I duck my chin to my shoulder, looking out from the cove, hiding my embarrassment before I turn to look at Hunter. A quick kiss is planted against my lips, surprising me, before he lets go of my hand. "Be right back."

I shift, watching him half jog away toward the crowd as a long exhale bursts from my lips, making my cheeks inflate. Aubrey comes up next to me, weaving her fingers through mine as Hunter navigates the crowd. He's giving high fives and happily accepting all the attention he gets as he makes his way over to Tag.

"I fear *stud* is your soon-to-be boyfriend's default setting."

I smile because she's not wrong.

"Yeah, and it's annoyingly hot sometimes. I just—I don't know—"

She bumps my hip.

"You okay, Sut? You've been weirder than usual."

Aubrey can always read me well. I turn my head, looking at my beautiful friend, wanting to spill everything because I don't think I am okay. *How do you stop feeling something?* That's what I want to ask her, but I'm cut off by Shephard.

He holds up the coolers he's carrying toward some logs in front of us.

"Drink?"

He's offering it to Piper, but we all answer.

"Coke." … "Water." … "Vodka." Piper and I stare at Aubrey, who smiles, changing her order. "Geez, fine. Sprite. But there is a whole party going on over there."

He gives us a little salute. The girls start chatting, Aubrey forgetting my weird moment as my eyes begin wandering around. I've lived here my whole life, and I never knew that this cove was even here.

How was I this clueless?

My hand shades my eyes because even with sunglasses, the sun is too bright as I look up at the cliffs that jut out where the cove opens to the ocean.

"Damn. Those are high."

A high-pitched scream comes as someone jumps from the lowest point, shooting down into the water, distant cheers erupting.

Piper links an arm through my free one. "So yeah. That's terrifying. No, thanks."

"Dude. That's the low ledge." Aubrey points out, drawing her finger up to a higher cut out in the rock. "That's the middle—where Hunty said he jumps from."

I nod, giggling a bit at Aubrey's nickname for Hunter, letting my eyes carry even higher.

"Oh shit. There's someone up there."

The girls follow my line of sight. Our lips collectively parted.

Hunter walks up, and the girls release me so he can put his arm over my shoulder. But I don't look at him, fixated on the speck of a figure standing at the top of the jagged cliff.

"Someone's up there," I whisper. "That's the highest point, right?"

Hunter stares up. "Yeah. Get ready to call an ambulance. That dude's crazy."

Shep laughs as he hands our drinks to us, but it's not funny. Whoever's up there could get hurt.

Aubrey nudges me, whispering, "I thought he said nobody jumped from there."

"Nobody does," Hunter answers back, having heard her. "Way back, like before we were born, some guy died. So everyone knows it's too dangerous."

All of a sudden, the guy in black swim trunks runs toward the edge. I suck in a breath, bringing my fingers to my lips. Oh, God.

The chatter on the beach goes silent. Even the music is turned down as he hurls himself off the cliff, doing a backflip. The kind where your whole body stays long rather than tucking knees to chest.

It's badass, like something you'd see in a movie.

Every person on this beach is watching with bated breath, frozen in place as he drops like he's falling from heaven for what feels like forever until a splash erupts.

Hearts start beating again, everyone collectively returning to life as people slowly stand, their eyes searching the water.

I'm counting in my head, waiting for the guy to surface, but there's nothing. It's too long. It's been way too long. I pull away from Hunter, my feet carrying me closer to the water as my heart begins beating out of my chest.

Reaching behind me, I'm about to tell Hunter to swim out when the daredevil pops up, garnering howls and cheers from the entire beach.

"Whoa," I whoosh out, before looking back over my shoulder.

Hunter and Shep start talking about the guy being crazy, but my eyes are on the water, smile fading inch by inch because as the daredevil swims closer to shore, all I see are muscular tattooed arms slicing through the water.

Shit.

Chapter thirteen

Sutton

Aubrey slow claps, drawing our attention.

"Okay, now that the drama's over and that dude's alive, let's swim."

Hunter pats my ass. "Come on, beautiful. Strip. Let's get in."

I turn around, a smile on my face, never breaking stride as I join back in. Because what else can I do? Shephard makes a joke, pulling a laugh from everyone as I look around, pretending to scope out the best log for our clothes. But really, my eyes are back on him.

Calder walks out of the water, droplets streaming down his chest as he makes his way toward the party, and I swear my body goes numb. Why is he here? I stupidly thought we'd never see each other again, but here he is—the walking definition of sin.

The chest I was obsessing over a few hours ago.

"We can put our stuff here," I half mumble, the confessional racing to the forefront of my mind.

I look down, staring at the sand, going through the motions, unbuttoning my jean shorts. I lick my lips, eyes darting over and back, knowing that Calder has seen me.

Because my whole body warms, feeling his eyes rake over me.

I give my hips a shimmy to pull the shorts down, step out, and bend down to pick them up.

Another glance, and I reach for my shirt. I hate and love Calder watching me because it feels unbearable either way. I lift my shirt over my head, left only in a black string bikini. It's smaller than my normal ones, but all Aubrey had are the ones that pretty much show your ass.

Hunter sweeps my hair over my shoulder as I start to sneak another glance, stopping me.

"Hey, you need more sunscreen on your shoulders."

I give a tiny nod, feeling his hand slide the cold cream over my skin. His name is called again, and I know he looks over his shoulder, so I risk another peek.

Calder's eyes aren't on me. They're on Hunter—boring into where he's touching me, Calder's fists squeezed so tight the veins on his forearms look angry.

I shiver.

But not because I'm scared. It feels like I took a hit of the shit Tag likes to smoke. I've felt Calder, and I want more. Even if I shouldn't. But now, seeing the hate in his eyes over another guy touching me just turned me into an addict.

No. Stop. What the fuck is wrong with you? You're a crackhead.

"You okay? You shivered, Freckles."

I swing around, staring Hunter in the eyes, desperate for him to replace the feeling in my body Calder gives with a single look. A small indent forms between his eyes as he looks down at me.

"I know you saw him. Do you think we should go?"

If this is his way of asking *"Do you still like him?"* then I'm going to give him the answer I should've before.

"Do you? Because I'll do whatever you want. I'm here with you."

That's the correct answer, even if it doesn't sit right in my gut.

Hunter rewards me with a grin, leaning in and kissing my forehead.

"Nah, let's stay. I kinda like showing you off."

Shephard calls Hunter's name, motioning with a football before I can push back. He runs a few feet away, catching the throw with one hand, giving me a wink and pointing the ball at me.

"That one's for you. Want another?"

I nod, saying, "Absolutely," before turning back to the sunscreen and the mindfuck I'm feeling.

"Catch" is all I hear before I'm pelted by Piper's shorts, making me giggle and snap out of the wicked amount of spiral brimming the edge of bad ideas.

"Thanks a lot. Jerk."

She comes up next to me, eyes shining as Aubrey closes in on the other side of me.

"You're welcome. Also, you're shit at hiding."

My brows draw together. "What are you talking about?"

Aubrey tugs my hair. "You're still hot for the town criminal. Can't keep your eyes off him. But now we know he really is a criminal, so says Shephard. Apparently, there's a rumor that his dad is in the mob."

I shrug it off.

"Whatever." The girls look at each other, half believing my false nonchalance. "I'm not hot for anyone except Hunter."

Just add another lie on top of the others.

"Are you talking about me again?" Shephard teases, coming up behind Piper just as Hunter takes my hand.

I smile, letting him lead me toward the water, never glancing back once.

Calder

Chapter fourteen

Red. It's all I saw from the top of that fucking cliff. Wild red hair, carrying in the fucking ocean breeze.

"Dude. That was amazing."

Tag raises his hand to high-five me, but I just look at it before catching the towel Roman throws me. So, Tag lowers his hand, taking a hit off the shit he called us out here for, exhaling his words in a cloud of smoke. "It was fucking crazy. But I got that shit on the GoPro. It'll make for some wicked footage."

I bend down, grabbing the speaker off the sand, and turn up the music before lowering myself down into an empty beach chair. Roman chuckles, passing me a joint.

"Remind me why the fuck we're hanging out with this asshole?"

Rubbing the towel over my head, I smirk. "Because he buys a ton of drugs. And neither of us is trying to hang out with Pops explaining the bruises on our faces. Let's just be glad he's got bigger fish to fry right now."

As I draw in and hold a breath, he grins. My eyes find her again before I exhale harshly, passing the joint back to Roman. She's walking up the beach, looking at me like I'm doing to her. Neither of us is hiding it well. My tongue darts out over my bottom lip, the sting still there from where it got popped a few days ago.

"Speaking of avoiding Pops, did you text West to get his ass down here? I never thought there'd be a day when he went to school for like days in a row."

I nod my head, eyes still on Sutton. *That bikini's too fucking small.*

"Yeah."

Roman's breath is held as he speaks. "Dude. You're fucking dumb. And a glutton for punishment."

"Fuck you. I'm just lookin'."

He chuckles, blowing smoke at me, "Yeah, for fucking trouble."

I shift my face to his. "I'm sitting in a chair. Not balls-deep in her. How the fuck you figure I'm looking for trouble?"

"You can't even help it. This doesn't end any other way than bloody, dude."

I wave him off. "You've been smoking too much. Paranoia's kicking in."

"Naw, that's bullshit. I know what I see. I saw that dreamy-ass look on your face when we left that party, then on Sunday, and again right now."

I tense my jaw, disliking where this is going.

Roman leans in, passing the joint back. "Every damn time we see that girl, you're staring at her like she's the only fucking thing you see. If she ain't shit to you, then why can't you take your eyes off her?"

How am I supposed to answer that? Not with the truth—that she is the only thing I see. *Fuck.*

"Roman. Relax. Nothing's happening." I point my finger at him. "And stop fucking talking about last weekend. It's not your business. Understood."

He laughs, shaking his head.

"Fine, tough guy. I've seen what you can do with a bat. I'm chill. But brother to brother—be careful. Don't ever make it you versus him, C. Because you know who he'll choose."

By *him*, he means our Pops. And I know Roman's right, but I can't stop this goddamn feeling—one that says she's mine. I want her. I'll have her. And fuck anyone who tells me otherwise.

I look over at her again, nodding, barely hearing the rest of what Roman's saying as I take another long hit, but no amount of weed could keep me chill right now. Because the war inside my head just got a victor.

All I see is Hunter's fucking bitch hands on silky skin that belongs to me.

I'm gonna break every bone in his fucking body.

"Calder—" Roman calls, but I'm lost in a fog.

Sutton turns, saying something to Hunter, and for her sake, it better be *"fuck off."* But my teeth grit so hard they may break because I know it isn't.

He runs a few steps away, her friends coming up next to her as I take my last hit, then hand that shit over to Roman.

"C. Should we bounce? You can't fuck up little Kelly—you know his father is too important to Pops right now."

"I'm good," I snap.

I'm not. Not even a little. I've crossed over from reckless to dangerous.

He hits my shoulder, trying to get my attention off her, but I don't budge. I can't. Hunter walks up, taking her hand, and I lean forward.

Don't you fucking dare go with him. Come the fuck here.

The minute she takes a step in his direction, I stand. Ready. Out of my mind.

"Calder," Roman barks.

I don't answer, taking a step forward.

"Calder." This time he's in my face, hand pushing me back. "Sit the fuck down. I told you—this shit is trouble. What the fuck are you doing? Trying to die? Let that shit go. Let that chick go. Remember your fucking place, bro."

I growl, looking at his face, and nod, realizing what I almost just did. What the fuck am I doing? I gotta get my head straight. And off this girl.

"Yeah. I got it." He frowns at me, but I push him back. "I said I'm fine. I got it."

He exhales harshly, watching me before grabbing some drunk bitch, who laughs loudly as he squeezes her ass and turns her in my direction.

"Here. Use this as a distraction."

I shake my head, but he chuckles and looks down at her trapped in between us.

"You know how to dance, sweetheart...because my brother's lap could use one."

The fit blonde with a set of double D's steps toward me, pushing a manicured finger against my chest until my ass hits the chair.

"Let's help you relax."

She swings around, sitting in my lap, grinding her cheeks against my dick. A deep groan leaves my chest, only because my body betrays my mind. Even still, I try like hell to give in to it.

Roman smirks, saying, "Keep him busy, mama," as he walks away, leaving me with this bitch on my lap and my mind fighting to remain elsewhere.

The high begins to take over, mouth drying, eyelids growing heavy, all my thoughts fading into the distance as taut skin warms under my hands. She's guiding them, rubbing them up her thighs as she circles her hips. But it doesn't feel like what I wish it did.

I pull one away, running it up her back into her hair, gripping at the nape and bringing her back to my chest.

"Make it good, and I'll let you ride my cock for real."

I don't like her on me, or me on her. I want the goddamn redhead in the water with the little prick. *Motherfucker.* I have to walk away and bury myself in as many fucking chicks as possible until Sutton Prescott becomes a girl I don't even remember.

Sutton

My hands come up in front of me as Hunter lets go.

"No. Hunter. Don't."

His eyes are narrowed on me, grin in place as he walks back toward me.

"Too late, Freckles. You said you wanted to swim. No takesy-backsies. You're going all the way in."

I'm hauled over his shoulder with a squeal and carried down into the water, hearing my friends yelling and cheering before he tosses me in. I go under, popping up just as fast and letting out a gasp. The water's cold but refreshing, and as I stand, I wipe my hands over my face slicking my hair back.

"You're a dick." I'm laughing as he wades toward me. "But you know that already."

He wraps his arms around me, caging my arms in next to my body. Water laps around us as he stares down at me.

"You really think I'm a dick?"

I shake my head but answer, "Sometimes."

It's the truth. Hunter leans in, his nose rubbing over mine as his next question's asked quietly, but it feels like a bomb going off around me.

"Are you really here with me, Freckles?"

My heart picks up its pace because suddenly, I'm feeling trapped. In the background, I hear Aubrey talking about the girls' cliffs being lower and less scary than she thought, so I turn my head, avoiding the question.

"Are you about to do something crazy, Aubs?"

She smiles, splashing water toward me. "Who, me? Never. Of course I am."

My chest shakes as I turn back toward Hunter, whose eyes haven't left my face. I hate every single thing about the way he's staring at me. Jesus. I can't even look at him—that's how guilty I feel on the inside.

I can't tell him the truth—that I'm trying my hardest to be here with him, but that it takes all the concentration in my fucking body not to look over my shoulder at the boy stealing my every thought. Hunter closes his arms tighter as I lick my lips.

"Last one there has to go first." Shephard howls, then laughs before diving in and swimming in that direction. The girls scream and follow, but Hunter holds us in place.

"Look at me."

God. I can't, but I swallow as I do. "Come on, let's go with everyone."

He shakes his head. "Why haven't you answered me?"

Because I'm tired of lying.

I roll my eyes. "I have answered. I already told you I was."

He turns me around so that my back is against his chest as he spins us to face the beach. His words are whispered into my ear, giving me chills.

"I'm not the dick, Sutton. He is."

I blink, feeling heat crawling up my neck, and not the kind I feel when it's in my core. This is anger.

Calder's sitting in the same place my eyes left him, except now he has company. One with huge tits and a lot of blonde hair, rubbing her ass all over him.

It doesn't matter that I don't have a right to be mad. I'm doing the same thing. I know Calder and I can't happen.

I shouldn't be jealous. Or even possessive.

But I fucking am.

I twist in Hunter's grasp, determined not to care, draping my arms over his shoulders. But I can still see that girl on Calder's lap even though my eyes aren't on them anymore.

Hunter's face is a challenge that I'm ready to meet. Because the hate I feel is so unnatural inside my body that I'm desperate to replace it with anything. Including Hunter.

"I don't care. I told you already. What's the point of all this?"

"Prove it to me, then."

I blink. Hunter drops his hands to my ass, lifting me up to wrap my legs around his waist. And I instantly feel him against my center—hard and ready.

Oh fuck. God, it's as if I've suddenly jumped into the deep end of the pool but didn't know until my feet never touched the bottom.

I lick my lips, gripping his shoulders, feeling nervous as I stutter out my words.

"H-how?"

His lips press to mine, but I don't kiss him back as he says, "Come for me. Right here."

My head shifts around, heart starting to race as he buries his face in my neck, breathing out a half-laugh.

"Our friends are swimming toward the cliffs. We're all alone, and the party on the beach is far enough away, so nobody will see what's happening under the water. I want to make you come, Sutton. Here. For me."

My breath hitches as I feel his hand run up the underside of my thigh toward my core. *Let it happen, Sutton.* His fingers brush the fabric of my suit as his lips find my neck, speaking words into my flesh.

"I want to feel you wrapped around my fingers. Hear you say my name."

I look over my shoulder, needing to see it one more time. It's the only way I'll be able to toe this goddamn line—Calder's hand is on her back, another in her hair, as he whispers in her ear.

My eyelids close halfway as I turn back. Hunter is running his fingers back and forth over and over, teasing me. He dips in under the seam, stroking my soft tuft of hair, making my body contract as his mouth finds my collarbone. I squeeze my eyes shut, trying to rid myself of the memory of Calder kissing me near there.

No. Get out of my head.

Hunter's fingers move down toward my entrance as my eyes open, locked to his.

"You really want to prove to me that I'm the one?"

I'm nodding, panting, willing to lose myself to the sensation. *Just replace him.*

"Yes."

His finger slides over, just barely rimming my slit as we stare at each other.

"Then let *him* hear you say my name."

Oh my God. My mouth pops open as my hands shove against his immovable shoulders.

"What the fuck? No."

His grip tightens around my waist as his eyes narrow.

"Why not? Scream it. Let everyone on the fucking beach hear you. If you don't give a shit about him, then you'll let him know who you belong to."

"Belong to? I don't belong to anyone that would treat me like this."

"We'll see," Hunter smirks, leaning in to kiss me but I draw back, scowling at him.

"Get the fuck off."

"Don't fight this. You know you want it."

His hand begins touching places it shouldn't, making me physically ill. I drive my foot into his thigh as I shove my hands against his chest, forcing him to drop back into the water as I sink backward.

"Don't ever fucking touch me again."

He's staring at me, not a fraction of remorse on his face. But I am sorry. Sorry that I actually let him touch me.

"Insecurity's a bad look, Kelly." I lock eyes with him. "You had your shot, and you blew it. I'll find a ride home."

"Get back over here, Sutton."

"No," I yell over my shoulder, half swimming, then wading out of the water.

Hunter calls my name the entire time, but he won't follow. Chasing's not his style. I walk out, wringing out my hair over the sand all the way back to grab my stuff, opting to pick my clothes up rather than putting them on. I'd grab my towel, but it's in Hunter's car along with my damn phone.

Fuck.

A growl tears at my throat as tears prick at my eyes because I'm so fucking overwhelmed.

I shake out my hands, trying to calm myself down, but I can't. I feel stupid because I did this shit to myself and hurt because I never saw that coming.

And to add insult to injury, all I want to do is beeline over to the dickhead on the beach chair to tell him what happened. Then demand that he ignore that stupid slut on his lap and take me away from here.

Which is ridiculous because Calder's a figment of my imagination.

Whatever connection I felt was me alone. That much is obvious. He doesn't seem to be in the middle of any kind of emotional war like I am. And it's just another reminder that I'm a fucking loser—out of my depth and gifted with the shittiest taste in men.

There is no magic. No Romeo. No prince. Just a bunch of dicks, ready to mindfuck you over.

I hate everyone.

Spinning around, I look up to see Piper and Aubrey waving from the cliff, so I wave back, wondering what the fuck I'm going to do. Shephard's still climbing up toward the lowest section, making me actually huff a laugh.

I have to get out of here. I shake my head, knowing precisely what I'm going to have to do. Shit. Securing my clothes to my side, I walk over toward where everyone is hanging to ask Tag to use his phone.

The closer I get, the harder it becomes not to look at Calder. The girl's gone. *Oh.* To West's lap. *When did he get here?* But Calder's in the same spot, drinking a beer. *Is that a bruise on his cheek?*

It's faded, like the one on his jaw. Now that I'm closer, I see that all the guys are banged up, West being the worst.

Calder's eyes meet mine, and I almost forget what I'm here to do. They're so blue, filled with a current that travels directly to every part of my body, but I look away because I'm not that girl—the one that begs for his attention. Nope. That girl is currently dry humping his brother.

Tag turns around, eyeing me as I slide between some people to stand next to him.

"Well, well. If it isn't the one that got away. You've got my brother spun. What kind of magic you got going on down there?"

He drops his eyes toward my stomach, but I know what he's referring to.

"You're disgusting," I snap but point toward where Aubs and Piper are still standing, waiting for Shep to jump. "How do I get there? Because after this conversation, I'd like to hurl myself off that cliff."

I'm really just asking so that I can go tell my friends I'm leaving. He isn't even offended, smirking as I add, "I also need to use your phone."

Tag motions a hand to an entrance at the bottom of the cliffs. It looks a lot like a cave, but he says, "It opens to the other side. There's a path up to all three. Can't miss it, beautiful." He steps in closer, making me step back. "And if you're looking for an upgrade—"

"Shut the fuck up, Tag," booms from behind me, pulling my eyes over my shoulder.

Hunter comes up behind, staring down at me.

"Can we talk?"

I let out a forced laugh, huffing, "Uh. No. Fuck off," before I spin around, heading toward the cave.

Ooo's follow us as the crowd around us splits.

"Sutton," Hunter calls to my back.

I flip him the bird, not looking behind me as I yell, "No."

"Then I guess we're jumping."

Asshole. I glance back, seeing Hunter stalk toward me along with a few of Tag's friends. But that's not what keeps my attention. It's Calder, West, and Roman following at the back.

A pack of Wolfes.

Fuck. Me.

Sutton

This isn't happening. Shit. I walk faster as the guys who were tagging along pass me by, jogging toward the front side of the cliff to what I assume is a shortcut. My eyes shoot over my shoulder again, seeing Hunter's closing the distance between us, pissed off and determined.

However, that's not what's making me nervous.

It's the three sets of soulless eyes behind him. Stalking. Not just walking or strolling. They're stalking him—focused and terrifying.

It's one thing to know Calder is dangerous. It's another to see it in action. I squeeze my clothes tighter to my chest as I hurry inside the cave, wanting away from everyone.

I hate Hunter. And Calder.

"Sutton. Just fucking stop."

Hunter's voice is closer.

I shake my head in answer, the light dimming the deeper I get inside the cave, making me shiver.

Halo-like light shines from the exit just around a set of large boulders that hides us from outside view. So I try to pick up my pace, walking between them, but I can't over the hard pebbles.

I wince, stepping on something sharp just as my elbow is grabbed by Hunter, who hurls his meanness through gritted teeth.

"Goddammit, Sutton."

I'm spun around, causing me to lose my balance and fall to the ground, hard. Heat shoots up my leg, accompanied by stinging, just as crimson spreads over my thigh. I shriek, trying to cover the gash with both of my hands, but I can't because Hunter still has one of my arms in his grasp.

Everything happens so fast that I don't have enough time to be scared.

Hunter's face swings to the left, forcing him to let go of me just as a trail of blood splatters over the rocks from his mouth. His body swings in the same direction, landing right on Roman's chest, who lets him drop to the ground before bringing his cold eyes back to me.

Oh my God.

My face shoots to see who hit him, eyes landing on Calder's heaving chest, fists balled at his sides, savagery in his eyes.

Oh my God.

Calder lifts his chin, licking his bottom lip. "Touch her again and I'll fucking kill you."

"Oh my God." This time I say it out loud as my chest begins to tremble. *Am I crying?*

Calder's face meets mine as he squats down, eyes softening. He holds out his hand for me to take as tears cascade from the corners of my eyes. It feels like I can't catch up. I don't understand what I'm seeing.

I stare at Calder's hand, trying to process.

Calder hit Hunter. My head swings to Hunter, seeing him unconscious, then back to Calder. *Why would he do that?* My eyes drop to my leg, feeling the pain. *Did Hunter throw me to the ground, or did I fall?*

"Look at me, Sutton." Calder's voice is calm, drawing my eyes. "Are you okay?"

But I can't move or answer. I'm blinking so fast that I think it's in time with my pulse. I open my mouth, but nothing comes out except stuttered cries.

I swing my head back to Hunter. Oh God, he's not moving.

Calder crawls closer to me, inching in. "Shh. Shh. It's okay. Just look at me. Everything's okay."

My eyes swing back to his. Calder snaps his finger at West as he stares at my leg. "Gimme his shirt."

West reaches down, ripping off Hunter's shirt as he wobbles, groaning and reaching for his jaw.

Calder locks eyes with me as he extends the shirt he's now holding.

"Press it to your leg."

My fingers curl around the fabric, pulling it slowly from him, bringing it to my leg, and pressing down. I gasp when I feel the sharp pain, eyes tearing up again as I shake my head.

"Why? Why did you do that?"

I'm not sure what I'm even asking, but I've never seen anything like this. Boys fight. I've seen that. But this wasn't your typical fight. Calder tried to take Hunter's head off, and if he never woke up, I'm positive Calder would've slept just fine.

He did that for me...I think.

I'm scared, but I'm not sure of who anymore. The boy on the ground or the one in front of me. I just feel blurry and untethered.

"Why are you here?"

His hand comes up, fingers brushing my hair from my eyes before he answers, making the world come back into focus.

"I'm here because you are."

The deepest inhale attacks me before I let out all my breath in a whoosh. I stare at him, and I know he just knows. He gets that of all the things I don't understand right now—that sentence isn't one of them.

"C'mere, baby."

My arms wrap around his neck so tight that I crush him. The scent of Calder mixed with sunshine fills my nose, so I nuzzle in closer to his neck as he tucks his strong arms under my knees, lifting me.

"Take me away from here," I whisper softly, crying into his skin.

"Put her the fuck down," Hunter groans, but Calder's eyes grow to the darkest blue as he speaks directly to Roman.

"Take him to the top. I'll be there in a minute."

Calder's arms tighten around me, carrying me out of the cave and back into the sunlight as he whispers his words into my hair.

"Sutton. Listen to me, okay. This never happened. You fell after Hunter went to the top. Do you understand?"

I nod against his skin, not lifting my eyes because I want to hide in his arms as he continues.

"Sutton." His voice is gravelly. "Did he hurt you in the water?"

My heart stops. Calder isn't an empty threat—he's a promise.

I lift my face to his bruised profile, wondering how to lie to him because I'm wholly compelled to do the opposite. How is that possible? I almost think, *I barely know him*, but that's not what he feels like.

I've known him over lifetimes.

That's the only real explanation for why the boy I just met makes me feel safer than anyone else. Or how I'll hate myself for eternity because I let Hunter touch me.

Calder feels like magic and forevers.

And if I'm only feeling this way because of this moment, I don't want tomorrow.

"He tried. I said no."

It's the truth without the shitty intention and the last favor I'll ever do for Hunter Kelly. I hear Aubrey yell my name, and my body tenses in Calder's arms.

"It's okay. Just remember what I said." He brushes his cheek over mine. "Do you trust that kid Hunter came with?"

"Shephard. Yes."

Calder nods, coming to a stop as my friends run to meet us. I can feel people looking at me from over by the logs, curious about what happened. My eyes lift to Tag, who's too busy downing beer than to notice that his brother's missing.

"Oh my God. What did you do to her?" Aubrey yells.

But I quickly counter. "Nothing. He helped me. I fell."

She snaps her mouth shut, only looking partially contrite as he wags his hand full of my clothes at her. I didn't even notice he'd grabbed them. Aubrey takes them as Calder shifts to look at Shephard.

"You carry her all the way to the car. And then take her straight to the hospital. The cut on her leg's gonna need stitches."

"Totally, dude, but Hunter drove. Soo—"

Calder's brows draw together. "He's not here though, is he? Take Tag's car. Tell him *I* said to let you. We clear?"

Shep nods a lot. "Crystal, man. Sutton goes now."

Calder holds me out to transfer to Shephard, but I don't let go, forcing him to cradle me again.

"You take me home," I whisper, hiding in him again.

I don't care if people notice or question it. This is where I feel safe.

His chest falls deeply as his mouth comes close to my ear. "I can't. You know that. But no matter what, I'll come to you tonight. Promise."

I nod before my arms slide off him, switching to Shephard, who says, "I gotcha, Sutton." But it doesn't feel the same.

Shep turns, my friends in tow, taking me back over the sand toward the cars, but my eyes stay on the broad tattooed back, making his way back to the cave.

Calder

Chapter sixteen

"*He tried. I said no.*"

Bullshit. But I'm not mad that she gave me a half-truth. That angel told me just enough to spare Hunter's fucking life. What did you do to my baby, motherfucker?

I take the last step, cresting the steep terrain, a smirk adorning my face.

"Hey, Hunter."

He spits the blood that's still pooling inside his mouth as he sneers at me.

"What the fuck do you think you're doing, Calder?"

Roman chuckles, looking at me as he crosses his arms, while West grins down from the boulder. They're flanking him, keeping him cornered for me. I walk toward little Kelly, motioning toward the edge of the rocky terrain.

"Well, I was thinking about throwing you off this fucking cliff."

His face pales, shifting between Roman and West before he points his finger at me.

"There will be hell to pay if you do. So stop now, and we can forget this —" He lifts his chin showcasing his busted mouth. "—that this ever happened."

I rub my hand over my jaw, smirking. "Pay to who, bitch? Nobody knows I'm here."

He takes a step backward.

"You think I won't tell my father once I swim back to shore?"

"Who says you'll make it?"

I stop in front of him and stare down before I slap him hard enough to make his fucking ears ring, sending his face flying before grabbing it and bringing it back.

"Do you think that scares me, Hunter? That you'll tell daddy?" My eyes narrow as I smile. "Mine's scarier than yours, and I still don't give a fuck."

He swallows roughly. "What the fuck? I didn't even do anything. She fell. I didn't push her if that's what you think. And why do you even care?"

"I'm sure that's what you want her to believe. But I saw, Hunter. I see what you hide."

I squeeze his face roughly, shaking my head as he keeps begging.

"It was an accident. Seriously. You can't throw me off a fucking cliff over an accident. I could die."

My hand glides over his face to the top of his head, gripping his hair, watching him wince like a pussy.

"You think I'm doing this because she fell?" I make his head shake no. "See. Now you're starting to get it."

Hunter's hands grab my wrists as I pull harder on his hair, forcing him to his toes as he groans, "Then why? This is crazy."

My jaw tenses before the question comes. "What'd you do to her in the water, Hunter?"

Hunter stills, eyes dropping from mine.

Son of a bitch. He's dead. "You piece of shit."

"C."

Roman says my name like a warning because he heard the switch in my voice, but it's too late for negotiation. The answer's in Hunter's eyes. I don't need the fucking details because whatever it was, he meant to hurt her.

That's all I need to know. Now I hurt him.

West and Roman close in behind me.

I chuckle. "You know what, Hunter? We were just gonna scare you. Because you're right—you're a protected little piece of shit. I can't really hurt you, not the way I want to unless I wanna play Russian roulette with my life. But we both know you deserve a fucking beatdown. So take it, and we'll call it even. Then you forget her fucking name."

I yank him closer, whispering in his ear, "Answer me, pussy, before I change my mind."

Roman grabs my shoulder, but I don't budge, staring down into Hunter's defeated eyes.

"Fine. Okay. Fine."

I let him go with a jerk of his head. He takes a few steps back, wiping the back of his hand over his snotty nose.

"I still don't get why the fuck you even care. It's not like she's fucking prime—she was going to let me finger bang her in the ocean before she freaked out. She's just an uptight wannabe slut."

A chain of *"whoa, whoa, whoa's"* ring out as rage suffocates my senses and brings me crashing into him.

My hand wraps around his fucking throat as I hover over his body.

"You touched her... My beautiful girl. You put your filthy hands on her. And then you call her a—"

I don't say it. Instead, I squeeze, wanting to break his trachea. Hunter's hands slap at my wrist as hot exhales rush from my body.

Roman and West are yelling at me to stop. To let him go. But I can't. A snarl rips through me as my words roar from my chest.

"You don't touch her. She's precious."

His face is purple. A cacophony of failed attempts at air and the deep bellows of my name mix together in the air swirling around me. There are moments in life when you know, way down deep in your soul, that the end of a story is set in motion.

My end has just begun.

Tears fall from Hunter's bloodshot eyes, trickling down onto my hand.

I half blink before my mouth opens with a growl, and I throw him off the cliff. His body hurtles down toward the water below as I lift my head to the sky, letting out a deep, relieved breath, closing my eyes, and seeing only her face.

West leans forward from the back seat, seeing our Pops standing in the garage, arms crossed, with two of his guys.

"Shit, man. News travels fast when you choke a kid out and send him hurling off a fucking cliff."

Roman looks at me, worry set on his face.

"Calder—"

I shake my head. "Nah, don't. I knew what I was doing. That little cocksucker lived—so will I. You two weren't there. You got me?" Roman grips the steering wheel harder, so I add, "Don't you even try to push back about this, Roman. I did this. I'll be the one that takes the consequence. Trust me on this—don't let him see you hesitate when he asks."

The car pulls to a stop, the three of us exiting, giving nothing away as we walk up the driveway and into the garage.

"Pops."

He looks at Roman and West. "Were you a part of this? Don't lie to me."

They look at me as I give them a hard look because he already knows the answer. Tyler Wolfe doesn't ask questions. And I'll bet my life and theirs on this lie—Hunter didn't even mention their names. They each shake their head before answering at the same time.

"No, Pops."

I lock eyes with him. "It was just me. But you already know that."

He nods, motioning to the goons next to him. They walk toward me looking like they're ready for a fight, but neither touches me as they surround me.

Pops keeps his eyes on me but speaks to Roman and West.

"You two get cleaned up. I've got a run for you later."

They walk past me through the garage, but I see the fucking torment in their eyes. They're my brothers. Loyal to the end. Turning their backs on me, wondering if I won't be able to fucking breathe past broken ribs tomorrow, will make for torture. But this is for their own good. Because Tyler's the kind of bastard that will leave the bruises where everyone can see them.

He won't kill me. If he was going to, we wouldn't be standing here. I can't promise the same for them.

Pops walks toward me, undoing his belt, tugging it from the belt loops.

"I don't care about the why, boy. I care that something like this will never happen again."

My eyes stay locked on his. The closer he gets, the more his eyes speak the cruelty he's about to administer. The leather belt wraps around his fist over and over as he speaks.

"If you would've killed him—" He pauses, letting the words he doesn't say hang in the air before continuing. "Well, I guess it's a good thing you didn't."

I offer nothing in return. It's futile. The decision's made. A pound of my flesh is required as retribution and goodwill. That's the service you get when your daddy owns a pharmaceutical company and is more than happy to partner with the Irish mob.

All I can do now is stand here and fucking take it. And hope that it's not bad enough to force me to break my promise to the girl.

"This never happens again, Calder. Do you understand me? Connor promised Michael Kelly he'd give to you what you gave Hunter times three. The next time you decide to be a prick because some little bitch likes that asshole better, you remember that when you think with your dick, it might be the last thought you have. Even if Connor O'Bannion's your uncle."

That little piece of shit. Before I can spout off at the mouth, his fist strikes my ribs once, then twice before my knees buckle, taking me to the ground. The goons grab my arms, holding me up enough to let him continue.

I stare down, head hanging as my father stands above me breathless. Oil stains mix with spit falling from my mouth. Pops brings his mouth close to my cheek.

"Now I'm gonna remind you who's in charge. Because it ain't you, boy. Remember your place, Calder. It's right under my goddamn boot."

His arm raises, the glint of brass on the buckle hitting my eye just before I see black.

Sutton

E veryone left hours ago, after spending most of the day doting on me. Piper and Aubrey grilled me about Calder the whole time we sat in the ER. Still, I denied that there was anything to tell, even when I let out an audible sigh of relief hearing that Hunter had called Shephard.

Fear spawned by my imagination played on a loop in my mind more than once today until I heard the story Hunter's told everyone. I don't really know what I thought Calder would do.

But no part of me believes Hunter jumped off that cliff by himself—he was either thrown or ran off because possible death was a better option. Both scenarios scare me.

Although now that he's okay, I wish someone would've checked his pants because I'm confident he shit himself. Fucker.

"Are you sure you're okay?" my mother questions, smiling down at me from where I'm lying on my bed. She holds out a bottle of water for me to take.

I nod, wrapping my fingers around the cold plastic, tucking it in next to me.

"I'm fine, Mom. Swear. It's just two stitches. I can't believe I've made it this long without any considering how clumsy I am. It barely hurts anymore."

The lie tastes sour, especially since it's for Hunter.

"That's the pain pills, but I'm happy you're okay. You scared us, darling." She looks behind herself at the door, then back. "Your father would be up here too, but he had some work to attend to because of this little...situation." She gives me a smile as if to say *don't worry about being a bother.* "Get some rest. I already emailed the school, so you can stay home if you'd like."

"Okay. Thanks, Mom."

She leans down, kissing my forehead. "We'll see you in the morning."

I sigh, getting comfy as she walks away until she spins around.

"Silly me. I almost forgot." Her hand reaches into the pocket of her long cardigan, pulling out my cell. "Hunter dropped this off with the house-keeper. Shame he didn't stay. I bet he feels guilty for not being there when you hurt yourself. You should call him tomorrow. Make him feel better."

A tight smile is all I can manage as I accept it, plugging it into my charger. She pats my cheek before finally leaving, closing my door behind her.

My eyes hit the ceiling. The adrenaline is long gone, all my emotions finally settling into my bones. Today kind of felt like a blur, but there are two things that I am completely clear about.

One—Hunter is a dick.

And two—I choose Calder.

Fighting how I feel is futile. That much was obvious to me yesterday because it wasn't until Calder wrapped his arms around me that I took my first real breath. I don't understand why I feel this way. I just know I do, and it's too strong to fight off anymore.

My fingers run over the edges of the bandage stuck to my leg, dropping my eyes I look at it. What would've happened if Calder wasn't there today? My eyes close, recalling his promise.

"...no matter what, I'll come to you tonight."

Will you? How?

The idea is beyond unrealistic, but that doesn't stop me from slipping the blanket off my body and placing my water bottle on the dresser before standing. I make my way across the room to the double french doors that lead out to my balcony.

"This is stupid. He's not coming," I whisper to myself, but I turn the lock anyway.

A warm breeze billows through my short sheer white nightgown as I open the doors.

A bright full moon greets me as I step out to hold the rail. My eyes drift from star to star, then back to the first one I saw, remembering what I used to do with my grandmother when I was little.

My lids drift closed, seeing only Calder behind them.

"Star light, star bright, first star I see tonight. I wish I may, I wish I might, have this wish I wish tonight."

"I wish for you to keep your promise," I whisper, eyes reopening.

But it doesn't matter how hard I hope for wishes on stars to be real. I've outgrown them.

Another breeze causes goose bumps to rise over my legs, reminding me of my injury. I step back, turning around, and make my way back inside before closing the doors behind me and leaving them unlocked.

He promised, and my heart wants to believe him.

I walk over to my bed and get back in, pulling my plush cream blanket over me. Reaching for the lamp next to the bed, I turn it off, making the room dark, with only the light from the night's sky coming in.

I lie there staring at the door, head tucked onto my pillow.

Seconds turn to minutes, minutes to hours, as my eyes grow heavy. No matter how much I fight it, the events of today bury me. I'm exhausted in more ways than one, so without permission, my eyes close, and sleep takes over.

He'll come.

My shoulders jerk, breath sucked in as I shoot to sitting, eyes rapidly blinking open. I fell asleep. Shit. I reach for my charging phone, but sunshine beams through my window, giving way for disappointment to weigh heavily on my shoulders.

I groan, hating myself a little for believing in fairy tales. Did I really think Calder was going to crawl up my balcony? Past all the cameras—without even having my freaking address?

"Jesus," I say to myself, rubbing my face and stretching my arms. I throw back my blanket, but my movements are halted as a piece of paper glides up into the air, winding its way down toward the floor.

What the hell?

My eyes pop out of my head as I scramble to get it, a very sore leg protesting.

Pressing my palms on the floor, I sit down mermaid-style, staring at that folded cream paper lying on the throw rug.

There's a capitalized S on the front.

I run my forefinger over the scrawl, almost too nervous to open the letter. *What if it's from my mom or dad and this day goes back to sucking?*

Lifting my eyes toward the balcony doors, a smile that bests all smiles graces my face. No way. He was here. I fucking know it. Plucking it up, I unfold and begin reading.

I couldn't wake you. I'm sorry. You looked like an angel, and honestly, I was fucking scared. You scare the shit out of me. Everything you've heard about me is true. You saw as much with your own eyes. I'm all that bad shit people say and worse, but I want you to know my heart. Read this. I wrote it the day I kissed you.

If you feel the same way, meet me at the confessional tomorrow around noon.

–C

Sunday—

Fuck. She's beautiful. The first day I saw her, I couldn't stop watching, and I didn't even know her name, but it wasn't her fiery red hair or the way her eyes seem to shine when she smiles. It was more than that. I thought I was crazy, just horny and dumb, but then I caught her with that fucking cigarette.

I couldn't stop myself. I had to touch her, be close to her—so I took it, but she'd already taken more. I was hooked that very moment and reeled in on the beach, watching her yell at the moon and smelling like fucking grapefruit.

But today—my whole life flashed before me. Playing so fast that I couldn't really see it, only feel it down to the depths of me.

Her lips touched mine, but my soul recognized hers.

I never believed in soul mates. I don't think I even believed in love.

But Sutton—she makes me want to.

I silently scream with my eyes closed, the letter pressed to my chest, before hearing the handle of my door turn. Scooting quickly, I shove the note under the throw rug and turn over my shoulder with a smile, meeting my mother's face.

"Darling, why are you on the floor?"

I shrug. "It hurt to walk, so I took a break."

She scowls but walks toward me, helping me to my feet. My eyes dart to the rug and back as she walks toward my balcony doors, opening them.

"It's stuffy in here. Let's leave these open."

I nod, holding my hands behind my back.

"I think I'll take you up on the offer to stay home today. It's not like there's anything to do the last week." *Because I kind of want to live in my head all day with this letter.*

She pauses, giving me a thoughtful look. "You could just be done."

"No," I blurt, scrunching my nose before I take it down a notch. "I'll go tomorrow. Just in case I want people to sign my yearbook. I just want a day to make sure my leg isn't sore anymore."

For fuck's sake, I'm a terrible liar.

She shrugs, accepting what I offer, pointing toward my closet.

"Do you need help dressing? If not, breakfast is ready downstairs— Rosie made a lovely quiche Lorraine. Come down soon."

I walk gingerly toward my closet to aid in my lie, smiling. "I'll manage. I'll be down in a bit."

My mother pats my shoulder as she leaves, closing the door behind her and letting my nerves relax as she does.

I scamper over to the rug as quickly as I can. Pulling it back, I grab the note before taking it to my closet, burying it in the back of my underwear drawer.

My cell rings, so I walk back out and grab my phone, seeing Aubrey's name flash. At the same time, a text comes through.

Piper: Do not ignore us. We're coming over.

What the hell? These two. I hit the call button.

"What are you talking about?"

Piper's voice blares over the speaker, making me turn my volume down. "I told you she was avoiding us."

"I'm not avoiding you." My eyes drop to the face of my phone, seeing that it's 10:00 a.m. "Shouldn't you be in class?"

"She's totally avoiding us," Aubrey snaps, talking to Piper like I can't hear her before adding, "but it doesn't matter, ho. We both skipped due to trauma."

"Trauma?" I snark. "From my leg? Are you serious?"

I hear Aubrey clap her hands together, yelling as Piper says, "Wheel," in the background.

"No, bitch—we're traumatized that our best friend keeps fucking lying to us. Your life has never been interesting. You're an open book, but now suddenly, you're shut tighter than a clam."

"Mmhmm. Unacceptable," Piper chimes in. "We ride together. We die together. Or have you forgotten?"

I laugh, running my hands through my hair.

"Isn't that what Vin Diesel says in *The Fast and the Furious*?"

Aubrey yells, "Don't change the subject," as Piper says, "Yeah, and it applies. Also, I just fucking love those movies. RIP Paul Walker. The man was fine."

I'm nodding. "Yeah, he really was taken too soon."

I come off speaker because Aubrey gets louder as she bitches at me. "Focus. We're on our way. Massage those lips, Sutton, because we expect them to be loose."

The line disconnects, and I roll my eyes. I knew that sooner or later, they'd figure me out, especially after the beach. But I was really hoping for later. What am I scared of? My brows draw together because I know—I'm scared they won't ride or die this one. I'm afraid I'll have to go it alone.

Crushed gravel under tires echoes through my open balcony doors, pulling me back to the present as I release a tiny growl.

Unbelievable.

On their way? They were literally around the corner. Assholes.

I walk to my closet, throwing on my favorite band T-shirt and a pair of comfortable lounge shorts. God. Where do I even start? They're going to kill me when they find out I've told them nothing this whole time.

Leaving the closet, I head into my bathroom and grab my toothbrush just as I hear their voices bust through my door.

"Hello." ... "We're here."

"We're here," I mock in a shitty voice inside my head.

I walk out, giving a half-assed wave, toothbrush in mouth. Piper follows me back inside my bathroom, jumping up onto the counter to sit, glaring at me.

I spit, lifting my eyes to hers.

"What?"

"What? The nerve you have."

I roll my eyes as she wags her finger at me. "You've got some explaining to do. Start talking..." She's trying to be the bad cop, but she's terrible at it because she adds, "Also, I brought up some breakfast for you. And how's your leg, babe?"

I smile before rinsing my mouth and patting it dry with a hand towel.

"Thank you, and it's much better today. Barely sore to the touch."

She follows me back out. I sit on my bed, accepting the warm plate she hands me. I tap the fork against the edge, watching as they both stretch out on the soft blush-pink chaise across from me.

We're silently staring at each other as I take my first bite, chewing on more than just the eggs. *Fuck.*

Aubrey's head drops back dramatically. "Oh, come on, bitch. Speak. I can't with you. I'm dying here."

Piper's eyebrows raise, so I drop the fork and let out a heavy breath. "Where should I start?"

"Are you in love?" Piper shoots out.

Both sets of eyes lock on me as I hesitate before shaking my head.

"No, but it feels like it's happening—I don't know if that makes any sense."

Aubrey frowns. "But did you fuck him yet?"

Piper slaps Aubrey's arm, making me giggle before she says, "So what you're saying is that you're falling for him?"

"Yes."

I've never been more nervous. I keep searching their faces for any hint of what they may be thinking.

"How long has this been going on behind our backs?" Aubrey says it snarky, but for a brief second, I see the hurt flash in her eyes.

Crap.

My face drops to my plate as I put it to the side before looking her directly in the eyes, saying what I should've from the beginning.

"Aubs. I'm sorry. I'm sorry that I lied to you. You're my best friends, but I was scared you'd be so mad at me that you'd hate me for being so reckless. You have to believe me, at first I didn't think Calder and I were even possible, so I kept the first moment we had locked inside of me because—"

I lift my hands before letting them fall back to my knees, at a loss for words, but she finishes for me.

"Because then you could at least dream about it without your shitty friends being judgmental and ruining shit."

Her bottom lip pushes out, pouting before she says, "I'm sorry too."

Piper rubs her arm, looking at me. "What changed, though, to make you guys possible?"

"Nothing else other than he kissed me. That's really it." I run my fingers through my hair, biting my lip. "I know how this sounds. But the minute Calder kissed me, it's like we became destined to happen. The stars aligned—" I exhale, before adding, "And that shit's impossible to fight. I know. I tried."

Shrieks and squeals. That's what happens. All the heaviness of the moment instantly changes as Aubrey slides down the chaise, making us all laugh.

"Bitch. That fine-ass man put his mouth on yours. Oh, my Gawd. Details. Immediately."

My teeth find my bottom lip before I pick my plate back up, tucking into my food. I start from the beginning, telling them every delicious and insane moment I've shared with Calder Wolfe as they stare back at me.

Piper steals my plate when I'm done, finishing my food, both enraptured as I tell them about the beach. Lots of "holy shits" happen when I get to the part at the church steps and how my father despises his. Aubrey's face pales when I confirm the rumors about who Calder's family is and then grows red with rage as I tell the story from the cave, lobbing a "fuck that dick" toward Hunter.

They sit patiently through all of it, mostly listening until I tell them about the note from this morning.

"What! That's perfect. It's right during the last mass for school," Piper yells, smacking Aubrey's leg, who's bouncing up and down. "Oh my God. I'm dying over this. It's like fucking Romeo and Juliet."

Aubrey claps her hands, but I shake my head.

"Uh, no. They die in the end."

Piper waves me off.

"Just skip that part, but, like, it's so fucking romantic. Calder might be scary, but he has my vote." She turns to Aubrey. "Right? Because he protected our girl."

Aubrey nods. "Absolutely. I guess your Romeo comes with tattoos, guns, and a taste for blood."

My hand shoots to my mouth, laughter popping out before a pang of reality hits, and I stare back at them.

"Oh my God. Is this stupid? Am *I* fucking stupid? What am I doing? This could end so badly. What do I know about anything? Especially falling in love."

Aubrey stands and comes to sit next to me, as does Piper. They each take one of my hands as my head volleys between them, but it's Aubs that speaks first.

"What's there to know? I would do anything for love. Anything for someone to love me so much they'd burn the world down. Do you think he'd do that for you?"

I answer without hesitation.

"Yes."

"And Sut," Piper interjects. "I'm going to say something hella controversial. I get that he's bad news, like a part of a criminal family or whatever, but that shouldn't define him. I think we can all understand how fucked-up that is—being judged by your name alone."

Aubrey snaps her fingers. Piper's right. It's a cross I understand bearing.

She kisses the top of my hand and smiles. "The way he looked at you when he had you in his arms—I've only seen that shit in movies. It's like everything we've all hoped could exist does in the way he stares at you."

I smile, understanding exactly what she means.

"I love you guys."

They hug me, sandwiching me between them, and whisper threats to my life if I ever lie to them again.

"Never again," I promise, knowing that I've already broken it because Calder going up to the top of the cliff with Hunter will die with me.

Sutton

chapter
eighteen

"**H**ail Mary, full of grace—" The familiar prayer rushes between my lips quietly from where I'm knelt reciting my contrition, but I'm barely able to concentrate.

Because during my entire day, there's been one singular thought commanding my full attention—Calder.

At least yesterday, I had Aubs and Piper. They hung out with me for most of it, overanalyzing, deconstructing, and plotting my escape upstairs today. It was perfect, but it didn't make me any more patient for this moment.

I look over my shoulder mid-prayer toward the front doors, hoping to see him sneaking in.

"Hey. Freckles. Psst."

My eyes spring back, prayer still on my lips, glaring at Hunter. He's such an asshole.

As if Wednesday wasn't enough of a reason to hate him. This morning he asked me questions about my leg during homeroom as if he didn't know anything. Then he let me look like a bitch when I ignored him.

"Hey. Will you please talk to me?"

Eww. Aubrey makes the sign of the cross, kissing her middle finger and blowing it at him as Piper leans forward, whispering, "Grudges, jerk. We keep them—forever. Don't talk to her."

Turned around in his place, he stares at me. "Can you call off the dogs? I want to talk."

"No," I whisper back.

"Freckles."

"Are something I have." I narrow my eyes. "My name is Sutton. And Hunter, I don't forgive you. At all. What you did—said in the water. You're gross. Don't talk to me."

He frowns, but I don't care, ignoring him.

"This is why men call women emotional. You're overreacting."

Three sets of pissed-off eyes dart to his face, effectively making his mouth snap shut.

Piper makes a blow job motion against her cheek before whispering, "Ferociously suck a dick, Hunter. How's that for emotional?"

A laugh, too loud, bursts out from me, garnering a harsh "shh" from Sister Agatha. But it's fine because it forces Hunter to turn around.

Asshole.

The music for the service begins, calling us off our knees and to sit. Aubrey taps my hip, motioning with her head for me to sneak out of the pew. We chose the row closest to the back to make my escape easier, but Hunter makes me nervous.

I don't trust him anymore. He might try and rat me out just to be a dick. I'm staring at the back of his head before I glance back to Aubs.

She pretends to punch his face and put him in a chokehold before mouthing, "I got it. Go."

I duck down, crawling over the lower benches we use for our knees before waiting at the end of the pew, looking back to Piper. She cranes her neck to make sure I'm clear before giving me a thumbs-up. The privacy of the hallway can't come soon enough as I keep my footsteps quiet, bent over as I dash away, sliding behind the wall.

Thumps reverberate in my chest. God, I could get so busted for this. I can't even think about how that conversation would go if my parents were called. My eyes close for a second as I cringe at the thought.

I check over my shoulder, walking down the short hallway, nerves growing as I sneak toward the stairs. *What am I doing?* My lips curl into a grin because even though I'm freaking out, the reward of seeing Calder insanely outweighs the risk of getting caught.

As my feet hit the stairs, each step is taken painfully slow, trying to ensure nobody hears. Not even a creak. Rote responses from the congregation rise to the ceiling in a chorus as I come to the top, making my way into the room, instantly not seeing him.

Shit.

I'm too scared to call his name or walk over by the organ—too close to being seen—so I stand in place, fingers finding the ends of my hair.

It's all romantic until nobody has a timeline. I check my phone, the time showing 12:45. *Shoot, what if he waited and then thought I didn't come?*

"Stop overthinking, dummy," I whisper to myself, leaning down and adjusting my knee-high socks.

As I stand, I shift my head, looking around the room, first to a dusty bookcase along the far wall and then to the stained glass, remembering the first time I saw Calder here. The colors from the windows aren't shining as brightly today, muted by the clouds outside.

The sound of Bibles opening and pages fluttering from below makes me feel exposed. If anyone were to come up, I'd be caught, so I turn, walk over to the confessional, and open the sculpted dark antique wooden door before slipping inside.

Darkness envelops me until my eyes quickly adjust.

"About time."

I jump, covering my gasp as Calder's face, shielded by the partition, comes into view. My eyes close, and I smile before I open them, teasing.

"You should've been more specific. You just said this room, not the exact time, so you only have yourself to blame."

He chuckles, "Fair," and I warm.

The silence stretches out as I sit, listening to him breathe, not really knowing what to say or where to begin. But I don't get a chance to try anything because he whispers, "Do you regret coming?"

Never.

"No. But I am scared. My father hates yours."

Damn. I should've only said the first part.

"Yeah, same...to all of it."

Oh. I lean forward.

"I'd do it all again though."

I hear him let out an exhale. His fingers touch the wooden screen. Tiny bits of his skin press through the cutouts, and on instinct, mine meet them.

"Every fucking time I see you, it's like this pull. I can't explain it—you pull me to you. Do you feel like that too?"

"It's like I've known you my whole life, except I haven't, but I like the way it feels. I feel safe..." I pause for a second, trying to figure out how to say the rest but Calder presses.

"But—"

I shake my head.

"No but. I was going to say that I never really feel safe. I keep all these thoughts locked up inside my head because I'm too scared of disappointing people or making them mad. But it's different with you. I just say things— all the embarrassing things. And the most honest ones."

He's quietly brushing his fingers over mine as words I think he means to keep inside fall out.

"How are you possible—real, even? This feels like life's cruel joke. Like I only get you because tomorrow I'll die or some shit like that."

There are so many things I want to say—like that I feel the same. That even though we seem impossible, the fact that a soul like Calder's even exists seems too good to be true.

But instead of any of that, I say the honest thought screaming in my head. Because I can't not—not with him.

"What if that were true? A relationship between us will most definitely come with conditions, lies, and deception. And it's still probably doomed to fail. So if you were dying tomorrow, would I still be worth the trouble?"

My heart drops into my stomach, terrified that he'll finally realize what I refuse to face—that we're a beautiful tragedy.

His forehead drops against the screen.

"I don't want to hurt you, Sutton, and I'm fucking terrified that's what

I'll do. But I lay next to you the other night, watching you sleep, trying to think of every fucking way to save us from ourselves, and I came up empty. And that's crazy because we barely know each other, but I can't stop thinking about you and wanting to be near you."

He lifts his eyes to mine, only partially visible through the screen. But the emotion behind them bleeds outs, holding me hostage as he says, "So yeah. If I only get today, then I'll take it because being without you feels like hell anyway."

It's in this moment that the headiest feeling washes over me—so strong and clear.

I don't want to be saved from ourselves. Fuck everything. I want Calder, even if it damns us to hell. It's selfish and hateful, but I don't care. I can't just forget him or walk away.

This time around, it's me reaching for the door first. I don't say anything, rushing out and pulling his side open. His beautiful, broken face fixes to mine as my heart pours out onto him.

"I want you too, Calder. None of the rest matters."

Strong hands reach for me the minute I step inside. I'm hauled onto his lap, straddling him as our mouths meet. We're devouring each other, kissing like it's the air we need to breathe.

Because this is how we'll say our story begins—with me, him, and this damn kiss.

Calder growls into my mouth as his palms cradle my face.

"Is your leg okay?"

I seal my mouth over his, our tongues dipping and swirling as our heads tilt from one side to the other before I pull back, breathless.

"I'm fine. Thank you for protecting me."

He leans in, but my hands in his hair force his crystal-blue eyes to mine. I just need to look at him.

Fresh bruises and cuts surround his eye, and there's a cut on his lip. I lean down, feathering a kiss to his brow.

"It never hurts, baby."

Never. Hate swells inside me for whoever puts them there. And as I think it, I also feel the realization finally cementing inside of me.

"I'm not turning back, Calder. I'm yours. And you're mine."

The anger that's always lurking behind his eyes falls away, and for the first time since we met, Calder looks at peace. He looks like someone who could love, believe in soul mates, and live a life full of magic. He searches my eyes, brushing his hands up and down my cheeks before weaving them into my hair as our foreheads touch.

"I'll never give you up, Sutton. Ever."

The world falls away as our lips meet again and our hands begin to roam. Calder's warm breath slides over my neck as I sigh, peppering soft kisses over his bruised face.

"Nobody ever touches you again. Promise it, baby."

We don't owe each other apologies, yet everything outside of him feels like sin, so I give him the oath.

"I promise."

Calder's arms wrap around my waist, holding me flush as his lips drag up my neck. He buries his face against my skin, sucking on a tender spot by the nape of my neck, making my body quiver.

"Promise me you'll never touch another girl," I pant.

Capable hands splay over my back as he answers, "I swear to God I won't."

I draw back, slapping my hands against his chest.

"Don't you dare swear to someone you don't believe in."

He grins, leaning forward for my mouth, but I hold him back as his eyes narrow.

"I do believe in God, Sutton. I just don't think he's all good. But I promise on our lives that I will only ever touch you. Because I definitely believe in me and in you."

Calder leans in again, taking my bottom lip in his mouth, letting it slide out agonizingly slow.

We stare into each other's eyes, and the air begins to shift, feeling thick on my lungs, forcing me to take slower breaths.

His hands feel warm under my blazer against the thin button-up blouse as he closes around my rib cage, pressing his fingers into me. I trace his jawline with a finger over to his soft lips, licking mine as he presses a soft kiss to the tip.

We feel electric, raw, like chemistry that's attracting and building the longer we stay connected. Eye contact is vulnerable. It's intimate. It touches you in places you don't expect. Rattles your emotions and fucks with your mind.

Ten seconds of staring at Calder feels like I'm floating in a starry sky—just us, surrounded by nothing and everything, as if we're the center of the universe.

There's no other sound than the beating of his heart and no other existence than the one inside this confessional. His hands drop to my hips, fingertips digging into the fabric of my skirt, silently desiring things we shouldn't.

But it doesn't matter that we're in a confessional or a church—*we* are the only sacrament that exists.

With his eyes on mine, he urges me forward, scooting me closer to him, my cotton panties catching on the roughness of his jeans. He guides my hips slowly, rocking them up and back, over his growing length as I weave my hands through his honeyed hair.

We say nothing, never breaking eye contact, leaving our bodies to speak for us.

My mouth falls open, wanting to taste his again, but he teases, coming close only to pull away before our lips touch.

The more I grind, the more I lose myself to the lust-filled heat that begins to soak through the folds of my pussy. My teeth find my bottom lip as I drag over his hard cock, shuddering, wanting more each time.

"Oh my God."

I just barely whisper it, almost unable to breathe past the pleasure. He's controlling me, leading me to heaven each time he urges me forward—the intensity of the feeling only matched by Calder's quiet growls.

"Mine," he grits out.

I clasp onto the back of his neck, shoulders lifting, losing myself to the sensation as I grind harder, staring into his ocean eyes. Short, quick breaths take over as I move, my words coming out in pants.

"I'm yours. Just yours."

"Fuck."

Calder rips a hand away, ardently bunching my skirt. There's no question or hesitation. He knows exactly what I want—I don't have to say a fucking word.

I dart down, helping him just as he slides underneath, straight to my center.

My lips press together, hiding the gasp from the exquisite bolt of need that racks my body as he pulls the cotton aside, running his finger through my wetness.

I'm pleading with my eyes as he rubs rhythmic circles over my swollen, begging clit. I'm lost, hips circling, as he stares at me with an intense smirk.

"You feel like silk on my fingers, baby. I'll never stop fucking touching you."

The old me would've never done something like this. But who I am with Calder overshadows my normal senses. I want Calder more than I understand, and not just sexually. I want to own every piece of him—no boundaries, living by only the rules we make.

"You wanna come like this?" He leans forward for my mouth, so I give it to him freely as he says, "Or like this," pushing his thick finger inside my warmth.

"Oh my God." I gasp as our eye contact finally falters.

My eyelids flutter as I squeeze against his finger, feeling it glide in and out—a welcomed intrusion making my heart race.

"God. You're so fucking beautiful."

He pulls out only to press back in slowly, letting my hips drive forward to meet him. Our mouths come together as his finger curves inside me again, touching just the right spot and pulling a soft mewl from my throat.

"More," he demands, kissing me with force as another finger presses inside of me, stretching the delicate barrier of my virginity.

My body tenses, hands shooting to his shoulders, nails cutting into him through his shirt. But he doesn't stop, and I don't want him to. I'm stretched, full, and fucking aching for more.

"Jesus. You're fucking soaked. Do you like my fingers in that beautiful pussy?"

I nod as sensations build, rising and falling, tightening my stomach, spurred on by his filthy mouth. Calder finger fucks me faster and faster until I'm almost bouncing, my sock-covered shins sliding over the edge of the wooden seat.

"That's it. Show me how much you like it. Come on my fingers."

I spread my legs wider, head falling back, giving him room to fuck me harder, wanting to feel that explosion my body's greedy for.

"Fuck. Sutton. Take what you need."

Tightness coils in my stomach with every thrust as I squeeze my eyes shut.

"Yes."

Calder's fingers glide in and out through my desire with force, engulfing us in the filthy sounds of my slickness and the heady smell of sex. We're a goddamn abomination, but all I want at this moment is for him to make me dirty and never look back.

His thumb presses to my clit, and my eyes open, locking to his. I feel the crescendo possessing my body accompanied by a sharp sting that makes me gasp. I grab his head, sealing our mouths together as a deep moan rattles my chest.

Calder's hand replaces his mouth, silencing me as he continues to dip his fingers inside of me, wringing every drop of my orgasm from my body.

I come so hard that I tremble over and over, legs shaking as waves of pleasure crash down on me. I ride his fingers until my head falls back again and my shoulders go limp.

His lips press to my neck as he drags his fingers from me, waiting until he's done to remove the hand over my mouth and grip the nape of my neck. I'm guided back to his face before he kisses me earnestly, whispering into my lips.

"I like the way dirty words sound on this mouth." A small peck wets my lips. "Are you okay?"

"Mmm. I am. And I guess I'll have to practice saying some really fucking dirty shit."

The smirk on Calder's face makes me want to do more than getting fingered in a confessional, but we can't have forever. Not yet.

"I don't want to leave."

His nose rubs over mine.

"I don't want you to leave."

"Take me somewhere tonight?" I rush out. "I'll meet you by my front gates after my parents fall asleep."

He nods, brushing soft kisses to my cheek.

"Gimme your phone."

I reach into my blazer pocket, pulling it out, still trying to slow my breath.

His face turns away from mine as he takes it from me. So I kiss his jaw, smiling as he groans when I rub over him again.

"Done," he says, bringing back his perfect smile and dropping my phone back into my pocket before he frowns again.

Neither of us wants to say goodbye, but we both know we have to. I hate this.

"Tonight?"

He nods, patting my hip with his hand.

"Go before you get caught."

I crawl off him, straightening my skirt, suddenly feeling the urge to pee. I reach behind myself and open the door, smiling shyly. It's stupid, but I can't help how I feel.

"Do I look okay?"

"You look like mine—so yeah. You look perfect."

He stands, crowding me, jerking his chin for my lips again. They're bee-stung, swollen but obedient as I lift to my tiptoes, pressing them to his.

"See ya tonight, baby."

I drop back down, opening the door, and walk out, glancing back over my shoulder at my beautiful villain until I'm too far down the stairs.

The chorus of song hides my steps as I walk quickly toward the bathroom, internally freaking out. This is where I'll hide until everyone files out so that I can blend back in. It was genius, really. I'm glad Aubrey thought of it. I push into the door, shutting it behind me, throwing my back against it.

"Holy shit." I quietly squeal before walking toward the toilet.

But the moment I pull down my underwear, I see a small spot of blood. *Oh my God. That's not my period. Calder tore my hymen.*

Embarrassment burns through me, realizing that it might be on his fingers too.

"Oh, God." I shoot off the toilet, not even thinking as I right my clothes and pull open the door.

I only take three steps outside the bathroom when he catches my eye.

Calder's standing in the entry, next to the basin of holy water. The congregation room doors are shut behind him, but he doesn't seem to notice because he's staring down at his hand, gently rubbing his thumb over his first two fingers.

Compulsion takes over, my feet hurrying quickly toward him as heat spreads up my neck. His face swings toward me, stopping me in my tracks, the intensity behind his eyes almost leaving me breathless.

My mouth opens to apologize, but Calder reaches for me, dragging me into him, snaking his other hand into my hair.

"Don't you dare fucking look at me like that. You will never feel shame or embarrassment. I demand all of you, Sutton."

My chest rises and falls so quickly as he stares down at me because I want to give him all of me, including my innocence.

"Calder. I—"

But nothing else comes out because Calder dips his tainted fingers into the holy water, never taking his eyes off me, bringing them to his forehead. I watch, feeling stripped, raw, and completely obliterated by him. His hand moves down to his chest, then to his left shoulder before finishing the sign of the cross.

"Now I'm baptized in you."

A heavy exhale leaves my mouth just before Calder's mouth meets mine, ravaging it. It's fitting because it feels like he's already done that to my fucking soul.

Calder

chapter
nineteen

Her: Why is your name Wesley in my phone?

Me: Because yours is Buttercup.

Buttercup: Again, I ask…Why?

Wesley: They're arguably the most iconic couple in film. How is this a question?

Buttercup: So in addition to being insanely attractive, intimidating, and exhibiting an overall lack of impulse control when it comes to punching people—you're a movie buff?

Wesley: Insanely, huh? I like it. And I'm a lot of things, baby. Wanna find out what else?

Buttercup: Yeah.

Wesley: Good. See ya tonight.

Buttercup: So, also a tease. Got it.

T he sound of knuckles rapping against my door forces my eyes up. I've been lying on my bed, rereading my texts with Sutton on and off all day, imagining the faces she makes when she writes them.

"It's open."

West peeks his head inside the door, smiling like a goofy bastard.

"Dude. Guess what?"

I raise my brows, but he doesn't continue, so I say, "How long are you going to make me wait, West?"

He swings the door open, barreling in like I've given him an invitation, and plops down on the mattress. So I sit up, pocketing my phone and snapping the journal in my other hand closed.

"I'm coming with you and Roman tonight to the docks. We're leaving in twenty."

The excitement on his face makes me instantly sick. *Fuck no, you aren't.* My brows draw together.

"Says who?"

"Pops himself. It's my time, bitch. I'm coming up."

He's staring at me for a reaction, but I offer nothing as I wipe my hand over the stubble along my jaw. West grumbles, shoving my shoulder.

"Come on, dude. Don't look like that. This is huge for me."

But I keep quiet, sifting through my thoughts, tapping a finger against the leather cover of my journal.

The docks aren't a fucking joke or a playground.

Barrels of ecstasy divert here, never hitting the New York Port Authority. And thanks to the hundred-year-old railroad that served as the only land transportation in and out of this fucking town, we're able to sneak a shit ton of little white pills right back into the city.

Roman and I handle the docks with Pops' number two, Aiden, who always arrives with the ferry. It's always just the three of us because if shit doesn't add up or someone gets squirmy, we do what we need to.

West isn't ready for that.

Fuck.

He shakes the mattress. "Fine. Be a bitch, but you should still totally let me sit in the front seat of the car tonight."

Goddammit, West. This shit's not a game.

I reach out, smacking his cheek playfully. "You're never sitting in the fucking front. And you're not going." I push off the mattress, standing up. "Where's Roman?"

The heavy book in my hand lands with a thud on my nightstand as West stands up too.

"Garage. Same place he always is. And yes, I am. The decision's above you."

I turn, walking out of my room, hearing West yell my name as he follows behind, talking a mile a minute. He's trying and failing to convince me he's ready the whole way to the garage, but I'm not listening. I'm only interested in shutting this shit down.

How I plan to do that, I haven't figured out yet. I can't say shit to my Pops because it doesn't matter if I'm his son. I work for him. Saying "*fuck you*" to our hierarchy is the highest form of disrespect—and a death wish.

"Bro. What the fuck? Let it go. You aren't changing shit," West yells from behind me.

A smirk pulls at the corner of my mouth just as we hit the garage. I look over my shoulder, his feet stopping quickly.

"Nobody ever said you had to make it out of the car. I'll put you in the fucking trunk if I have to."

I swing open the door. The resounding thump of bass from the rap music playing greets us as we enter. Half of Roman's body is hidden under the GTO we've been tag-teaming.

"Romes," I bark, turning down the music.

He slides out, wiping his greasy hands on a rag as he looks up at me before darting his eyes to West.

"He must've told you about the docks."

I nod. "Then you already talked to Pops."

"Yeah, dawg, but he wasn't hearing it. West is coming tonight whether we like it or not. You wanna throw him in the trunk?"

I love that we're always on the same page. West throws his arms up in protest, making Roman chuckle as he sits up.

"You ain't ready for the docks, little bro. Just trust us. We ain't trying to have you get us killed. Or yourself clipped."

Maybe we're protecting him for good karma. God knows Roman and I could use all that we can get, but the way we grew up, the shit we've seen—that's not West's story. He's not ready for this chapter yet.

West grew up in an orphanage, picked up by my father at thirteen and shielded by Roman and me ever since. He's always been our little brother, following behind us, mimicking everything we do. I feel responsible for him, and I've done a lot of fucked-up shit in my life—helping West die before he's ready won't be one of them.

West crosses his arms, looking between us.

"This is bullshit. Both of you started younger than me. I'm fucking ready—stop treating me like a kid. I'm not going to fuck up. I'm gonna prove myself."

"Men don't have to prove themselves," I cut in, crossing my arms, irritated that Pops put us in this position.

Roman hops to his feet, shoving the rag in his pocket, looking at me as I shake my head, but before we can say any more, West hurls an empty motor oil can across the room.

The clang on the concrete is the only sound in the room as Roman mirrors my stance, our eyes locked to West. *What the fuck?*

West runs his unruly hair back under his loosened cap, not looking at us, nostrils flaring. He stabs a finger toward the ground as he paces, voice raised.

"Men do have to prove themselves, Calder. It's how we become them. If you two never let me dip more than a toe in this world, it'll be your fault when I get clipped."

I lift my hand, waving him off as I hurl, "Shut the fuck up with that. Don't say that shit. That's not happening."

Roman steps forward as West kicks the tire on the car, barking, "Settle down, dick."

West locks eyes with Roman's. "No. You settle down and fucking listen to me."

I've never seen him get this worked up before other than when he was hitting that kid on the ground with the bat—it's as if everything he's stored inside of him is about to explode.

Looks like West has shit to say to us.

A deep grumble rocks my chest as I catch his eyes. "You got something to say? Say it. But don't expect us to treat you like a grown man when you're having a fucking tantrum. This is real fucking life, West. With real motherfucking consequences."

"I know that."

"You don't know shit," I bark.

His face lifts to the ceiling as he shouts, "You two can't protect me forever."

I start forward, but Roman's hand on my chest stops me, pulling my eyes to him as he shakes his head.

"Let him speak, C."

West looks between us, spreading his arms as he speaks before letting them drop.

"I don't want you to protect me. I want to know what the fuck I'm doing so I can take care of you the way you do for me."

His eyes swing to mine. "You told me that men in this family never let anyone else fight their battles. So then, stop now."

Roman's face shifts to mine, eyebrows raised.

Fuck.

We stand in silence for more than a few seconds, their eyes on me. Roman would never give him the green light before me, but that's precisely what we have to do. My voice is deep and clipped as I hurl my words at him.

"You do what you're told. Or you go in the trunk."

He nods, shoulders relaxing, eyes darting to Roman as Roman says, "You listen. Don't speak."

"Or you go in the trunk," I add.

"Got it." West smiles, clapping his hands and rubbing them together.

But I frown. "West—" My eyes lock to his, a deep indent forming between my eyebrows, "I can't protect you out there. Do you understand that? The dock is real business, not the dime bags of weed we let you sling to rich assholes with money to burn." I motion to Roman. "We have a say over what happens to you right now. But once you cross this line, I can't—"

He's nodding, but what I'm trying to say won't come out—*stop you from dying.*

Roman's hand falls on my shoulder, patting it twice, but I can't shake the feeling I just signed off on my little brother's death warrant.

He closes the distance between us, patting my cheek the way I did to him earlier.

"I got me, Calder. Stop worrying. I'll be fine. You should worry about that little piece you can't stop texting."

I push his face away from me, and West laughs as Roman throws an arm over his neck, pulling him into a headlock, talking shit. But I turn and walk out past the garage door opening, not feeling as celebratory.

The hairs on the back of my neck stand on end as my head swings to the left, sensing eyes on me.

Pops.

He stares back at me, seated on the porch, an apple in one hand, knife in the other. I don't have to ask. He heard everything.

The knife spins round and round as we stand in silence.

His eyes search mine, questions I don't like behind them. He may be my Pops, but I don't want his attention—none of us do.

The sound of the knife piercing the apple is crisp, popping the skin as he takes the chunk straight from the blade before saying, "You boys don't be late," and that impenetrable wall falls back over his face.

If there was ever anything I've learned from my father, it's that you can always spot the Devil among demons.

Calder

I roll my Mustang to a stop a few **houses** down from Sutton's, engine killed, headlights off as I pull the **hood of my** sweatshirt over my head and lower my face to my cell.

> Wesley: You comin' or what?

> Buttercup: Shut up. You're early. Patience. I need to be cute.

> Wesley: You're already fucking cute. Get out here.

> Buttercup: And what are you going to do if I make you wait? Huh, tough guy?

> Wesley: I'm gonna knock on your door and tell Baron that I'm the daddy now.

> Buttercup: OMG! I'll kill you.

My eyes lift to the gate before dropping back to the screen. Fuck, this girl has me all twisted up. I want to text her again, even though I know she's on her way out, but now that I have a direct line to her, I'm a fucking addict.

There will never be enough Sutton.

My thumbs hover, about to say some more dumb shit, when something catches my eye, forcing my head up.

Red hair tucked inside a black hoodie paired with black leggings slips through the gate. Sutton ducks down as soon as she's clear of it, running toward my car. I chuckle, dropping my phone into my lap because she's fucking adorable.

It's midnight, on a street chock-full of old people. Who the fuck's watching?

I lean over, shoving the passenger-side door open, laughing as she throws herself in the car and scoots down super low in the seat.

My head is turned in her direction with a grin on my face as I stare.

"What are you doing?"

She blinks up at me through her thick lashes, smiling brightly, pulling the strings on her hoodie to make it tighter around her face.

"Go before someone sees us."

My hand slips under her arm, hauling her up as I shake my head, loosening her hood with my other hand and pushing it off her head.

"First, kiss me."

Her chin lifts immediately as I lean down, brushing a kiss onto her lips and breathing her in, feeling peace for the first time tonight.

"And second," I say against her mouth before I pull back, "how many people in this neighborhood do you think sit on their porches watching traffic after midnight?"

Her face relaxes as she thinks, embarrassment coloring her cheeks.

"Plus, I cut the wires to your cameras."

She slaps my arm, giggling, "Liar." But then her eyes grow wide. "Wait. Are you serious? What if someone tries to break into my house?"

I lean over again, wanting more of her mouth. "Baby, I'm the scariest thing on this island. I wouldn't worry about it, and you're right. I'm lying. Now gimme."

The vibration of her giggle gets lost between our lips as we kiss again.

Fuck, her mouth is the worst kind of temptation. I could kiss her all day long, and it'd be worth every minute lost to everything else.

"That's better," I whisper, opening my eyes as I only just barely pull away.

She smiles, fingers coming to my stubble, her eyes on mine.

"Better?"

I take a deep breath, feeling what I always am around her—honest.

"I had a shit night that I can't tell you about. I'm worried about my younger brother, West, and I almost put him in my trunk twice tonight. Shit sucks with my Pops. And I feel like a pussy because I couldn't stop counting the fucking minutes until I got to see you. So yeah, now that I kissed you, I feel...better."

The smile on her face could only be rivaled by the feeling it gives me.

"I missed you too," she whispers like it's a secret as she crawls over the console.

She straddles my lap, wrapping her arms around my neck, tucking her face into the crook as my arms engulf her, sinking into her hug.

"Better?" she mumbles again against my flesh.

Fuck. So much.

I nod, not wanting to let go because I can't remember the last time someone hugged me. Although it's just *her* hugs I want. My face burrows in her hair, our chests rising and falling together in the silence.

After a few moments, she whispers, cheek on my shoulder, "Is it weird to feel this connected? To feel like I know you even though you're a stranger?"

I shrug, enjoying the smell of grapefruit on her hair.

"Fuck it. Let's just be weird."

I feel her smile as she snuggles in. "So, where are you taking me?"

"Nowhere if you're on my lap," I tease.

An arm leaves my neck, fumbling for the door as she says, "'Kay, it's been fun, see you later."

Aw, she thinks she's funny. I wiggle my fingers against her ribs, tickling her sides, making her squeal. Her body jerks as she tries to protest through her laughter until two small hands smack down onto my cheeks, garnering my attention as she brings her lips to mine.

I stop tickling her—full stop, because this kiss has heat behind it.

Her tongue slips inside my mouth as my hand slides up the nape of her neck, weaving into her hair. Our lips glide in between each other's, tongues teasing, becoming more and more fevered until I growl, reaching down, gripping her leggings at her hips. I raise her up a few inches as she squeaks out a sound.

"Unless you want your neighbors hearing you scream my name, your beautiful little ass better find the seat and buckle up, Buttercup."

She shakes her head as she plops down. "No. Don't make me leave." Her arms wrap back around my body, speaking her words back against my neck. "Drive with me like this because you make me feel better too. You're like the sun—I want to soak you up for as long as possible so that I can feel you lingering on my body later."

It takes me a second to answer because she's knocked the wind out of me.

There's an ache in my chest from this fucking feeling she gives me. It's that visceral. I don't even know how to label it, but that doesn't matter because she keeps serving it every damn time I see her.

My mouth opens to speak, but I don't even know what to say back. So, instead, I do what I can—give Sutton what she wants.

I kiss the side of her head, wrapping one arm around her as I turn the engine over.

"Only on the local streets, okay? Once we hit the highway, you sit."

She nods, somehow molding her body even closer to mine as I pull out, driving past her house with her in my arms, like a goddamn thief.

We drive down street after street, too slow, but I've got precious cargo, and I don't really want this to end either. All I feel are Sutton's contented sighs feathering my skin until we pull to a stop at the sign for the main highway.

"Ride's over, baby."

I smile as she lifts her head, looking like she's waking up from a dream.

"Better," she breathes before crawling back over to the passenger side.

She spins around, her ass landing on the seat, laughing as she brushes the hair from her face.

"Fuck, you're beautiful," I rush out, smiling as I catch myself saying shit I didn't mean to say out loud.

Her eyes drop, shy as ever, but lift back to mine. "Where are we going?"

I lean over, pulling the seat belt across her chest, buckling her in. My face is close to hers as I frown, teasing.

"I thought you had a plan?"

The tip of her tongue is caught between her teeth as she narrows her eyes on me.

"Liar."

I nod, slowly grinning before I wink, hitting the road with a quickness she doesn't expect.

"Holy shit," she screams as we barrel down the dark empty highway.

After a few miles, we turn down a dirt road with tall grass on either side and towering oak trees that block the view I've brought her here for.

I pull into a hidden turnoff, the kind that if you don't know it's here, you'll pass it. I'll never tell Sutton how I know it's here. The Mustang bounces over the bumpy path for a few minutes until the gigantic trees and grass give way to nothing but an empty clearing.

Her face turns to mine.

"Did you bring me out here to make out?"

I shake my head, stopping the car and reaching for the button to slide the top back.

"Nah, I brought you here to see stars, baby."

The top begins moving backward, her head lifting to look at a crystalline sky as I kill the engine.

"Whoa."

Sutton

chapter
twenty-one

A billion twinkly lights fill the blacks of my eyes as I stare up, a smile etched on my face. I unbuckle my belt, grabbing the windshield, and stand, keeping my neck craned toward the midnight blue overhead.

"This is amazing, Calder. Everything's so clear without the town's lights."

My hair falls forward, framing my face as I look down, the stars making him just bright enough to see.

"Hey."

He grins as our eyes lock.

"Hey, back."

"Thank you for the stars."

He draws his bottom lip between his teeth, releasing slowly before he says, "They're almost as pretty as you."

My cheeks heat, knowing he means what he says because I don't think he's looked at the sky, just at me.

"False. How would you even know? You haven't looked at them yet."

He grabs my waist, hauling me into his lap, coaxing a giggle out of me. My head lies back against the top of the door, cradled in his arms.

Calder brushes a few errant strands of hair from my face, his eyes solemnly fixed to mine. Butterflies explode in my stomach.

"Why would I need to look? When to me, you look just like heaven."

My eyes close. I want to memorize this moment as he leans down and kisses me under the stars, an unsaid promise of forever on his lips.

I open my eyes, feeling lost in a haze. His eyes are so blue even in the dark, and the golden stubble over his face scrapes my fingertips as I sigh.

"Have you ever grown a beard? I mean, you are almost a man. I hear they do that sometimes."

"Almost?" He laughs. "Yeah, I do. Want me to grow it out?"

I nod, biting my lip, tipping my face to the sky. The idea of Calder with a beard does tingly things to my body. Who am I kidding? Just the idea of Calder makes me tingly.

We sit together, me cradled in his lap, looking up at the stars in comfortable silence. Oh my God, that's what he is—immediate comfort. The kind I usually feel when I'm all alone because I don't have to be "on" for anyone. I feel like I can just be with him.

His thumb brushes back and forth over my arm as I stare at the sky, lost in thought. I look at him, finger lifting, tracing the top of the inked constellation on his neck. It's peeking out from under his hoodie.

"What's this one?"

He grins with a sparkle in his eye before dragging the hoodie over his head to give me a better look. I smile as his motion crowds us, pressing us together, before he tosses the sweatshirt to the passenger side, tilting his head for me to get a better look.

"Wanna hear a cool story?"

"Yes," I rush out dramatically, lifting up to kiss his neck softly. "I thought you'd never ask."

He chuckles, and I swear I'm mesmerized. He's just so perfect—down to the tiny scar right under his jaw. Even his flaws are beautiful.

His eyes search the sky before he points to a cluster of stars.

"There. Right there—you see that?"

I nod, recognizing it as the same one on his neck.

"That's Draco—" he muses.

My head shifts to his. "As in Malfoy?"

He sneers playfully. "No, nerd. As in Latin for 'dragon.'"

"Oh." I giggle, mouthing, "Fancy," as he ignores me, looking up again.

"There's this story in Greek mythology—" He pauses as a look of surprise crosses my face. "What? I don't just throw people off cliffs."

My mouth drops open, trying not to laugh because I never thought he was stupid. But who just knows random stories about Greek mythology? Before I can say just that, he winks, continuing.

"A chick named Hera married a terrible dude named Zeus. As a wedding gift, he gave her a tree that had golden apples."

"Wow, setting the bar high, Zeus."

He grins, nodding. "But Hera was terrified someone would steal them. Because golden apples, right? So she placed a dragon at the base of the tree to breathe fucking fire on anyone that tried."

I'm staring up at him, waiting for the rest, but he doesn't say anything, staring back at me like he suddenly remembered something sad. I raise my eyebrows.

"But?" I rock my body, making us shake. "There's always a but in these stories. What happened? The dragon got the apples and made off with Zeus? Because rumor has it, those gods fucked everything around."

Calder laughs, and I exhale at the sound, drawn into him.

"No. He was killed. With a poison dart, and the apples were stolen."

My bottom lip pops out.

"That's the saddest story. Why would you get that on your neck?"

He shrugs, the easiness of his laugh from before growing muted in tone again.

"Because before she died, my mom was into Greek mythology and all that kind of shit. She had this book, and in it, she had Draco circled. I don't know why...maybe she liked the name. But sometimes, I feel like I was that dragon, sent to protect my brothers and our family tree. So I got it to remind me of her."

My fingers follow the lines on his neck from dot to dot, lingering on each.

"I don't want you to be the dragon. Because that means you die in the end."

His face hardens, but his eyes are soft as he speaks to me. "We all die in the end, but at least I had purpose."

There's so much he's seen that I'll never experience. I can't even put myself in his shoes. *I wonder what baby Calder was like before life got a hold of him.*

"Was it strange growing up without a mother?"

He looks up at the sky.

"I wouldn't know the difference."

But something about the look in his eyes makes me think there's more sadness inside him than he realizes. He takes a deep breath. As I drop my hand, his face turns down to mine.

"Are you close with your family?"

I shrug, adjusting in his lap to sit up. I don't want to talk about my family because it makes me feel shitty. *Who am I to complain?*

"Close is a deceptive word. Because yes, we know each other, and I know they love me." My shoulders tense as I look down at my fingers. "But given a choice, I wouldn't choose my life—no."

An indent forms between his eyes as he huffs a breath. "Says the girl in the castle."

My face swings to his, fear imagined. He thinks I'm a bitch. My eyes narrow because I'm gutted.

"That's not fair. I know how it looks from the outside. But my mom and dad never ask me what I want or if I'm okay with their plan for me. They just tell me how to be for the cameras and the crowd. They discuss my future as if it's a press release, including who I should date or where I should attend school. They don't even really know me. So yes, I live in a castle, but the walls are cold, and the rooms are fucking empty. I'm alone."

Calder grips my jaw with his hand, making me look into his eyes. Why do I feel like I'm going to cry? Fuck. Because being with him feels like I'm stripped down and unprotected. The cut hurts more when he's holding the knife.

"Hey—" The way he says it is gruff, with all the gravel in his voice, but it doesn't scare me. "I didn't mean it like that."

I try and move his hand, but he doesn't let me.

"I said it like I agree—like 'even says the girl in the castle.' My world, your world. It's all fucked. Baby, we're the same, you and me. Damned by our last names. But don't you ever fucking think for a goddamn second that I'd believe anything less than perfection about you. Do you understand me?"

I nod against his fingers, re-seeing how he said it in my head. Feeling stupid. But Calder shakes his head.

"Do you want to know what I think about you?"

I blink because I didn't even realize that I do until now. He starts to speak, but I cover his mouth, needing to say my part first.

"I'm scared of how I feel. It's so intense. And it's like we got here, under these stars, at a lightning-fast speed." He frowns, but I grab his wrist. "I know what you said before about me being worth the trouble. But I'm scared now that we have time to get to know each other, you won't like me anymore." My voice raises. "Because maybe I am just some spoiled rich little princess. And you're all this real life that I don't know anything about." I drop my eyes and let out a half-laugh dipped in the rawest truth. "So you'll leave—and how can I blame you. But then I'll be left trying to figure out how to unfeel this."

"Look at me."

I do, not shying away from how I feel.

"Baby, I wouldn't know how to walk away if there was a gun to my head. You're mine. And I'm yours. That's the deal."

He tugs my face to him, pressing a messy kiss to my lips, melding our mouths as I shift in his lap straddling him, never breaking our kiss. This one isn't like the others.

We're all over each other, tongues, lips, hands—an inelegant mess of lust. Calder's hands run up and down my back as mine slide through his hair.

I'm breathless, dying more and more with every glide over his tongue, rocking my hips into his hardened length below me.

"Sutton," he growls as I rub my tits over him.

"Be my first," I whisper into his mouth.

The kiss deepens as he backs me up against the steering wheel. My head drops back as he molests my neck, sucking and biting at the flesh.

"Calder," I breathe. "Fuck me."

His breath whooshes over the dip at the base of my throat before his eyes lock on mine.

"I will be the only man that owns that pussy." My eyes roll back into my head over his words. Calder leans in, licking my fucking mouth, breathing quietly. "But tonight, baby, we walk before we run."

I'm still, staring back, burning for him.

"Teach me how to walk?"

His nose rubs over mine. "Mmm, the first lesson. You come first."

Calder

I reach for the door, opening it and flipping on the headlights before taking her with me. She wraps her legs around my waist as I step out, my mouth still on hers as I carry her toward the front of the car.

"I've fucking dreamed of this—you on the hood of my car," I rush out as I pull away. Her chest rises and falls faster with each of my words. "All spread out for me to feast on."

Her hands grip my shoulders as I place her slowly on the hood, watching her tongue drag over that perfect mouth. She swallows, biting the inside of her cheek as she looks at me.

"Nervous?"

"No..."

I raise my brows because she's pretending there wasn't a question mark at the end of that.

She grins. "Maybe."

My hands trail down her legs to her sneakers, pulling them off her feet, letting each drop to the ground with a soft thud.

"Tell me what you're thinking."

She's watching me, taking it all in. And it's fucking sexy.

"What if it tastes weird?"

"Impossible. Baby, I want your cream all over my fucking face. Trust me. Everything you got is everything I want."

She sucks in a breath, biting her lip. I lean forward, palms against the metal, retaking her mouth, tugging that goddamn lip from her teeth to suck it before letting it go with a pop.

"What else?" I push inches from her face.

Her green eyes blink at me as she reaches for the bottom of her hair. My hands leave the hood of the car, fingers dipping into the top of her leggings. I motion with my chin for her to lift her ass.

She does, saying, "I don't know what I'm supposed to do. I don't want to be bad," as I strip off her pants.

But the minute I pull them off, my eyes drop to her pussy, and I growl, "Fuck," because she's not wearing any goddamn panties.

Her pussy is perfect, that small patch of hair calling for me to separate it with my tongue and tease her clit. Fuck me. *If she owns any fucking underwear, I'll burn them.* I'm staring down as I speak.

"Baby, your job is to lie back and let me lick you until you scream. Now spread your legs. I want a better look."

My head lifts to hers as she slowly lowers herself back onto her elbows. I take a step back, adjusting my hard cock in my pants, gritting out, "Open for me."

Hesitantly, she spreads her legs before gasping as the air hits her in delicate places. I smirk, enjoying every fucking minute. Sutton's head drops back as her legs open wide, giving me a full view of her wet pussy.

Something dark stirs inside of me as I look at her. Possession. More potent than anything I've ever felt. This fucking girl is mine, for better or for worse, and I'll kill any motherfucker that tries to take her away from me.

I step in closer, running my fingertips down her thighs, splaying my hands against her pelvis. Her head darts to mine just as I lick my lips and say, "Mine," taking what I want.

A deep inhale fills her body as I flatten my tongue, licking straight through her folds.

My tongue rolls over her clit as her thighs try and snap closed, overwhelmed by the sensations.

"Oh fuck. Calder. Oh my God," she gasps, ass scooting back, but I follow her up the hood, greedy for more, growling into her pussy like a fucking animal.

My hand slaps the top of her ass as I tear my face away, dragging her back down the warm metal hood.

"I knew you would taste like sugar. Sit still."

She's already convulsing as I dive back in, hands finding their way to my head.

"Fuck yes, baby." I hum against her clit, making her jump again.

"Holy shit. I can't take it."

I flick my tongue over her clit, pushing her thighs open, spreading her wide. High-pitched whimpers and mewls tumble out of her as I devour the sweetest fucking taste.

"It feels so good. Oh fuck. Don't stop. Please. Like ever."

I switch between flicking and rolling over her sweet fucking clit, teasing her as I hold her open. Sutton's body bucks, her moans growing louder as her hips begin to rock. The hand she has on my head grips my hair as she pushes me closer to her pussy, wanting more.

That's it, baby. Fuck my face.

She's unabandoned, all the worry she had gone. Lost to the fucking moment. My tongue moves faster and faster in time with her panting, until she's begging.

"Ohmygodohmygodohmygod."

Her thighs begin to shake as her entire body tenses before she screams, back arching off the car, sweet juices exploding into my mouth. The hand not in my hair slaps against the hood as she comes, wave after wave, each a little smaller than the first.

I lick her slower, laving my tongue in lazy swipes, listening to her gulp for air, her breath slowing.

Sutton lifts her face back to mine, jaw slack, watching as I lick her pussy slowly, letting her come down. My tongue dips to her entrance, sliding inside her slit, wanting more of her pleasure.

Her eyes roll back again, but she doesn't stop watching. I fuck her with my tongue, slowly and gently, as her hips begin to circle, the fire reignited.

Goddamn, she was made for this—for all the filth and the luxury. *One day I'll give her both.*

My tongue glides out, running down toward the seam of her ass where she dripped her sugar. She tenses, breath hitching, but there won't be any fucking part of her that I don't taste or fuck.

I nip at the inside of her thigh, making her grin before she relaxes, opening her fucking legs even more. I make figure eights with my tongue over the skin, stopping just before her most innocent part, teasing until she's breathing hard again.

"All clean," I whisper against her skin before I raise up, pressing a kiss to her swollen mound.

"Oh, shit," she groans, stomach sucking in.

I crawl over her, lowering my face, and kiss her with cum-smeared lips. She wraps her arms around me, tongue diving into my mouth, letting out a moan before I pull away.

"You like the way you taste?"

She nods with a blush on her cheeks, my hand on her ass.

"Me too, baby."

Sutton

C alder pulls me back up so that he's standing and I'm sitting again. Goose bumps prick my skin as he steps back from between my legs before looking to the ground, bending down to grab my stuff.

Holy hell. That just happened. All of that just fucking happened. The smile on my face feels permanent because it was amazing.

"Will it always be like that?" I breathe quietly.

He nods with a smirk, shaking off my pants and turning them right side in. My knees swing open and closed lazily as he steps back up to me. The way he's looking at me like we're not done, it makes my hips rock forward before I squeeze my legs shut.

He licks his bottom lip, taking my ankle in his hand, extending my leg. His eyes dart to my center as he does it. "I like you bare. Do that shit all the time. I want to know that if I were to reach my hand up your skirt or down your jeans...that all I'd feel is your wet kitty."

My lips purse, blowing out a breath because—fuck. The way he talks about my body makes me feel hot all over. I nod, biting my lip as he pulls the leggings over my bare feet, running them over my legs.

"Lift, again."

My palms press against the hood, raising my ass so he can tug my pants back into place, but not before he places a soft kiss to the Band-Aid on my leg. His body wedges itself closer between my thighs as he does it, and I swear my back arches, hoping to feel him against my center.

Jesus, I'm so horny that it's embarrassing. But he did say "the first lesson." So there has to be a second.

It's as if he can read me because he chuckles.

"Did I create a monster?"

Kinda.

He's putting my shoes on, not saying a damn word, and I'm freaking dying as I watch. Every single part of Calder's body is attractive. The way his shoulders move. The muscles that ripple under his T-shirt.

It all makes me shiver as I watch him.

He switches to my other foot, and his bicep flexes as he lifts my leg. My eyes run the length of his forearms, the veins on display as he wiggles my foot back into my sneaker.

He's making me weak.

"So what's—" *lesson number two,* I was going to ask, but I'm silenced because as Calder stands, he reaches down and adjusts himself. He's hard.

The length of his cock is strained against his pants, hypnotizing me because I *am* a monster. A lusting over Calder one.

God, I wonder what his dick looks like?

Calder's hand comes to my face, calling my eyes to his. He smirks, thumb brushing over my cheek.

"How do you feel, baby?"

I shrug. Amazing. Addicted. Ready for more. But I don't say that, opting for flirtation.

"Eh, I've had better. Maybe you should give it another shot?"

Calder laughs loudly, and it makes me join in before he attacks my neck, gently biting and sucking my skin in between breathing his words.

"If I didn't know it was a lie, someone might die tonight. I'm all fueled up on testosterone. High because I made my girl come so hard. I'm an animal. You don't know what I'm capable of."

I sag into his lips. Fuck. His voice touches me in all the right places. I wrap my legs around him, pressing myself as close as possible, wanting what he won't give.

"Oh, but I do know..." I purr, lifting the sleeve tucked over my hand, biting my lip to hide my smile. "Because you've got something... right...here—"

I wipe his whole mouth as he pushes my hand away, giggling again. He grabs the front of my hoodie, tugging my face to his. Enviable long lashes brush together as he blinks, hiding his blue eyes for milliseconds at a time from mine.

God, I can't get enough. I want more. Right fucking now. I want him to be my first. Screw walking. *One little french kiss south of France, and I've become a sexual beast.*

I rub my cheek against his hand that's gripping my sweatshirt, batting my damn eyelashes. He lets out a long exhale.

"Who taught you to flirt like this? Because baby, you can have anything you want if you keep looking at me like that."

I smile demurely, bringing my face closer, rubbing my nose to his.

"I want you...inside of me."

His eyes search mine as his hand runs up my chest to my neck, wrapping it around my throat, pushing me back gently. A rush of wetness coats my pussy as he holds me in place, staring, his chin lifted, looking down at me like I'm at his mercy.

He's right. I am at his mercy.

"Baby," he levels, bringing his other hand to cradle my face. His thumb drags over my bottom lip. "Tell me what you saw that night in the cabana."

I blink, sucking in a breath. Vivid memories flick through my mind as I stare back at him.

"Lesson number two. Be specific when you ask for what you want. I'm gonna be inside of you, but it's not your pussy I'm filling tonight."

He steps back as I begin speaking, sliding me off the hood with him so that I'm standing in front of him. Fuck, I'm so turned on. I don't even recognize my voice as I speak because it's husky, drenched in lust.

"I saw a girl on her knees. Her hands were on his hips."

Calder places my hands on his hips, eyes not leaving mine. I lick my lips, feeling overwhelmed with need.

"His hand was gripping her hair."

A quiet moan escapes my mouth as he grips the base of my hair, forcing my head back.

"Oh my God."

He winks. "Keep talking."

"Um." I swallow, already feeling weak in my knees. "She had his—" I hesitate, but he scowls. "—his dick in her mouth."

Two fingers, the same ones he had inside of me earlier today, push inside my mouth as my lips close around them. The taste from the salt on his skin bursts over my tongue as he slowly glides them in and out of my mouth.

"Did you watch her suck dick, Sutton? Did you watch her head bob?"

The deep voice is a bass of gravel, making my nipples harden under my hoodie. My eyes are on Calder's as he jerks his chin for me to show him, stopping his movement.

I do, circling my hand around his wrist as I lower my head, sucking on his goddamn fingers.

"That's my good girl."

My thighs squeeze together, shivering as he says that. Calder watches me before he reaches down, rubbing himself through his jeans.

Sweet Jesus.

"Hollow your cheeks. Suck them good," he directs, smiling as I listen.

My pussy aches as I grip his wrist harder.

"That's it, baby. Fold your lips over your teeth."

I'm obedient, sucking harder, making sure my teeth don't touch his fingers as my head bobs faster. I feel on fire. God, I want him so fucking bad. The sounds coming out of my wet mouth filter into the night, mixed with his groans as he watches.

"Fuck, you're gonna suck me so good."

Calder guides my head, holding tightly to my hair, as he pushes my head further down his fingers. My hand on his hip digs into his jeans as he says filthy words that make me feel like I'm going to explode.

"Did she gag on his cock, Sutton?" As he says it, his thick fingers press further toward the back of my throat, making tears spring to my eyes, but I don't gag...I moan.

His fingers leave my mouth, arms dropping to his sides. "Fuck. Baby. Suck me."

He looks drunk...on me.

I drop to my knees. Because I've never wanted anything more than to have him in my mouth. Fumbling with his belt, I unlatch it, but he moves my hand, pulling it from the belt loops, gazing down at me before he lets it drop to the ground.

He unbuttons his pants, lowering the zipper, his bulge immediately coming into view.

I reach up, rubbing over the protruding length behind his boxer briefs. It's so hard, and it pulses as I touch it. His head drops back to the sky as I look up, hearing a whoosh of breath releasing from his lips—*my god at my mercy.*

My impatient fingers brush over the elastic band, folding it back. The tip of his cock shines with cum that's beading at the top.

I don't know if I should. But I can't stop myself. I dart my tongue out, hungry to taste him, taking a lick.

"Fuck," grits from between his teeth. His fingers pinch my jaw, holding me in place. "Give me a second. You're fucking killing me, baby."

Not listening, I tug his pants down, face held still because I want to see all of him. Calder releases me, reaching down, gripping his shaft. My eyes are locked on the motion.

I'm mesmerized, watching how his thumb rubs over his smooth tip, smearing his juices over the head before gliding his palm over and down his thick cock.

His dick is beautiful.

I don't know if people think things like this, but his cock is the most beautiful thing I've ever seen.

I'm hungry to taste him as I look up from my knees. "Just like your fingers, right? With my hand like yours?"

He nods, jaw slack.

I look back to his dick, slowly leaning in, replacing his hand with mine. My palm drags down, but he stops me.

"Get your hand wet. Spit on it."

I let him go, bringing my hand to my mouth, looking up at him as I take a long stroke of my tongue over my palm.

"Oh fuck. You're a...very. Good. Girl."

A strangled groan bursts from his mouth as mine covers the tip of his cock. I wrap my wet hand around the base, moving in tandem.

"Fuck yes."

I suck down his thick shaft, jacking him off, again and again. Each time, I get braver, finding a rhythm and bobbing my head as I hollow my cheeks.

"Your mouth is pure fucking velvet." He groans, hand finding my head.

His fingers weave between my locks, and I can't help but remember how that girl looked when she was like this. I want that. I want Calder to fuck my mouth.

Whimpers vibrate between my lips as his grip tightens.

I take my hand away from his dick, holding on to his hips, letting him move my head faster. *Yes. Fuck my face.* His moans fill my ears as his dick slides in and out of my warm mouth. My thighs squeeze together, clit begging to be touched.

"Fuck. Sutton. You're sucking me so good."

Without thinking, spurred on by his dirty mouth, my hand drops from his jeans to my center, rubbing as I blow him.

"Oh shit. Baby."

My eyes lift to his like he called them. Calder's face is dark and animalistic. He's locked on me like a predator lost to its need. His hips rock toward my face, moving faster and harder into my mouth.

His words are spoken through gritted teeth, making my fingers move faster.

"Rub that greedy little clit. You like sucking my dick, huh?"

Need barrels through my body. Calder pulls my hair so tight that I feel stinging as he fucks my mouth.

"I want your throat. Trust me."

It's not a question. Because he doesn't need to ask. I want everything he gives.

His face is strained as he presses my head closer, filling my mouth with his cock. Back further until it feels almost like I can't breathe.

"Swallow."

Tears leak from my eyes as I do, making him growl before pulling back and looking down at me. *More.*

"Again."

My entire body starts to shake as he pushes back in, clit throbbing as I rub faster and faster until I'm humming on his cock. I swallow his dick back, launching into an orgasm, screaming around the thickness.

"Oh shit," he bellows, pulling back as warm cum shoots into my mouth, spilling onto my chin as he pulls out of my mouth.

"I'm sorry," he says in a ragged breath, milking his dick with his hand around his cock.

My head tilts up, fingers wiping over my chin, gathering his pleasure. I'm staring up at him as his chest rises and falls, his eyes barely open.

I'm yours, and you're mine.

His head lowers, eyes piercing mine. I lift my fingers to my mouth and run my tongue over them.

"You tasted me. It's only fair I taste you."

He blinks but says nothing before swallowing.

"I don't expect—" He shakes his head. "I wouldn't expect for you to do that. You just brought me to my fucking knees faster than I anticipated."

I smile, happy and proud.

"Well, now you know my answer. So, I guess there's always next time."

That smirk he wears so well peeks out. He reaches behind him, dragging off his T-shirt, showing off his flawless body before he hauls me to my feet.

"Another lesson?" I say, almost breathless, but he laughs, wiping his hand off before tossing the shirt on the hood.

"Pace yourself, killer."

Calder leans down, kissing me senseless until my lips feel raw and my body feels ready all over again before pulling back, locking eyes with me.

"When can I see you again?"

Sutton

My eyelids flutter open, streaks of light filtering in as I yawn. I stretch my arms outside of the blanket, body still warm from sleeping as the sides of my lips tug up, remembering...last night was not a dream.

"When can I see you again?" His words lie over me like the naughtiest invitation.

"Holy shit," I whisper, covering my hands over my center before lifting my fingers to feel my swollen lips.

I draw the comforter over my head as squeals erupt, partnered with my kicking my feet.

Aubrey's ringtone blares from my nightstand, causing me to scramble out from under the blanket. The last text she and Piper got from me said I was sneaking out with Calder. So I know they're dying to know what happened, but first, I have to text him.

I sit up, brushing my hair from my face, hitting Decline as my fingers race through a text.

> Buttercup: (*heart emoji) I really wish I could see you rn. But I'll settle for tonight. I'll leave my balcony open. P.S. I'm playing hard to get...is it working?

Giggling, I throw myself back onto my bed, staring at the ceiling, just as my cell rings again, making me quickly hit Answer.

"Bitch. Did you decline me?"

"Aubs. I don't even know how to explain to you how amazing last night was."

"Well, you'd better figure it out because we need to debrief stat. While you were finding the Bonnie to Calder's Clyde, Piper got pipe laid by the one and only Shephard. Picking you up in ten, beotch."

"Oh my God."

The line disconnects, and I jump out of bed, rushing to my closet to get dressed. I reach for some overalls as a thought crosses my mind.

I have a boyfriend.

No, that's not the right word.

When Calder dropped me off last night, I almost never made it out of the car. We couldn't leave each other, coming back for more kisses each time we said goodbye. It's as if each time we're together, the stronger the impulse grows to never be apart.

"I won't make it a whole day. Tell me I can see you today."

"You can see me today and tomorrow and the day after that, and the day after that."

Calder's hands cradle my face as he stares into my eyes.

"Tell me I can have you forever."

Smiling at the memory, I toss the overalls and grab my cute jean cut-offs. I shimmy them on, catching sight of a cropped T-shirt I bought last month but haven't dared to wear. But today's the day. I slide it right over my head, turning to look in the mirror.

My lips are bruised. A blush only Calder gives shades my cheeks. My hair is wild. Sexy. I look like the hottest version of me. I'm different. Changed. He touched me and made it so.

I grab a hair tie off the center dresser, pulling all my hair into an on-purpose messy bun. I look at myself again, remembering all the most delicious parts of last night.

Until the signature sound of Aubrey driving too fast has me hustling to shove my feet into my high-top Converse. I run to the bathroom and brush my teeth, grab my bag, then jet out of my room.

My hand hovers over the rail as I take the stairs, hearing a singsongy "Hi, Mrs. Prescott."

I'm not even paying attention to what my mother says back as I bound down, buzzing with excitement.

"Hi, Mom."

Her eyes dart to me as I pass. I push Piper backward, hoping to leave quickly before speaking over my shoulder.

"We're going to get coffee and then maybe do some shopping. I'll be home later."

"Freeze."

Shit. I turn around slowly, smiling.

"Firstly. Good morning, Sutton. And no, you will be home in an hour. We have the fundraiser itinerary to discuss and a tasting to attend. Lastly —" She narrows her eyes. "—do we think this outfit is the best choice?"

I drop my head to the front of me, then back to her questioning face. Granted, I'm typically more conservative, mainly because her voice is always in my head, like, *"Darling, would we want someone to receive the impression being given? Probably not."* But this time, more than ever, the answer is *"Yes, we freaking would."*

If Calder sees me, I hope the impression I'm giving is *hot girlfriend*. My arms cross in front of me as my lips part to say something I shouldn't, but the girls chime in.

"I love it. It's so on trend." Aubrey smirks as Piper nods.

"Exactly. It's like Sutton has her pulse on today's youth. What an asset to have."

I try and hide my smile. Such conniving little geniuses. I give my mother's frowning face a wave. "My outfit's fine. I'm going for coffee, not a press conference. Bye, Mom."

Taking Aubrey's hand, I tug her away, Piper following. The minute we shut the front door behind us, laughter erupts, and Piper imitates my mother.

"Is this outfit the best choice?"

Aubrey answers, grabbing her car door. "Uh, yeah. Because Sutton isn't worried about what America will think, Elizabeth. She's hoping her outlaw thinks she's smoking hot."

I shove her shoulder as we all pile into the car, me in the back. My hands slap down on the soft camel-skinned leather in Aubrey's Range Rover, shifting between them.

"So, is Shephard's staff as big as expected?"

Piper screams. I laugh. The car starts, and music blares.

Aubrey tears out of my driveway as Piper sticks her arm out the window. I can't remember the last time I felt this free or this happy.

And it's all because of him.

The closer we get to downtown, the more my eyes start to wander. First to the basketball courts, not seeing anyone, then to every possible place he might be. I can't help myself.

"Did you text him? Or are you doing that Sutton thing and waiting for serendipity to strike?" Aubrey snarks.

I smile, pulling my cell from my bag and rolling my eyes because my messages are always silent to avoid my mother's glare. So I should check to see if he texted back yet.

"Yes, I texted him. But he's probably still sleeping."

But when I open my messages, I suddenly realize there was one waiting...above the one I sent. "Oh my God. You guys. There was a message waiting from last night. I typed mine so quickly that I didn't even check the one above. Why am I so embarrassing?"

They laugh as I read it.

> Wesley: You're probably already sleeping. But I wanted to say something fucking poetic for you to wake up to. All I could come up with is
> —Better.

My heart straight up leaps out of my chest. It's one simple word, but to us, it has the biggest meaning in the world. Calder's right. Last night made everything better in the most dramatic freaking way. Jesus, even the sun seems to shine brighter today.

The music fades when I don't say anything, so I look up before I type back. Piper turns to look at me.

"Either read that text or start talking because that goofy smile on your face is too much. We're dying over here. Tell us everything."

I giggle, dropping my phone into my lap.

"Last night was...earth-shattering. Life-changing."

"You fucked him," Aubrey yells, making me look around because I'm sure people outside the car just heard.

"No," I blurt as I shush her. "But—" My hands cover my reddening face before I peek through my fingers. "—he went down on me."

Our bodies bounce as Aubrey hits the parking space curb.

"Shit." She laughs before killing the car and turning back to stare at me. "Where? Like where were you?"

Piper grabs Aubrey's shoulder, eyes fixed on me as I drag my hands down my face.

"On the hood of his car."

Aubrey's eyes get wide. "Holy fucking shit. That's so hot. You bitch."

I nod bigger as Piper cuts in. "Did you...go down too?"

The high-pitched and somewhat inappropriate words fly from their mouths when I say, "Yes," until we're all laughing.

I'm the first one out of the car, making them follow me into the coffee shop as our laughter dies out. Piper goes to the front to put in our orders as Aubrey and I grab a table. As soon as our coffees arrive, we hold court at our small table, taking turns telling each other war stories from our nights.

"So," Aubrey cuts in, "when are you seeing him again?"

I close my eyes for a second, thinking about the text again. "I don't know. It's funny because that's what he asked me last night. I basically played hard to get and said every day."

My mother's demand filters back into my head as they both giggle. Shit. She'll monopolize my time for most of today, so only tonight works, but maybe I can sneak out again this week...unless my father starts doing late-night meetings like he usually does before these events. *Shoot.*

Piper raises her brows. "I know that look. Where'd you go? What are you suddenly thinking?"

"Just about how to see him. My mother's going to have me bogged down all week with errands. And it's not as if he can just come over and hang out. I have to think of something covert."

Aubrey giggles, licking whipped cream off the top of her Frappuccino.

"You're like sexy secret agents. Strangers in public and freaks in private."

"More like vampire secret agents because it's the same with his dad. He can't know about me either. Midday meet-ups are looking impossible right about now."

"Right. Edward and Bella cannot sneak over to his side of town either."

She nods along with her words, voicing the "shit that complicates Sutton's life" checklist. *Thanks, Aubs.*

"Exactly. We can't be seen here, there, or any-fucking-where—it's like my life just became a maudlin Dr. Seuss poem."

I laugh, but it isn't genuine because I'm feeling a little doomed right now. Piper puts her chin on her hand, staring at me.

"Do you have a plan? Because before you start really investing in that frown...put me in coach. I'm ready. I have all kinds of calculating shit saved up. I've been waiting for you to become a badass." She pretends to cry as she adds, "Welcome, friend."

This time my laugh is genuine, and so is my smile.

"You're insane. I feel unprepared for badassness, but I'm all in. I know that I'm punching above my weight. You guys know sneaking out last night was a first for me. And the only reason I could relax is because I knew my mother had taken a sleeping pill. But I did it. And it was more than worth the risk. He is worth all the risks."

Aubrey leans, giving Piper a discreet high five.

"Sutton, there's a reason the Lord introduced us. We're terrible influences. He knew you'd need us, eventually. My parents are gone again Fourth of July weekend. I know it's like a month away, but you can totally use my house to satisfy your lady boner. But...make your boy bring his friends. I can't be the only bitch without a fun story."

Piper claps her hands together before almost bouncing in her seat. "And...you said your mom will have you tied down this week, right? That's perfect. Give me your list for Tuesday. I'll do everything for you. You can sneak away. I refuse to believe Calder won't know how to hide in broad daylight."

I press my hands to my cheeks, feeling grateful for these two.

"Really? Be serious. Are you sure?"

"Yes," they say in unison until Piper adds, "Dibs on West for the Fourth."

Aubrey and I swing our heads in Piper's direction. But she shrugs, taking a sip of her coffee.

"Shephard and I said we weren't official. We're just summertime fun. I feel no guilt."

"Piper Jean," Aubrey teases, bringing a full smile to my face. "I'm shocked. Such a little whore."

"Shut up." She laughs. "And my middle name is not Jean... What the hell?"

Aubrey smirks. "I know, but it should be because you're as trashy as Miss Britney Jean Spears circa barefoot at a gas station bathroom. And I'm here for it."

Laughter erupts as I pick up my coffee and take a sip, but Piper turns her head toward me.

"I'm proud of you, Sut. It's about time you went for what *you* want."

Agreed. I chew on the brim of my cup, staring at them talking because I hope for the rest of my life, I never forget who these people are to me right now. There are no better friends.

Aubrey lifts her cup. "Here's to a summer full of bad ideas."

Piper joins. "With good times."

I raise mine, tapping theirs. "And a badass destiny."

Calder

> Buttercup: (*heart emoji) I really wish I could see you rn. But I'll settle for tonight. I'll leave my balcony open. P.S. I'm playing hard to get…is it working?

F uck. I run my hand over my morning wood, pushing it into my hand. Damn, if I don't know exactly how she's feeling today. She was my first thought when I woke up twenty seconds ago.

Last night was the kind of perfect I never wanted to end.

I sit up, cracking my neck, before leaning over to grab my journal. My fingers brush past all the filled pages as the pencil tucked between them falls out, but I swipe it up, writing the truest thought in my head.

She tastes like the kind of temptation I'm never fucking coming back from.

The pages snap together as I close it, tossing it back on my dresser before grabbing my phone.

> Wesley: Did you just booty call me?

> Buttercup: Don't be offended. You're at the top of my rotation.

I hit Dial. Sutton's laugh answers **the phone for** her.

"Keep laughing, punk."

There's background noise I can't **make out, but** her voice dominates the line the way a phone that isn't on spe**aker does.**

"Shut up. Did you just wake up? **Your voice is** all—"

"Mmm," I rumble, interrupting h**er, "I did. This** wild chick had me up late last night. She smelled like grape**fruit and taste**d like bourbon, and after I ate her pussy, I felt drunk on her."

Silence. Just the sound of her breathing**.**

"I hate you." Her voice drops to **a whisper.** "I'm literally standing in a room full of event planners with my **mother, prepar**ing for a cake tasting."

Now it's my turn to laugh before **I make my** voice huskier.

"Lemme eat your cake."

The sweet sound of her giggle m**akes my eyes** close. I could get used to this.

"Sneak away."

"I can't." Her voice becomes hushed**. "I have a** thousand dumb errands. And I'll be with my mom for most of **them. But Pi**per said she'd cover me for Tuesday. And I'll leave the door un**locked tonigh**t."

My eyes open, chin lifting to sta**re at the ceil**ing as a growl leaves my throat as I think.

"Oh, God. Quit it," she rasps.

"Tuesday's too far, and tonight's **not good.**" I smirk as an idea pops into my head. "Share your location with **me. I'll find th**e perfect time to steal a kiss from those lips. Nobody will se**e me. I prom**ise. I'll just take what I want and go."

"Done," she breathes out before **adding,** "Coming," to someone in the background. "I've got to go."

"See you later, baby."

The call ends, and I lie back, **eyes only** lifting as the ping comes through my phone to accept the invi**tation to see her** location.

I'm staring at my phone as my **door swings** open and Roman pops his head in.

"Dude, get up. We got business w**ith Pops.**"

I nod, pushing off the bed, but as I turn my back to him, he adds, "Where'd you go last night?"

My face swings over my shoulder to Roman's stare. He's guessing correctly, telling by the look on his face. But I'm not listening to a fucking lecture. West's face comes into view behind him, a grin from ear to ear.

"Yeah, Calder, where'd you go?"

"If I wanted you to know, I'd have taken you with me."

West looks at Roman, who seems less amused by the answer, saying, "Oh shit. I think our boy got laid. Was it that stripper from the beach?"

Fucking West. I almost laugh. Instead, I walk toward the door, slamming it closed just as he says, "Can I hit it too?"

"Tyler. Please sit," Michael offers from his patio table chair, backdropped by his pool.

Roman, West, and I stand behind my father as he sits. That's our job. To watch, listen, and ensure nothing happens that Pops doesn't want to happen.

As we rode over, he gave us the warning to behave today, wholly aimed at me, but he also gave me a gun.

Michael wipes his mouth on his napkin before giving my father his attention.

"Connor wants a date for the product."

Michael doesn't answer. Instead, he shifts his face to look at me.

"I see you brought your sons." Michael's eyes flick over the bruises on my face. "I'm sorry to see it came to that, Calder. Lessons can be hard learned sometimes."

Was that a flex? He better be fucking joking talking to me like that. I motion to step forward, but my father holds up a finger, halting me in my place. Even with his back to me, he knew that I'd react.

I stand in my place, eyes on Michael, as Pops lowers his hand.

"Mr. Kelly, lessons *can* be hard learned. I suggest you answer my question, or I'll arrange for Calder to show you how we teach them. Maybe he can recreate your son's."

Michael blanches, stuttering, "This is no way to treat a business part- ner. It's not as easy as a date...I own a whole company that produces more than just your street drugs. I have to be careful. My reputation is on the line if I'm caught. My family's name is a founder of this country."

Pops chuckles, reaching out and grabbing Michael by the collar before slapping his face, fucking hard. *Damn. Shit just got real for you, Mikey.*

"Please," he cries out, lifting a hand in front of his face.

I don't even need to look at my brothers to know they're grinning the same way I am. Michael sounds a whole lot like his bitch-ass son. Pops lowers his voice as he leans in.

"This isn't a partnership, Michael. We don't give a fuck about your family name. You're just the whore we use to get what we need. You let us fuck you for a few dollars because you don't have a choice. That's why you sought us out—desperation. Imagine what the world would think if they knew the kind of trouble you're running from."

Pops lets go of Michael's collar, straightening it out for him.

"Now, Connor gave a little with our sons' beef, but if we don't get our product, there will be no fucking grace for your family."

We take a step back as Pops pushes from his chair to stand.

"You have one week to get us our shit, or one of your little prick sons won't just be tossed off a fucking cliff."

My eyes meet with Michael's, and I give a wink before my father turns, and we follow. The moment we're clear of the house, Pops turns to look at me.

"Change of plans. I'll take West to the docks tonight. You and Roman keep eyes on Kelly. He's scared. And fear makes people do very dumb things."

Sutton

"Sutton, make sure a sample of the lemon cake is brought to the table," my mother directs curtly, turning back to the event planners sitting around the table.

I nod as I make my way past the glass cases of desserts and pies all stacked neatly, making my mouth water. The man behind the counter smiles, already pulling out the cake, having heard her.

"Thank you," I mouth as I walk by.

We've been at this bakery for the last hour and a half, debating desserts for my father's fundraiser. And what could've been fun was introduced to my mother. She scrutinizes everything as if people are more generous after cherry pie versus lemon meringue.

I get it. Securing election funds is a year-round hustle, and my mother knows how to do it best. And I've already heard the lecture about this re-election being key in my father's political career. But it's cake.

She's just exhausting, and because of that fact, I just lied and said I had to go to the ladies' room so that I could escape, scroll Instagram, and text my friends.

Or just text Calder.

I pull my phone out of my mini crossbody bag as I walk down the short hallway. There are a ton of texts in my group chat, so I open the chain as I reach the bathroom door. But a swishing noise pulls my eyes to the right just as the kitchen door of the bakery swings open.

Crystal-blue eyes arrest my heart.

A smile breaks out over my face as I'm pushed—no, shoved—into the ladies' room, barely in time to hide his lips meeting mine.

"What are you doing here?" I rush out, pushing him away only a little.

"Exactly what I said. Now shut up and kiss me back."

My arms wrap around his neck, and I press my lips to his, letting him lift me off my feet. He reaches back as our tongues taste and locks the door before winding his arm around me, the other hand in my hair as we kiss and kiss until I start to lose track of how many seconds have ticked by.

I pull back, breathless and happy, but his eyes are hooded as he stares down at me.

"Baby. You're gonna need to be very quiet for what I'm about to do."

The way he says that makes my heart start to beat faster, as does the smirk on his face. I nod as Calder sets me to the ground, turning me around, gently pushing my back against the door.

My eyes stay on him as he lowers down to one knee, running his hand up my skirt before hooking my leg over his shoulder. He raises it, revealing my bare pussy, smiling before he lifts his eyes up to mine. *I remembered.*

"Oh fuck. Such a good girl. Now give me the kiss I really came for."

That's the last thing I hear before I'm forced to clamp a hand down over my mouth. Because Calder's eating me like it's his fucking mission, and my muted gasps are the only sound filling my ears.

His fingers grip my thigh as my eyes roll back. God, it's like the first time all over again. My body is instantly overwhelmed, every nerve ending short-circuiting. Without thinking, I push down on his head with my free hand because it feels like I can't take it.

"It's too much. Oh my God," I mumble.

But he growls, gripping my leg hard, flicking his tongue faster over my clit.

Fuck.

Calder's holding me in place, up against the bathroom door as my body begins to quiver. His finger pushes inside my pussy, rough and fast as his tongue works me over.

I'm being thoroughly fucked. A second finger pushes in, and I bite down on my hand to stop from moaning. He's pushing in and out, faster and faster, touching me in just the right spot as he kisses my swollen bud.

My hand curls into his hair as the divine feeling begins to take over, building and building, until my thighs shake uncontrollably. I moan into my hand, rolling my hips into his face, hearing him hum his appreciation until I explode, squeezing my eyes shut as the waves of my orgasm feel like they're drowning me.

Calder licks me, drinking me in as I drop my hand, panting with a smile on my face.

"I can't believe you just did that."

He smiles up at me, kissing the inside of my thigh, before standing and licking his lips.

"Baby, that was as much for me as it was for you."

He straightens my skirt before turning me back toward the door and whispering in my ear, "Go be a good daughter. Until you can be my bad girl later."

"When?" I rush out, but he's already turning the doorknob, pushing me back out.

I run my hands over my hair as I walk back down the hall to the table, fighting the urge to look over my shoulder.

"There you are," my mother calls, standing alone, the others having clearly left.

Jesus, how long was I in there?

"Sorry, I'm not feeling well. I thought I was going to throw up. I hope no one was offended."

My mother's discerning eyes rake over me. "You do look flush." She feels my forehead. "We're heading home now anyway. You can lie down before dinner."

I nod, smiling weakly before glancing over my shoulder, only catching a glimpse of tattoos as Calder ducks back through the kitchen.

Sutton

Wesley: Did you dream about me last night?

Buttercup: Yes

Wesley: Was it dirty?

Buttercup: Is there any other kind?

Wesley: Then you should spend some extra time in confession today.

"You look chipper this morning," my father muses, staring at me.

I shrug. "It's a nice day."

But all I'm thinking about is yesterday in the bathroom and how Calder better be at our spot today. I think that's what his text meant. Either way, I can't stop smiling.

"There doesn't seem to be any press today. I'm surprised since we're so close to the fundraiser. They usually turn into vultures around this time," my mother snarks, ripping me from my daydream.

"Huh? What?"

My parents stare at me like I've lost my mind. I have—completely and totally over Calder Wolfe.

"Are you okay, darling?"

I nod, feeling heat crawl up my neck. *I'm fine, Mom. Just a brazen hussy embarrassed by my wet daydream. Jesus.* My head swings toward the window just as the cross on the steeple comes into view. *Call, and he comes.*

As the car slows, I reach for the door with my smile firmly in place.

"Do you mind if I sit with Piper and Aubrey today? I mean, since there isn't any press."

My mother raises her brows, dropping her eyes to my bouncing knee—the one I stop bouncing immediately.

"I suppose that's fine," my father offers as his door is opened by the driver before he adds, "This wouldn't have to do with a young man? Would it?"

My heart stops beating for a moment before I kick it back into gear.

"Dad. Seriously?" I roll my eyes like a typical teenager, hoping to quell any further questions.

Because I know exactly who he's talking about. At least Hunter's good for something.

He holds up his hands, eyeing my mother, who's smirking.

"Go. But model behavior, Sutton."

I don't wait for further conversation, nodding as I duck out of the other side, immediately spotting my friends. My legs go as fast as they'll take me, all but running toward Aubrey and Piper as their smiles grow.

Aubrey appraises me, shaking her head as I come to a stop in front of her.

"He's here. Isn't he? You are all shiny and happy. Like a puppy."

I nod, quickly answering, "Yep," as she grabs my hand, turning and pulling me up the steps as Piper chuckles behind me.

We walk inside the mostly still-empty church as Aubs spins around.

"You have ten minutes, ya whore. We'll cover for you until the service starts."

I smack a kiss to her cheek and sneak into the hall, rushing up the stairs, looking back to see them take a seat at the bottom. Best friends ever.

The minute I get to the top of our hiding spot, Calder's eyes lift to mine from where he's sitting, flipping a Bible in his hand. He stands, tossing it on the table next to him before closing the distance.

"Hi," he breathes, wrapping an arm around my waist, lifting me up as we instantly kiss.

His lips break from mine again, dragging down over my jaw as I hold him tighter.

"Hi. I only have ten minutes before someone notices I'm gone. The girls are covering for me."

He pulls back for a moment, breath warm against my neck. "Why does it always feel like it's been a hundred years since the last time I saw you?"

God, he's right. We've been apart for half a day. And it feels like forever.

Blue eyes connect to mine as my feet touch the ground, but I wrap my arms around his waist, refusing to break away.

"I wish you could just steal me away. Is that dumb to say? But I just want to be with you without an expiration date."

Calder sweeps my hair behind my ears, forcing me to step back as he looks down at me. And I know he feels the same. I can't get enough of him to last me. It's impossible.

"I would, baby—if I thought I'd get away with it."

My smile blooms at his teasing as I weave my fingers through his. "We have Tuesday. And the fundraiser is Saturday, and I'll say I'm sleeping at Aubrey's. So we only have to make it a week before we can sneak away for a whole night. Can you find a place for us?"

"Only a week, says the girl that owns my fucking thoughts. But beggars can't be choosers. I'll find a place. But if shit doesn't work out, I'll just have to burn your fucking house down...because I'm gonna see you."

He bends down, tucking his head into the crook of my neck as he growls. My hands find his hair, and I let out a giggle as his face rubs against my shoulder.

"Fuck, I just want to bathe in your smell so that I can keep you with me. How am I supposed to watch you walk away? When all I wanna do is pin you the fuck down."

I blink, pushing his head back, as a deliciously bad idea comes to mind. Oh my God, what am I doing? Licking my lips, I slowly begin gathering my long maxi skirt.

Calder takes a few steps back, his eyes locked on the movement, watching, narrowed, as his lips part.

"Mmm. If you're doing what I think you're doing, then I'm absolutely gonna lose my mind this week."

I pull the fabric all the way up to my waist, revealing my white satin panties. Calder raises his brows, but I shrug, looking up at him innocently.

"I'm in a church. I have to wear them here."

His eyes half blink as he steps toward me again, voice lowering.

"I am gonna steal you. I've decided. And I'll never give you back. Because you are mine, Sutton. Do you understand how deep I mean that shit, baby? I will never fucking give you back. Ever."

Right now, no matter if what he's saying started as teasing, it's my every wish that his promise is true.

"Swear it," I whisper.

He grips the back of my neck, pulling my lips to his roughly before he says, "On my life."

I'm released, eyes on his as I shimmy off my panties. We stand silent before I take his hand, flipping it over, palm up. The silk folds over itself as it drops over his greedy fingers.

"Now, you can take a piece of me with you until you take all of me. And I hope you don't mind, but all I've thought about is you—so they're wet."

Church bells sound like the clock striking ten, making him scowl as I lift to my toes, kissing his lips quickly before turning and running back the way I came.

But before I take the stairs, I look over my shoulder as Calder raises the white satin to his face and smells my goddamn panties.

Calder

"Hi," she answers, and I can tell she's smiling.

"Hi, back. I missed you all damn day, baby."

She sighs into the phone. "How are my panties doing? Are they helping your cravings?"

"Not at all. Monday usually sucks, but this one's been the fucking worst. I want you on me. Now."

"Today is almost over, and tomorrow Piper will cover for me—so we have four whole hours in the afternoon."

I groan because patience is not a virtue I possess when it comes to Sutton. She giggles, but my smile fades because I'm staring out the window, watching Michael Kelly help his wife into the back of their town car. Pops told us to follow him and make our presence known tonight.

"You got quiet. What are you doing right now?"

My head shakes as I answer. "Just stuff."

"Ah. Stuff. Stuff you can't tell me."

"Stuff you don't want to know."

Roman taps the hood from where's he sitting outside, grabbing my attention. My arm dangles out the window, and I give a wave as Roman and I stare down Michael's car as he passes. *We're watching, motherfucker.*

I turn my attention back to my call as Roman pulls out his cell to let Pops know we said *hello*.

"Okay then, tell me this," she muses. "What would you do if you weren't born into the life you're in?"

My head tilts, a smile returning to my face.

"We're getting deep. All right." She giggles again. "I'd probably work on cars. Like maybe restore old cars. I like taking something that somebody overlooked and seeing what's beautiful in it."

She laughs but not as if what I said was funny, and I don't like it. I can feel her mood change.

"What's that laugh? What's wrong?"

The sound of her sheets rustling fills the phone before she says, "Nothing. Just what you said kind of hit me hard. Today was a shitty day with my mom, and as you were talking, it felt like you were describing me."

My brows pull in. "Bullshit. How?"

I'm gruff. I don't mean to be, but it pisses me off that anyone would make her feel like that.

"No, seriously." She half-laughs. "I've always felt kind of overlooked, obviously by my parents. But even by my best friends. Don't get me wrong, they love me so much. I know that. And they're amazing friends, but they've always been closer, the two of them. I've never really been special to anyone until you."

Until me. My eyes drop to my lap because she just fucking guts me when she says shit like this. I swear to God, our feelings double in intensity because they're the same. Nobody's ever truly seen me until her.

I draw my bottom lip between my teeth before I let it slide out.

"You're not just special to me. You're the one on every level." My hand runs through my hair as I lift my eyes. "Nothing compares or competes. It's just you that I think about...that I want. And a really shitty part of me is happy those people don't see your worth because then I'd have to share you. And I want you all to myself, for as long as I can have you."

She's so quiet that I push my face closer against the phone, trying to listen to her breathe before saying, "I wanna kiss you right now."

"I wish that too," she whispers back.

Another beat of silence goes by, and then she says, "I have to go. My parents have donors coming for dinner, so I need to change... But...I don't ever want you to share me either. I like being yours, Calder."

I say nothing as the line dies, trying to internally catch my breath. She feeds the darkest parts of me. The possession, the selfish adoration I have for her. I'm falling for her, more and more with each breath she takes, and it feels like euphoric doom. A death I'd welcome.

Roman pulls the car door open, sliding inside as he looks at me.

"You good?"

I ignore him, staring ahead, deep in thought. *I want to fucking kiss her.*

My eyes narrow as I think. I bet I could sneak right the fuck in, and nobody would be the wiser. Doesn't matter that it's still light out. Her house is enormous. It's not like they could hear us from where her bedroom is tucked away.

And her security system is a fucking joke. I always thought senators had fancy bodyguards until I learned that's only for when they're in Washington. If I wasn't here on this island, I'd tell her to make her father get a better system because he's making it too easy for Connor.

All my bad ideas must be evident because Roman laughs as he stares at me.

"Dude. Whatever it is you're thinking right now looks like fucking trouble. You don't even have to tell me. The answer is hell no."

I grin, lighting a cigarette.

"I just need to make a quick off-the-books stop before we visit Tag."

Roman scowls. "I fucking knew it. This is about the redhead."

I shrug, sucking in a drag, "So? It's nothing."

"What the fuck, C? You got your ass beat because of her. Did you forget that?"

The cigarette spins to the ground as I flick it before shifting to face him.

"Careful. I said it's nothing."

Roman stares back, stubborn as fuck. This is how everything goes down between us. We always make it back on the same page, but sometimes it has bloodstains.

"You should take your own advice and be careful. Business before pussy. Or have you forgotten?"

My hand darts out for his throat before I stop myself, wiping it down my face instead.

"Watch your fucking mouth, Roman. I won't warn you again. You won't ever call her that. Am I understood?"

He's staring at me, doing that fucking thing he does, trying to read me before he settles back against his seat.

"Roman." I barely contain my anger. "Say you understand. Because if I have to bash your fucking head into that steering wheel to make sure you get it, I will."

He nods his head, jaw tensed.

"Yeah. I get it."

"But?" I toss out.

His fist thrusts forward into the dash, and he raises his voice.

"But... 'It's nothing?' That's your answer. Even though you're ready to fucking kill me?"

"That's what the fuck I said, isn't it?"

My blood is boiling. Roman needs to fucking leave this alone.

"Fuck you. You can't be into her like this. It can't ever work. What the fuck are you doing, C? You're not *for* this girl. She doesn't even fucking know who you are."

My voice is thunderous, filled with rage.

"Nobody tells me I'm not for her. Or that she's not for me. Nobody, Roman. Not even you." I stab my finger at him. "What I'm doing is none of your fucking business. So, you will leave it alone. Because just like I remember my place, you need to fucking remember yours."

I should've just hit him. Because that blow was worse.

Roman kicks the fucking door open before the keys hit me square in the chest. "Fuck off, asshole. Drive yourself, then, boss."

I smack the dash, then shove open the car door, stepping out into the street.

"Roman."

He stops, turning around to look at me. I can't tell him how I feel because then I put him at risk. Doing this, sneaking around, being with her, without anyone knowing, keeps him safe.

"This is on me. All on me. You have to trust me. I take this on the chin alone."

I know he knows what I mean, but he shakes his head anyway.

"No. Nothing is ever all on you. We're brothers, Calder. I don't fucking work for you. I stand next to you. No matter what. And I'm telling you to cut her loose. Trust *me*."

Trust him? Even if I did, there's no going back now. Maybe there never was.

"She's not some stray I picked up off the street, Romes. This girl means something. She knows exactly who I am—better than anyone. I don't hide from her. That's the truth."

Anger sets on his jaw again. "Tell me you're joking. You're a fucking fool. She doesn't love you—"

"She will," I bark back, but he doesn't stop.

"You're just fun. This bullshit could get you hurt, man. What happens when Connor wants Prescott six feet under? Huh? You gonna kill him or Connor?"

My head is shaking as my hands ball into fists, ready to crack his fucking jaw.

"C, I'm sure she's great. One in a fucking million, but she ain't my family. How am I supposed to protect you when you're fucking sleeping with the enemy? I watch your back. Not hers."

"There's no difference." I spit it out so fast that his head draws back. "If you protect me, you protect her."

Roman stands ten feet away, staring back at me. The gravity of what I've just said imprisons us in our places.

I could argue how wrong he is, tell him that I know everything she feels because it's as if we share the same goddamn heart. Tell him that loving her isn't an *if*. It's a *when* …maybe even an *already*. But this world doesn't afford men love. We only get violence and allegiance. So, I'm claiming her as mine —if he protects me, then he protects Sutton.

"You've known this girl for—"

My hand raises to stop him. "How long doesn't matter, Roman. You heard me, and I mean it. You will carry my truth as your burden. Forever. She is mine, forever, Roman."

What I just said will change everything. Our whole story. Because I've condemned her to a family she may not want.

But I don't care.

Sutton belongs to me. Now she belongs to us.

My eyes haven't left my brother's, but I don't have to say shit because he gives me a nod.

"You got my word."

Sutton

chapter
twenty-nine

I pull my hair into a messy bun as I walk into my bathroom and turn on the faucet, letting the water run into the tub. As I make my way out, I open my balcony doors, letting in the ocean breeze. It's still light out but already cooler than the afternoon.

My eyes close as I stand there, thinking about his words, enjoying the breeze that's feathering my face.

He said I was the one.

Taking a deep breath as my shoulders shrug, I open my eyes and walk outside, looking up. God, it's so clear, not a cloud in the sky. A perfect blue canvas.

Still, it's nothing like the night Calder took me to the field. That was magical.

I rest my forearms on the banister, staring up as I close my eyes, dreaming about that moment again. It used to be that I'd shut my eyes and dream about all the things I'd hoped would happen, but now my real life trumps the imaginary one.

My tongue darts across my bottom lip, wetting it as I remember him kissing me. And the way his lips are always so soft against mine. The memory is so visceral that I can almost feel the warmth of his breath.

Oh my God. My eyes spring open, a squeal erupting from my throat as I push away from lips pressed to mine. But I'm halted by a hand in my hair and the scent of the man I was just dreaming about.

I smile big and wide as Calder kisses me. Our faces are so close that he's blurry for a second as he pulls back.

"What are you doing?" I say, hushed, looking down over his shoulder to see him standing on a small ledge against the façade of my house.

"Climbing up your balcony. What does it look like?"

His grin makes my heart want to jump out of my chest.

"You can't be here. We'll for sure get caught." I glance over my shoulder, suddenly scared someone might just walk in before I look up at the cameras on the house. "It's not dark enough. You'll be seen."

He shakes his head. "In case you didn't realize, baby, there isn't a risk I wouldn't take for those lips. And don't worry, that camera is pointing toward the tree. But if you want to play it safe..."

I bite my bottom lip, watching him descend back down, peeking over the rail.

"Wait. Just one kiss?"

He smiles, gripping the rail again, launching himself back up. "I like you bad. Kiss me a hundred more."

I lean forward without hesitation as he cradles my cheek. My arms wrap around his neck, pulling me even closer.

"You're crazy," I say, practically breathless.

"About you."

He's smirking as he rubs our noses together, but the sound of my door makes me spin around, almost knocking him down the wall. A faint "Oh fuck" is all I hear as my mother walks inside, eyeing me on my balcony.

"Sutton. Come inside. You'll let bugs in."

"Okay." I nod, desperately wanting to look behind me.

Instead, I close the doors, just as my mother extends a typed piece of paper toward me.

"What's this?"

"Your father wants you to look over these talking points for Saturday, especially the one about his 'Clean the Streets Initiative.'"

My face drops to the paper, brows pulling together. "Why would I need talking points?"

She smiles wide. "He'd like *you* to head a youth anti-drug and alcohol platform. We'll handle the day-to-day, so it won't conflict with school, but PR thinks it will be very successful in making a statement. And your father is going to use it to spearhead a push on the Hill for stricter regulations. They won't even see it coming, because 'from the mouths of babes.'"

My eyes lift to hers. "What does that mean?"

She huffs. "I thought you'd be pleased to help your father. Why don't I feel any excitement from you? Sutton, now is not the time to argue the benefits of marijuana or whatever cool statement drug Aubrey likes to partake in, pretending she's backing a cause."

Her judgment of my friends is unwelcome.

I shake my head. "First off, I don't do drugs. Neither does Aubrey. Second, I just don't understand why anyone would be interested in what I have to say. Why me? You've never needed me before."

Suddenly her demeanor shifts, her smile dropped, the ease in her stature lost. Now she's all hard jawline and crossed arms. Gone is the mother that's selling me on the virtue of good deeds, and in walks my real mother—the woman with strategy and a purpose.

"Because you are a beacon of good values and upbringing. That's what we're selling. You make him look good. Perfect daughter equals perfect candidate. And that all lends to people wanting to back his cause. It checks all the boxes. Don't be dense." She tips a smile in my direction. "He's asking Hunter too. Does that give you more of an interest?"

I cross my arms.

"No. I'm less interested. Also, he does drugs."

I think. Probably. Who cares?

She narrows her eyes. "Does anyone know?"

My head tilts, eyes opening wider.

"Mother. Seriously?"

She snaps her fingers at me when I don't answer, making me blink before I let out a whoosh of breath.

"No. Nobody knows that would tell. And I'm not sure he does them. I just hate him."

Her hands find her hips, the way they do when I've clearly made her angry.

"Then keep your mouth shut, Sutton. That is exactly the kind of unhealthy gossip that should stay dead. The two of you, together in a campaign like this—you could be the next Caroline and John-John."

I frown. "Who?" She waves me off, but I press. "I can handle it alone. Whatever it is."

She snatches the paper back from me to set it on my desk.

"We'll circle back to this later. In the meantime, you'll be speaking about this Saturday night. I expect you to be fluent."

I nod as she walks back to me and puts her hand on my shoulder.

"This is a wonderful message for our community, Sutton, while being helpful to your father. The trash that's washed ashore, living among us, needs to be thrown out. You'll be proud knowing that you're responsible for ensuring that happens because once he gets you on the air, all eyes will be ready to watch those filthy Wolfes."

My head swings to her. "Dad's targeting the Wolfe family?"

"Of course, Sutton, and you could really spur the cause. We know they've tried selling drugs at the park. A park where you and your friends hang out."

I shake my head. "No, they haven't."

She walks toward me. "Listen to me. That family is scum. Together, you and your father will rid us of the Wolfe family and that goddamn O'Bannion curse that hangs over his head. Remember what you just demonstrated. Facts don't always have to be true. They just need to appear that way. I'm sure you've seen a thing or two that was suspicious, right? And if you haven't, you've always excelled in the field of imagination."

Oh my God. No. Is she fucking serious? I hate her.

I swallow, feeling panicked and angry.

"I can't...I don't know...I'm—"

What are the words? I can't seem to find the right words. Because what

I won't say is that I'm falling for the boy I shouldn't and that hurting him feels physically impossible.

But I also don't know how to say no to her.

And that's the gut punch that's left me silent.

She rubs my arms, smiling at me. "People listen to today's youth. Especially when they're personally affected."

My mouth drops open. *Just fucking say something, Sutton.*

She shakes her head. "And between us, mother to daughter, I think it's time you found a place in this family—brought something to the table, so to speak." She pats my cheek, pointing to my bathroom. "Don't let the bath run for too long. Dinner is at seven sharp, darling."

The moment she walks out, I remain imprisoned in place. Of all the shitty things just said to me, it's the last that's making it hardest to breathe.

"I think it's time you found a place in this family…"

It almost knocks me to the floor—that familiar feeling. The one that reminds me that I'm just a cog in the wheel.

That words like *daughter* are for sound bites, not proud moments in private. That hugs are relegated for the cameras, not to console or display love.

I just fucking work here.

And if that wasn't bad enough, apparently my new job is to ruin my boyfriend.

The lump in my throat grows thick, but I suck in a breath, pushing it all down, suddenly remembering Calder. I turn around, walking quickly to open my balcony doors.

As they sweep open, Calder's eyes lock to mine from where he's seated just inside, ass on the floor, hidden from view.

He heard everything.

It's evident by the way he refuses to let me look away, head tilting, catching my eyes as I try and look everywhere but at him.

But I'm embarrassed and ashamed. It's one thing to tell someone the secrets about your life. Having them witness the tragedy is a whole other kind of evil.

When he frowns, I smile and shrug. "Remember when your face was full of bruises? You said it never hurts. Same. I guess my bruises are just on the inside."

He doesn't say a word as he stands. But the way he's staring at me, cataloging my body, makes everything I just said feel like a lie. Because it's as if he can see all the cuts and scars below the surface, on my heart.

The bluest eyes fix to mine, with only the promise of the truth behind them.

"Do you want me to hurt her back?"

My lips part, but I shake my head. Every damn part of me is sickly comforted by his words but also equally afraid of how easily he said them.

Even still, I'm undeserving of his brutal kindness. Because I hate myself for my silence. He heard everything—my cowardice and humiliation. And he's still protecting me.

Calder walks inside my room, straight to the bathroom, before I can say any more. I turn, heart already pounding as I follow, shutting the door, then twisting around to lock it.

He can't leave before I say what I should. Except, everything I want to express is all jumbled inside, refusing to come out.

Pressing my back against the door, I start with the easy part, but it's the wrong order, even though I mean it.

"I'm sorry. I'm so sorry you heard that."

"No," he whispers. "You don't say that to me."

He turns off the bath before grabbing my waist and hauling me forward, unlocking the door behind me. My hands coming to my chest, feeling like I can't catch my breath.

"Please don't leave me," I whisper.

Calder reopens the door as he looks down at me.

"Wait here."

I nod, numb and confused as he moves past me, walking out into my bedroom. It's almost like I'm feeling too many things at once, and I can't focus.

God, why didn't you make them love me the way other parents love their kids? Or make me not care? Because this feels cruel. She'll make

Calder hate me. Because he'll see what a coward I am. I just want him to know that I'm sorry. And I need him to stay because—

I suck in a shaky breath as my forefinger picks at the polish on my thumb, trying to keep everything bubbling inside of me down. But I just as quickly stop, remembering I must be presentable for tonight.

"Perfect daughter equals perfect candidate."

Perfect daughter. Be the perfect daughter...but how would they know if I was? They look right through me. Calder's the only person that sees me.

I peek around the doorjamb, hearing a click before seeing him returning. My head swings back inside, waiting and trying to breathe, but as soon as he's in the room, all my words rush out, spilling over onto him with urgency.

"Calder, I won't do what she's asking. I swear. I'm sorry. Please believe—"

He cuts me off, brows pulled together, his finger pressed to my cupid's bow. "Shh. You don't ever fucking apologize to me for them."

He reaches behind him, dragging off his shirt, then stares down at me. But I'm not moving.

My eyes drop to the floor, but his fingers gently press under my chin, lifting them back to his.

"Let me make it better, baby."

He steps in closer, lifting my arms, pulling my T-shirt over my head before he kisses my forehead. My breath hitches as I stand silently, watching him undress both of us.

There's nothing sexual about what he's doing. It's care. And it feels so good that I almost break.

Calder takes his time, kneeling, helping me off with my shorts before pressing a kiss to my hip bone just above the rim of my panties.

He doesn't even say anything about me wearing them, leaving them on as he stands.

A drip of water plinks into the tub, and I blink as he toes off his shoes before undoing his belt.

My chin lifts, trying to keep everything I'm feeling at bay.

I hear the zipper sliding down on his Dickies before he pushes them to the ground.

"Look at me, baby."

I do. We're standing in our underwear, vulnerable and half-bare. But I've never felt safer in my life. I shut my eyes, unable to stop the wave of emotions crashing in on me, but my mouth keeps opening and closing, wishing I could just speak. But nothing comes out.

There are no words. No apologies. Nothing.

He didn't just strip me of my clothes. He's stripped me of every barrier. All that's left is to feel it—all of it.

His fingers brush down my face as he looks at me with so much care behind his eyes that it nearly splits me in two.

"We're alike, Sutton—bound to our names. Held down by our obligations. Robbed of love. Until we found each other. That's why we're so connected, because I am you, and you are me."

A ragged breath shakes my chest as I throw myself at him, arms hooking around his neck. He lifts me off the floor, whispering into my ear as tears fall from my eyes.

"She doesn't have to be dead for you to know what it's like to be without her."

There have never been truer words. I've lived without a mother for so long, grieving the loss of something I never really had.

"Shh. It's okay. I got you. Everything's okay now."

Calder steps into the tub, taking me with him, arranging us so that we're sitting face-to-face. Our legs are entwined, mine over the top of his. The water's hot, stinging my skin, but I don't care if it burns. I'm not leaving him.

His hands come up to my cheeks, wiping wet thumbs over them as he cradles my face.

"Don't cry. Not over her. She doesn't deserve your tears."

That's not wholly why I'm crying. I shake my head, tilting my head to press my cheek into his palm as I speak.

"How can I do something that hurts you? Even if it's supposedly what's right."

He says nothing as I stare up at him. "Do you think you can care for someone so much that right and wrong stop existing? Like what's right for them is wrong for you. Because I think I feel that. I don't care what you do. What you've done. I won't hurt you."

He leans in, feathering kisses over my cheeks, then my eyes, traveling over my nose before he locks eyes with me again.

"You should care, Sutton. Run us off. It's okay. I'm not going anywhere. My place is with you...not them. Be the dutiful daughter. As long as you're with me, nothing matters."

My chin trembles as I climb onto him, sloshing water outside the tub, our bodies flush.

"I hate them. I'm sorry. I'm sorry for both of us," I whisper into his ear.

I cling to Calder, feeling crushed by everything stacked against us as his hands run over my back, in soft strokes up and down, comforting me, holding me.

"We don't get forever, do we?" I breathe out onto his shoulder because it all suddenly feels impossible.

His stubble scratches my cheek as his head moves.

"I don't know, but I know we get right now, and that's what matters. Because if we only had today, it would be worth it."

It's the answer to the question I asked him in the confessional that day. I pull back, looking at his beautiful face, staring at him.

I love you.

"Better?" he whispers.

I lean in, speaking my answer into his lips before I kiss him. "Better."

Sutton

"Taste," Calder growls, smearing my juices across my lips with his middle finger before pushing it into my mouth.

His lips find mine, sharing the sweetness as his two fingers thrust back inside me. It's only his breath I inhale because our mouths are sealed, desperate for one another.

After last night, the way he held me, bathed me, before we were forced to say goodbye—Jesus, we felt like live wires the moment we snuck away today.

My back arches off the leather, from where I'm lying on the back seat of his Mustang. We're hidden under a carport, a tarp used as curtains to keep our dirty doings a secret.

"That's it. Come all over my fucking hand."

Fuck. Me. He's relentless, pushing in over and over as my eyes begin to roll into the back of my head, gripped by the sensations pooling in my center.

The build starts to compound as his rough hand covers my breast, rolling my nipple through my shirt between his fingers.

"Oh fuck."

My hand smacks against the window above me, leaving finger marks on the fogged-up glass. Calder's lips drag over my neck before he stops just below my ear.

"I wanted to fuck you last night in that tub. Bury my dick in that tight pussy until you screamed my name to heaven and left your blood on my cock."

My fingers curl into the fabric of his T-shirt, gripping him as he hovers over me, spreading my legs wider, carried higher into ecstasy by his dirty mouth.

"Fuck me, Calder. Please. Right here."

I'm begging. I want him inside of me so badly.

"Back seats are for bad girls," he growls low and quiet. "Is that what you are, baby? My bad girl?"

The wet slaps of his fingers thrusting inside of me, mixed with his wicked question, tips me right over the edge.

"Oh God. I'm...fuck. I feel it."

His eyes meet mine as he grips my jaw, holding me in place.

"Look at me. I wanna watch you come."

Oh my God.

"Yes," I scream, tightening around his fingers as I explode.

His eyes bore into mine, watching in exaltation as I quiver. My mouth hangs open as the long, drawn-out mewl echoes inside the car.

A smirk forms on his lips, and my thighs shake before he covers my mouth, thrusting his tongue inside as I happily accept.

We kiss slowly, savoring each other until my breathing finally matches the pace. Calder pulls away, eyes on mine.

"This is the best date, down at the docks, I've ever had."

I giggle. "Nobody has dates at the docks."

But as he smiles, the words I thought last night come back to me. *Is this what love is?* I've never felt it, but if it's despising being apart from someone and only really feeling alive when you're with them, then I love him.

"How long has it been since we met?" I ask, staring at his grin.

Calder leans down again, chastely kissing my lips before dragging his fingers slowly out of my pussy as he answers.

But I barely hear because of the gasp I've sucked in.

"Three weeks or so. Why?"

"Oh my God. Why does that feel so good?"

He chuckles as he reaches into the middle console and pulls out the panties I gave him. I bite my lip, watching as he wipes his fingers on them.

Fuck. He's so sexy. Everything he does drives me insane.

My legs drop off the seat as I push to sit, giving him room to do the same. But his eyes drop to my bare center, and I can't help but spread my legs just a bit.

"It feels so good because you were made for my fingers." He leans forward, kissing my mouth again, breathing, "And my lips," before he cups my pussy, groaning, "and me."

I sigh as he pulls away, letting my head drop back against the seat as he speaks.

"Is that why you're asking how long we've been together? Is my baby ready for another lesson?"

"When?" I say breathlessly, perking up, making him laugh.

He sits back, grabbing my shorts off the floorboard before he smiles at me, placing them in my lap.

"Do you remember the night we met?"

I nod.

"That girl deserved magic. So I'm gonna give it to her. And that's not the back seat of a car." His eyes drop from mine down to his hands.

Oh my God. He looks scared. And it seems as unnatural on him as I think it feels.

His eyes lift to mine again. "There are things I want to say, Sutton...shit that I need to say before—"

I cut him off, crawling over onto his lap, pressing my lips to his.

He's afraid of me. Because I feel it—Calder loves me too.

A few weeks ago, sex was a transaction. It was something to check off my list. But it's different with him. He's made me different. So, if he wants to give me magic, I want to believe in it. It's that simple.

His fingers weave into my hair, forcing me back as his eyes search mine. "I'm gonna give you the stars, and the moon, and—"

"Love. You're going to give me love."

It's not a demand. Just a statement of fact. One we both feel.

His lips part to speak, but instead, he nods before touching his forehead to mine, whispering, "Yes, baby. All I have to give."

"Where have you been all afternoon?"

I stare innocently at my mother before placing the bags in my hands down on the foyer floor.

"Running errands. Where else?"

My head tips toward the bags to stress my point. She rolls her eyes.

"Forgive me, but I didn't think the dry cleaning and a few other measly items would take hours. You missed Hunter. He came by with Michael...to speak with your father about the initiative."

I swear to God. She's never going to stop hoping we happen.

I shrug. "Shame."

Her eyes narrow because I definitely didn't pull off anything close to genuine, so I quickly segue.

"I was stuck forever waiting at the cleaners because they hired someone new. And you know how that can be."

Thank you, Piper, for that little detail.

She eyes me suspiciously, or maybe I just think that because I'm a big fat liar. I almost smile. Best lie for the best reason.

"Well, leave all the bags there. I'll get Rosie to put everything away." She turns toward her office. "I've set out some dress options for the fundraiser on your bed. Remind me never to plan another garden party again. Everything appropriate is bound to burn us alive. Take a look-see so I can approve."

I'm nodding with a smile on my face like I care about what she's saying. Because I need her happy for what I'm about to ask.

My mouth opens, but she dismisses me by ignoring me to speak to the housekeeper. Shit. The window of opportunity is lost.

I start up the stairs but pause. Fuck it. With my back to her, I squeeze my eyes shut, asking, "Hey, Mom, would it be okay if I slept over at Aubrey's after the main part of the fundraiser is over?"

She hums in acknowledgment that I've spoken but doesn't answer, so I turn around, pressing the issue.

"We wanted to brainstorm more ideas for the initiative Dad asked me to head. I'm actually pretty excited about it. And I figured I'd get out of your hair so you guys could mingle and not have to worry about me."

Her head pops up from where she was looking, eyes on mine. Now I have her attention. I watch all the pros and cons pass over her features until she smiles.

"I'll need to speak to her mother, but yes. And make sure you let your father know. I like the team playing, Sutton."

"Thank you," I rush out. "I will."

My grin is almost too wide. Not because she's happy but because I got my way. Saturday night, I get Calder and magic for a whole damn night. I pull out my phone as I trot up the stairs, immediately texting Calder, letting him know I pulled it off, giggling as he responds.

Wesley: Goddamn, I like you bad.

Calder

> Buttercup: Everything is set for tonight. I'll be at Aubrey's at 6:30 sharp.

A smile tugs at my lips. Fuck, I think I'm already feeling the adrenaline pumping through me. I can't fucking wait to get my goddamn hands on her. The last four days have been torture, even though I snuck in another kiss on Thursday while she was in town.

I type out a quick text, letting my tongue drag over my bottom lip.

> Wesley: I'll be there. If I don't fucking die waiting first.

She's giggling. I can hear it in my mind.

I push off my bed, cracking my neck, thinking about all the dirty shit I'm gonna do to her as a warm-up when my phone pings again. There's a smile already in place as I look down. But it fades quickly as I read what's on the screen.

> Roman: Trouble's coming. He knows. Delete this.

What the fuck?

I don't hesitate, swiping to erase his message before scrolling quickly and deleting my entire chain with Sutton. Because there's only one thing to know. One damn secret.

Her.

Looking around, I grab a pair of jeans slung over a chair, pulling them on and throwing on a black T-shirt just as the front door slams. Fuck. I slip on my boots before sliding a hand under my pillow, pulling out my Glock.

That message meant one of two things: my father or Connor.

Neither option means anything fucking good. I've never lived inside a fairy tale that either man wouldn't kill me in cold fucking blood if I crossed them.

Sutton crosses every line.

My mind races, looking for any mistake I've made over the last few weeks, flipping through moment after moment.

Goddammit. I've been fucking methodical. Her name's not in my phone. I've made sure I wasn't followed. I know I've never been caught on camera sneaking out. And there's no fucking way Roman or West said shit. So how?

I tuck my phone into my back pocket as a steady breath leaves me. *Get your shit together.* My mind settles, forcing my entire body to calm as I listen, waiting, with my eyes on the door, but there's nothing but fucking silence.

Whoever's out there is waiting for me to come to them.

I've never killed a man. But today might be that day.

"Hey, West?" I holler to cover the sound of my doorknob twisting. "I got the greatest story to tell you about last night."

Silence.

I slowly open the door, peering into the empty hallway before slipping out quietly.

"Dude, there was this chick..." I throw out quietly, taking the safety off my gun. "She did things you've never seen."

I creep down the hall, stopping before I enter the great room. With my back against the wall, I stare across at the thermostat. No way Pops is around the corner. He'd have answered me. Someone wants me off guard.

I close my eyes, heart pounding because there's a chance that when I turn this corner, I may not come back. But nobody's gonna hurt Sutton. Even if that means I put a bullet between their eyes.

So, I step, gun raised. Locked right onto my father.

"Good mornin', boy."

Pops is leaned against the back of the couch, alone and unnerved. There's no doubt he's seen the end of a gun before, but the way he's looking at me—like he expected this—is throwing me off.

What the fuck is going on? And why the hell did Roman say "trouble"? Because there are no goons in sight.

I hesitate to lower my gun, staring back at him as he waves a hand for me to drop it. Because what did I just fall into? There's nothing right about this. My gut and my head are at war. Is this about Sutton?

My arm drops, suspicion on my brow. "What the fuck are you doing? I could've killed you."

He uncrosses his arms, narrowing his eyes before a smile spills out over his face. I shove my gun into the small of my back as he stands, walking toward me, grinning like the devil. He grabs the back of my neck hard, pulling me forward, locking his eyes to mine.

Air sucked between his teeth before he speaks.

"I needed to see what you're capable of...in *her* name."

The feeling of ice pollutes my veins. In an instant, all my fear is confirmed. He knows about Sutton. This *is* trouble. So much fucking trouble.

"You know, I wondered how you'd take Roman's message. But killing me..." He lets out a hard whoosh. "There's more of me inside of you than I expected."

My jaw hardens, realizing I was set the fuck up.

"Ah, Calder." He sighs, letting me go, stepping backward toward the couch.

I wipe a hand over my jaw as he does, itching to pull my gun. But he's right. I am like him, even if I hate it. Because at this moment, I know exactly what I have to do.

In the back of my mind, I've always known. Since the moment I laid eyes on her. There was always only one end. A destiny we could never return from.

Our fall is destined.

Tyler wags his finger at me. "Love makes men act like fools and poets, Calder. But it's the villain I needed to see."

"How the fuck did you find out?"

He eyes me suspiciously before smirking, as if he likes the game he's playing. "Calder."

The look on his face is fucking sinister as he reaches down to the couch seat. My eyes follow, a hollow feeling growing in my chest as he says, "From you, boy."

In his hand, waved like a Bible from a preacher on a pulpit, is my fucking journal. His Irish lilt coats the words I wrote about her as he spits them back at me.

"Her lips touched mine, but my soul recognized hers. I never believed in soul mates. I don't think I even believed in love. But Sutton—she makes me want to."

Her name is spoken through gritted teeth before he snaps the leather closed.

Only she had that paper. I ripped it the fuck out of my journal because I wrote it for her. To give to her because it's the only time I ever mentioned her by name or in a way she could be discovered.

Has he been in her room?

My mind splinters.

Did he send someone?

They say before you die that your life flashes before your eyes. All the moments you've collected play like a movie until *bang*. You're gone.

It's still only her I see.

The wild way her red hair flies in the wind. And the smiles that feel like a gift. All the seamless curves of her body and the pattern of her freckles. The way she melts in my arms so that there's no me or her—we're always one.

She is my life.

Everything begins in slow motion.

Me reaching for my gun. Tensions exploding. Tyler lunging. Our voices bellowing.

I swing my arm around, aiming for him, but he crushes the leather journal against my hand, forcing the gun to the floor as he rumbles, "Ya' fucking little prick."

The sound of metal scrapes the floor, moving everything into fast-forward until we're hurling ourselves onto each other.

Tyler drives his shoulder into my ribs as I bring an elbow down on his back. But he grips my throat, throwing me against the wall, pinning me to it.

His nostrils flare, face red as spit flies from his mouth.

"You want me to kill you? Is that what you fucking want?"

My airway's cut off, but I try and choke out my answer. Fuck him. But my head is already feeling dizzy.

"Shh. Shh. The more you fight, the faster you die."

He's staring at me, watching me choke. My eyes begin to sting from the force of the pressure, but I stare back, feeding into his anger before his hand finally gives, and I suck in life.

"What am I supposed to do here? Kill my only son?"

He's laughing to himself like a lunatic as I tip my head back, letting more oxygen in.

Tyler sidesteps, checking how far away the gun is before he looks at me again. He moves toward me, and I flinch as he grabs my cheeks, cradling them. He's unhinged. And that makes him capable of anything.

"No. No. Don't be scared. I won't hurt you. Unless you make me again. You listen to me, boy. That filthy bitch will ruin you. Do you understand? She'll tear down everything we've built. Her family looks to destroy everything we stand for. There's no loyalty. No allegiance. They discard what they can't use."

I'm silent, trying to control my rage as he nudges my head back against the wall with more force than necessary.

"Do you know the evils I've committed? The unforgivable sins in your name? It's all for you. My only son. For you to be king, Calder."

I can't look at him, so I stare to the side.

"Look at me," he rumbles.

My eyes lock to his, chest heaving as we stare at each other.

"It's like looking in a mirror," he breathes out. "Except one of us is more dangerous than the other. I still don't know which."

He narrows his eyes like he just decided.

"You walk away and this dies. Not even Connor has to know. Do you understand?"

When I don't nod, he leans in, fingers gripping my hair so hard it stings.

"But if you don't do as you're told, your lass will be found in the river, filled with so much cum that the police won't even be able to match it to anyone."

I will kill him. Now I'll make sure he suffers.

I swallow, feeling my chest crack wide open because this is the end.

"I'm seeing her tonight. I'll end it. But give me tonight."

His eyes search mine, so I say it more forcefully.

"I'll fucking end it. Okay. Just give me tonight."

I'm released, but the weight on my shoulders remains. Tyler steps away, straightening his shirt as he turns toward the door, barking, "Come in."

The meatheads he's usually with stalk inside, dragging Roman and West in with them. My fists ball at my sides, seeing West's lip fucking busted.

"Boss, this one tried to get by." The dick motions to West. "Things got a little rough."

They shove them down on the couch as Tyler chuckles.

"My boys are handfuls." He shrugs, running his hand through his hair. "Clean the place. Take the guns. Wouldn't want anyone getting any more bad ideas."

Tyler looks at Roman, who seems almost as angry as me. He should be. Tyler's a cocksucker.

"You and West will go with Calder tonight. As insurance. If he fails, then you all fail." Tyler's eyes drift to West. "It would be a shame for West not to see eighteen."

Sutton

chapter
thirty-two

"We loved hearing what you said tonight. I wish more young people had their heads on their shoulders like you."

I smile as the shapely woman sips her martini. I don't know why my mother worried so much about the desserts and food. All anyone wants at these events is the booze.

She smiles, turning toward her husband, giving me a moment to reach into the pocket of my dress to eye the time on my phone. 5:30. *Jesus, I'm going to combust.*

Time is slithering by so slowly that I'm losing my mind. God, I can't wait to see him. My mother calls me from across the room, beckoning me with her perfectly manicured fingers.

"Please excuse me. My mother's calling," I offer to the woman before I step away.

My eyes drop to the ground for a moment as I cut between two groups before lifting them, connecting right on Hunter's face.

For fuck's sake.

"I'm so pleased Hunter agreed to help Sutton," my mother gushes as she and Marianne air-kiss.

Everyone is pretending to be the very best of friends. My father and

Michael Kelly pat each other on the back while my mother and Marianne throw around compliments like confetti.

And I try not to puke.

But no matter how disgusted I am, I stand with my eyes up and a polite smile fixed to my face in an elegantly appropriate knee-length sleeveless black halter dress.

I'm the embodiment of a good upbringing. Their perfect daughter. Because I have a half hour until bliss, and not even a deal with the devil, aka my mother, is stopping me from escaping.

"Sutton, darling. Let me introduce you to Hunter's mother."

Marianne's eyes drop to me.

"Hello, Mrs. Kelly, so nice to see you again," I say in response.

Marianne runs her hands up my arms before cradling my face. "Well, I can see the appeal. Your daughter is gorgeous, Elizabeth."

I'm right here. Marianne drops her hands as my mother beams.

"Thank you, but I think she's the lucky one here. Hunter is quite the catch."

My skin crawls. *Oh my God. I've thrown him away. Over and over. Get a clue.*

Hunter's arrogant face comes into view as he walks around Tag, beelining straight for me. His hand slides against my lower back as he leans down, kissing my cheek, making our mothers swoon.

I almost scream.

"Freckles. I was sad to have missed you the other day."

Oh my fucking God.

I stare into the void before I snap back and lift my chin to look at him.

"Yeah. Such a shame."

He smiles charmingly toward our mothers, shrugging. "But who cares about that? When Sutton looks so incredible today."

I hate you so much. Dear Kellys, your son is a complete dick, and I hope that my boyfriend throws him off a higher cliff.

Our mothers turn away, probably planning our wedding, so I take the opportunity to lean in and whisper, "Thanks for the compliment. I wore black because I thought it best to prepare for your funeral. I'll kill you if you touch me again."

A pinch to my back makes me jump before I glare at him, but he gives nothing away as he leans down toward my ear, whispering in it.

"Play nice. Or I'll tell your parents who you're really dating."

I turn my body toward him, putting my back to everyone else.

"Then I'll tell them you're a small-dicked rapey douchebag with a giant ego."

He chuckles, trying to brush my hair from my face with his middle finger, but I slap it away. We both immediately look around to ensure nobody saw.

"Easy. Don't act like they'd actually believe you." He licks his lips. "It's better to have me as a friend than an enemy, Sutton."

"Eww. No, thanks. You're a psycho."

Hunter grins. "And you're a rich little slut that likes to slum it across the tracks. We're all a lot of unlikely things."

"Oh my God. Just get out of my life," I spit quietly.

From behind me, my mother calls my name, but we don't move.

"I'm out, you narcissist. But my mother stays off my back because she thinks I'm breaking yours. Go along for the ride, Freckles."

My face distorts in disgust. "My name is Sutton."

He rolls his eyes. "Whatever. I'll stay quiet if you do, Sutton. Because if I had to guess, you've been eyeing the time on your phone because a certain greasy scumbag is waiting for you."

Hunter raises his eyebrows in challenge. And I wish I could punch him.

Instead, I take a deep breath, turning around to whisper my contempt.

"Let's just get this over with."

His hand slips onto my back again, just like the smile on my face. He leads me to follow our families outside to the garden deck, where a smaller group is mingling.

As we make our way closer, the conversation between our fathers seems to have everyone's attention. My father points his finger at Hunter and me.

"These two are a great example of why I'm so passionate about reforming New York."

Great. He's found a launch for another podium speech.

"St. Simeon is a perfect example of the values I'm hoping to spread across this entire state. Trust me. I've seen the evils that these crime families commit in the streets of our fine communities."

Michael Kelly postures, wrapping his arm around my father's shoulder.

"You have our support. There's nothing we want more."

My father nods as he continues, putting his hand in his pocket. Oh geez. He's going for the *"every" man* angle. My hand slips into my pocket, but Hunter taps my back, forcing my attention to my father's face but not before I cut my eyes to Hunter.

He raises his brows, but I know I can't say anything, so I turn my attention back to my father.

"I wasn't always a senator. Or a wealthy man."

Lies. His father cutting him off until he inherited a fortune isn't exactly the American dream.

"I started my career on the streets." *In an office.*

"Working for the FBI, on the organized crime task force."

Funny, Mom's always said his official title should've been barista because he was sent for coffee so often. I look around the small crowd of people, watching them eat it up.

"I've seen firsthand the horrors committed by families like the Wolfes." My eyes dart back to my father as he continues, "and the O'Bannions. This is why I pledge to run them out of this town. And then the state."

Michael Kelly begins clapping, the crowd joining in, making my chest rise and fall faster. I hate this, but I don't let on, joining in with the applause.

My mother looks at me, giving me a wink because she thinks I'm smiling over my father's speech. But I'm not.

I'm just playing the role. Something she's taught me how to do far too well.

Calder

I'm staring down at the small box in my hand as I wipe my fingers over the top, dusting it off. It's been years since I've looked inside, but today feels like a good day to do it.

"Hey."

I look up at Roman standing in the doorway as he steps just inside.

"I didn't send that text. He snatched my phone and then me."

I'm already nodding, because I don't have to grill my brother to know he's telling the truth. I trust him with my life.

"Those assholes still out there?"

He nods.

When Tyler left, the guards stayed to make sure I did what I said I'd do.

"What are you gonna do, man?"

I half-laugh, as if there was ever a question.

"What I have to."

My eyes drop back to the wooden box, and I flip the lid. The wood top creaks as I open it, half smiling as I take in my mother's possessions.

"This was all I got...after my mom died. This stupid shit is all I have to feel connected to her."

I pick up the book about Greek myths, handing it to Roman as he sits next to me.

"I don't know. I know I'm doing the right thing by walking away. But I can't help it...I just want to keep her fucking connected to me. Ya know? Letting her go—it feels impossible. So I'm sitting here trying to find something to give her so she'll remember me."

West leans into my room, hands on the doorjamb. "Then we'll make tonight epic. At least you guys will have the memory."

"Hey," Tyler's goon barks. "I said, hey. What the fuck is that in your hand?"

The ugliest of the two guards is yapping at me as I turn a tarnished gold coin over my knuckles.

"I'm talking to you, dick."

I still don't answer as Tyler walks into our place, raising his hand to quiet his bitch.

"It's fine. It was Calder's mother's." Tyler holds out his hand, so I hand over the St. Michael coin. "She loved the saints. I've never met a woman that prayed more." He hands it back to me, walking past to look at Roman and West.

"Help your brother make the right decision tonight. This family is counting on your loyalty."

They nod, saying, "Okay, Pops" and "Yeah" simultaneously.

I stand, tired of his fucking bravado, but he calls my name, forcing me to turn around.

"She loved you." His eyes drop to the coin between my fingers. "Remember whose family you belong to, Calder."

My cold eyes meet his soulless ones.

"I never forgot, Pops."

Sutton

Piper squeezes my hand as the Mustang pulls up into Aubrey's driveway.

"I know you wanted him all to yourself, but I'm so fucking excited to go into the city."

I smile because I'm excited too. Calder never ceases to amaze me. The only thing better than just me and him is to not be a secret.

Tonight, he's giving me a carnival in Bensonhurst, the unofficial Little Italy of Brooklyn. All the way in the city. We couldn't be more anonymous.

He's giving me all the magic he promised, and I honestly couldn't love him more.

I push my phone into the back of my cut-off shorts, feeling the breeze blow my midriff T-shirt up just as Calder pushes out of the car.

God. He should have his own personal soundtrack. That's how hot he is.

Maybe it's knowing I get him all night or knowing what's going to happen at the end of it, but my body is already on fire. He saunters over, flicking the cigarette from his fingers as he lets his eyes rake over my body.

Goose bumps fucking explode as he licks his lips, coming to a stop in front of me, hovering. Calder always stands just a little too close, and I love it. There are no boundaries between us.

"You ready, baby?"

I nod, biting my lip, feeling all eyes on us. I don't know if he's even noticed though, because he hasn't looked at anyone but me. His hand lifts, fingers brushing my hair behind my ear.

"I fucking missed you. Ride with me. The girls can take West so they don't get lost."

Aubrey clears her throat, pulling a smirk from Calder's lips, but he doesn't stop staring down at me.

"Um. What if we don't want West?"

My head snaps to hers, but she's grinning. *Fucking Aubrey.* Before saying anything, Calder leans down, kissing my cheek, and then asks, "Which one's Piper?"

Piper's eyes become saucers as I turn to look at her. She stares back at me, cheeks turning red as I giggle. Because she knows I told him what she said about West.

Calder looks at her as she gives an embarrassed wave, but he offers nothing, taking my hand. Before he starts tugging me back toward the car, he gives her a wink.

"Yeah. You look like his type. Have fun."

I'm laughing as Piper shoots daggers at me. She's not really mad because West is already giving her an abundance of charm, circling her like she's prey.

Oh shit.

We load into the cars, Calder guiding me into the back seat, next to him, as Roman turns the key. This feels surreal. All of us together.

"Roman, Sutton. Sutton, Roman," Calder offers, tucking me under his arm.

I stare at Calder for a second because he's gruffer than I've seen him. Maybe he's trying to be cool in front of his brothers.

Roman stares back at me through the rearview. *Just as unfriendly as I remember.*

"Hi," I rush out, feeling nervous. "Calder's told me almost nothing about you." I can't help but giggle because it's the truth before I shrug. "I mean, understandably so. But it's nice to meet someone so important to him."

Roman says nothing, just stares before dropping his eyes. "She always like this?"

Calder chuckles, but it's empty. "Yeah. It's kinda fucking amazing."

My face swings to Calder's, watching him as he stares at nothing out the window. Something's not right. I feel it.

Roman looks over his shoulder with a frown, backing up. "I get it now."

I don't know what's happening, but my mouth drops open to say, "Stop the car" because my heart is screaming. As if it feels the sword coming near.

"Calder," I whisper as he turns his face toward mine, sorrow behind his eyes. "What's happening?"

His brows pull together as he tugs me closer, leaning down to my ear, whispering, "If we only had tonight, would it all be worth it?"

My heart begins racing in my chest. Because for the first time since we said that to each other, I don't want to say yes.

I don't just want tonight. I want forever.

My body shifts so I can wrap my arms around his neck, hugging him close to me.

"Promise me you'll ask me again tomorrow."

Calder

Watching her stare up at the Ferris wheel, the kaleidoscope of colors in her eyes, makes me want to kiss her and never stop. *But we have to.*

That's why tonight is so important. I can give Sutton one night of magic. One epic fucking night so she'll always have it to carry with her.

Then it won't feel like a loss—that's what I keep telling myself.

I reach into my pocket, rubbing my finger over the gold coin before looking at her.

"You wanna go on?"

She shakes her head. "No. I've always been too scared."

"Come on." I grin, tickling her side. "I'll protect you."

She pushes my hand away, giggling before weaving her fingers between mine and following me to the platform. I hand over some tickets to a guy whose eyes dart to Sutton, then to mine before he turns around.

Good idea, dick. She curls in next to me, head leaned against my arm.

"I can't believe I'm holding your hand in public. I know I keep saying that, but it's—" My eyes drop to hers as she speaks. "It feels like a miracle... something sacred and spectacular. You know?"

I nod, giving her a half-smile as the Ferris wheel comes to a stop. The door is opened as another dude waves us on. She scrunches her nose at me before moving because she's nervous. But I shake my head, pushing her forward with a laugh.

She's fucking spectacular. So beautiful as she walks ahead, all that hair of hers flipping over her shoulder as she looks back at me. As I follow her on, my attention is pulled, hearing a quiet whistle come from that slimy-dicked fucking carnie.

Motherfucker. His eyes are glued to her ass as she steps in.

"Hey," I bark, gripping his chin and jerking it to my face. I lean in close, but everyone can still hear. "You put your eyes on her again and I'll rip them the fuck out of your head. You get me, dickhead?"

Sutton steps back toward me, eyes open wide. But I pat his cheek.

"We good?"

"Yeah, man." He breathes out shakily. "We're good."

I feel her hand on my back, so I spin around, hooking my arm around her waist, and pick her up.

"You ready, baby?"

The worry on her face is replaced with a smile before my lips press to hers. She wraps her legs around my waist, giggling as I walk us into the red-and-silver bucket.

"You're kind of different in the daytime."

It's eight o'clock at night, but I laugh because I know what she's saying. This night feels like we're seeing each other for the first time.

"I don't like people looking at what's mine. That hasn't changed since the beach, baby."

The minute I drop her into the bucket and the door closes, she taps her feet on the metal floor, gripping my hand again.

"Oh my God. It goes so high. I don't want to look. What if we fall out?"

I laugh. "We're not falling out. C'mere. You need another lesson."

She grins, shifting to face me.

My thumb runs across her bottom lip. "Nobody looks...the whole point of a Ferris wheel is the making out."

She blinks, a blush peppering her skin. "But everyone can see us."

I shrug, grabbing her bottom lip between my fingers and pulling her mouth to mine. "Then we should put on a good show, baby."

She sighs into my mouth as we lock into a kiss, not breaking once as we circle the sky, lost in each other.

Sutton

"Does the beautiful young lady want the kitten or an angel?"

Calder's grinning down at me as I clap my hands together because he's won me a prize. At a carnival. Everything feels perfect. His brothers, my best friends—it's been nothing but West making jokes and Roman being quietly intimidating, even though I caught him grinning from time to time.

I'm like the main character in a movie right now.

Calder leans in, taking my lips before answering for me. "Angel. Because she is one."

I'm forced backward as he snatches the prize, growling into my mouth as we kiss.

"Get a room." Aubrey laughs as we break away.

My head tips back as Calder lays his arm across my shoulder. I stare up at the sky, closing my eyes to make a wish on the brightest star, but Piper grabs my attention.

"Is that Tiffany Astor?"

"Who's that?" West questions as my head pops up, panic taking over.

Why would she be in this neighborhood? That was the whole point in coming here. I swing my head around as Piper laughs. "Never mind. False alarm." She turns to West. "She's just some random chick we know."

He shrugs as Aubrey snarks, "Jesus, Piper. Sut's having a heart attack."

But she's quieted as Roman stares down at her. My eyes cut between Aubrey and Roman because you can feel the tension. What's surprising, though, are the glances exchanged between Aubrey and West. Not that Piper seems to notice. Her interest fizzled quickly. I think she's more into Shepard than she wants to admit.

"So, what's next?" I breathe out, looking around as we walk.

Calder's playing with my hair as **he says,** "**The** night is yours. Whatever you want."

People are in line everywhere fo**r the different** rides. Some I'm all in for, but others there's no way in hell I**'m going on.** A group of guys walks by, catching Aubrey's and Piper's attent**ion, making** Roman playfully put his hands over Aubs's face.

She laughs as my eyes drift from **one bright-co**lored ride to the next, all the neon lights illuminating the dark **sky.**

I'm just taking it all in, never wan**ting it to end.** My eyes close just like that very first day I saw him on the b**asketball cour**ts. I let myself get lost in the smell of popcorn and powdered **sugar from the** zeppole because it feels like I'm making a memory—of what **being in love f**eels like.

My eyes open, compelled to say **what I've been** holding back. I turn my head, staring up at Calder's profile—**his strong jaw** and growing beard, and the way his lips part as he licks th**e bottom one** before the words just tumble out.

"I love you."

Calder's eyes shoot to mine. E**verything** around us, the lights and sound, it all swirls around and aroun**d, turning in**to streaks encircling us into a bubble.

The arm over my shoulder slips off **just enough** for him to grab the back of my neck, pulling my lips to his. **They press to** mine, forcefully, as if he can't control the emotions inside him.

My mouth opens as his tongue **slips inside,** circling over mine as our heads tilt one way, then the other befo**re he pulls b**ack, crystal-blue eyes not leaving mine.

"Promise me you'll never forget th**is moment, S**utton."

My head draws back, but he stands **quietly. C**alder's eyes are filled with so much regret and sadness that I feel **it too.**

Every fear I felt in the car earlier **pulls forward** so fast it feels like I've been punched in the stomach. Tears **threaten to spring** to my eyes.

We're staring at each other, all the **words unsaid** killing us.

Because it feels like he's at the **end of our s**tory while I'm still in the middle.

"Calder."

He leans down, softly kissing my lips before saying, "It's time to go home."

My head shakes. "I don't want the night to end yet. Please. Just a little more time."

Oh God. I can feel my hands shaking.

"I love you," I whisper again.

Aubrey's voice cuts in as she grabs my hand, popping our bubble. "Holy shit, Sut. It's that witch. Remember? From the tea shop. We have to do another reading."

I gasp, blinking quickly as she begins tugging me away. I'm pulled away faster, feet stumbling as I look over my shoulder. Calder takes a deep inhale before shoving his hands into his pockets, following behind me and the others.

As we near, my gaze roams over the black tent. It's tucked away from the crowds of people, back next to dark shadows and a dead end.

"What's that smell?" Aubrey giggles, but I don't answer.

It smells like patchouli oil, incense, and unease if that had a smell.

Roman and West joke about Aubrey finding out her future, and Piper laughs along, but I'm staring at the lady.

She stands in front, with those same dark eyes that feel like she's hiding the secrets of others. Her long, curly salt-and-pepper hair trails down her back, and she's wearing the same kind of long flowy skirt she wore before. She picks her hair up, fluffing it, making her bangles clink as she eyes Aubrey.

"Back so soon? Hoping for love again? Or just trying to choose between them?"

Her wrinkled, frail finger motions between Roman and West, making Piper tuck her lips under her teeth, trying not to laugh. Aubrey smiles as West and Roman glance at each other.

"Is it still ten dollars?" Aubs rushes out, letting go of my hand.

Piper eyes me, but I barely smile back because the heaviest sense of déjà vu takes hold of me. And I'm scared. It's ridiculous, but I am. I'm suddenly chilled all the way down to my bones.

The woman's dark eyes shoot to mine before she steps back, shaking her head.

"No more readings tonight. I'm closed."

She then looks over my shoulder and back to me as her face grows cold.

"Come on. I'm a returning client," Aubrey whines, making Piper laugh, but I want out of here.

"Let's just go," I offer, pulling Aubrey's shirt to force her to come with me, but I run into a rigid body as I turn.

Calder's behind me, looking down as his hands find my waist. I let go of Aubs, spinning around so that my back is to Calder's front.

Aubrey's still trying to negotiate, offering more money. But the old woman brushes open the fabric hung as a door, stepping inside her tent before looking over her shoulder at Calder and me.

"You share an aura. That's very rare. It means your destinies are intertwined."

As West tries to make a joke, I lean back into Calder's arms, brows drawn together.

"Ooo, spooky. Auras."

Aubrey giggles unconvincingly, accepting West's arm over her shoulder because we're all kind of weirded out as the woman simply stares without reaction.

I turn my head to the side against Calder's chest. "I want to go."

He nods, but as my head turns back, the old woman walks toward me quickly, making my pulse quicken. A faint "What the fuck?" is whispered from beside me as she reaches down to take my hand. But Calder darts out, grabbing her hand before she does, sliding me just behind him.

"Careful, old woman. You don't touch her."

She's staring at him, pupils so dilated they look like saucers in her eyes. She twists her wrist, grabbing his hand, holding on tight as she tugs him close.

"Whoa, lady," Roman calls, stepping in closer as Piper says, "Oh my God."

But she's staring into his eyes as he stares back, neither breaking before she shivers.

"Ah. You're the end of her story. I told this girl once that you can't save her but that she could save you. She's your fate, you know? But *death* is your destiny."

My eyes lift to his profile, tugging his shirt, urging him backward. But he looks angry, full of rage.

He tries to pull his hand away, growling, "That's enough lookin', old woman. Go back to your tent."

But she digs her nails in deeper, laughing. "The devil already knows your name, Calder Wolfe. And one day, even he'll be afraid of the king."

What the fuck? How does she know his name?

She lets him go, laughing, making the hairs on the back of my neck stand on end.

I hook my finger through his belt loop, pulling him backward as everyone looks at each other. Her voice rises as she stares, a lump forming in my throat.

"Tragedy awaits you. Death is knocking. And it's on her doorstep."

Calder turns around, grabbing my waist and spinning me to take me with him. His face is dark as he guides me away.

Everyone follows behind us, mixing back among the crowd of people. Each of us glances over our shoulders the further away we get, our silent discomfort accompanied only by carousel music.

Piper crosses her arms, rubbing the top of them. "Maybe it's time to go? The freaks are definitely coming out now. How'd she know your name?"

Calder shakes his head but then nods. "Yeah, okay. Let's go."

I grip onto Calder's hand as we walk back toward the exit.

"What the fuck was that?" West levels, hitting Roman's shoulder, who shrugs as West continues. "Well, it was fucking creepy. Like some voodoo kind of shit."

Roman looks at Calder. "You good, C?"

But he doesn't answer. He just walks, staring straight ahead.

Piper nudges my shoulder. "Are you okay? Obviously, she's crazy, but man, does she like to pick on you. It's so weird. I bet she's high."

West glances back. "Maybe she's got extra?"

He's trying to lighten the mood, but nobody really laughs.

My eyes raise to Calder's face, feeling afraid because he seems lost in thought. I've never seen him look so worried.

"Hey," I whisper, tugging his hand. "Don't listen to that kooky old woman."

His head shakes as his eyes meet mine. "I'm good, baby. I'm good." But he's not. I can feel it. *And he just lied to me.*

I start to push, but my shoulder is bumped. I jerk my head over my shoulder, saying, "Rude," under my breath.

Calder pulls me to a stop, looking back before turning around.

"Watch where the fuck you're going, asshole," he rumbles, garnering interest from passersby.

A guy, maybe in his mid-twenties, turns around, facing Calder as the rest of us stare between them. *Fuck.*

Calder kisses the top of my hand before he lets it go, stepping in front of me. I want to protest, but it's Roman's reaction that makes me silent. He's shaking his head, speaking under his breath.

"C. You know better than to fuck with him. Cool it."

Aubrey grabs my hand as Piper squeezes in next to me. "Oh my God, Sut. What's happening?"

I don't answer, keeping my eyes on Calder.

"Fuck that," Calder growls to Roman before facing the guy again. "I don't give a fuck about him. Apologize to my girl. You don't fucking get to bump into her and not say shit. I'll break your fucking jaw."

West looks panicked as Roman tries to step between the guy and Calder, but Calder doesn't care, pushing Roman back. *Oh shit.*

"Calder. Stop," I rush out, reaching for him, but he jerks his arm away, throwing me back as his head darts over his shoulder with nothing but anger on his face.

"Know your fucking place, Sutton."

I blink, shaken to my core as I lower my hand. My eyes drop to the ground, hating everything about this moment as he turns back around.

"Oh my God. Did he just do that to you? What the fuck?" Aubrey hisses, staring at my face, but I can't look at her.

The guy steps in closer to Calder's face. He doesn't seem to be intimidated.

"What the fuck are you little Irish pricks doing in my neighborhood? You know better." He looks around Calder. "And with these little high-society bitches to boot."

I shriek as Calder lunges forward.

Aubrey rushes out, "Oh my God," pulling me back as Roman wraps Calder in a bear hug, forcing him backward. West steps in between them, holding his hands out. "Hey, Matteo. We're cool. Just a misunderstanding. No harm, no foul. Why don't you tell Antonio we say hello."

The guy gives a tight nod before looking right at me.

"Sorry for bumping into you, kid. Let your boyfriend know I said it."

I don't answer as he turns around and walks away. Because my head has already swung in the direction that Roman carried a belligerent Calder, just a few feet away. My mouth falls open, not knowing what to say before Calder stares back at me.

"What?" he barks, making my shoulders jump. "That guy was an asshole. Stop looking at me like that."

I feel embarrassed, looking around at people staring as they pass, as I remove myself from my friends.

"No, you're the asshole," I say quietly, closing the distance between us. "Why are you acting like an animal?"

Calder shakes his head, running a hand through his hair. "Because I am an animal. You just conveniently forgot."

My eyes glance again at the random people paying attention, snapping back to his as he says, "What's wrong, Sutton? Are you afraid people might see? Know that you're slumming it. Daddy's little princess likes it dirty."

"Stop it," I snap, brows furrowing, "What are you doing? Is this because of what that old lady just said? Is that why you're acting like a lunatic?"

I reach for him, but he steps back, shrugging.

"Does it matter? Does any of it fucking matter? We're too different, Sutton. It just took me until now to see it."

My eyes search his, swallowing before I answer.

"Quit acting like this. This isn't who you are."

His eyes are so cold as he looks at me before wiping his hands down his face, walking away. My heart begins racing as Aubrey reaches for my hand, saying, "Sut, let him go. He's a dick." But I don't, glancing at her before following behind him.

"Calder."

He doesn't turn around, walking deeper into the crowd as our friends follow us, so I call his name louder with more force.

"Calder."

He spins, locking eyes with me. There's so much anger behind his eyes that it makes my hands ball into fists, bracing myself for what he's going to say.

"Take it back."

My lips part in confusion before I say, "Take what back?"

He grabs my face, bringing it close to his. "That you love me. Un-say it. It makes me fucking sick to hear it."

I grasp his wrists, trying to pull them from my face, feeling the burn behind my eyes.

"Let me go," I rush out, my voice barely above a whisper.

He releases me as my feet carry me backward, putting a few feet between us. God, the way he's staring at me. It splits me in two. My chest begins shaking as ragged breaths leave me.

Because I already know what he's going to say.

He steps forward, eyes dropping to the ground. Oh my God, he can't even fucking look at me.

"How can you love me when you'll only ever get half of me?"

I shake my head as his eyes lift, wishing I could cover my ears. Because it doesn't matter that people talk as they walk past us or that the music grows louder in between screams from the rides.

All I hear are the words that break my heart.

"There will always be a whole side of me that you don't know. That old witch was right, Sutton. My destiny is death and destruction. Are you sure you can love that? Can you really?" His face grows cold again. "Because any chick that's with me would always know her fucking place."

Pieces of me break off like I'm slowly dissolving into nothing instead of crumbling all at once. Because that's how much I love him—I'll take his anything just to have him, if only for a moment longer.

"Why are you saying this?" I yell, tears beginning to stream down my face, eyes pleading with him. "You said I was the one."

His hand grips the back of his neck as he hurls his words at me. "God-dammit, you're so fucking desperate to be special to someone, anyone, you'd lay down with the devil. Wake the fuck up, princess. You don't belong in my world. Not because of cursed moons or fortunes from some fucked-up old woman—"

I'm sobbing, fat tears blanketing my cheeks as he stops mid-sentence, just staring at me. He sneers before letting out a vicious growl toward the sky.

My friends yell my name, arguing with his brothers to make him stop, but I'm numb. My heart is dying.

He takes a step away, and I suck in a breath because it feels like a piece of me is being ripped away.

"Tell me you don't love me back."

It's all I can think to say.

Calder looks me dead in the eyes, and suddenly he's someone I don't recognize. Seconds that feel like minutes pass as we stand in silence before a V forms between his brows.

"I never believed in love before you."

My heart waits, hoping to beat again until he pushes a sword directly through it.

"And you weren't enough to change that."

I scream inside of me, wild and angry, scratching the walls of my heart before my entire body gives out. I collapse to sitting on the dirty asphalt as my hands cover my eyes. I can't look at him. I can't see his face as he walks away.

My friends race to be at my side as sobs rip from my chest. Aubrey screams at Calder, calling him a fucking lowlife asshole as Piper wraps her arms around me, whispering that they're going to take me home.

"Everything's going to be okay. We're here," she keeps saying.

But I don't stop crying. Sitting on the ground, in the middle of a fucking carnival. Not until there aren't any more tears left. Because that's how I know he's gone.

I feel empty.

"Are you sure you want to be alone?"

I nod weakly, standing in the entry of Aubrey's house. "Yes. I just want to sleep. I'll be okay. I just..." The tears start up again as I wipe my cheeks. "I want to cry without anyone seeing. You know. In my own bed."

Aubrey hugs me, kissing my cheek. "I get it. We'll conspire on revenge strategies when you're ready."

Piper nods, sticking out her bottom lip. "Love you, Sut. If you need us, we're here. No matter what time."

I squeeze her hand before walking back out with my keys in hand. I click my lock, pulling open the door of my Mercedes SUV, and slide in. The moon roof draws my eyes up to that full globe in the sky. Tonight, it has a yellow ring around it—like a halo.

But it doesn't feel benevolent. It just feels like the moon.

The key slides in, and the car starts to life as I whisper to myself.

"Time to go home."

Calder

My father's standing on the porch, watching as I stumble out of the car, a bottle of Jack in my hand.

Roman and West get out, trying to help me walk, but I shove them off.

"Fuck you. Get off me." I spread my arms, liquor sloshing everywhere. "Are you happy, Pops? The prodigal son has returned. I did what you asked. It's done." I bring the bottle to my lips, throwing back the amber liquid before letting it drop as my voice grows quieter.

"I did what you asked. We're done."

He says nothing, looking at Roman and West, who nod before he taps the railing in front of him. "Let him sleep it off. He's earned that much."

My brothers follow me back to our house and all the way to my room in silence. None of this is their fault, even though I can feel how they wish shit were different for me. I fall on my bed, face-first, keeping the Jack upright.

West clears his throat. "Nothing's gonna be the same now. Is it? He's not coming back, is he?"

"He'll be fine, West," Roman levels. "We'll all be fine."

I listen as they make their way out of my room, closing the door before I roll over and stare at the ceiling. West is right. Nothing will ever be the same.

My mind spins in circles, looping back around to that old woman and her dark words.

"Death is knocking, and it's on her doorstep."

My eyes are fixed to the ceiling as I take a deep breath, dropping the bottle onto the floor as my eyes close.

Not anymore, baby. You're safe now.

Sutton

The heat from the hood of my car warms my palms as I scoot myself back onto it and stare up. It really is beautiful out here—this place. *Our place.*

My palms rub up and down my thighs as tears well in my eyes. I haven't stopped thinking about what Calder said to me in the back of his Mustang.

"If we only had tonight, would it all be worth it?"

"Promise me you'll ask me again tomorrow."

How can I be without him? It doesn't matter how much anyone tried to cheer me up. Nobody could ever understand the emptiness I feel when he isn't around.

Thankful that I found a hoodie in my car, I tuck the sleeve over my hand and wipe my cheeks, looking back to the stars, and whisper to myself.

"I love you, Calder."

The tiny white dots in the sky blur as more tears fill my eyes, distorting my vision. I drop my head between my arms, pull my knees up, and rest my head on them, wishing for the hurt to stop.

But how can it? He's not here to make it better.

My shoulders start to shake, the devastation of tonight taking over again until I hear it. *Hear him.*

"Don't cry, baby."

My head pops up, swinging over my shoulder to Calder's face. He pushes back his hood, smiling as he quickly closes the distance. I launch myself at him from the hood as more tears erupt, wrapping myself around him as he catches me.

"I got you. Fuck. Baby, I got you. Don't cry."

I draw my head back, my hands planting on the sides of his face.

"I was so scared nobody would believe us. Or that you wouldn't come."

His lips find mine before saying, "Nothing could've kept me from you."

Calder pulls back, frowning as he stares at my face...at my tears. "I hated how convincing it all felt. I hated saying all that shit to you. You knew I was lying—" I'm nodding, feathering kisses over his face as he speaks. "—that I didn't mean a fucking word. But, still, watching you cry like that. It felt too true, too real. Fuck. Telling you to take back what you said. I'll never stop seeing the look on your face."

I wrap my arms around his neck, whispering into his ear.

"Shh. No. Forget it all. I'm not just crying to mourn the people we're saying goodbye to. Calder, I'm also crying because I'm happy—now, we get forever."

He grips my hair, tugging me back, eyes locked to mine. I've never felt loved more than in this moment.

"I love you, Sutton. And I hated that I couldn't say it back. But if I had, there was no fucking way I would've been able to walk away like I did. So, I'm saying it now, baby."

My chin trembles as his free hand cradles my cheek. "I love you. I've always loved you—my whole damned existence, even before. And I'll love you after I die. The world will have to dedicate stars to us. Because you will always be the only fucking one for me."

Our mouths crash into one another, whispering *I love yous* as his fingers weave through my hair, pulling me in closer, needing more of me. My head tilts, tasting Calder mixed with my tears as we kiss until we're breathless. Until there's nothing left but the love we feel.

He pulls back, eyes so blue they're like the ocean, touching our foreheads together and asking me the same question he did earlier.

"Tell me you're sure? Because there's no turning back."

Our conversation floods my mind because I'm doing what he's asking of me—being sure.

"Calder," I whisper as he turns his face toward mine, sorrow behind his eyes. "What's happening?"

His brows pull together as he pulls me closer, leaning down to my ear, whispering, "If we only had tonight. Would it all be worth it?"

My heart begins racing in my chest. Because for the first time since we said that to each other, I don't want to say yes.

I don't just want tonight. I want forever.

My body shifts so I can wrap my arms around his neck, hugging him close to me.

"Promise me you'll ask me again tomorrow."

"I can't."

My eyes shoot to his, but he leans back in his seat, pulling me close, whispering in my ear.

"Stay here. We're in Roman's blind spot. The things I'm going to say next are going to be hard to hear, baby. You're gonna want to cry. But you can't, Sutton. You have to act like everything is chill. Tap my hand if you understand."

I do, feeling like I can't breathe, but nobody would ever know. If anyone can detach, play a role, it's this girl. I guess I have the senator and Mommy Dearest to thank for something after all.

"My father knows about us. About you. He's told me to end it. He threatened you and my brothers if I don't walk away."

My eyes search the empty space ahead, soaked in fear. Don't scream, don't cry. Be cool. He's trusting you to handle this, Sutton. Don't let him down.

"Everything's going to be okay. I'm gonna take care of us. But we're gonna break up. Tonight. And we're gonna make sure people see. You'll know it when it happens, so just go with it. It's better that you're in the dark so it feels real. Just remember I'm lying. No matter what I fucking say—it's a lie, baby. But I'm gonna make it hurt. That's the only way Tyler will believe it."

I tap his hand, letting him know I understand, even though I'm already shaking on the inside.

"When your friends come in for the rescue, say you need to be alone and *pretend to go home. Lift up your shirt."*

I swallow as I do, exposing my bra. Calder begins writing on my breast, so I glance down, seeing he's writing directions.

"Drive to our field. I'll meet you there."

He lowers my top, kissing my temple.

"First thing tomorrow, you tell the senator that you think someone's tried to break in through your balcony doors. Take a screwdriver or a butter knife and dig into the wood to make it look like someone tried. Because no matter what my father says, I don't trust him. Then you cry. Cry a lot so your friends talk about how sad you are. So everyone knows something's up. But we don't know each other, Sutton. Erase my number. Erase me."

I tap his hand, feeling like I'm going to break.

"Here's the but..."

Thank God.

"On the Fourth of July, this town will be packed with families in for the holiday weekend. You meet me at the church when the fireworks start, and we'll never look back. This is the only way I keep you and my brothers safe. I have to keep them in the dark and give enough time for my father to believe that I'm loyal. He'll be comfortable enough to not see this coming. That means you can't tell your friends either. Do you understand? Listen to me—I had to let Tyler almost kill me tonight to make him believe he holds power over me because if I didn't, we might not be here. This is the only way, but I don't want you to do anything that you—"

He doesn't finish because I turn around, sealing my mouth over his, whispering, "Yes. Forever, yes."

My hands brush over his beautiful face, giving his lips another peck before I smile as the memory washes away.

"You are the only thing I'm the surest of. I love you, Calder, and if running away is the only way for us to be together, I'll say goodbye to everyone. I can't live without you."

The smile on his face could power my heart forever. He bites his bottom lip before his voice drops lower.

"I have a surprise. I know it's a lot after tonight, but—"

I cut him off, saying, "Show me."

I'm set to my feet before Calder walks a few steps back, grabbing a duffle bag I hadn't noticed before. He motions with his head for me to follow as he walks out into the empty field, squatting and unzipping the bag.

A small camping lantern is pulled out, along with a yellow blanket. It billows as he throws it open, spreading it out onto the ground before he turns the tiny lamp on, illuminating the space in a soft amber hue.

I see his entire face as he turns back to me, looking up.

"This is our real night. Under the stars."

I sigh before taking quick steps back into his arms. Exactly where I've always belonged.

"Baby." He says it so tenderly that I suddenly feel fragile.

Calder's hands skim down my arms, stopping at the bottom of my hoodie. His eyes connect with mine before he slowly bunches it. My arms lift as the cotton sweeps over my face, my hair falling onto my back when he pulls it off.

We don't speak as my fingers tuck under the bottom of his sweatshirt, mimicking his actions. He bends down to help me as I tug it off, letting it fall to the ground.

Our eyes lock as we breathe in tandem. God, I'm already overwhelmed, and nothing's happened, but it's still everything I'd wished for.

He reaches for my crop top, letting his fingers skim the underside of my breasts, making goose bumps tickle my skin. The moment it's off, his eyes drag over my body, making me arch my back under his stare. Because I want him to look at me.

I lick my lips, reaching for his T-shirt, but instead of letting me take it off, he reaches over his shoulder, gripping the fabric and dragging it over his head.

It makes his hair messy and tousled, so I smile as he does the same.

Calder's finger traces the length of my arm, up to my shoulder, hooking a finger under my bra strap before he tugs it down. He lets it hang as he leans down to press a kiss where it once lay.

"I cherish the feel of your skin on my lips. There won't be any space on you that I'll leave unkissed tonight, baby."

I sigh into the feeling, reaching out to touch him, but Calder drops to his knees, fingers skimming my calves as my hands fall to his shoulders. He takes off my shoes one by one, pressing a kiss to my thighs before his head lifts, looking up at me.

I brush my fingers through his hair, staring down. He makes me feel so loved. So fucking worshipped. I watch as he unzips my shorts, pulling them off.

The moment I step out, I'm doubled over, hands slapping his back as his mouth connects with my clit through my panties.

"Oh my God."

"Mmm. Fuck, I love the way you taste."

Calder groans before standing, running his hand over my breast as he smiles.

"I want to defile your body. Teach you how good it can all feel. So, we're gonna start slow until we've done everything. Until I've broken you in and ruined you for anyone else. Because you're mine. And I'm forever fucking yours."

My lips part, drawing in a breath as he massages my tit, making the lace scratch as my nipple hardens under his palm. His other hand slides over my sternum, up to my neck, fingers closing around it.

Fuck. My body's exploding. I'm already wet, painted in goose bumps and want, staring up at him.

"I *am* yours, Calder. I want everything you are. All you have to give." Fuck. I feel high. Entirely owned by him. "I love you."

His head dips, tongue pushing into my mouth, kissing me like the first time. Except instead of prayers chanted in the eaves of a church, we have the heavens looking down on us.

The kiss is rough and demanding. We're desperate for each other. So completely fucking magnetized that I don't know where I begin and he ends.

I reach for his belt, wanting it off, along with his pants as he kicks off his shoes. His hand wraps around my waist, walking us toward the blanket. The feel of the soft fabric tickles my feet as he pulls me onto it further.

"I love you."

It doesn't matter who's saying it because we're both repeating it over and over as he lays me down. Calder's lips run over my jaw as his heavy thigh lies between my legs.

My chin lifts, giving him more room as my eyes open, looking up at the bright speckled sky. His hands roam my body, leaving a trail of heat behind as I suck in a breath. He's igniting my entire body with every touch.

"Goddamn, I just want to fuck you and lick you...and then die next to you. Do you know what I mean?" he says, almost breathless as his lips devour my neck.

I nod, running my hands over his back, feeling a tingle in my center each time his leg moves. My hips press up, rubbing my clit against his thigh, seeking the delicious friction again.

"I never want to be apart from you, Calder. I won't ever fucking leave your side. Not even in death."

A moan escapes as his hand dips between my legs, rubbing my clit from the outside of my panties. His fingers press lightly in a circle as his dick grows harder against my hip. I'm panting, gripping his shoulder, feeling hungry for him.

"I want you inside of me. Please."

His tongue runs across my clavicle, and I feel his growl against my skin.

"Not yet, baby. You're gonna come first because then when I fuck you, it won't hurt as bad."

My hips rock forward into his hand, but his face comes to mine, locking eyes with me.

"Not like this."

He pulls his hand away, running it up to my stomach, stopping at my nipple. It's rolled between his fingers as he stares down at me.

Oh God. He's watching me writhe under him, back arched off the ground as he pinches the hard bud.

"Calder," I gasp before biting my lip.

"Those lips. Fuck me. Those damn lips make me think the dirtiest shit."

He reaches up, tugging it from my teeth, before he leans down and draws the plumpest part of my pout between his lips, sucking and letting it go with a pop.

"Take off your panties, baby. Let me watch."

He moves his leg from between mine, sitting up and shifting his body so he's facing me as I roll onto my back, doing as I'm told.

I hook my fingers into the band, sliding them off my body, looking down at him. He's watching, eyes on my pussy as I draw my knees up, pulling them off.

Calder scoots closer to me, leaning in.

"Open your legs."

The leg closest to him lies flat as I leave the other bent, but he's impatient. His palm presses to the inside of my knee, dropping it open, holding me spread wide.

"Fuck, that's so pretty."

My eyes roll back because the air hits all the most sensitive places.

His lips part before he leans in, fingers spreading my soaked lips apart. I squirm, but he doesn't move. He just stares.

God, he's so close that it makes me want his mouth on me so badly that I could die.

"Ah, Calder. Please," I practically whine, undulating beneath his touch.

My head drops to the side, racked with need, as I'm immediately fixed to what's in front of me.

Calder's cock is growing harder behind his briefs as he rubs himself. His hand moves inside his briefs, making them ripple and shift with the motion.

There's something so dirty and sexy about watching him do what he's doing inches from my face while he's staring at my pussy.

"Oh fuck. You just got so wet, baby."

He lets go of my leg, letting his finger slide through the slickness before he dives down, tasting me. I suck in a breath, mouth opened.

"Oh my God."

I reach for his cock, brushing my hand over where he's rubbing himself, itching to touch him. Jesus, I'm on fire.

"I want..." I breathe out. "I want to—"

Calder growls, making me gasp before I finish what I'm saying as he eats me. He's rude and animalistic, pressing my leg to the ground harder, devouring me. The sounds of him sucking and licking my clit sends shivers over my body. He's possessed with need, attacking my pussy with his desire.

"Fuck. That feels so good. Don't stop."

Calder licks and kisses me everywhere. Between my folds, the inside of my thighs, up the ridges of my clit until he drags his tongue back down, pushing it inside of me.

He draws back briefly before sucking my clit and speaking into it.

"I can't wait to feel you all over my cock."

I want to fucking taste him so bad. Moving closer, I grip the band of his briefs, tugging them down to his thighs. I lick my lips, stopping his hand with mine before darting my eyes down to his because I feel him staring at me.

His eyes are hooded, lips parted as he looks at me. One of his fingers makes decadently teasing brushstrokes over my clit as he licks the wetness off his lips.

He draws his bottom one between his teeth, then lets it out slowly.

"Are you my bad girl, baby?"

My words are raspy, almost ragged, because I feel like I'm going to explode.

"Yes."

Calder's stroking his cock in front of my face. He slides his hand up his shaft slowly, before running it down.

"Lemme get it wet."

I part my lips as he guides the tip of his cock into my mouth. A bead of saltiness explodes against my tongue as I swirl it over the head.

Calder lets out a deep exhale.

"Oh, baby. I love you bad."

His hand drops from his dick, coming to my head. I moan, gripping the side of his ass, pulling him into my mouth.

"Fuck," he growls. "Don't make me come, baby."

I don't listen. I want to swallow him down, so I suck, remembering everything he's taught me from all the times I've done this to him. My cheeks hollow as his hips rock forward, going deeper each time.

He groans. "Baby, I'm gonna make you come, hard, so I can bury my dick inside of you."

His arm hooks around my thigh, tilting me toward him, so that I'm on my side, as he seals his mouth over my clit. It's so intense that I almost scream in pleasure, but the sound is muffled by his dick, deep in my mouth, and that pushes me closer to the edge.

Calder fucks my mouth, eating me at the same time.

We're all need. Filthy fucking need. Wanting more, chasing our ecstasy. His hand pushes against my thigh again, opening me wider as he relentlessly licks my pussy. And I pull him closer, wanting to deep-throat him, begging to gag on his cock.

Breathless, lips glistening, he breaks away, pumping his hips into my face.

"Fuck, yes. Take that cock deep."

I moan, choking on his dick, before his tongue connects with my clit again. But I can't get enough. I want to taste him, swallow his salty cum as he fucks my face.

He's gripping my hair, bobbing my head faster, making messy slurps mix with quiet moans. But I can't concentrate because my stomach begins to tighten, wanting, needing, begging for more until I'm quivering.

Coming on his face.

"Oh my God," I scream.

He buries his face in my pussy, holding my shaking body as I keep coming. Calder doesn't release me, coaxing my body into another wave as my head drops back.

I'm breathless, entirely spent as he kisses my pussy softly, laving his tongue over all of me, chasing my pleasure down to my slit.

"Calder," I breathe out because it's so sensitive. "I can't take it."

"Shh," he whispers against me, making me shiver before his tongue runs lower, gently brushing over my tight hole.

I gasp, but he growls. "All of you. I'll kiss all of you."

Nothing comes out of my mouth except for pants as I'm enveloped by the sensation of Calder licking cum off my most forbidden place.

Because I'm a slave to my body and to Calder.

"Every part of you is mine," he breathes against my thigh before nipping at it.

I jump, but I hear him chuckle as he presses his rough hand to my hip, rolling me onto my back. My tongue darts over my lips, watching him shift around, stroking his dick again as he kneels between my legs.

His knees push my legs apart as my chest rises and falls faster because this is it.

This is the moment I've always wanted. Calder's face, like a damn bruised angel, stares down at me with the stars at his back. Like he was cast out of heaven.

"I love you," I whisper, bringing my hands to his face.

He swallows, suddenly looking scared. "I love you too." The way he says it, as if he can barely speak, makes a lump form in my throat. "You're my everything, Sutton. And I've never felt like this... You're my purpose. My only reason for breathing. There's nothing I won't give you. But it could never match what you're giving me."

My beautiful monster. His eyes are so crystal blue as he stares down at me with such reverence.

"You're not just giving me your body—" He can't finish, overwhelmed with emotion because I'm giving him my soul, and he feels it.

I lift my hand, placing it over his heart, staring up.

"Forever, Calder. We're forever."

His head lowers, lips pressed to mine, staying there as a tear leaks from my closed eyes. I feel him reach down between us just before the pressure springs my eyes open.

"Oh, God."

Calder's face doesn't leave mine, his words whispered so gently.

"We'll go slow, baby. If you want me to stop, all you have to do is say stop."

I'm nodding, but I don't want him to stop. He pushes inside of me a little more, and the sting makes me gasp as I dig my fingers into his shoulders.

"Breathe, baby."

I inhale through my nose, blowing out a shaky breath, locked to his eyes.

"It hurts, Calder."

He stops, jaw tensing. But his eyes are filled with love. Calder's fore-arms are anchored by my head, but his hand strokes my hair.

"I love you, baby."

We wait there as I take a deep breath before saying, "More."

I bite my lip as he pushes inside again, stretching me as wide as the girth of his cock. Seconds feel like minutes as we stay locked onto each other, me letting out stuttered breaths and him groaning as he forces himself inside of my tight pussy.

He lets out a whoosh of breath, dropping his cheek next to mine.

"Baby. Fuck. I'm all the way in."

It feels heavy and full, but mostly I feel something else. A tingling. My hips want to move.

"Move a little. Rock your hips and let my cock drag in and out. It'll start to feel good."

I listen, doing what I'm told. The stinging makes me suck in a quick breath, but I feel my desire coating us as I push him back in.

So I keep going, rocking my hips as he lets me take over.

Calder's face looks pained. He closes his eyes, and the hand in my hair tightens.

"Are you okay?" I whisper.

He nods, blinking his eyes open, lowering his head to brush his nose over mine.

"You feel like fucking silk. Your pussy's so tight. I'm gonna fucking come if I don't concentrate."

I lick my bottom lip, turned on by the idea of Calder coming. What does that look like? My words rush out without thought or consideration. Because I want him.

"I want to see you come. I want to feel it inside of me."

His eyes close again as a deep rumble vibrates in his chest.

"Baby. Unless you want me to fuck you so hard that you forget your name, I'd keep those fucking thoughts to yourself."

I half-laugh, but Calder drags his dick from my sore pussy and pushes back inside, making me gasp.

"There we go. Behave."

I nod, a smile tugging at my lips because the pain is subsiding. My arms drape over his shoulders. He pulls out and pushes back in again as I meet his movement.

Fuck, this feels good.

"Kiss me."

His head lowers as my lips part. The taste of me is still on his tongue as it pushes inside my mouth, making me feel naughty. I run a hand up the back of his neck, fingers weaving into his hair, feverishly kissing until we grow sloppy. He growls, pushing deeper inside of me making me moan into his mouth. But I want it. My legs wrap around his waist, feeling him move faster.

"Oh my God," I whimper.

"You okay?" Calder whispers just as I add, "It feels so good. Fuck me, Calder."

Calder presses his palm on the ground, pulling away, breathing hard as he looks down at me. My lips try and follow him, but his eyes drop between us, making mine follow.

"Move your legs off me. Open them wide."

As I do, all I see is Calder's huge cock nestled inside of me. It's glistening with my wetness, moving in and out.

"Look at us. Me, inside of you. You're mine, Sutton. I took your blood. Made your pussy my home. And I'm gonna fill you with my cum. I swear to God, if anyone ever fucking touches you, I'll kill them. Do you understand that? That's how fucking deep I love you. You are always and forever fucking mine."

My jaw is slack as Calder fucks me slowly. His face lifts toward the sky as he yells, "Not even you can have her."

He's speaking to God.

I lift my body, wrapping my arms around his neck, and press a kiss to his jaw.

"Not even He can have me," I whisper back.

Calder begins pumping into me as I cling to him. It hurts, but the pleasure outweighs the pain. His face buries into my neck as he fucks me harder and harder. Until I almost can't take it.

"Touch yourself," he rushes out.

Without hesitation, I reach down, rubbing my clit.

"Fuck, baby. Fuck," he grunts, lowering to his forearms.

I dig my nails into his back, feeling my body tightening around his cock because I'm coming. Racked by a wave of my orgasm, stealing the breath from me.

"Oh fuck, you're so tight."

His muscles are tense as we fall back onto the ground. Calder grinds inside me two more times until he's deep, curled around my body, hand gripping my hair as a guttural moan leaves his body.

I'm filled with warmth. His cum.

Goose bumps explode over my body, feeling his lips against my neck as I try and catch my breath.

His eyes lift to mine.

"Are you okay?"

"I'm better than okay."

Our smiles match before he kisses me again. I giggle, feeling his dick twitch inside of me.

"Mmm. I don't want to pull out."

"Then don't."

We lie there, staring into each other's eyes, not moving even when he grows soft and eventually slips from my body, leaving me feeling empty. Something I never realized I'd hate until now.

Calder pulls me into his arms, dragging the blanket folded over us. We're face-to-face, noses almost touching, saying nothing until my eyes begin to close.

"I love you," he whispers.

"And I love you back."

Calder

chapter
thirty-seven

"Two weeks."

"Two weeks," she whispers back before kissing me again.

My fingers press into her waist before I push her back, "Get the fuck out of here, or this plan is going to hell."

She giggles, taking a step, as I mouth, "I love you." The early morning makes her eyes impossibly green as she says it back, holding up the gold coin I gave her last night so she could keep me close to her over the next two weeks. She almost cried when I told her it was my mom's.

She turns around, walking away. My eyes stay locked on my girl as she slips into her car and drives away.

Last night was so much more than I thought my heart could ever carry, but Sutton makes everything possible.

I squint, looking up at the dawning sun before I hustle my way back through the fields, letting her scent fade from my clothes but not from my memory before sneaking back into my house.

"Connor was pleased you were able to find a resolution to our problem."

Michael nods weakly, handing Tyler a small bag full of pills with a shaky hand.

"Here's the sample. The entire haul is already on the ship, scheduled to arrive next Friday."

Roman's staring at me. He's been doing it all morning. I think he's waiting for me to erupt. It makes sense. He thinks I'm on the brink of losing my shit. If I could tell him, I would, but ignorance and time will be his savior. It's all I can give him before Sutton and I cause a shitstorm. I drift back to last night, holding Sutton in my arms under the stars.

"Do you think your brothers will hate you for what we're doing?"

"No. But I think Roman will be pissed that I left him behind. We've lived our whole lives making all the same decisions, living the same life—"

"If he loves you, he'll forgive you, Calder."

The sound of pills spilling out onto the table brings me back to the present. Powder-white little round pills scatter, all with a red heart stamped on the front.

Tyler holds one up, looking at it closer.

"Your idea?" he levels, staring across at Michael, who hasn't stopped looking nervous.

"Yeah," he responds, clearing his throat. "Designer drugs are making a comeback, so it seemed smart to be a niche player."

"Niche," Tyler repeats, looking back at me. "You believe this guy?"

I give half a shake of my head, not saying anything. Tyler only has me here to make a point. Which is why I'm the only one without a gun.

Tyler pushes from the table, nodding. "You made good. Your sons are safe. Let's not make a habit of being late." He looks over his shoulder. "West, bag these up. You boys take these out this week for a test drive."

Michael huffs, staring up at Tyler.

"You're going to sell these in our community?"

Tyler smiles. "No, your sons are. Tag's gonna throw a party. My boys will sell to him, and he'll sell to whomever he wants. Business as usual."

The look on Michael's face is priceless. Guess he didn't know what his oldest has been doing. Tyler's accompanied by his fucking goons as he leaves without saying another word.

West goes about doing as he's told as Roman and I stare down Michael Kelly, staying to do the grunt work of babysitting him until West is done.

"Make it quick, West," I mutter, crossing my arms as I hear the front door close.

Michael is fidgeting with his collar, and I can't help but notice the sweat line on it. Fuck. But I can't blame him. Until a few minutes ago, he didn't know if he would be left with sons or just a son.

Roman glances down at his pocket before putting his eyes back on Michael. A few seconds later, he looks again.

What is he doing? I watch him look down a third time as he cracks his neck.

"What the fuck?" I level, turning my head to stare at him.

His jaw tenses before he reaches into his pocket and pulls out his cell. It's vibrating in his hand, but he doesn't do anything, just frowns.

"Are you gonna fucking answer it?"

He doesn't though. Instead, he extends it over to me, eyes narrowed as he tilts his head to face me. "Maybe you should answer it, C."

I glance down at the screen, seeing "Aubrey" flashing. *Shit.* I shake my head, looking away, but as soon as the call stops, it starts again. *What the fuck? Why is she calling?* Sutton knows not to tell her friends.

"She's calling again," Roman pushes, glaring at me.

"Why the fuck would I answer it? That's your bitch. Your bad for giving some crazy stalker your number."

My nerves are fraying, worry beginning to take over. I stare down at Michael, watching as he tries to make conversation with West, who ignores him, but there's something off.

Roman clears his throat, so I swing my face back to his. "What?"

The phone starts buzzing again.

"Seriously? We're doing this?"

The look on Roman's face is pissing me off because he's too curious. He can smell the lies I'm telling. Goddammit.

We're just staring at each other as the call stops and starts again.

Fuck.

"Calder," he barks, but I don't move until he says, "You'll never forgive yourself if something happened."

I snatch the cell from his hand, pushing past him, stalking out to the backyard, and shutting the door behind me before I hit Answer.

"Why the fuck are you calling?" I growl, slipping back into the asshole I was last night.

Aubrey's voice rushes out, biting back just as hard.

"Fuck you too. I don't even want to do this, but something's happening. I need to talk to Calder."

"You've got him."

"She called me, maybe by accident, I don't know. But I heard her mother and father screaming, then her mother was yelling at just her, and I think she slapped Sutton. And after that, all I could hear was her begging not to be taken away. Saying that she wouldn't leave you. I've never heard her sound like that. Whatever the fuck happened last night isn't important because she needs you. And Calder...fuck, I hate even saying this, but I think I heard Hunter's voice—"

I hit End, turning back toward the house, breathing heavily. Rage courses through me.

Why the fuck is Hunter at her house? Is that why Michael's so nervous? I knew something felt off the minute we walked in today.

Goddammit, I tried to do this clean—so nobody got hurt. I wanted to save her, not condemn her to my world. We were going to start fresh, just live for each other.

I'm a fool.

Dark words said by that old woman lay themselves out like some kind of fucking prophecy in my mind.

"You can't save her, but she could save you."

She already has. Sutton's the reason I live because she showed me how to love. But that doesn't mean I've forgotten how to kill. So fuck what that old bitch says, I'm going to save my baby.

Because I'm not afraid of death. I'll take that motherfucker back with me if I have to keep her safe.

Michael's bringing a glass of water to his lips as the back door slams behind me.

"Where's Hunter?" I rumble, walking toward him.

His eyes grow to saucers as he drops the glass on the floor, trying to stand from his chair. That's what I thought. Motherfucker.

Glass shatters, water spilling out everywhere as he begins to stutter. My voice booms through the house as I repeat myself, closing the distance.

"Where the fuck is your son?" I look at Roman. "They've done some shit to Sutton."

Michael scrambles to his feet, stumbling backward, face shifting between Roman and West for help. But they don't try to stop me. West quickly clears the pills as Roman closes around the other side, grabbing Michael by the arm.

"Calder asked you a fucking question. Answer him before he tells me to make you. Don't think I won't enjoy that, you motherfucker."

Michael's shaking his head, holding up his hands as I stand in front of him. I can hear the ragged fury my breath makes, scraping in and out of my lungs. I'm a fucking animal.

If he's hurt her... I slam the palm of my hand against his face, gripping it, taking his body back against the fucking wall with a thud.

My mouth comes close to his ear, gritting the words from between my teeth as I press against his skull as hard as I can.

"I'll gut you. And leave you for your sons to find. Don't fuck with me. Answer my question."

"What about your father?" he mumbles under my palm. "I'm protected."

"The devil already knows your name, Calder Wolfe. And one day, even he'll be afraid of the King."

Today's that day.

I squeeze his face harder, digging my fingertips into his temple, listening to him scream like a little pig before I let him go.

"Look at my face, Michael. If you think there's anyone that I'm afraid of, then you haven't been paying attention. I'll kill everyone if she's hurt. Including my fucking father."

He's still blubbering, not fucking answering me, so I turn, swiping a ballpoint pen off the table, and stab it into his goddamn stomach.

I slap my hand over his mouth to force him to swallow his scream, throwing the rest of the broken pen to the ground.

"Michael. It's important to trust me. I'll never lie to you. If you hurt my precious girl, I won't just kill you. I'll dig up the fucking roots of your family tree and make it so you never existed."

His tears spill over my hand as I stare at him before peeling it off his mouth.

"Please," he mutters, covering his stomach as crimson bleeds out on his shirt. "He's at Sutton Prescott's house. None of this was my idea. You have to believe me. It was my wife's. She thought of all of it. Please don't kill me."

My head swings to Roman's. We're thinking the same thing. He's setting us up. Roman snaps to West and motions around. This motherfucker tried to run a game on us. Twenty says he recorded everything with Tyler and us.

"All of what, Michael?" The tone of my voice alone is a goddamn threat. I barely contain my rage enough to ask the questions I need to.

Michael coughs, so I slap him so hard his teeth rattle.

"All of what?" I thunder.

"Found it," West announces, holding up a small lipstick-sized video recorder. I fucking knew it.

Michael's crying, fucking blubbering like the bitch he is. "We just wanted out. The camera's just for protection. The plan is really Sutton, as a means to an end. A way to deliver Baron to Connor. We thought you'd be forced to walk away...because your father had that note and then—"

I almost black out.

"It was you...you gave my father that letter? You went into her room?"

My head shifts around, looking for something to crack his head open with. He's dead.

"Hunter...Hunter did it. My wife made him do it. And he's setting her up with drugs too—they're going to send her away."

Roman reaches into his pocket, handing me his keys. "Go. We got this."

My hand closes over his, taking **them from him** as I stare back at him. I'm never coming back. This is it. I **don't have to** say anything because he already knows. So, I give a nod as his **eyes search m**ine.

"We'll be fine, brother. I'll look aft**er West. Just** get your girl."

I back away, jaw tense, as West **comes up in my** place before I turn my back on my brothers.

The last thing I hear is Roman sp**eaking.**

"Here's what's happening. First, **we're calling** Connor, and you get to confess. And then, if I had to guess, **we're gonna ha**ve some fun."

Sutton

chapter thirty-eight

"**N**o," I scream. "Let me go."

Two security guards grab my arms, throwing me to the ground. Shock reverberates through my body, leaving me momentarily breathless. But I don't stop fighting, forcing breath into my lungs, making my feet kick and body flail.

I can't believe this is happening.

"This is in your best interest," my father hisses, standing behind my mother like the coward he is.

This isn't in my best interest. It's in theirs. I hate them.

"Fuck you," I spit. "I'm not doing drugs. Hunter's a liar."

My eyes dart to Hunter, who's watching, transfixed. He looks pleased and like he's sickly enjoying this.

Tears spill over my cheeks as I'm dragged. Literally dragged toward the front door.

"Stop fighting, Sutton," my mother yells.

The grip from one of the assholes holding me loosens, so I squirm harder, jerking my arm from him.

"Fuck. Grab her," he yells to the other guy as I pull away, kicking at them before standing up and running.

Footsteps and yells follow me as I tear through the foyer. I'm running barefoot and aimlessly because I don't know what to do. But I'm scared. I'm getting fucking shipped away.

I won't leave him. Not without a fight.

"Sutton," my mother screeches, followed by my father yelling, "Stop right there."

My feet carry me quickly up the stairs as I look over my shoulder. The two guards stand at the bottom, looking at my parents for direction.

It's my mother that nods her head. Fucking bitch. But I don't see them follow me up because I'm already bursting into my room, locking the door behind me.

I swing around, eyes landing on my desk.

Fuck. Everything on top gets hurled to the ground before I grit my teeth, pushing it in front of the door. My face stains red with the pressure as I use all my strength to barricade myself in my room.

Bangs erupt against the door as I get it in place, making me jump backward.

"Open the door, Sutton." … "Don't make us break it down." … "It doesn't have to be this way."

All the yelling mixes together, crashing down on me. I slap my hands over my ears, trying to escape. I won't go.

"Calder," I whisper, hearing my own voice. "Please come."

Please, Aubrey. Please have called him. I need him.

"Open the door, Sutton."

It's Hunter's voice.

"I hate you," I scream back, dropping to my knees as I sob.

A half hour prior

I'm jolted from sleep as my bedroom door hits the wall, my mother busting in.

"Oh my God." I blink, the light hurting my eyes. "Mom? What's going on?"

My mother begins opening the drawers on my desk. Papers fly everywhere as I try to catch up.

"Mom. What are you doing?"

She looks over my shoulder just as my father walks inside with two men dressed in black.

"What's going on? Who are these people?"

"We know everything, Sutton," he levels as I draw my brows together. *How can they know about Calder? Oh my God. Lie, Sutton.*

"Know what?" I snap back, but my heart is pounding as I see my mother walk into my closet. *She'll find the letter from Calder.*

I jump out of bed in nothing but a tank top and underwear as my father snaps at me.

"Cover yourself. Have some decency. Or is that long gone by now?"

I ignore him, grabbing my phone and rushing toward the closet. As I get to the doorway, my mother walks out.

The look on her face can only be described as hate.

If ever I wondered if this woman loved me, the answer is no. No person could ever look at another one the way she's staring at me right now.

Her words are delivered with an eerie calm, punctuated with hostility.

"You. Little. Bitch."

My eyes drop, not because it hurts but because my mind screams at me to call Calder, but I erased it. *Aubrey. Call Aubs.* I know she exchanged numbers with Roman before our fake breakup went down, so I hope she understands what I need her to do.

I hit the number, keeping it at my side so that mother doesn't know.

"How could you?" my mother spits, holding up a clear bag of white pills. What the hell?

I shake my head, but she shrieks, her palm slapping my face. My head shoots sideways as my hand covers my cheek. Tears well in my eyes as the sting smarts my skin.

"I should've had an abortion."

My eyes dart to hers, mouth fallen open as I stand holding my face.

"I didn't do anything," I whisper, trying not to cry.

I'm grabbed by my arms from behind, causing me to drop my phone. Everyone's talking at once.

"You'll get the help you need." ... "I can't believe you've done this to your father." ... "How could you fall so far from grace? I'm ashamed of you."

My head is shaking as I plead. "I didn't do anything. Where are you taking me?"

But as I'm turned around, Hunter stands in the doorway. He walks toward me, and I can feel anger—no, hate—fill my body.

"Freckles, one day, you'll thank all of us. A year will go by faster than you think, and I'll be right here when you get back."

I hate him. Oh my God.

My head draws back before I spit in his smug-ass face.

"Fuck you, Hunter. You're a dead man."

Hunter wipes his face, smirking as he comes close. "Your boyfriend's never going to find you because he'll be behind bars. I told you it was better to have me as a friend."

He looks up over my shoulder, behind me, to my parents.

"I'm so sorry this is happening. But I love her, so I know it's for the best."

I scream as he steps aside, and I'm hauled out like a criminal.

Calder

The engine growls, tires squealing as I take the corner faster than I should making the ass end of the car fishtail. I correct it, knocking into a higher gear as I speed down her street.

My phone rings just as I hit the brakes. Her gates are closed, but there's a black van and Hunter's fucking car in the driveway.

I kick open my door, getting out in the middle of the street, pulling the phone to my face.

"What."

"Check the glove box."

I don't wait to end the call, knowing Roman will. I shove it into my back pocket, stalking back to the car and ripping open the door, making the hinges strain before I lean inside, popping the box open.

My fucking gun.

I open the chamber, gritting my teeth when I see only one bullet before I slide the safety off and tuck it into the back of my Dickies.

All the dark swirls of rage begin to still inside me as one foot steps in front of the other toward her front door. Because I finally understand all of it—my destiny and hers.

"Tragedy awaits you. Death is knocking. And it's on her doorstep."

Yes, I am.

Sutton

My hands drop from my head as I crawl toward my bed to hide underneath it.

"Sutton. Can you hear me? It's just you and me, Freckles."

I scowl, looking over my shoulder, hearing Hunter through the door.

"Go to hell, Hunter."

"Now, why would I do that when it's more fun here?"

My body freezes because we're definitely alone. There's no way he'd talk like that in front of anyone else. I sit back on my ass, my hand brushing past my phone.

Oh my God. I swipe the screen, but it cuts my finger because it's cracked from me dropping it. Fuck. I can't get it to work.

"Why did you lie?" I yell, tossing the phone back to the ground.

"Because I had to. Why'd you choose him?"

"Is that what this is about?"

He laughs. "No, you egotistical bitch. But if you're regretting it, I can make all of this easier on you."

I don't answer, looking at the ceiling.

"Because, Sutton, this isn't even the hard part. See, setting you two up was easy. All it took was one little peek in your room and, of course, your panties drawer because that's where all bitches like you keep shit."

What the fuck? My mind is spinning in circles. Why would he want to set us up? Why is this happening? I don't understand.

"Then it was a matter of presenting the plan. I let Tyler Wolfe know his only son was fucking the enemy."

Oh my God. My head swings toward my closet—he took the note. I feel sick. My eyes fill with tears, wishing I could stop him. Just stop him from speaking.

"Then I told him that I could connect you two, in a way that's public record—rehab. And I hid a little white bag of goodies in your room. So, not only will everyone know Calder popped your cherry, but they'll think he's helping you pop pills too."

My head's shaking as my cheeks grow wetter.

"I'll tell everyone you're lying."

This can't happen. They can't send me away...I can't leave him. I won't.

"Tell them the truth. Because that seems to be working so well for you. You can't do anything except watch the O'Bannions blackmail your father while mine is set free as payment. If you think about it, you kind of whored yourself out for me. I guess I should say thank you."

I push to stand, trying to process what he's saying. *What does Hunter's family have to do with the O'Bannions and Calder?* I can barely understand my own thoughts, running my hands through my hair.

I'm trying to hold on to one thought as another crashes down onto me as my chest shakes.

"I hate you. Stop. Just stop it, Hunter."

"Do you want to know the best part, Freckles? Now that you two are broken up—"

"We aren't," I snap as my eyes land on the bag of little white pills.

I stand, swiping them off the bed, yelling my words through ragged breaths and tears.

"There's a flaw in your plan, Hunter. You left the evidence in here. No pills, no proof. Fuck you. I won't let you hurt him."

There's a bang in the distance like the front door slamming, but I don't slow my stride, walking toward my bathroom and opening the baggie as Hunter says, "God. That's even better. Now you can watch him hate you."

I freeze before spinning around, stalking toward my bedroom door.

"Why would Calder hate me? That would never fucking happen. Ever."

Ignore him. Don't listen, Sutton.

"You're so dumb. Do you think he'll still love you when he's arrested for rape? Because a photo of you kissing on the Ferris wheel is gonna be what helps do just that."

"Lies. Shut up."

Walk away, Sutton.

"Is it a lie? Come on...you're smarter than that. There won't be a judge out there that we can't make believe that your drug dealer wasn't grooming you."

My heart stops beating because I don't want to believe Hunter, but I know what these people are capable of. And suddenly, I'm not just afraid of what they'll do to me.

"No. You can't do that. I won't let you."

He laughs. "Yeah, we can. Have you forgotten my last name? Or yours? It was just luck that Tiffany saw you and sent me the photo. Though, lately, that seems to be on my side. Because it's really the pièce de résistance. Don't you agree?"

I can't breathe. Oh fuck, I'm having a panic attack. Stop. Please, God. Make it all stop.

"He loves me. It doesn't matter what you do to us. You can't stop that."

The tears won't stop, and my goddamn feet won't move to run from this door. Hunter laughs again, and I close my hands over my ears, wanting all my thoughts to just stop.

This is my fault. All my fault. I've done this to Calder.

"I don't have to stop anything. Time will. You'll never see him again, Sutton. By the time he gets out of jail, he'll fucking despise the bitch that put him there—you. I hear that place really likes pretty boys too."

It's like I can't focus. My heart is beating too fast, and I can't catch my breath. How did this happen? Tears stream down my face, the saltiness bleeding between my lips.

I love him so much, but it's all my fault. Hunter would have nothing on him without me.

"You might as well be dead, Sutton...because that's what you'll be to him after he lives his life in a six-by-eight prison cell."

My eyes half blink as my body feels like it's curling in on itself. I've lost track of the tears I've cried. I'm overwhelmed by the emotion. I can't speak to fight back or feel anything other than grief. This is my fault. I've hurt the only person that's ever loved me.

The bag in my hand feels heavy as my head drops down toward where my hands have fallen, Hunter's words sounding far away because my mind is numb.

I can't live without Calder. But without me, he gets to live.

No pills, no evidence. No me, no setup.

The plastic tears under my fingernails. I bring the bag to my lips, letting the contents fill my mouth, swallowing as many as I can before I hurry to my nightstand and grab the water bottle left from last night, chugging it back.

Everything drops from my hands as another sob racks my body before I slide down the side of my bed to the ground.

"I'm sorry, Calder. I love you. So, I'll save you."

Calder

Chapter
forty

The front door slams behind me, pulling all eyes to the entry as I walk inside. Everyone stands silent in the living room, fear on their faces—murder on mine.

Two assholes in all black start toward me as Sutton's father begins yelling for someone to call the police.

"Where is she?" I roar, pulling my gun from the small of my back.

The guards put their hands in front of them like they're trying to defuse the situation, taking a step toward me. I look between them as my teeth fucking grind.

All my words are growled. "I said, where's my fucking girl."

"She's already gone, buddy. Let's put the gun down."

"Fuck you. Where'd you take her?"

The guy not talking steps in closer, so I pistol-whip him, sending blood flying as Sutton's mother begins screaming. He falls to the floor, hands on his face, trying to stop the blood gushing from his broken nose.

My gun points at the other dipshit left standing, who takes a step backward. Sutton's mom is still fucking screaming, so I point the barrel at the senator.

"Shut that bitch up before I put a bullet in her fucking head."

She immediately goes silent, shaking as she stares back at me.

"You're lucky I don't take your fucking hands for touching her."

Her face turns to ash as Baron puts his arm in front of his wife. I'd bet it's the single bravest thing he's ever fucking done.

"Now, I'd answer my question if I were you. Or I'll let Sutton choose whether or not you live or die. Because that feels like justice—judged by the daughter you mistreat."

Before I finish, her mother's already blurting out, "We don't know. They wouldn't tell us. It's part of the program."

"Bullshit," I rumble.

"It's true," Baron rushes out, eyes darting to something behind me before he swallows, looking indignant.

My head swings over my shoulder as I lock eyes with Hunter, who's standing by the front door.

"You did this," I spit, turning around. "And like a fucking coward, you were gonna sneak away. Where? Back to daddy?"

His eyes grow wide as I shake my head. He knows what I mean.

He's dead. Just like you're about to be.

One step after another gathers speed as I lift the gun, feeling the kick as his shoulder's thrown back, hit with my bullet.

Screams erupt around us.

Hunter howls in pain as he stumbles, back hitting the door. I run toward him, raising my arm and bringing the butt of my gun down on his fucking skull.

I'm drowning in a red mist of fury, giving him what he deserves. He's done this to my baby—taken her from me.

"You're fucking dead."

Spit flies from my mouth as my hand comes down over and over, blood erupting underneath each hit as he tries to fight back. But I throw him to the ground, gripping his hair, holding his head in place, knocking the metal into his face.

"This is what you get for what you've done."

Bone cracking under the gun's handle echoes in the hallway, becoming the only sound mixed with my grunts as Hunter stops fighting back.

"She could've died because of your fucking little game."

I hit him harder each time, smashing his face until I can't see him past the blood. I hit him until his body goes completely limp and then after.

I hit him until he's dead.

Hard, abrasive breaths drag from my body as I stand, stumbling backward, blood splattered over my shirt. I heave out as much air as I take in, hovering over his body. I'm staring down, filled with my hatred, fueled by it.

I suck in a breath through my nose and spit on his fucking body before I step away. The noise in the room, all the shit being yelled. The cries. It all begins to reach full volume.

They're going to tell me where she is. Or everyone's going to suffer.

As I turn, bloody and cruel, I see the security guard halfway up the stairs. My eyes shoot back to Baron, who pales, backing away, taking his wife with him.

Fuck.

I drop the gun to my side, feet taking the stairs three at a time, pushing past the fucking guy.

"Baby," I bellow as I get to the top of the stairs.

My hand pushes off the wall as I rush down the hallway, attacked by a sense of emptiness that suddenly fills my body, making my hands almost shake.

"Baby," I yell, coming in front of her door, banging on it. "Everything's okay now. Baby, open the door."

Bust it open.

The thought starts out quiet until it's screaming inside my head.

Bust it open. Bust it open. BUST IT OPEN.

I throw my shoulder into the door, but it barely moves, so I do it again, and again, groaning as the pain grows with each hit.

"Sutton," I holler, throwing myself into the door a fourth time, feeling it start to give.

I'm a machine, bashing into the door until it opens just enough that I can get my hand in and fucking push. I shove harder just as it gives, making me fall inside past the desk she pushed against the door.

"Sutton," I yell.

But as my eyes lift, I see her.

Oh God. No. No, no, no, no, no.

I scramble, half crawling to her body, lying lifeless on the ground. My hands hover over her, almost too scared to touch her small frame.

"No," I grit out, feeling my chest split open. "No, baby."

I touch her arms, then her stomach, before I cradle her cheek, staring down at her peaceful face. My palm presses to her skin, hoping to feel warmth as I move it over to stroke her hair. Fuck. She's so pale. *Why is she so pale?* I don't understand. This can't happen. *Not my baby. Please.*

My forehead drops to hers. "Wake up. Wake up, Sutton."

Everything inside of me feels broken as I kiss her lips, praying to feel her breath before I pull back, looking at her face. I seal my lips over hers, blowing into her mouth, pulling back to look at her before trying again, but nothing happens.

She doesn't move.

My entire body is vibrating, shaking with the emotion I feel. I scoop her up, gritting out, "Please, baby. Don't leave me."

I tip my head back, holding her lifeless body in my arms as a guttural cry erupts from my chest. I scream until my voice gives. Because all I can do is weep, rocking her, folded down over my beautiful girl. My chest shakes as my voice cracks, and tears pour down my face.

"Not you. It wasn't supposed to be you."

Back in the recesses of my mind, I hear commotion, people yelling, footsteps falling quickly, but I don't care. Because I'm praying.

I'm praying for God to take me with her. To forgive me of all my sins and let me go with her. Please take me with her. Please, God.

"Our Father, who art in heaven—"

"Step away from the girl. Hands up."

"Hallowed be thy name —"

"We need paramedics." ... "Step away from the girl or I'll shoot."

Her face flashes in my mind, moment after moment relived.

From the rock I'm seated at, I watch her dramatic little moment unfold, lifting my cigarette to my lips, readied to light it as she whispers.

"I hate you, moon."

"What are you doing here? How'd you get here so fast? I just saw you—"
    "I ran."

"Now I'm baptized in you."

"I'm gonna give you the stars, and the moon, and—"
    "Love. You're going to give me love."

"I've always loved you—my whole damned existence, even before. And I'll love you after I die. The world will have to dedicate stars to us. Because you will always be the only fucking one for me."

My body shakes as I hug her to me before placing her body back to the ground.

"Forever, baby. I'm coming," I whisper before my voice raises. "Thy kingdom come. Thy will be done. On earth as it is in heaven—"

"Show me your hands."

I swing around, quickly lunging forward. Searing hot pain shoots directly through my chest as all my breath is torn from my body. I collapse, falling backward to the ground. My head falls, facing Sutton.

"I'm coming," I whisper, straining to touch her hand as blood begins to pool around me.

"Medic" is called out, and I feel myself being jerked around, eyes beginning to close as people kneel next to her. But my eyes remain on her. Her beautiful face.

I'm coming. I feel it.

"It's an overdose. Narcan."

We'll have forever now.

I feel cold, eyelids closing longer and longer. They don't want to open anymore. I just want to go. Be with her. I blink one last time, staring at her face, death gripping my shoulder.

A needle is shot into her arm, and I close my eyes.

"Calder."

Baby. She whispered my name, but I can't open my eyes.

Baby, I scream inside my mind, but it's too late...

Everything goes black.

sinning
like hell

USA *Today* Bestselling Author

TRILINA
PUCCI

Roman

I slide my hand through the long strand of beads forming a curtain, lined neatly in a row as I pass through the doorway, hearing only the sound of them rattling around my face.

Each year is the same. I come to this dark room, thick with the smell of incense in the back room of a Queens candle shop, to meet with familiar dark brown eyes that see all.

"I was expecting you," she says with a rasp that comes from too many cigarettes and a decaying body.

I don't answer, just smirk as the old woman takes a deep breath, sweeping her long gray hair over her shoulder. She brushes her hands over the colorful scarves draped over her small wooden table, whispering to herself. Maybe praying before she reaches for the deck of tarot cards next to her.

My fingers curl around the top of the old wooden chair, dragging its feet over the floor before I sit.

"I'm here. Like you expected. So tell me the future, old woman."

Her perfectly arched brow raises as she flips over the top card. One I've come to understand represents the past.

"Five of cups..." Her eyes lift to mine. "Grief over what is lost."

I lean back into the chair, legs spread, hands joined in my lap.

"You say that every year."

She shakes her head gently. "That's because the past never changes."

I stare across at her, waiting for the next card. She turns over two nude people with the label *The Lovers* underneath.

"Looks like the present doesn't change either," she says under her breath.

It's always the same. The Romani woman tells me they still grieve the past, that their fate is intertwined, but in the end, the future is always just out of reach. Unseeable. Like it's being guarded—kept secret by the devil himself.

As the third card flips, the one that represents the future, her eyes narrow, and I tilt my head to the ceiling, waiting for what's a foregone conclusion.

Fuck. I don't know why I come, and yet I still do, every damn year. Bullshit—I'm struggling to hold on to that lie because the reason's etched onto my bones.

That night, the night when she called Calder by his name at the carnival. A part of me wondered if the witch cursed him to his death with all those things she'd said. And in case she really is that powerful, the other part of me hopes that somehow their story, Calder's and Sutton's, can be resurrected. And that all the wrongs that happened can be made right.

I vowed to him that if I protect him—I protect her. And I won't break a promise to my brother.

So here I sit, hoping this witch can tell me what's coming.

Hold up. Why hasn't she said anything?

My head drops to hers, but what I see has me sitting up straighter. Magda's frozen, staring down, her lips moving ever so slightly as if she's speaking. But no sound's coming out. What the fuck?

"Magda?"

She says nothing, fixed to the card, lips moving faster. So I snap my fingers toward her face.

"Hey. Witch. What the fuck do you see right now?"

My eyes dart to the card before looking back at her. It looks like a tower on fire as people fall from it. That's never what she pulls.

"Hey. What does that card mean?"

Silence.

I reach across the table, grabbing her arm as a whoosh of breath leaves her, eyes fluttering back. She falls back against her seat, pulling from my hold, eyes locked on mine.

All I see is fear. It's so potent that I can almost smell it.

Her sun-soaked leather skin is pale, and her breath comes out in ragged draws as she makes the sign of the cross.

"So much death. So much destruction..." She trails off, shivering, reaching for a wrap that's slung over the back of her chair.

"Death always waits for men like us," I level calmly as I sit forward, chasing the fear on her face. "As does hell, Magda. What have you seen?"

Her head shakes, eyes avoiding mine as she pulls her wrap tight. The sound of her chair scraping the floor pierces the silence with the quickness of her standing up.

"Take your money and go."

My brows furrow as I slowly stand.

"You will tell me what you saw first. Because I ain't leaving until you do."

Her eyes grow cold as we stare at each other. "*O maćho o baro xàla e tikinen.*"

My hand slaps down on the table, making her shoulders jump as my voice bellows, "In English."

The old woman takes a step around the table, moving like the slither of a snake.

"I said, 'Men are like fish,' Roman Wolfe. 'The great ones devour the small.'"

She stops in front of me as my chin drops so that I can see her.

"And which are we?"

"You are the madness he creates. You are the great fish. But Calder"—she shivers—"he's the ocean, and he'll swallow everyone whole. This is the last time I will speak his name. Because to say it calls to evil. But you are wrong. Death isn't waiting for Calder. It's listening for his instruction."

Chapter one

Sutton—Present

My body feels like it's floating, but my eyes are so heavy that it feels impossible to open them.

Am I dreaming? Or have I died? I always thought death would be peaceful, but all I feel is fear. It's coursing through me, holding me by my throat, and all I can think is to call out his name.

Calder.

Cold rushes into my body, and I feel my eyelids begin to flutter. Oh God, I can feel my heart beating and my lungs burning. I don't think I'm dead, but then why am I so scared? It's as if my mind knows something irrevocable has happened—something worse than death.

Because I'm afraid to open my eyes. Fearful of what will be in front of them.

Calder.

Muted voices fill my ears, but I can't quite make sense of what's happening around me. They get louder and louder until it feels like they're yelling at me, making me wince and try to lift my arms to my ears.

Pins and needles shoot through my arms, making me gasp, and this time I feel my lips mouth his name.

Calder.

"Can you open your eyes for me? Hey. Come on...what's her name?"

From behind me, someone says, "Her name's Sutton."

The next voice is closer, as if it's hovering above me.

"Sutton. Can you open your eyes?"

I blink them open, eyes unfocused, lips trying to move, but still no sound comes out of my mouth. My tongue feels like it's coated in chalk as I try to swallow.

Memories flick through my mind, causing my pulse to quicken—Hunter making unimaginable threats to Calder. Me swallowing pills. Then everything's gone.

"No, no. Stay with me, Sutton."

I feel my arms rubbed vigorously. So I drop my face toward the feeling, only to realize my eyes have closed again before I reopen them as wide as possible, letting my head fall to the side.

My entire world slowly and painfully comes into focus, making my body shudder with fear. I want to scream, but I'm held hostage by the scene in front of me as stuttered breaths draw from my lungs.

Calder's tan skin is gray, hair slicked across his forehead, his eyes closed before they're forced open by the men working on him as they shine a light on them.

They're jerking him around like a rag doll, tearing his blood-spattered shirt open. The paramedics press something to his chest, scrambling to stop the blood from leaking out as they shout directions over him.

Oh God. No.

Blood seeps closer to me from Calder's lifeless body as I stare, unable to see anything but him.

"Calder," I whisper, slurred and too quiet.

"He's bleeding out," I hear yelled out, but unsure from whom.

My mind feels detached, unable to make my body listen because I need to get closer to him. I have to. He can't leave me.

"No," I drag out, feeling like my stomach might turn over.

Every bit of the panic I felt swallowing those pills descends upon me in full force, electrifying my nerves and jump-starting my heart.

"Calder," I say a bit louder, but I'm drowned out by louder voices around me.

"Let's get her on the stretcher. Narcan's working. Vitals are stable."

The sound of fingers snapping in my face makes me blink rapidly.

Calder. The gauze on his chest is soaked with his blood. *Oh God. Please no.*

"Sutton. Focus on me. Can you tell me what you took?"

My head turns toward the men kneeling over me, my garbled words rushing out. "Why is he bleeding? Why is Calder hurt? Make it stop."

"Tell us what you took."

"Make it stop," I all but scream.

I reach for Calder, ignoring the question as I'm slid onto a stretcher. But my movements are slow, making my hand land in thick, wet crimson pooled around him instead of his arm.

My wrist is yanked away and tucked in next to me as the rip of Velcro cuts through the air.

"No," I breathe harshly, trying to reach for him again, but I'm strapped in, unable to move.

They're taking me away. *No.* Adrenaline pumps through my body as I grind my teeth together before gritting out, "Stop."

My head swings uncoordinatedly back and forth as I try to shake it.

"I can't go. I need to stay with him."

Voices bellow from the side, calling my attention.

"I don't have a pulse. Paddles."

Oh my God. No. Calder. Tears cascade down my face as I try to struggle against the hold of the straps, but I'm so weak.

A voice at my feet says, "Try to relax, Sutton," but I ignore it, wiggling, hoping it will force them to leave me where I am.

But I'm just too weak.

A pulsing sound echoes around the room, sending the fear of God through me as I clench my fists tight, begging, protesting as the legs of the wheeled gurney click into place.

"Leave me here. Please. Leave me with him. He can't die alone. Please, God. Anyone. Please."

The paddles in the EMT's hands are pressed to Calder's chest, sending the voltage straight to his heart. I stare as his back arches off the ground and then relaxes, feeling as if I'm fracturing into pieces.

He's dying. This isn't real. This can't be happening. No. I won't believe it. This is a nightmare. It has to be.

A voice carries. "Nothing. Again."

I strain to see him, but he's disappearing as they roll me away.

"No," I say through my teeth, voice cracking as I begin to sob, looking between the men on either side of me now. "Help him. Leave me and help him. Please."

He can't die in this room without me.

Another click of the paddles, and then the sound of his body falling back against the floor pulls a gut-wrenching sob from my chest.

"Calder. Stay with me. Please. I love you."

My vision blurs from the tears pouring down, soaking my cheeks, as I stare at the ceiling. Panic infused with fear wracks my body as my head shifts, looking between the walls of the hallway.

I have to go back.

I did all this to save him. I tried to save him. Please, God. Please don't take him from me. Not like this. Not with me still alive.

"Her pulse is through the roof. Sutton. Look at me, take a deep breath. We need you to calm down."

"No. Take me back to him," I growl, trying to stay awake, feeling like I'm going to be sick.

But they just keep carrying me down the hall. Farther away from him. Until I can't even hear what's happening, and all I'm left with is the unthinkable.

I can't do this. I'm not strong enough. I need you...please, Calder. I love you.

"If you're taking him, let me go too," I whisper through my tears. "Please, please, please. You can't be this cruel. I've listened and prayed. I do what I'm asked, what I'm told. You can't punish me like this. I'm begging you. I can't *live* without him."

"Calm down. They're doing all they can. Focus on breathing. You're going to be okay."

It doesn't matter what anyone says. My words are for God. They're a prayer because nothing will ever be okay again.

My eyes close, wishing for the darkness I felt before to come again and take me away. My lips part, whispering the words I know he'll never hear.

"It was all worth it. You are mine, and I am yours."

The lights above my head pass in a flash as I drift in and out of consciousness. I'm rushed down the hospital corridor as people speak above me, talking about an overdose and spouting medical terms that I don't understand.

"I couldn't let him be hurt," I slur, but nobody's listening.

My eyes land on a man in a white coat. He's looking at the EMTs as he places a hand on the metal rail of the gurney.

"Mrs. Prescott."

I blink, trying to focus. Wait. He's not looking at me. *He said Mrs.* My head turns to the side to see my mother standing beside me.

"Sutton will be escorted to our psychiatric ward. We'll assess her and keep you informed. I've spoken with the senator. Rest assured, we'll keep this matter private."

I shake my head, wanting to speak, to scream at her. To tell her I hate her, but none of my words come out fast enough.

The movement of the bed rolling jostles my body, pulling my attention back to the doctor. "Wait. How long are you keeping me here? What about Calder?"

The doctor looks down at me. His cheeks wear a warmth that his eyes lack.

"You're lucky to be alive, Miss Prescott. But you'll need to speak to someone because not everyone had the same fortune as you."

My entire chest feels like it's cracked wide open as I try to refuse what he's saying.

"No. No. They were helping him. He's not dead."

The doctor ignores me, nodding to the orderly. "Let the staff know we're holding her until further notice."

"Listen to me. He's. Not. Dead."

But nobody hears me. I'm shaking, tears falling into the corners of my mouth, leaving the taste of salt on my tongue as I shift my head from side to side.

The doctor speaks over me. "Call psych and tell them we need a consult. And that it's hush-hush."

"No. I'm not crazy. You can't keep me here."

Both men flick their gaze to my panicked face before looking away, continuing with their instructions. Oh my God. My breath turns into short huffs as I begin to break into a full-fledged panic attack because I'm alone. Terrifyingly alone. They're locking me up and throwing away the key just to keep us apart.

"Calder," I rush out as loud as I can before taking a deep breath and calling for him again.

"Miss Prescott, calm down."

There's no more time for that. They forced me from the room, away from his side. But I won't let them steal him from me now. I'll never let them do that.

"He's not dead...I prayed. I asked God. He can't be dead. I won't believe it. It's not true."

Both men stare down at me, saying nothing. My chest rises and falls faster and faster until this time, his name leaves my lips as a scream.

There is no me without him. No world I'd be forced to exist in without him in it. The thought is unbearable. Physically fucking unbearable.

I keep screaming because it's a herald's cry. I hope the heavens fall to earth and the devil rises to imprison it here.

Because there are no stars and no purpose.

Without Calder, nothing exists.

Chapter two

Sutton

"**N**o," I scream, kicking my feet as I buck off the bed. "Get off me."

"Hold her. Tighter," the nurse directs with a needle in hand.

Male orderlies grip my arms and legs. One on each side of me, struggling to hold me down because I'm a maniac—screaming through ground teeth, spit flying from my mouth as I flail all over the rigid strip of a hospital bed, tears streaming down my face.

"Let me go."

My head thrashes from side to side as I groan, straining all my muscles, trying to break free. Because I don't need another fucking dose of that shit that turns me into a zombie.

I want to get to him, even if I have to tear through everyone here.

Calder's not dead. Fuck their lies.

"Screw you. Your lies won't keep us apart," I growl. "Why are you doing this?"

I scream again, deep and guttural, trying to pull my arms free. My scalp stings as my hair's caught under the hand of one of the orderlies holding me down. But it's nothing in comparison to the pain inside of me.

He's not dead. I won't believe it. I'll never believe it.

"You're sick, sweetie. Still affected by the drugs you took," the nurse lies because I've been here for days, and those drugs are well out of my system.

But this is what happens every time I refuse to cooperate. Apparently, being locked up and isolated isn't enough. They have to dope me up to keep me quiet.

I buck again, fighting as before while she snaps at the men, "Hold her still. She's tiny."

"No. I want Calder," I scream, knowing he won't hear me but needing to say his name.

"Stop fighting, Miss Prescott. Just give in and rest."

"Calder," I yell again, feeling a prick on my hip, making my sob draw out along with my protest. "No."

Tears rush down my face as I stare up at the white, ugly dropped ceiling tiles, familiar with the next sensation—the warmth that will wrap my body in its vise grip, making me mute.

But only on the outside. Inside, I'm still screaming his name. Over and over.

The drugs work swiftly, coursing through my blood, pulling me deeper into the mattress, making it impossible to move or fight.

"I want Calder," I whisper.

The last of his name bleeds out, almost slurring as my eyes blink away the wetness left over on my lashes.

"He's dead, Sutton," the nurse says under her breath, wiping my eyes as she stares down at me with sympathy etched on her face. "You can let her go, gentlemen. She's not any trouble for us, now."

If they do release me, I can't tell because my legs feel like lead. My head falls to the side, feeling as if it's sinking into oblivion.

"Close your eyes now," the nurse instructs. "That's it, sleep away this nightmare."

I do as she says, only because I know it's his face I'll see and his warmth I'll feel because Calder's with me in my dreams. And my nightmares. He's always with me, protecting me, loving me. Until I open my eyes again.

"Better," I whisper as my dreamworld begins blending with my reality, and everything fades into darkness.

Sutton

Chapter *three*

I can hear them speaking—the doctor and my parents—but I don't roll over from where I'm lying.

Instead, I'm motionless, staring at the sweat beading over the cheap mauve plastic hospital cup that's next to my bed.

It's been ten days since my psych ward incarceration, isolated from everyone I know. This is the first time either of my parents has come to check on me.

Not that I expected them any earlier.

But it's weird to think that I ever believed either of them truly loved me. I knew there was a line to toe and that I wasn't their top priority, but I never realized that I wasn't one at all.

They really don't love me.

My mind drifts back to the day everything happened, to my mother's words and the cruelty that played out in her eyes as she said them.

My head shoots sideways as my hand covers my cheek. Tears well in my eyes as the sting smarts my skin.

"I should've had an abortion."

I blink, the memory fading but the pain lingering. The way she looked as if she was relieved to finally tell me the truth, and the sneer of her lip as her eyes dismissed me. I'll never forget that. Jesus, I'm not sure anyone can ever prepare for knowing that you've always been alone. Unwanted. That the joke's been on you your whole life.

My hands curl up under my chin as I try to reason with the despair I feel. I won't let them beat me. I won't. My chin trembles, but I squeeze my eyes shut, giving a small shake of my head.

No. Calder will come. Just hold on.

He has to because he's the only person that fills all those cracks and crevices inflicted on my heart.

God, I don't know if I'm strong enough to endure this...this reality without him.

More hushed talking ensues behind me, and I keep ignoring it. Because I don't care.

Nothing I have to say matters anyway. That's the lesson I've learned.

I'll stay locked in this fucking room until I stop fighting for him.

They're trying to beat him out of me. But I'll never pretend he's dead.

He's not. He's just not.

Cold spreads over my body as I squeeze my eyes closed harder, refusing any thoughts born from *their* deceit to stay inside my head.

The taste of bile taints my mouth, my stomach sick with panic, as I begin telling myself the same story I've held firm to since the moment I was committed to this hellhole. It's a mantra of hope.

Calder will come for me.

"He will," I say under my breath.

And he'll make them pay for what they've done to us.

Then he'll take me away from this nightmare, just like we planned.

My shoulders begin to tremble, fingers curling around the blanket as I pull it closer to my face.

I just want to tuck myself away and disappear so they can't see me anymore because I want to be left alone. Left to fade away, into my memories, locked inside my own mind until he frees me.

Go back, Sutton. Go back to the day you first met.

My eyes close as I try to remember how blue the sky looked when he graced our off-limits basketball court.

I take a deep breath in, wishing I could smell the ocean or the faint scent of cigarettes that always lingers on his neck.

We were perfect. All the beauty of beginnings and him—the possibility of love.

The doctor starts to speak louder, but I keep my eyes closed, concentrating on Calder's beautiful face.

"She's clinically depressed. And it's getting worse. She's not eating. She's combative with the staff, refusing to speak. The hospital has been very accommodating, Senator Prescott. Inventive even, considering we didn't have cause to hold her this long. Now we need to talk about real solutions. Because your daughter—"

My father's gruff voice commands the room, interrupting the doctor, barging too loudly into my mind, tearing down the walls I built.

"Thank you for your input, Doctor. But we *have* a real solution. Sutton will be fine once she gets to Madison Prep. They're aware of the situation."

"Good luck getting her there without putting a feeding tube in her. A prep school isn't exactly a hospital, Senator. I don't think you understand the gravity of the situation."

I squeeze my eyes tighter, trying to feel the breeze or hear the sounds of birds chirping from that day. My head shakes, anger building because I'm trying like hell to imagine the thunder of his basketball hitting the ground, but I can't. It's slipping away.

Goddammit. I can't hold on to him.

Another image flashes in my mind.

It's him behind the confessional screen. *Yes, come back to me.* Even in the dark, his eyes are so blue. His lips tug into a smirk at the same time mine do. As if he's feeling the same emotions I am. He is, and we do.

Can you feel me now, Calder? Because I love you. And I need you. I'm trying to be strong, but I don't know how long I can live this hell before I break. I'm so tired. Please come. Please.

My mother's voice comes from behind me, yanking me from my thoughts, throwing me to my knees in the present.

"Sutton. Roll over and look at me when I'm speaking to you. You need to let this go. Calder Wolfe is dead. And you need to move on for all our sakes."

My fingertips wipe the tops of my cheeks, smearing the constantly flowing tears over my dry skin as I bury my heart down deep.

I just wanted to hold on to him for a moment longer, but I need to not feel so that I can be as cruel as she deserves.

Because I hate her, and I wish I could strangle every last lie from her throat until she chokes on her fucking entitlement.

For all our sakes? As if she has a place here.

"Save the faux tough love speech," I breathe out. "He's not dead. We both know that. So I won't go along with this bullshit. Fuck *your sake*...I only care about him."

"How dare you speak to me that way," she hisses.

My lip lifts into a sneer, hating the show she's putting on as if she's a good mother deserving of my respect.

I twist, shifting around quickly so that I'm facing her, locking eyes before she draws back.

Her brows draw together, disgust staining her features.

"That's right. Take a good look, Elizabeth. This is your handiwork."

At least she has the moral compass to pale. She's seeing what I do every single day in the tiny, smudged plastic mirror they give me.

Can't have me slitting my wrists with glass, after all.

I search her face as her gaze drifts over the dark circles under my eyes.

"The dark circles are from the nightmares. They have a way of keeping you awake. But I bet you can't relate. You probably sleep like a baby since you *are* the nightmare."

She swallows, jaw set in anger, but her eyes drop to my cheekbones which are too pronounced because I'm gaunt.

"It's hard to eat when people are always sticking you with needles to shut you the fuck up. Then again, lying bastards never want to hear the truth. Do they, Senator?"

My father clears his throat, looking away like the coward he is. But she doesn't. No, my mother is never one to cower from confrontation.

I push myself up to sit, lifting my chin to give her a better look at the scratch marks clawed over what used to be smooth and unmarred skin.

"This is really the best part. See, sometimes, I want to crawl out of my skin. That's how unbearable life feels without him." My voice cracks as it begins to tremble. "And no matter how strong I try to be, sorrow is fucking drowning me. It won't let me breathe, so I dig my nails into my neck and try to tear myself apart."

Her lips part as if she's going to say something, but I throw back the covers, hanging my legs over the side of the bed, punctuating my words.

"I *bleed* for him. Calder isn't something I move on from, you callous whore. This is what misery looks like. But then, what do you care, right? You wish I were dead. Remember?"

This time she looks away, crossing her arms, staring at my father. Silence suffocates the space as everyone looks anywhere but at me. I guess the outcome of their evil is hard to witness.

Good. I hope it fucking haunts them.

I laugh, but it's tinged with rage. "If you're not letting me out, then go. Just. Fucking. Leave."

The doctor clears his throat, closing the distance between us, worry on his brow.

"Sutton. Grief takes many forms. Your parents care deeply about you—"

My head shoots to his, feeling myself snap.

"Fuck grief. That's not what I feel." My fingers claw at my chest as I spit my words, screaming them at his face. "The absence of him makes death favorable when I'm fucking weak."

My fists ball in front of me, lifting to my head before pounding down to the mattress. "I love him. Don't you understand that? I love Calder."

I place my bare feet on the cold speckled tiles, hurling my words, crying them out of my body.

"He's not dead. He's not fucking dead. You just accepted the lie they told. You're a fucking puppet."

My father turns toward me with anger behind his eyes. In the past, it would've terrified me, but this time I smile back, full of animosity and spite.

Because there's nothing more they can do to me that would be worse than how I feel right now.

He hurls his words at me with vicious intent.

"How could you do this to our family? Look at where we are, Sutton. In a goddamn psych ward because you tried to kill yourself over a drug dealer. You're acting like a selfish child. And now you look like this...like some kind of... Jesus, what will the press say..." His voice trails off as he turns away.

But I huff a laugh, tucking my hair behind my ears, feeling unhinged, unpredictable.

"What do I look like, Senator? Like a girl who's lost everything? And don't kid yourself—my childhood died the minute you locked me in here."

My hospital gown brushes my calf as I step forward, wanting to hurt him. To say everything I've kept quiet, locked inside of myself because I loved my parents.

But I've been surrounded by monsters, and now I see them for who they really are.

My finger stabs into the air, shifting between them.

"I'm in this place because of *you*. I look like this because of *you*. Blame yourselves," I spit, face distorted, neck burning red from my anger. "Then you should figure out how to repent. Because when Calder comes—"

My mother steps in front of my father, swiping her hand in the air harshly.

"That's enough. Stop this," she snaps, but I don't, shouting over her as I shake my head.

"No. I won't. When Calder comes for me—"

"He's never coming," she hurls.

"Yes, he is," I scream back.

Her teeth grind as her hand darts out, gripping my chin roughly between her fingers. Our eyes are locked as she speaks her words with quiet, sinister violence.

"Don't you dare speak that filth's name ever again. He. Is. Dead. And may he burn in hell."

I lunge, screaming, hearing her shriek as I reach for her neck to choke the life from her. The doctor throws himself between us, thrusting me backward.

"I'll kill you," I howl as I'm pinned by his body against the bed, still trying to reach for her.

Orderlies rush the room as my mother breathes, "Jesus Christ. She's crazy. You're not my daughter."

"Oh yes, I am, you bitch. I'm just the daughter you deserve."

My chest is heaving as my wrists are restrained, but my eyes stay locked to hers. I'm wild, filled with hatred.

"One day, everything you've built will burn to the fucking ground. And I'll be there to strike the match."

My father wraps an arm around her waist, pulling her backward out of the hospital room door, but our eyes stay locked on each other the whole way out.

It's not until the door closes and they disappear that I fall to my knees, arms held above my head by the men surrounding me. Sobs thunder out from my opened mouth as I dangle, unable to escape my emotions.

"It's okay. Let her go," the doctor says quietly as I cry.

My arms fall to my sides, palms smacking the ground, making them sting as I hang my head, barely holding myself up. Water pours from my eyes, spilling over my cheeks onto the floor, blurring my vision. But it doesn't matter because I can't see past this feeling.

This fucking sadness.

"I hate them. I hate all of you," I scream.

My fingers curl into the ground before I slap it.

"Where are you? Goddammit. I need you. You're not dead."

I hit the tile again.

"You're not."

And again.

I hit the floor faster and faster as I repeat, *You're not dead*, until my arms give out, and I slide down to my belly, feeling the chill on my skin.

My head lies to the side, staring at the empty floor next to me, remembering everything about him.

A part of me is scared that the longer I'm here, the harder it will get to find him when I close my eyes. But at this moment, he's staring back at me, eyes the color of the ocean, lips the same blush of my cheeks.

He's here with me.

"I love you, baby," he whispers before disappearing piece by piece into the night sky like the stems of a dandelion blown away to make a wish.

I reach into the space, feeling nothing but emptiness, closing my eyes because I'm alone again.

"Hold on for a little longer," I mumble to myself, feeling the needle pushing into my hip again.

Sutton

Chapter four

"**C**alder," I rush out, sitting up quickly from the stiff hospital bed as I wake from my dream.

I wish it *were* only a dream and not a memory because the pain that sears straight through my heart kills me every time I wake up.

It's too visceral to remember the way he looked on the floor of my bedroom—the emptiness in his eyes, the way he was so still even as they tore his shirt, scrambling to stop the bleeding... there was so much blood.

My hand comes to my forehead, feeling the dampness beaded over my brow before I lower it, noticing my tremble.

Jesus, my hands are shaking.

I lift my eyes to the darkness of my room, save the light filtering through a small rectangular window in the door from the hallway. It must be late because it's quiet.

God, how long was I asleep this time?

Looks like they doped me up nice and good after my parents left this morning.

My feet kick out from under the blanket, trying to rid myself of it, but I'm still slow from whatever they sedated me with. *I hate this feeling.*

Twisting toward the table next to my bed, I reach for the cup filled with water. But as I do, I'm suddenly halted, body frozen in place.

sinning like hell 301

There's a man next to my bed.

He's in a black suit, jacket open, sitting in the corner of my room with one leg casually crossed over the other, hands folded on his thigh, staring back at me.

"Who the hell are you?"

He takes a deep breath but offers nothing.

The light from the door cuts across half his face, spotlighting it just enough to see him. But he tilts his head, bringing his eyes into view, making me frown.

There's something that feels familiar about him, but I know we've never met. Or maybe we have. I can't count the number of doctors and shrinks that have been through my room. All with the same bullshit questions.

His eyes search over my face as I grab my cup, gulping down the coolness. The way he's looking at me is like he's hoping to discover an answer to a question he hasn't asked yet.

My eyes roll as the thwack of the cup back to the table accents my words.

"You must be the new shrink? I'm surprised you guys even pretend to evaluate me, considering you're going to say whatever my parents want you to. But like I told the other guy, I'm not unstable. My parents are just assholes."

He shakes his head, and for whatever reason, goose bumps spread over my neck.

What the hell is going on? Why the mystery?

Butterflies flicker in my stomach, but I'm not nervous. Maybe they're trying to run away. I narrow my eyes, wondering if I should too.

My voice is cautious, laced with my unease, uncomfortable with our sudden game.

"Okay then, did my parents send you?"

He grins, and it pisses me off. *Oh, fuck them.* I should've known.

"I know Calder's not dead. So you can save your breath and leave."

He licks his lips, seemingly deep in thought. So I spit my words at him, feeling all the familiar anger from earlier soaking them.

"I said, get the fuck out."

"Ha." He chuckles. "You're a firecracker. I would've never believed it from the way you were described. What a nice surprise."

"Life's full of those," I huff.

I scoot back up against the wall, pulling the blanket back over my lap dismissively before I scowl, adding, "So, how about you try to surprise me now and listen? Get out of my room."

He hums a laugh.

"I suppose life is full of those, but it's not often I feel that way. And in answer to your question—no, Sutton, I don't work for your parents. In fact, it's quite the opposite. And I'm not a shrink either. Care to take another guess?"

My shoulders tense as all the tiny hairs on the back of my neck rise up like hackles. The longer I look into his eyes, the more violence I feel behind them, and I'm scared.

Because it's as if he's patiently waiting to be unmasked.

Suddenly, everything Calder said about his father begins to flood my mind. What if Tyler sent this man...here...to hurt me? It's what he promised would happen.

I exhale, teeth finding a raised piece of skin on my dry lips as I inconspicuously begin to slide my hand over the bed for the button to call the nurse. But he smiles, eyes flicking to my hand as I do.

"Go ahead, call for help." He's completely unbothered. Almost amused. "It won't change my presence. People tend to give deference to a man like me." His eyes lift as he leans forward, his entire face coming into view.

Oh my God. How could I have missed it?

It's in the eyes—they look like Calder's. Not in form or color. It's the lack of fear behind them they share. Ordinary people don't have that trait. I saw it once before in Tyler's eyes when he argued with my father on the steps of the church.

It's something I've come to envy.

"You're Connor O'Bannion."

He grins. "And she's smart. No wonder my nephew likes you so much."

"Loves..." I correct boldly.

If Connor's here, then he knows **everything**. And no matter how scary that is, love is what we feel. And not **even** *he* gets to say otherwise.

"Oof. Fearless too, I see. My God. **You are something**," he offers, staring in predatory awe.

I wish that were true, that I was **fearless**. Because my heart is beating out of my damn chest, and I feel like **I'm going to** throw up. The only thing keeping me from screaming for help **is that I'm** desperate to know where Calder is, and I bet Connor knows.

"Where is he? And don't tell me **he's dead. I'm** tired of the lies."

He takes a deep breath like he's **choosing his w**ords carefully.

"You're so sure he's alive."

He's not asking a question. He's **stating a fact as** if it's remarkable.

My chin lifts as chills cover my **body because I** won't back down. I want to know where Calder is. I want to **hear Connor** make liars out of everyone.

I need to hear that my life isn't **fucking over**—that the man I love is alive.

Connor smirks, his hands clasping **together**.

"You remind me of my sister, Lena, **Calder's** mother. I can see why he's so taken by you, Sutton. She was strong-**willed, committed** to her faith. And stubborn. Oh, the arguments we'd have**. I miss her** every day. So for that, I'll give you something you want."

He cocks his head as he straigh**tens the cuff** of his shirt, adding, "A gift...before I take everything away."

Oh my God. I blink, heart thud**ding to a stop**, because absolute fear snakes around the organ, holding it in **a vise grip**.

My gut was right. Connor's here to **hurt me**.

Calder. His name rings out in my **mind, calling** to him like a lifeline.

Connor bites his bottom lip, eyes **narrowed**, as my voice comes out barely above a whisper.

"Are you going to kill me?"

The answer that takes seconds **feels like an** eternity because life is cruel. I know that now. My lips part, **wanting to beg**, *I can't be taken. We've fought so hard.* But I don't. Calder **would be strong**. He'd never let anyone see his fear. So I'll do the same.

Connor shakes his head in answer, never breaking eye contact, but I don't feel relief.

My mind is screaming at me. No part of me believes Connor isn't here to hurt me. So, if I'm not dying today, then he's going to make me wish I were.

"Let's get to the gift...you're right, Sutton. He's alive."

My chest caves the moment he says it, a whoosh of air emptying my lungs. My entire body begins shaking as I stare down at the blanket over my lap, clenching it, trying not to let the tears fall that are pooling in my eyes.

I want to scream, to weep, to fucking explode because he's alive. He's alive.

All the fractured pieces of my mind fall back into place because I'm not crazy. They're liars.

I take a deep breath, steadying my breathing as Connor continues.

"He took a clean hit right through the chest but hasn't woken up yet. The bullet barely missed his heart. I guess the saints were lookin' down on him that day. I had him quietly airlifted into the city and out of this..." He motions around the room with a look of disdain, not offering any more before he continues. "It's as if he was never here. Calder doesn't exist in St. Simeon anymore. He's a ghost."

I search his eyes, my brows furrowing, wanting more information like why he was shot, who shot him, and what the fuck happened that day?

But he offers nothing else, and I won't ask because survival keeps my mouth shut. If he wanted me to know more, he'd tell me.

Silence fills the room as I nervously rub the stiff white sheet between my fingers, focused on the only thought owning my body—Calder's alive.

My eyes close, filled with tears that want to fall, but this time it's not because I'm drenched in sorrow. It's because I know he really will come for me. I feel it in my bones.

If death couldn't hold him, nobody can keep him from me.

The side of Connor's mouth tugs into a grin as I reopen my eyes. He wags a finger at me before standing, drawing my eyes up. He's tall like Calder, just not as broad.

I watch him as he walks to the foot of my hospital bed.

"She was wrong about you, you know. One look and I can see that you'd never roll over. There's a fire burning behind those pretty green eyes. It's a shame he can't keep you. Because you, girl, might be the most dangerous fucking creature I've met."

What the fuck?

"She, who?"

His vile grin turns into a smile as his fingers curl around the smooth edge of the footboard as our eyes stay locked.

"Sometimes enemies are forced to work together for a common goal. Your mother was so sure you'd be easily manipulated into believing Calder died. Seems she was wrong. I think the only real pussy in your family is your father."

They're working together? Oh my God. I'm struck silent, lost to the million thoughts flying through my head as heat creeps up my neck, spurred by the anger I feel. My head drops, staring at my lap.

All this time, she was plotting. It's not like I didn't know, but...no... I *didn't* really know.

I couldn't say those words—that he was dead. That it was true. My body rejected it, and I clung to that, telling myself it was a gut feeling. Promising my heart that he would come.

But I didn't *really* know. Because lunacy was preferable to reality. And all this time, I suffered while she was plotting, sticking the knife in deeper, hoping I'd die.

Because that's what I was doing...dying without him.

My head lifts, eyes locked to Connor's.

"The day Calder comes will be everyone's reckoning. And I won't even pray for your souls."

Connor's jaw strains, muscles rippling as he looks into my eyes. His whisper is sinister as he leans in.

"There it is...that fire. The anger. But I still can't tell if you're a scared little animal backed into a corner? Or a wolf ready to eat?"

Connor grips the footboard with one hand, reaching inside his jacket with the other, by his ribs, and pulls out a gun.

My eyes drop to the piece, blinking too rapidly as my mind begins racing, my heart pounding in my chest. *He said he wasn't going to kill me. Did he lie or change his mind?*

Even in his large hand, the black metal looks heavy, but he holds it like he's familiar. I'm staring at it, nerves feeling like I've been hit with an electric jolt as adrenaline courses through me.

Connor slowly taps the gun barrel against the footboard, making a tapping sound as he speaks.

"You wanna know what he said as he lay dying on that stretcher?" I swallow, lifting my eyes to his face. "It was your name, Sutton. He said it over and over. He begged for you."

"He loves me," I whisper, breath hitching. "And I love him."

I do love him so much that even now, here, faced with a gun, I can't lie. I will never stop loving him. It's impossible, like it's woven into my DNA.

"See, that's the problem," Connor grits out. "Love isn't for men like us. We're too selfish."

"He's not like you," I cut, anger still brimming.

The tapping stops, and Connor tilts his head. "But are you?"

My chest rises and falls quickly. My soul is engulfed and darkened by my rage. This is why Connor is here. It's not to take my life—he's taking Calder.

Connor places the gun at my feet, laying it down gently, smoothing a hand over the top. There's a challenge on his face as he takes a step backward, lifting his hands in the air.

"Let's see what you're made of. What are you willing to do to keep him?"

I don't hesitate, scrambling forward over my knees to grab the gun, jerking the heavy metal up toward his face, finger on the trigger. My hand shakes uncontrollably as tears fall from my eyes.

"Tell me where he is."

Connor smirks. "It's one thing to sacrifice yourself. Quite another to have someone else's blood staining your hands."

"Tell me," I snarl, spit flying from my mouth. "Tell me, or I'll shoot."

Connor's eyes grow wide like he's feeding off my anger.

"Will you? Because you look more like that scared little animal."

He takes a step toward me, so I stab the gun in the air.

"Tell me where Calder is."

The silence stretches out as we stand off, rooted in our places.

But then he lunges.

My shoulders jump, tensing, prepared for the bang as I press the trigger, but all I hear is an empty click. Connor laughs, grabbing the barrel of the gun, pressing it to his forehead as I shake, eyes wide with panic, clicking it over and over again.

No, no, no, no, no.

Our eyes meet, and before I can say anything, the gun's ripped from my hand. I open my mouth to scream, but barely a sound comes out as I scramble backward because Connor's already around the side of my bed, his hand clenching my throat as he hauls me farther back, throwing me into the headboard.

"So brave," he growls, "and foolish."

I can't scream or cry because he's choking me. All my breath is trapped inside my body, burning inside my lungs, clawing to escape.

"Did you think I'd really give you a loaded weapon? Even weak bitches bite."

The mask he wears is replaced by sadistic amusement as he watches me flail and kick my legs. My hands circle around his wrist before slapping at him to let go, but he gives my neck a jerk, smashing the back of my head against the wall, making my eyes roll back as he tightens his grip even more.

I'm dazed, head wrung, as my mouth falls open, feeling myself begin to fade. My hands slap against his wrist slower and slower until I can't lift them anymore.

"This is what it looks like to be a wolf, little girl. This is Calder's birthright. I am who he'll become. And you don't fucking change that."

He squeezes tighter, making my eyes sting from the pressure before they begin to flutter closed, lungs burning. I'm losing consciousness.

Calder.

Warm breath tickles my face before Connor suddenly lets me go, whispering, "Not yet."

I release a breath in a whoosh, sucking in another just as quickly, feeling the color drain from my cheeks. My head hangs forward, eyes watering, staring down at the sheet-thin blanket as I press my palms into the bed, trying to hold myself up.

The heavy scent of cigars makes me want to gag as Connor sits next to me, pressing a finger to my forehead and lifting my head before wiping my hair from my face.

"You can't have him. Don't you understand? His allegiance is owed to this family, not you. And yet…"

Connor searches my face, maybe because he sees I know the rest.

When push came to shove, Calder left everyone to die, for me. He never thought about his brothers or himself. Only me. I am where his loyalty lies. Not to his name or the family.

I swallow, wincing past the pain as Connor continues.

"He risked this family for some little whore he's known for ten seconds. If I didn't love my sister so much, I would've killed him for his betrayal."

My shoulders shake, staring back at him. I close my eyes, wishing that this was a nightmare.

"No, don't do that. You're braver than that. Look at me, Sutton."

My chin trembles as I reopen my eyes to his cold face. Connor reaches up, taking a strand of my hair between his fingers and lifting it to his face, and inhales.

"Tell me that you understand that you have to let him go."

I nod, exhaling ragged breaths, saying whatever he wants me to as I stare past him at the wall.

He pulls away, looking up from my hair and tsking.

"I don't believe you. Let me explain what will happen if you don't obey me."

My hair falls back against my shoulder as my eyes meet his again.

"I will gut your whole useless, shitty family and those innocent little bitch friends of yours. Do you understand? They'll die, sweetheart, one by fucking one until you submit. It would be a shame to condemn that pretty little pixie of a blonde named Piper to a life of being passed around, fucked, and used up until we stick a needle in her arm and toss her body in the trash."

A sob tries to escape my lips, but I slap my hand over my mouth.

"Calder will find you, I'm sure of that, but what I also know is that you're the only one who can end this."

My hand drops from my face.

"How am I supposed to make him believe I don't love him?"

There's no version of us where Calder could ever believe that. Connor has to know that.

"You don't have to make him believe a lie. He just needs to see that love isn't enough to make the nightmares go away."

He is enough. He's all I need. Connor knows that too. Which drives fear straight to my heart.

"What nightmares?" I say on unsteady breaths, feeling led to ask the question.

Because I feel it coming—the destruction, the desecration of our love. All the evils of the world conspiring to ruin us.

Connor smiles before it turns into a frown. He reaches into his pocket, saying, "Shh," before caging me in as I dig my heels into the mattress, trying to scoot away.

His cell phone fills his palm as he brings it from his pocket. Our eyes meet again as his other hand slaps against my forehead, holding me in place.

"Stop. What are you doing?" I shriek, but his finger pulls at the skin around my eyes to keep them open as he holds the phone in front of my face.

"Providing the nightmare. Be a good girl and watch."

I flick my eyes to the screen just as laughter sounds from the video. Two men fill the screen, one older and the other... *Oh no. Please, God. Don't let this happen.*

My head tries to tug sideways, but Connor's fingers dig into my skin, keeping me facing forward.

"I don't want to see this, please," I cry, but it falls on deaf ears.

I try to close my eyes but only manage to half blink as they begin to burn. The guys on the video are walking down into a basement.

"It's right around that corner," one of them says.

"*Where?*"

My body goes numb. I stop tensing and fighting because I know what's going to happen. I see what Connor's showing me. And the pain, the unimaginable pain that's welling inside, makes my stomach turn, bile rising in my throat.

"He'll hate you for this," I whisper, tears pouring down my face.

My vision's blurred, eyes unable to blink, but Connor still forces them open.

"Sweetheart, this wasn't me. This is your fault. This will break him because how many people have to die for your love?"

My entire body shakes as I chant, *I'm sorry*, in my mind, over and over, wishing for this to all stop. Hoping and praying that what I know is coming won't.

Calder will carry this for the rest of his life. Connor's right—all I have to do is let him see me. Because I'm not sure love *will* be enough. Not for the horror burning into my memory.

The camera pans to the right as West comes into frame, fear on his face.

He's my age. He's too young.

Please, no. No, no, no.

"*You had a job to do. Tyler told you to watch your brother and get him away from that fucking little bitch. He warned you what would happen if you didn't listen.*"

West shakes his head, hands reaching out in front of him as he backs up, pleading,

"*I didn't know he was still talking to her. I didn't know. You have to believe me. I don't want to die.*" His head swings to the right. "*Please... Pops, don't let him kill me.*"

My mouth falls open, sobbing, saying West's name through heavy tears, feeling his fear. Knowing he was alone with nobody to protect him.

Because of me.

I begin to whisper a Hail Mary because I'm hoping beyond hope that this is all a warning and not a consequence.

Until the bang.

West's body falls to the ground, a single hole burned into his forehead. I gasp, then again, catapulted into shock, hyperventilating as Connor lets me go.

My eyes squeeze shut, arms covering my head, trying to erase what I just saw. But I can't. All I see is his face when I close them.

I see West's sweet face, the floppy golden curls, and that smirk he wore like he knew a secret nobody else knew. And the way he looked at Calder like he was a god, always staring up because he wasn't quite as tall—like the little brother that tries on his big brother's clothes to pretend what it's like to be cool. He loved him so much. I saw it that day at the carnival because no matter the risk, he never stopped smiling at me as if he was happy I loved Calder.

Connor stands, silent, tapping a finger to the same place the bullet killed West.

"His brother's death is on your hands. Is that enough of a reason now?"

A hate-filled scream rips through my throat as I tilt my head back to the ceiling. Connor buttons his jacket and walks straight past all the people dressed in white, filling my room.

My mind isn't my own anymore.

People grab at my wrists, yelling, trying to calm me. But I don't care because I'm already dead.

A part of me died right there on that floor with Calder.

And the other died today.

We'll never run away. There won't be stars or blue skies filled with heavens staring down on us. All we have is death and destruction.

A life sentence, forced to survive within the absence of our love.

Calder

Chapter five

The sound of beeping feels like stabbing on the inside of my fucking ears. Like nails being hammered inside my eardrums.

I'm struggling to open my eyes, blinded by the light as my tongue darts out over my dry lips.

"Sut—" I'm trying to say her name, but only half comes out because the word scratches my throat.

"Oh shit. C—"

Footsteps gather closer to me as I blink my eyes open, everything fuzzy before slowly coming into focus.

"Nurse," I hear someone yell from my side as I shake my head, eyes closing again.

The lights are too bright. Fuck. *Where am I? What the fuck happened?*

"Sutton," I breathe out, deep and raspy.

A warm hand touches my shoulder, but I'm slow to react, lagging before turning my head to Roman's face.

Fuck, everything hurts—breathing, blinking, my whole goddamn body. What the fuck happened to me?

Roman's leaning in, staring at me.

"C, can you hear me? Can you see my face?"

I nod, feeling confused and out of focus, until a sharp pain shoots

sinning like hell 313

through me, making me groan as the beeping in the background grows faster.

"Fuck," I grunt, trying to reach for my chest, unable to because I'm caught around a mass of wires and tubes. "Romes... what is all this shit? Where's West? Tell him I need—"

My face falls heavily to my arm, seeing a needle piercing my skin along with a black band wrapped around my bicep. My eyes lift to where they're all connected, piped into machines next to my bed.

I'm in the hospital. What the fuck? The last thing I remember is Sutton. Where is Sutton?

"Get this shit off me."

Hot breath leaves my body as my mouth hangs open while I clumsily struggle to rip the tape on my arm.

"No. Dude. Don't touch. Calder. Stop."

Blood beads on my skin as the needle tugs from my veins, hitting the floor. Roman holds his hands out in front of him before running one through his hair, turning in a circle to look back at the door.

"Where the fuck is she, Roman?"

I rip the Velcro band off, and alarms begin to blare, making me wince and Roman panic.

"Brother. Come on. You gotta relax."

I blink, trying to get my bearings, feeling hazy and weak. But I don't give a fuck. If I have to crawl to her, I will.

"Sutton. I want her." I try to push myself upright, only to fall back down. "Fuck."

"Okay. Okay. But you got shot, C. Please chill. You ain't no good to anybody dead."

I got shot. Fuck. Do I remember that?

A flash of images imprisons my mind as I shake my head. They're coming on so fast it feels like the breath is knocked out of my lungs. I heave in short gasps of air as the memories descend.

Her beautiful face is so pale. All her wild hair spread out where she lay dead...pills scattered around her.

"*No,*" I rush out, loud, vibrating my rib cage as I push myself to sit, immediately feeling the pain rock my chest again.

"Goddammit," I grind out, unstopping. "Where is she?"

Roman stares back at me, and for the first time in our lives, all I see is fear on his face. Straight up fucking fear.

"Roman," I bellow. "Don't you tell me she's dead. If you say that, I'll kill you."

I hold up a hand to say something else, but I have to stop moving to catch my breath. People begin quickly filing into my room, all speaking at the same time. But my mind is only on one fucking thing. Sutton.

My head flops down as I drop an unsteady leg over the side of the bed, blood dripping down my veiny forearm.

"I have to get to her."

Someone touches my arm, but I jerk away, almost falling over.

"Where the fuck is she?" I yell through slurred words.

I blink, trying to get rid of the white dots in my vision. But they're multiplying.

Baby, I'm coming. I love you.

"Calm down, Calder" and "You need to lie down" are hurled at me. But my entire body is fueled with the rage I feel.

She almost died. All those pills...my precious fucking girl.

And it's all because of that little motherfucker Hunter, and my pops, and her fucking parents.

I already killed one of them. The rest better run.

Some asshole grabs my wrist.

"Settle down, Mr. Wolfe. You're still fresh from surgery."

I swing, hitting only air, feeling hot pokers branding me from the inside out.

My hand wraps around the hospital bed rail, holding me steady as I groan out a breath before putting my other foot on the ground. Fuck, it's so hard to breathe.

"Where's Sutton?"

The room is packed full of people, all with worried eyes fixed to me, but they don't fucking know what I'll do to every goddamn person here if I'm ignored.

"I heard her whisper my name. I know she's not dead. I've been chasing her voice back here from hell. Because no-fucking-body keeps *me* from her."

My hand curls into the sheet as I try to push to standing, bellowing my words.

"Bring me my fucking girl."

Another unbearable pain sears me, buckling my knees. Everyone lunges toward me, but it's Roman who catches me, arms wrapped around me, holding me as we sink to the ground, dragging the sheet off the bed.

"She's alive, C. She's okay, brother. I got her. Rest. You'll need your strength. Because everything after this will be a fight."

My breathing slows as he nods, repeating the last part over and over until my eyes close and all the sound fades into nothingness until I'm back, trapped inside my mind.

Swirls of black fog curl over and into itself, almost as if it's crawling toward me. It pools at my feet as I stare down into the vacant nothingness.

Where am I? What is this?

Sutton.

My head shifts around the empty void, stepping backward, but no matter which way I turn, it's all the same—endless black space vibrating with rage and hate.

This is hell.

Baby.

Frost chills my feet, rooting me in place as the dense black mist begins winding up my legs, creeping over itself to my arms, cold and blistering hot simultaneously.

It slithers and glides over my flesh, searing me as it does, scorching my skin.

I jerk my arms, but it has a hold on me, almost as if it's born from me, back to claim its space.

It wraps tightly around my neck, engulfing my face until plunging inside my mouth. My lungs feel like they're filled with tar, robbing me of any breath, drowning me in scorching liquid.

I'm devoured from the inside out by the profane feeling of desecration and violence.

But my only thought is Sutton.

I need to get to her.

I want to yell. My fists tighten as pain wracks my body, making my skin crawl and my stomach sick. Because I feel like I'm being burned alive and squeezed to death at the same time.

But I don't stop fighting, trying to reject my fate.

I hear my own words gritted between my teeth.

"She's my fate, you motherfucker, not this place."

If this is hell, the devil should worry because I won't be fucking kept from her. It's not my time to go, not when she's alive.

"I won't go."

I tense my shoulders, grinding my teeth. Devil, you can't take me from her. My eyes close, seeing her face, hearing my name whispered from her lips.

Her sweet voice fills my ears, "I love you," quelling the scorching fire inside of me as I focus on it, holding it tight inside of me like my lifeline.

All I see is her. All I want is her.

My chest begins vibrating with a rumble as I stretch my arms wide and cry, "Sutton."

Her name draws out until there's no more breath left to say it, and I fall to my knees.

The thick cloud of soot inside expels from my mouth with wicked retreat, arching my back until I fall forward onto the palms of my hands.

My head lifts as I stare into the void, kneeling before standing.

"Sutton," I breathe out again as a voice from behind whispers in my ear.

"She doesn't belong here, Devil. If you claim her, she'll be damned."

I suck in a quick breath, overcome by the pure goodness at my back. It feels like her, like love and devotion. Goodness and life.

My thoughts sound too loud, hissing in my head.

Heaven or hell. Heaven or hell. Heaven or hell.

I have to choose. My eyes close, knowing there never was a choice for us. The only place Sutton belongs is with me.

"Then let her be damned, God, because I told you. Not even you can have her."

Chapter

Six

Sutton

I t's been two full weeks since Calder was shot. Four days since I was visited by Connor. And zero hours that I've felt whole.

But how could I feel whole? Nothing will ever be the same again.

I was a dreamy girl, staring at the moon. A good girl caught halfway between childish dreams and a shiny future. Always seeing my world through rose-colored glasses.

But it was all a lie.

Everything I thought about who I was is inextricably false.

Because that's not who I really am.

I'm selfish.

Connor was right. I'm willing to do anything to keep Calder—including loving him when it means ruin.

I'm the evil.

When I close my eyes, all I see is West, with fear marking his face.

I hear the way he pleaded with his own father. Scared for his life.

But something happened to me when Connor walked away, leaving me screaming for West's life on that hospital bed.

I shattered. Crawled into a corner of myself, too scared to come out.

My eyes half blink as I stare down at my lap, almost paralyzed by my numbness. He's dead. West is dead. And all I want is Calder. I'm so scared that if I let myself really feel this...this guilt, and heartbreak—all the fucking devastation of what we've caused—I'll shatter into too many pieces that can't be put back together.

And I hate myself because I've seen that we're unholy, condemned to our family names. Destined to destroy everyone around us because our love only begets hate.

And still, I love him.

The feel of beads fills my upturned palm as I lift my eyes from the back seat of the black SUV. This morning, I was released to my parents, quietly escorted to their car, where a bag was already packed waiting inside for me.

The single bag I'm allowed to take to my new home—Madison Prep, all-girls academy.

"Why are you giving me this?" I whisper, looking up at my father's face, closing my fingers around the rosary.

"You're going to need it in a moment."

His eyes don't meet mine as he speaks. Not that I expect them to. Neither of my parents have uttered more than two words to me since I saw them this morning. But what's there to say?

They've won. I'm doing as I was told.

My brows furrow, head shifting to look out of the tinted window. I always forget how tall the buildings are and how wide the streets are in New York. It's a place you could get lost in.

I turn my head to look out of the window past my mother, suddenly feeling uneasy.

"Shouldn't we be crossing the George Washington Bridge? I thought we were flying out of Teterboro?"

My mother's profile turns to mine, eyes locked.

"We're making a stop before you fly to Madison."

My father clears his throat as I look down at my hand. My heart begins to beat faster as my eyes search my lap. *Why did he give me these?*

"Where are we going?" I say quietly but with purpose as goose bumps spread over my arms.

My mother's voice is level, calm, and filled with her distaste for me.

"To see your boyfriend."

"Room 304," my father directs.

I nod, remembering that's what the nurse said at the station when we arrived, but I'm surprised I even heard her because it's almost as if there's nothing but buzzing in my ears.

Mount Sinai is a foreboding building with cold hallways and doctors in crisp jackets. It's a place where people escape death's grip, but I feel my heartbeat slowing with each step I take down the long corridor.

I feel like I've woken up inside one of my nightmares, and I can't escape.

"To see your boyfriend," my mother said casually, like it's just another day.

Not the day they're going to force me to look at the man I love and say unspeakable things. To tell him I killed his brother. That our love is a curse. That we can never see each other again.

This moment will leave an indelible mark. One branded on our hearts, turning the memories of our first kiss into ash and our touches into regret. Because today is when I condemn us to hell.

How can I do this?

The familiar panic that's permanently settled inside of me wells. I wrap my arms around myself as I walk, trying to stave it away, digging my nails into my sides, hoping the pain will win.

I can't do this. Oh God. I can't.

My eyes blink faster. I feel light-headed.

I give my head a slight shake, taking a deep breath because I have to do this. There's no other choice. We're not strong enough to beat them, not when they'll take someone like West.

My head bows, feeling my chest shake.

This has to be goodbye.

I glance over my shoulder at my parents following behind me, eyes dropping to where my father's arm is gently tucked behind my mother's back, guiding her.

We look like a family united to anyone watching, but all I feel is hatred and sadness. For myself, for them, for everyone. But I need to hold on to the hate. I need to dig my nails in, wrapping my arms around tightly, refusing to let go.

Or this might kill me.

My head swings back, eyes ticking to the gold plaques affixed to the sides of the doors. I count them quietly to myself as I walk past. Like a countdown to a bomb exploding, the steady ticks a person would hear before they know everything they've ever known and loved is about to eviscerate.

298, 300, 302...

My chest jerks as a singular thunderous sob attempts to crack me open. My hand darts over my mouth before I look around to make sure nobody is looking as I try to slow my breathing.

You're okay. You're okay.

But I'm not.

How can I destroy him when he never did the same to me?

My eyes flick to a nurse across from me, who smiles kindly as I drag the back of my hand over my lips before smoothing my hair. Her eyes dart away as she busies herself with some folders, giving me my dignity.

I suppose I look like every other person she usually sees. But losing Calder feels bigger than death.

"Keep a hold of yourself," my mother whispers from behind as I half blink, swallowing my self-pity.

That's what it is—selfish pity for a love I can't have.

West is dead. So it's fitting our love should die too.

I swallow, closing my eyes as I push the taste of bile back down my throat, along with the sadness.

"This is it: 304," my father offers, reaching past me for the door handle, forcing me to the side.

"I hate you for this," I whisper, turning my face to my mother, feeling nothing.

Hold on to the hate, Sutton.

My mother huffs a contemptuous laugh.

"One day, you'll thank us, Sutton."

My head shakes as I answer with **nothing but h**onesty.

"The only thing I'll ever thank y**ou for is dying.**"

The heavy hospital door sweeps **open, but I st**and there still, too much of a coward to lift my head.

This is it. Our end.

The last line in the book that will **linger, leaving** its mark on my heart forever.

"Come, Sutton," my father command**s like I'm** a dog as he walks inside.

My eyes lift, locking with the face **staring back** at me from the hospital bed.

Oh my God.

My head darts back over my sho**ulder to the sm**ile on my mother's face.

"What have you done?"

She walks past me into the room, **whispering,** "What I had to do to please Connor. Just like you will."

The walls around me feel like t**hey're caving** in as my breath shortens dangerously close to a panic attack. **I search the** room, eyes darting from face to face, before landing on a man **with a pad of** paper and pen in hand.

A reporter? *Why is there a reporter here?*

I blink as a flash from a camera **catches me off** guard, making me drop my eyes and tuck my chin to my chest. **My mind** races, trying to put the pieces together as someone speaks.

"You must be so relieved, Miss **Prescott, to k**now that your boyfriend will make a full recovery. I bet he's **your hero.**"

My boyfriend? Full recovery? This isn't happening.

I dig my nails into my palms, nee**ding to feel** something visceral to pull myself back into reality as I blink **down at the floor.**

My feet are moving. I've entered **the room.**

Jesus, my body's on autopilot.

"It's not every day I get to report **a happy** ending to such a horrific beginning."

What the fuck?

My eyes dart to the unassuming **man who's** speaking, eyes narrowed, brows drawn together as I search his face. If he only knew what he was saying...the kind of disgusting fallacies he is spreading.

I want to scream at him, but my mouth won't move. I'm in shock because I know what's happening. I just can't fucking believe it.

"She's still in shock since the robbery, and with—" my father offers, not elaborating at the end.

A robbery?

Oh my God. That's their story.

The one I'm expected to bear, like a goddamn cross.

Everyone gets what they want. Connor, my parents. Tied up all nice and neat with a little bow, and I can't do anything but smile as they dredge me up to hang on that fucking piece of wood, nails in my hands, bleeding out.

I turn my head back to the hospital bed, walking closer, feeling my rage build.

"Of course, of course," the reporter responds. "I'm sure it was traumatizing seeing your boyfriend taken away by the ambulance. What was your frame of mind during that time?"

He's waiting for a response, but all I can manage is to stare forward as all the memories come crashing back to me.

Motherfucker.

Hunter's face looks almost unrecognizable, mouth swollen, cut open, and stitched back together. He's battered and bruised in deep shades of black and blue everywhere I can see.

Purple and yellow peek out from bandages on his forehead, stained from the inside out with blood. And his arm is in a cast, held up by a contraption, making it impossible for him to move from the position he's in.

Calder broke him into pieces. This is why Connor wiped him off the map.

But I have no doubt that Calder did it for me. To protect me.

My heart almost leaps out of my fucking chest as I stare into Hunter's eyes, wishing like hell that Calder had broken his neck.

Everything Hunter said that day plays like a damn record in my head.

All the vile and disgusting things he threatened, pushing me further into despair.

"We'd love a photo for the piece. It's scheduled to run on the front page...we're leading with the unfortunate sailing death of Mr. Kelly and tying in how these two brave kids have leaned on each other through tragedy. It's a real Romeo and Juliet story."

I don't turn to look at the reporter as he speaks, for fear they'll see the look on my face—morbid satisfaction.

I hope the whole Kelly family goes up in flames.

Marianne Kelly's voice fills the room, lifting my gaze. I didn't even notice her when I walked in. She's staring at me with the same hate I'm looking at her with.

"Take a photo of just their hands...joined. Hunter's been through enough. Memorializing his wounds doesn't suit the narrative," she directs, narrowing her eyes on me.

I look over my shoulder, seeing the reporter nodding vigorously before jerking his head toward Hunter and me for the photographer to get to work.

"Miss—" That's all the prompt I hear as I pick up Hunter's hand, staring into his eyes as the cameras click behind me.

Hunter's eyes search mine, but he doesn't speak. They're filled with disdain, not that anyone would notice past the blemished skin and bruises, but I see it.

I remember who you are, Hunter Kelly. And I won't forget.

My father clears his throat. "Sutton, you wanted to say a prayer for Hunter, remember?"

The side of my lip tugs into a grin.

Such a masterful manipulation they've conspired. The world will see me on my knees, at Hunter's bedside, praying for a love that doesn't exist.

Our families linked forever. And Calder, a ghost.

I reach into the pocket of my pants, pulling out my rosary, letting my thumb skim over the beads before staring into Hunter's eyes.

I don't have to look behind me to see the smug mask of victory my parents are wearing. Because it's in front of me, on Marianne Kelly's face.

No one's asking the right questions or second-guessing the story because they've handed the world precisely what it devours. A fairy tale.

Except everyone here is a fucking villain backed by the devil himself.

My hand rests against the mattress as I lower myself slowly to kneel at the side of Hunter's bed, bringing the rosary to my lips as I close my eyes.

Clicks of the camera go off in a flurry as I silently say the last prayer to God I will ever make.

Our Father who art in heaven. You abandoned me. Left me to this cruelty. You've taken the only man I love from me and allowed innocent people to be punished in the name of their hate. So this is the last time I'll pray to your name. If you're real, if you ever loved me, then commit Hunter to hell. And let them burn with him.

My eyes open, palms pressing to the bed as I stand, retaking Hunter's hand and wrapping my rosary around it. I lean down to his ear, whispering so that only he can hear.

"I wish he'd killed you. And one day, Hunter—he will. *That* was my prayer to God. For you to burn in hell."

The hate in his eyes follows me as I pull away. But I smile, lifting his battered hand to my lips, pressing a kiss to the top before saying,

"Amen."

Calder

Chapter seven

My body's sore as I blink, bringing my hand to my chest. I don't know how long I've been asleep since the last time I woke up ready to brawl, but the hot pokers inside of me aren't there anymore.

"Nice to have you back, brother."

My head swings to where Roman's watching me from a brown leather chair in the corner of the room. The last time I saw his face, I was falling to the goddamn floor while he warned me about what was coming.

"How long have I been..." I trail off, looking around, realizing I don't know where the fuck I am, as he finishes my thought.

"New York-Presbyterian."

My eyes lock to his again as he says, "It's been three weeks, five days, and a couple of hours."

Three fucking weeks?

I run my hands through my hair, taking a deep breath.

"What do you remember?"

"Everything," I level, throwing back the blanket. "How come I'm not in cuffs?"

I push into a sitting position and swing my legs over the side of the bed. But Roman stands, patting the air with his hand.

"Whoa. C, you need to take it easy."

Fuck taking it easy. I'm going to get my girl.

My head shakes as I rip off a black band that's Velcroed around my arm.

"You need to get me some clothes." My hand drops to the hospital gown I'm in. "This shit ain't gonna fly when I walk outta here."

Roman closes the distance between us, and my head draws back.

He looks like he hasn't slept in weeks; his clothes are rumpled and disheveled. But that's not what's hitting me hard in the gut.

Roman's staring at the ground as if he can't look at me—shoulders turned in, hands shoved into his pockets.

My brother looks fucking defeated. And that's not something he's ever carried.

"What the fuck is going on, Roman? Tell me she's okay. Because I swear to fucking God—"

An unfamiliar feeling courses through me as I take a step forward. It's fear.

I'm scared to death something's happened to her. And it fucking shreds me. I'll never fucking forgive myself if... No. Fuck no, I can't think about it, or I'll lose my mind.

Roman nods. "She's alive. They've got her upstate at some fucking prep school called Madison. And you ain't in cuffs because of Connor."

I nod, fully understanding Connor pulled major strings to keep my ass out of jail. Strings that will come with shit attached. But right now, I don't care about that. I just need to get to her.

"C, a lot of shit went down that day. You need to chill because what I gotta say—"

He exhales harshly, not finishing his thought, as I take another step, pulled backward by the needle stuck in my vein. I grab the line, yanking it from my arm before tossing the whole thing on the bed.

"You can fill me in while we drive."

"Stand fucking still, Calder," he barks, drawing my eyes. "I gotta say this...fuck, how do I say this..."

Roman runs his hand over his head, shaking it before he drops his eyes, mouth opened.

"What the fuck is going on, Roman? Spit it out."

He can't even look at me. His hand grips the back of his neck as he speaks.

"It's my fault. I shouldn't have left him alone."

Oh, Roman. Don't say that. Oh fuck.

Rage courses through me. My mind pleads with itself. Begging for what I'm thinking not to be true. But as Roman looks up, the fucking devastation on his face fills every fucking pore of my body as my teeth grind.

My fingers curl over the side rail on my bed, squeezing so hard that pain shoots up my forearm. I raise the bed, letting it drop with a bang.

"*Who?* Who did you leave alone?"

Roman doesn't answer as he lets out a heavy breath. That look, it takes me back to when we were children.

To when we were twelve, and he'd found out his father died. It didn't matter that the dude was a deadbeat who'd abandoned him. Roman felt responsible. Like he could've somehow saved him if he was just better. He's worn that shame for the rest of his life.

And that's the look he has on his face right now. Like he should've been better.

"West was found—"

I take a step backward, colliding into the machines behind me, hit in the chest like that fucking bullet with his words. Shit falls, crashing to the ground around me as I try to steady my feet before pushing off something hard next to me. The heavy equipment careens to the floor with a thunderous bang.

"No." My head shakes as I stab a finger at him. "You shut the fuck up. No."

He doesn't stop though, pulling his hands from his pockets, wiping them down his face as he steps toward me.

"His body was dumped on the side of Highway 27."

"Goddamn you," I grind out, feeling like I'm out of breath as I bring a fist to my forehead. "He was fine, Roman. He was going to be fine."

Roman's shoulders shake as he blows out an unsteady breath, eyes locked to mine.

"We take care of him, Romes," I growl, turning toward the heavy metal at my back.

I'm wild, murderous, destroying anything I can get my hands on.

A crash echoes through the room as I hurl machine after machine to the floor before pitching a metal rod holding an empty bag of fluid across the room, bellowing, "No."

The hospital door flies open, but Roman pulls his gun.

"Get the fuck out. He does what he needs to do."

My fists hurl against the wall, denting the drywall as I grunt and growl. I want to hit something until it's destroyed. Because that's what I am. Fucking destroyed.

My brother is dead. He's fucking dead.

And it's my fault.

"I did this. I fucking did this," I shout, feeling the wall give under my fist. "It wasn't supposed to be him. Not because of me."

Roman catches my arm as I connect a fist to the wall again, jerking me toward him.

I shove him away, but he fights to pull me back, gripping the back of my neck. We're eye to eye, pain to pain as he presses his forehead to mine.

"You gotta let it hurt, C. I got you. I got you. You can let it hurt."

My arms raise at my sides as my mouth opens, growling the pain of this loss, wishing I could make it all right. Knowing I fucking can't.

"Fuccckkk," I grind out, body shaking. "It wasn't supposed to be him, Romes. Not him. I was supposed to protect—"

My body shudders as wetness coats my face, the rest of my words turning into sobs. Men don't cry. That's what everyone always says, but I'm not crying. I'm weeping. Hoping that if I suffer enough, he won't ever have to.

If I couldn't protect him in this life, then I'll give a pound of flesh to protect his soul.

Roman holds me as I grieve. He doesn't move as I begin to shout again, throwing my fists against him, cursing God and myself until my arms can't move anymore.

We stay there, locked together, because we're all we have.

My head falls against his shoulder, muscles weak. He wraps his arms around me tighter.

"Pops put a bullet in his head because West protected you. But his death isn't your fault, C. You can't carry that. This life ate him up, but seeing you and her together—that was what he talked about all the time when you weren't around. It's like he never knew people like us could be loved like that. He saw the change in you. We both did. That is what you gave him, not death. So don't you fucking dare turn your back on him now. He wanted you to live, C. You gotta do that for him. Swear to me, Calder. I fucking mean it. You don't let his death be in vain."

I pull away, staring at Roman, holding back the overwhelming agony I feel, burying it deep inside of me so it can fuel the anger I'll need.

"I'll make every single one of them pay, Roman. They'll suffer for what they've done to West and to us. I swear that to you."

He nods, stepping back away from me. Both of us take deep breaths, owning the men we are and what we have to be, before he says, "Let's get you to your girl. Because everything after this is gonna be a fight."

Those words echoed from before fill me with purpose. I know exactly what I need to do because nobody will ever take another person I love again. If death and destruction are my destiny, then I'm ready.

"First we see Sutton, and then we find Pops."

All it is, is dark outside. No lights, just sky. I don't think there are even stars out as we drive down the highway, windows down to try to mask the sound of my ragged breaths.

He's dead.

My brother is dead.

Roman was right. This life eats us up. But I should've saved him. I should've done what I needed to do, claimed my birthright, been the man I was born to be. Because then none of this shit would've happened.

I roll my window up as Roman glances over.

"You good?"

"Tell me everything I don't know."

His hands grip the steering wheel harder.

"C—"

He only gets my name out before I repeat myself.

"Tell me everything I don't fucking know."

The car slows, pulling to a stop as he shifts to look at me.

"All right, but you gotta stay chill."

I know he means because of my stitches and shit, so I nod.

"Fuck." He breathes, rubbing his shaved head before he lays it out. "Connor's working with her parents. He owns the fucking senator now, and Kelly's wife was happy to step into place. And...Hunter's alive."

"The fuck he is. I beat that little bitch to death."

"No, you didn't. He made it. Barely. But he did. And *he's* their story— they made her pray at his bedside. Put that shit in the papers, called them a Romeo and Juliet story because he saved her from some bullshit break-in. That's the take, man. They're linked."

My vision blurs, black spots appearing in front of me before my fists hurl into the dash over and over as I growl.

"Fuck."

Roman lets me explode, staying quiet as I heave breaths staring into the darkness behind the windshield.

"What else?" I grind out.

Roman hesitates then locks eyes with mine. "Connor showed her West. He has a video that Pops shot of..." His face drops, and I squeeze my fists so hard pain shoots up my forearms before he takes a breath and finishes.

"He showed her. Threatened her friends, her life, yours. He told her she had to walk away. And he ain't playing."

"And he told you everything to make sure I got the message."

Roman nods.

My hands wipe down my face as my body stills. Because I know what I have to do. And so will she. I can't just kill all of them, because Connor's made it clear that I can't run from my birthright. There'll always be a bounty on my head. We'd never know freedom.

"I'm gonna end this, Roman. For all of us. But I'm gonna kill them all for her."

Calder

My head hangs, feeling the weight of my love crushing me as I stand in Sutton's moonlit dorm room, staring down at her sleeping body.

She's thinner, shadows under her eyes, hands tucked under her chin like she's haunted even in her sleep.

I did this to her.

Fuck. The shit she's endured, all the fucking pain she's gone through over the last few weeks. And I couldn't save her...or West.

I lift my head to the ceiling, still feeling raw over my brother as I grind my teeth together.

If I ever deserved any goodness, God...give it all to her.

I blow out a breath and open my eyes, looking around the room. The thought of her stuck in this fucking place with no pictures of her friends on the walls and only an empty twin bed across from her makes me want to burn it down and steal her away.

She shouldn't be here. *Goddammit.* She should be staring at the stars, red hair blowing in the wind with that fucking gleam in her eye that's a little bit trouble and a little bit heaven.

My hand wipes over my mouth, thumb carrying away a stray drop of grief falling down my cheek.

"I'm so fucking sorry I failed you. But I'll never do it again."

I think back to everything Roman told me as we drove here. The fucking details were like a knife to the heart.

He was right to do it. To be straight, no watering shit down. Because my brother knows I'll need that hate to have what I want. But every hour felt like torture because I gathered more and more rage, knowing I'd have to let it eat its way through me, patiently waiting until I could make them all pay.

Pay for every goddamn indiscretion and sin against her—from the psych ward to her parents working with Connor.

I'll make them eat their fucking tongues for the lies they told her, and destroy their goddamn names. Until they're splashed all over the front pages like that bullshit story about Hunter saving her.

And the next time I see him, I'll put a gun in Hunter Kelly's fucking mouth and make sure I do the job right.

Sutton rustles, sighing in her sleep. She rolls onto her side, gorgeous red hair spilling over her pillow, making her look like a fucking angel. Because that's what she is.

My angel.

Fuck me. I want to scoop her up in my arms and kiss every fucking place she hurts until all that's left is the wet imprint of my mouth on her flesh. I lean down, drawn into her as my eyes drift over her neck.

"Baby," I whisper.

My knees feel weak, palms coming to the mattress as I drop down to them, staring at faded scratches on her neck, darkened by faint bruises. My fingertips hover, scared to touch her because she might hurt, before they curl into fists, lowering down to the bed.

Anger boils inside my veins because I know this is Connor. He marked her, put the bruises here for me, as a reminder of my place.

He'll hurt the worst.

He threatened to take everything from her, but by the time he notices that I've done the same to him, it'll be too late.

Fuck. I can barely breathe. I'm gonna gut him from dick to throat for touching my precious girl.

"Baby." My voice breaks as I lean in, pressing a kiss to her lips. Anger and love are at war within me. "He'll find no peace in this life or after. I promise you that."

My head bows, eyes closing as I stay knelt in front of her, rocked by the fucking war inside of me. By all the goddamn love I feel for this girl.

How do I leave her alone?

I lift my head, ready to kiss her again but not ready to say goodbye as shiny emerald jewels framed by thick black lashes stare back at me.

All the air inside my body is robbed from me.

She blinks, unbelieving, like she can't trust her own eyes. Slowly, almost too cautiously, her hand comes to my beard. It's as if she's afraid I'll disappear, a shaky breath leaving her gorgeous lips.

"You're here."

Aw, fuck. That voice. It guts me, cracks me right the fuck open. My eyes close as my lips part, feeling like I just took my first real breath as she says, "I'm not dreaming?"

"No, baby," I whisper, bringing my eyes back to her. "I'm here."

We stare at each other, the world drifting away, not saying a fucking word. Hands brush over cheeks and palms press to faces, needing to feel the warmth on our skin to prove we're not in another fucking dream. One that'll become a nightmare the minute we wake up.

A tear from her eye pools against my hand before flowing over my skin as her shoulders shake. Her eyes drop, as if she suddenly feels the weight of the world on her shoulders.

Because she does. I see it in her eyes—the fucking agony and torment she's wearing over West.

"Calder..." Her voice is so shaky she can barely get her words out. "West—oh God..."

Her face draws in, devastated as I gather her hands between mine, pressing kisses to her palms.

"No," I growl. "That shit isn't your fault. Don't you fucking do that."

My face raises to hers, my hands cradling her face.

"Look at me. I know what Connor did. What you saw. I'm gonna make him pay for it. But baby, *they* took West. Not you. Not us. You understand me?"

Her voice is so quiet, so fucking delicate and raw that it cuts me open.

"I'm sorry. I'm just so sorry. I'm a curse."

I wipe my thumbs over her reddened face, bringing my lips close to hers, brushing over them with mine as I speak, the taste of salt lingering between them.

"I love you, Sutton. *You're* my magic. My forever, baby. Don't take that away from me."

She lets out a breath, fingers crawling along my jaw, pulling me closer.

"I love you too. So fucking much."

My mouth seals over hers, holding still, only for a moment, letting the divinity of her taste fill my body like my communion as her tongue dips inside my mouth.

I tilt my head, drawing her bottom lip between mine, letting it drag out. I'm high on her after one hit. We kiss like we're starved for each other, needing another taste, just to satisfy the hunger.

This is heaven. And she's the only version I'll ever want.

She blinks up, breathless, as I pull back, her words rushing out.

"I thought I'd lost you, Calder. I was so scared."

I grip the nape of her neck, pulling her forehead to mine, hating how strong she had to be as I grit my words out.

"Not even death, baby. Not even then."

She pushes her mouth back to mine, tongues dancing, craving more, as I grip her hair, wanting to devour her. To kiss her senseless. I love this girl so fucking much that nothing else matters—not her family or her friends.

I'd let them all die tomorrow to keep her.

A quiet moan pulls from her throat as her tongue licks over mine, her back arching toward me. The kiss grows faster, our heads tilting, lips crushing against each other.

I kiss her like it's the first time, rough, soaked in need.

Because I want it to last. Forever. *Fuck.* I feel rooted in place, knelt by the side of her bed, hands in her hair, pulling her closer. And floating all at the same time.

The taste of salt coats my lips, seeping into our mouths. She's crying.

I start to pull away, but she grabs the sides of my face, keeping me in place, breathing ragged breaths against my lips.

"What's going to happen to us?" she whispers.

I'll never lie to her. But I wish I could.

I press my lips to hers one more time, closing my eyes as I answer.

"You're always mine, baby. Even in goodbye."

Her breath hitches as her hands shake. *Fuck.*

"You're my home, Sutton," I whisper, slowly pulling back. I put my hands over hers and look into her eyes. "And I'll always come back. But we can't have magic and forever until *I* make the rules. Until *I'm* king."

A sob shudders through her chest before she shakes her head, growling no. My heart is physically fucking breaking, but she knows this is the only way. This is how I protect her and give her what she wants—our future.

She takes a deep breath, dragging her hands away from under mine before wiping them over her wet cheeks. Our eyes stay locked as I watch the girl I love trying to become the woman she'll need to be.

"Sutton," I whisper, wanting to tell her everything will be okay, but she shakes her head, bringing a finger to my lips.

"I would wade through hell to be with you, Calder. No matter how long it takes."

This beautiful fucking girl is stronger than she'll ever know. Everything I do for the rest of my fucking life will always be for her.

"And if we only had tonight—" she breathes.

I push her hand out of the way, grabbing her lip, and tug her mouth to mine, kissing the fuck out of her.

"Then it would be worth it."

Chapter nine

Sutton

Calder's palms press into the bed, pushing him back to standing as he stares down at me.

My bottom lip folds between my teeth, then drags out slowly, and my chest rises and falls quickly as I sit up.

This is our goodbye.

I reach for him, grabbing his belt with my hands as I tuck my knees underneath me so that I'm kneeling on the bed.

"Don't go. Please. Don't leave me yet."

He lets out a heavy breath, dropping his eyes to the floor for the longest second before meeting mine again.

"Baby, I'm not anywhere near brave enough to walk out that fucking door with you watching me."

The way he says it like he can barely get the words out past his emotions almost makes me break. Calder reaches behind him, dragging his shirt over his head.

God, he looks so strong, untouched by death, but I remember how close he came.

I lift my hand to the bandage covering the right side of his chest before leaning in to press a kiss to it.

"I'm okay," he offers, voice low and gravelly. He runs his hand down the side of my head, tucking my hair behind my ear.

But I'm still staring at the white square piece of gauze taped neatly over his pec, suddenly remembering every detail of that day. My lips part, needing air, feeling the familiar panic buzzing over me as I whisper to myself, "How am I going to exist without you?"

Calder gently grips my jaw, bringing my face to his, our eyes locked.

"You don't. There is no fucking difference between where I begin and you end. Not now, not ever. So we'll do what we have to so that we survive until we're together again."

He leans in, brushing his lips to mine so gently it makes my soul cry. My hands run up his chest, resting on the sides of his neck as he speaks against my jaw between dragging long kisses over my skin.

"It doesn't fucking matter what happens in the in-between, Sutton. Because I've seen the world without you, baby." His eyes meet mine. "And on my fucking life, we won't die before I know it with you again."

I suck in a breath, holding back more tears that are begging to fall.

"Promise on us," I whisper.

He's staring down at me with those blue eyes, piercing and haunted, not answering, making my chin quiver. A deep v cuts his brows as I shake my head.

My lips part, but before I can speak, he growls, grabbing my hand before forcing me to stand quickly.

"C'mere."

Calder steps backward, eyes on mine as I follow, our arms outstretched.

He stops in front of the bay window on the far side of my room. I blink up as Calder draws back the heavy polyester navy curtains, letting in all the moonlight.

My eyes glisten as I stare out at the night sky. The moon is full and bright, tucked high in the sky, shining down on our faces and bathing us in cool light.

"You want me to promise? I'll do you one better, baby."

My face turns back to his as he takes my other hand. We stand facing each other, fingers interlaced, silent as the world cracks and breaks away around us, leaving only the stars and that moon.

His voice is quiet and deep, filled with the reverence of his love as he stares down at me.

"You told me once that this moon was a curse. You remember that?"

I smile weakly, biting my bottom lip, and I glance over as he continues.

"But I don't think it is. I think its magic is only for us. It was waiting for us to find each other. That's why it felt unlucky before."

His face is so earnest as he says it that I'm stripped of all my fears of the future. None of them matter because he is love, and he is mine.

A tear escapes, running down my face as I look into his eyes.

Calder blows out a shaky breath, eyes dropping to the floor, squeezing my hands tighter. His ocean-colored eyes, banked in the moonlight, lift to mine again as he speaks.

"I vow to always love you above all others. No matter what."

I blink as my heart races, realizing what he's doing. I'm almost unable to speak because his love is so big, so all-consuming that I drown in it.

My lips part, but only a shaky breath comes before he smiles down at me. Before he says anything else, I repeat his vow back to him as my own.

"I vow to always love *you* above all others. No matter what."

He brings my hands to his lips, kissing one, then the other before pressing them against his cheek.

"I will always protect you, even with my life."

My shoulders shake because I know he will. Always. He drops my hands back down, still holding them.

"And I will always protect you, even against yourself."

I lick my lips, tasting the saltiness left behind from my tears.

He lifts his hands to my face, cradling my cheeks. "I promise to die by your side when we're wrinkly and fucking gray. So that we'll never be apart again."

My hands grip his forearms to give me the strength not to fall to my knees as I stare up into his eyes.

"And I promise to love you even after death."

His lips come to mine, breathing his words against them, leaving them to burn into my heart.

"I'm yours. And you are mine. Not even death does us part."

"Forever," I whisper back, leaning into his kiss.

But this isn't just a kiss. It's the consecration of our love—our vows.

A declaration to the universe that we're fated and nothing can keep us apart. Our mouths meet again, reverently, lip over lip, as we fall into each other deeper. Existing only for one another.

No end, no beginning.

I don't know how much time will pass before I see him again, but I know deep down in my soul that I will.

And that's all I need.

Calder

ten

I'm struck silent, too filled with emotion to open my fucking mouth.
Because I love her down to the depths of my soul.
So fucking much that it makes me dangerous.

One day I'm gonna say these vows to her in front of a goddamn priest. But if I open my mouth right now and try to say that, I'll just take everything back that I shouldn't.

I'll tell her that we're running away and leaving the animals to fight it out alone.

That's how fucking wicked this girl holds my heart.

I already lost one brother, and I'm mired in fucking guilt and still only a breath away from risking another.

Those eyes stare up at me, begging for things she shouldn't, saying it all with a bat of her lashes as she licks her lips.

"Tell me what you want, baby. Because tonight I'll give you everything."

Sutton reaches down between us, fingers coming to my belt, making the metal clank as she pulls the leather from the clasp. It falls open as we stay locked on each other, feeling the crackle of energy that passes between us.

Fuck. The connection I have with her is palpable, as if it vibrates off us.

Soul mate would be the easy word, but what I feel is deeper. I recog-

342   *sinning like hell*

nize *my* soul in *her*. Like it's split between us, and we're only whole when we're together.

My hips jerk as she pulls at the top button of my pants, unfastening my Dickies, saying nothing and everything all at once.

Her hands still as she blinks up at me.

"I want *us*, Calder. It felt like there was nothing between us when we did this before. We didn't have to be strong or brave. We were just raw, stripped down, and so in love. I want to feel that, the real us, before all the fucking tragedy. I just want to be that girl that gets stars and magic, just one more time before we say goodbye."

Only the sound of my zipper crackling open echoes around the room as I lean down, cradling her head in my hand, lips so close to kissing that our breath mingles, hot and fevered.

"No goodbyes. Ever."

If she wants magic, that's exactly what I'll give her.

She starts to tug at my pants, but I grab her hands, pulling back and shaking my head.

"Naw, you know better. That was your first lesson. You first. You're always first."

My pants hang on my hips as I bring a finger to the strap of her sheer tank top, lowering one side before brushing my lips over her shoulder.

I drag my lips, across her clavicle, listening as her breathing picks up as I nudge the other strap down with my mouth.

"Calder."

I know, baby. I got you.

My lips travel up her neck, holding her at the nape, fingertips weaving through the red strands as her head falls back. I lick and suck my way under her chin, feeling goose bumps spread against my lips.

"Tonight, we do it all. I'm gonna touch, lick, and fuck every part of you, Sutton. You want stars, then I'll make you see 'em."

She's breathing so hard she's almost panting as she answers, "Yes."

My lips meet hers again before letting her go, bringing my hand to the front of her tank. It's draped over the tops of her tits, straps hanging down, nipples pebbled underneath.

"Where should I kiss first?" I rasp, dragging my hand over the soft material, exposing what's underneath.

The slip of cotton falls to her waist, but her eyes never leave mine. She stands stock-still, letting my eyes drift over her gorgeous body as she draws her bottom lip between her teeth, pulling her arms from the straps.

Fuck, she's beautiful, skin kissed with freckles, eyes so green they're hypnotizing, and nipples begging for my mouth.

I step in closer, our bodies almost flush. The feel of her skin grazing mine as we stand there feels like streaks of fire searing us with every brush.

My hand comes to her face, cradling it as I drag my thumb over her bottom lip.

"Should I kiss your mouth first?"

Her tongue darts out, licking the pad of my finger, making me freeze. I press it past her lips, slowly dipping into her warm mouth, letting her lips close around my knuckle.

"Suck."

A groan rumbles in my throat, watching her full lips drag over my skin as she hollows her cheeks and her head bobs forward.

My cock strains against my boxer briefs, wanting free from behind my low-hung pants. My beautiful girl might just fucking kill me tonight.

It's a death I'd welcome.

I reach between us, bringing my middle finger to the space between her tits, tracing a line down her stomach torturously slow. Soft skin pebbles under my touch as I run all the way down past her belly button, dipping just inside the band of her panties.

She grabs my wrist, twisting her head before running her tongue up the underside of my thumb.

"Someone misses my cock in their mouth. Is that what you want? To be on your knees, swallowing me back?"

She moans as I shove my hand all the way inside her underwear, cutting through her silky patch of hair, parting it as I glide over her clit. Her mouth falls open as she gasps, letting go of my thumb. I move my hand to her neck, lifting her chin as our eyes lock.

"You first. Remember." I circle my middle finger slowly, bringing another next to it as her hips move with me. "I kiss *her* first."

"Oh my God," she breathes as I stare down at her.

Our bodies are so close that my arm brushes against her stomach as I rub circles on her needy clit.

My bottom lip draws between my teeth, then glides out slowly, mesmerized by this beauty.

"Calder," she whispers. "Oh fuck."

Her body jerks, stomach contracting as I pick up my pace, rubbing the swollen bud faster. She's gripping my arms, circling her hips, as slickness coats my fingers.

"Fuck. Do you feel that?" I groan. "You're fucking soaked and throbbing. Do you know how hard it fucking makes me knowing that your pussy begs for me?"

She'll never understand the possession I feel. The straight up fucking dominance she breathes into me every fucking time she quivers under my touch.

I'm an animal stripped down to my basest fucking instincts.

I don't give a fuck how long we're apart. If any man touches her, I'll take their hands, then their life.

Her hips rock forward, eyes closed as I slow my hand and change my rhythm, dragging my fingers up and down each time a little closer to her entrance.

"Oh. My. God."

Sutton's mouth hangs open, staring into my eyes. Her tits are on display, swaying with her movement as my hand moves so slow, so leisurely, teasing under the panties that it's almost cruel.

"Fuck me," she rushes out, rocking her hips forward as my finger rims her entrance. "Please."

I press a finger inside, lips tugged up at the side as she gasps, squeezing around me.

"Yeah, baby. Tell me how good it feels."

"So good," she mewls, back arched, smashing my arm between us.

My words growl out as I move my hand off her neck, weaving into her hair, thrusting two fingers inside her.

"How fucking good?"

"Oh fuck" bursts from her lips, but my mouth seals over hers, tongue dipping inside her mouth, hungry for her pleasure.

Her arms wrap around my neck as I devour her, the sound of my fingers fucking her wet pussy echoing around the room.

"Fuck me," she says in a ragged breath against my lips.

"Come, baby. Then I'll fuck you. So it doesn't hurt."

She grabs the side of my face, holding us almost nose to nose, our lips almost touching as she opens her legs wider.

Goddamn. I wanna fuck every hole. Brand her so everyone knows she's mine. That's how fucking deep I feel.

My fingers dip in and out of her pussy, palm rubbing over her clit, our bodies flush as she pants, looking into my eyes.

"That's it. Feel it, baby. Open those legs, and let me fuck that sweet pussy."

Her lips quiver as her body tenses.

"Ohmygod. Ohmygod."

Her pussy contracts around my fingers before her mouth opens against mine.

"I'm...I'm..."

Stuttered breaths gather as her eyes open wide. She grips the sides of my face, her entire body contracting as she drags out my name before she squeezes them shut, a whoosh of air warming my cheek.

A gush of warmth releases, filling her panties up over her clit, onto my palm.

My eyes close along with hers because it's the sexiest fucking thing I've ever felt. My forearm slows until it's not moving, veins bulging.

I drag my hand out of her panties as she sucks a hiss between her teeth, letting go of me. Her eyes are heavy, chest rising and falling as I stare down at my fingers.

I'm covered in her. My fingers glisten in the moonlight as I raise them to my lips, eyes fixed on hers as I push them inside my mouth, dragging them back out, licking her clean off me.

"More," I grunt, hands coming to her waist, forcing her back as I drop to my knee, mouth assaulting her thigh.

She gasps, contracting over me as I drag my tongue up her thigh, devouring her pleasure.

"Hold still. I'm not fucking done."

Chapter eleven

Sutton

His mouth closes over my sensitive clit as my fingers run through his hair, gripping it as I try to step back. But he paws at me, pulling me closer, licking and sucking as I squirm.

"Oh my God. Calder, I can't take it," I rasp, bringing one hand down hard against his shoulder.

"Mine," he growls, doubling me over again.

He's an animal, dropped down to his knee in front of me, eating my pussy as I gasp for air. A slight squeal pulls from my throat as I feel him nip my inner thigh before his hands fall from my waist.

Calder stands, broad shoulders covered in tattoos, stomach muscles so hard they look flexed as he stares down. I'm panting, eyes on his, dwarfed by his size, as he wipes an arm across his mouth and reaches for me.

"C'mere."

His mouth crashes down against mine, letting me taste myself as he swirls his tongue over mine.

We're kissing frantically, as his palms hold the sides of my face. My fingertips press into his skin, gripping his hips as my feet are forced backward, each step mirroring his forward ones.

The back of my knees hit the bed, buckling as we topple down onto the mattress.

"Oh shit."

He catches us, palm pressed to the bed, softening our fall as his mouth chases me. I scoot backward, tongues dancing, lips gliding, breathless.

"Fuck, baby."

I feel it too. We're an explosion of emotion, feeling everything that's been embedded inside us like shrapnel. We're hands grabbing, nails scraping over the flesh as his hard body smothers my petite frame.

We're fucking brutal and violent, grinding against each other as my hips lift, rocking forward, dragging up his length.

"You keep doing that, and I'm gonna fuck that tight little pussy until it screams and cries thick tears all over my cock."

My eyes roll back as he licks his lips before mine part, voice husky in a way that it only gets when I want him to do dirty shit to me.

"Fuck me, Calder. Make me scream."

He exhales heavily, running his rough hand up the side of my body.

"Aw fuck, baby. My good girl's bad. Real fucking bad."

My head falls back, chin tipped to the ceiling as his lips drag roughly across my neck. His hips press forward, making my swollen clit throb.

I reach down, hand rubbing the imprint of his cock behind his boxer briefs.

"Only for you...and always for you."

Calder stills. He's hovered over me, staring so intensely into my eyes that it feels like we're sucked into an alternate universe where only we exist.

Neither of us move, overwhelmed by what we feel.

It's possession. I know because I feel it too. No matter how long we're apart, we'll only ever exist for each other.

No man will touch me. And no woman will ever touch him.

We just stay locked on each other as everything passes between us, all the love we feel, the devotion. Flashes of moments I'll never forget mix with heavy grief over what we're losing.

"I love you, Calder. Forever."

He lowers himself down, kissing me softly before whispering against my lips.

"It'll always be you, Sutton. You're mine, and I'm yours."

My fingertips dip inside the band of his underwear, dragging them over his ass as he holds himself up with one arm, helping me with the other. He kicks them off, leaving us naked, his cock nestled against my wet pussy.

I moan as my hips rock forward, legs wrapping around him. Our noses brush as Calder reaches down, positioning himself at my entrance.

But he doesn't move, bringing his eyes back to mine.

They're so full of love that it takes my breath away. *This is magic.* He's all the fucking magic, and it hurts how much I fucking love him.

I claw at his lower back, pulling him closer, lifting my hips as I do, desperate for him to make me feel something other than the sadness welling inside.

"Never goodbye," he whispers.

A shaky breath leaves my body as I nod. "Never."

Calder fills me. A tear rolls down my cheek as I suck in a harsh breath, saying, "Yes."

I'm stretched by his cock, the fullness felt in my stomach.

My body arches off the bed, hands on his shoulders as my eyes lift to the ceiling. He groans, seated deep inside of me, holding there, his eyes lidded as if he's taken a hit.

He pulls out only halfway before pushing back in, inch by fucking inch, making me lift my hips, begging for more.

"Baby, your pussy is heroin. Pure unadulterated fucking heroin. And I'll never get enough."

My hands roam gently over his chest as he leans down, bringing his mouth over my beaded nipple.

"Don't stop," I whine, pressing my tits forward.

My hips rise to meet his as he reaches behind, grabbing my knees, spreading me wide. Calder raises his body, fucking me slowly, pulling his cock to the very edge of my entrance before sinking back inside.

His eyes bore into mine as his veiny shaft drags in and out, glistening from my cum.

"Fuck. You're so tight. Touch yourself, baby."

I'm heady off the feel of his cock filling me as I stroke my clit, hips circling.

Calder's ass caves in with each thrust as we stare at each other, his rhythm gathering speed until his hips pump forward with so much force that he shakes the bed.

His fingers dig into my thighs as his jaw grinds. And my fingers move faster, gliding around my juices, before lifting my hand to his lips, watching as he runs his tongue over the pads of my fingers.

"Yeah, baby. Gimme that pussy."

Fuck. We're so intensely connected, his blue eyes so hypnotizing, it's as if the edges are blurred around us.

Our bodies are flush, already thick with sweat as we fuck.

"It'll never be enough." He groans.

Calder grabs my free hand, pinning it above my head, falling over me.

The smell of sex is thick in the air, like a fog. And the sound of our bodies slapping fills the room as he breathes heavily, mouth hung open.

I pull my hand from between us, letting that sacred space between his abs and cock create friction.

"Yes. God, yes."

His mouth closes around my nipple again, sucking the tender bud as he fucks me hard.

We're building, combusting, clawing our way toward release. His mouth leaves my nipple with a pop as he presses my wrist harder against the bed, tucking his other hand under my lower back. My hips lift as his cock pushes inside.

"Calder," I moan.

The feeling is indescribable. My mouth falls open as my eyes roll back, and my stomach tightens. Calder holds me in place, grunting, strumming something deep inside of me again and again.

"Oh...I'm..."

Everything inside of me explodes.

"Oh God," I scream, muffled by his mouth.

I'm coming. Stars in my eyes, my entire body lit up like a firework. He drops my hips, digging his foot into the bed as he grips my thigh, pulling it up over his hip, grinding into me so deep that I suck in a breath.

"Oh fuck, I'm coming," he grits out, rutting into me one more time.

My pussy strangles his cock as he jerks, coming so hard that no sound falls from my lips.

I'm silently shaking, with my hand fisted against his back.

His pants fill my ear as he drops his face to the side of mine, breathing hard. My arm is freed, so I wrap my arms around his neck, gently peppering kisses to the side of his face.

We stay like that until his arm gives, smothering me with his full weight.

Calder rolls to the side, taking me with him, draping my leg over him so he stays inside of me.

I tuck myself in close to his chest, kissing the bandage again.

His breathing slows, as does mine. But neither of us speak. Maybe he's as scared as I am.

"Say something," I whisper against his sweaty skin, tasting the salt as I kiss his chest. "Tell me what you're thinking."

He shakes his head, licking his lips. I nudge my nose against him, seeing a sad grin grace his face.

"I wish I wasn't a fucking criminal."

The memory of him sitting across from me in that confessional flits through my mind. Two people damned by our families, doomed to end tragically, unable to walk away.

He exhales, brushing his fingertips up and down my arm.

"What are you thinking?"

I scoot closer, feeling him drift out from inside of me. And something feels so sad about that. Like every connection we have is falling away.

"That I'm a liar."

His eyes close. "We're back where we started."

Calder pulls me closer, shoving his arm under me, hugging me so tight that I almost can't breathe. We're sealed, legs intertwined, arms wrapped around each other.

"Why are you a criminal?" I whisper, wanting to relive the moment, wishing I could go back and recreate it over and over until the ending is different.

"Because it's my destiny," he grits out, chest shaking.

"Why are you a liar?"

"Because I said I'd walk away. But if you tell me to follow you, right now—this very moment—I won't look back."

His lips press to my forehead, and I can feel his tears on them. A sob escapes my body as my shoulders lift, trying to crawl inside of him and never leave.

We lie in silence, just listening to each other breathe before his deep voice breaks the bubble.

"Connor will kill you. And me, if it came down to it. I won't risk you. So we have to be strong for this part of our story. Strong for each other and ourselves."

My mouth falls open as I weep, not holding back.

He kisses my head again and again before whispering, "I don't want to say goodbye either. Fuck, I already feel like I can't breathe just knowing you'll be outta my fucking reach. But Connor will do everything he promised you, baby. And you'd never be the same. I won't let that be something that happens to you. Because I can shoulder this...I will, for the both of us. I'll make it all right."

He pulls my head from his chest, holding the side of my face as I stare into his devastated face.

"So we're gonna walk away, and we're not gonna fucking look back."

My heart physically aches, a pain shooting through my chest, but I force myself to take a breath, chin quivering as I nod.

"It's not forever, Sutton. *We* are the forever."

Sunshine fills my room as I slide a hand across the empty space next to me, dragging over nothing but a cold sheet.

"Calder."

His name is whispered from my lips, but I don't open my eyes because I know what I'll see. I squeeze them tighter, plummeting back into my darkness, lost to grief again.

Because he's gone.

Calder

Chapter twelve

"**H**ey. He's ready for you."

I push off the wall, and so does Roman, but Connor's guard waves him off.

"Just him."

Roman's face shoots to mine, but I give a reassuring nod before taking a step forward. It's all I can do. The hate I feel is consuming me. Trying to hold me under until I explode, but this is what I have to do to get her back, even if I want to give in and destroy everything around me.

The guard turns, opening the door to the suite and gesturing for me to walk inside. Connor's been at this hotel in New York since I was admitted to the hospital.

No part of me believes he stayed because he wanted to make sure his nephew was okay. Nah, he stayed to keep his ear to the ground and to be close enough to tighten his fucking foot on my neck if needed.

As I enter, my eyes immediately lock with Connor's. He's sitting at a desk, like a king on a throne, looking back at me with the same hardness I have on my own face.

"Nephew."

"Uncle."

I close the distance, my heart pounding, violence screaming into my ear to act in her name. But all I do is blink as the door clicks shut behind me.

Connor motions for me to sit as I jerk the chair to the side and lower down, picturing myself reaching over and wrapping my hands around his throat as I choke the fucking life from his body.

"I assume you've seen her."

"Last night."

He reaches for his cigar case, pulling one out and running it under his nose as he inhales deeply.

Get her out of your head, Calder. She can't be here. You can't think about her.

"And you've said goodbye?" he levels.

My jaw sets as the muscles in my body tense.

"You act as if you gave us a choice."

His fist comes down hard on the desk, thwacking the glass on top.

"And you're barking like you gave *me* one."

I smirk, adding fuel to the fire, wanting a fight because then maybe I could get away with killing him.

"Careful, Connor, you might cut yourself. I'd hate to see you bleed."

Before I cut you open and let you spill over this fucking table.

His eyes bore into mine, the real him oozing out before he blinks and sucks in another breath, reaching for the cigar that flew from his hand.

He grabs his cutter, snipping the top as he sticks it in his mouth to wet it.

"You're angry with me. And that's fair, but you're almost smart. This is your future I'm protecting. Let's be real, the more of this world you peeled back, the more she would've hated you."

All I can focus on is breathing. In, out, in, out. Because I need him to trust me, at least enough to take me home—to Boston.

"Calder, I did what needed to be done for this family, and one day you'll do the same."

One day, I'll slit your throat and burn down every fucking thing you've built.

Connor sucks in a drag, puffing as smoke billows. He points at me with the cigar in his hand as he continues.

"You put this family at risk. Almost killed the son of a supplier we're in deep with. Undermined the outfit in St. Simeon. All for what, Calder? A girl. And not just any girl—for the daughter of a man I fucking hate, who's looking to send me up the river. What exactly did you think I'd do? Because I would've done worse if you weren't my fucking nephew."

I don't offer an explanation as he stares at me. Because I want to slap his fucking mouth for even mentioning Hunter.

"Calder," he says thoughtfully, "this is your birthright. She doesn't belong here. Your loyalty has to be to the O'Bannion name."

"It is," I lie, staring into his eyes.

He shrugs, leaning back into his chair. "It's not just me...the other families, they need to know you'll be loyal too."

I let out a breath because there it is. What I came for.

My fists, squeezed together, slowly open, letting my hands feel life again.

"I said goodbye. I walked the fuck away. What more do you want from me?"

He stares me down for a long minute before stubbing out his cigar and lifting his eyes over my head.

"Tell the boys we're coming to the warehouse, and let them know to have the package ready." His eyes meet mine again. "I have something for you, nephew. Because what I want is peace for this family."

"Yeah?" I throw back at him. "Then you show me what you showed her."

He blinks, eyes narrowing before he reaches over, grabbing his phone, never taking his eyes off of mine as he flips it over.

"Go ahead, look for yourself."

I swipe the phone across the desk, eyes flicking back to his because the fucking video was already ready.

He had it fucking queued.

I stare down at the triangle on the screen, before I touch it hitting play to watch my brother die.

Chapter thirteen

Sutton

Three hard bangs on my door **wake me** from the dead, forcing my body to shoot up in bed, my **eyes springing** wide open.

What the fuck?

Another few bangs accompany a **woman's voice**.

"Sutton Prescott. Open the door."

"Hold on," I yell back.

I pull back my blanket and stand, **eyes searching** my room as I walk toward a chair, grabbing a pair of gray **sweatpants** labeled Madison on the sides and lifting my foot to put them **on**.

I'm still in just my underwear and **tank top from** last night.

What time is it? How long was I out after crying myself to sleep?

I step into the other leg and shift **my head over** my shoulder to look at the clock on my nightstand when my **eyes catch**, held hostage by something there.

Oh my God.

The sound of a key thrusting into **my lock** makes my heart stop before the handle twists and the door swings open.

"What the fuck, lady?" I bark, tugging **my** sweats over my ass, turning to stand directly in front of her.

The school's headmistress stands in my doorway, foreboding, with a bun twisted so tight that it makes her features look harsh and angular.

"You will not use that language here."

She walks toward me, stopping just short of uncomfortable as she stares down.

Fuck you. I'm done being intimidated.

My mouth falls open as I huff a laugh.

"I'll cut to the chase, Miss Prescott. We know your felon was here. So I hope you made your goodbye worthwhile because if he sets foot on this property again—"

I step in closer to her, blocking the view of my nightstand.

"You'll what? Have him shot? Others have already tried. What exactly do you need at noon on a Sunday? To tell me that you know I let a boy in my room? I'm a whore, didn't my parents tell you? I like to spread it nice and wide for bad boys that do terrible shit."

I bat my eyelashes as her jaw sets firmly, hands clasped in front of her.

"Get fucked," I cut before taking a deep breath and stepping backward until I feel my nightstand behind me. "I'm done with my parents' puppets. You can tell them I followed all the rules. They all got what they wanted. Now, get out because I'm going back to bed."

Her eyes narrow to slits. This bitch is mean. But I'm starting to perfect that myself.

"Your parents require you to attend mass every Sunday. Next week, you'll be ready by 8:00 a.m."

I shake my head. "No, I won't. I don't believe in God."

I cross my arms as she keeps her eyes on me for a long moment before she turns toward the door. Her voice travels over her shoulder as she glances back.

"They said you'd be a challenge." She stops at the door, hand holding it open. "I expect you to fall in line."

I say nothing, leaning back against my nightstand, hands gripping the wood on either side of me, mocking her with a sneer.

But my heart is racing, body impatient as she shuts the door behind her.

I don't know how long I wait to turn around because it fucking feels like forever. But she has to be gone.

Giggling passes outside my door, making me smile as I spin around, staring down at the beat-up brown leather journal.

"Calder," I whisper.

My fingers brush over the long leather straps wrapped around it, fastened tightly like they're holding secrets inside.

I guess they kind of are.

I don't know how he got this back or when he left it here. All I know is it's mine now.

My hands wrap around the book that's as big as a Bible, picking it up in one hand and smelling the faint scent of his cigarettes, before unwinding the long leather straps with the other.

My ass hits the bed as I place it in my lap, letting it fall open.

I have to close my eyes for a moment because I instantly want to cry. They drift back open as I bite my lip, fingers tracing over his messy handwriting. I flip the pages to more drawings and scribbles until I get to the last entry.

My life was always about you. Before I knew it.

You saved me. Gave me purpose. Led me to be the man I was supposed to become.

Because for an angel to walk on this earth, it'll need the protection of the Devil.

There are a lot of empty pages I'll never be able to fill in, so now it's your turn.

Tell me everything. Yell, scream, and cry in here, baby. Because one day I'll read it all.

Soon. –C

Calder

chapter
fourteen

R oman and I walk in step into the dark warehouse. The sound of
feet shuffling comes from the shadows as a man appears thirty
feet away. He's forced forward by one of Connor's men, hands
tied behind his back, a sack over his head.

"What the fuck is going on?"

My uncle smiles, stepping ahead as Roman's face turns to mine.

"C," Roman whispers because he sees what I do.

"I know," I say back as the man is forced to his knees, the sound of him
hitting the cement cracking around the room.

No sound comes from his mouth, probably because it's taped shut
under the hood.

"This isn't good, C. We gotta get out of here."

My head shakes because there's no walking away. I turn my face to
Roman's to say just that when one by one, the lights begin to flicker overhead, clicking consecutively, sounding like thunder gathering.

Ten men stand in a semicircle around the one kneeling. They're facing
us. Dead, soulless eyes behind cold faces.

This is the Council.

My eyes fall on each face, recognizing them as the heads of the different Irish families, from the East Coast to the West and all the way to fucking Ireland.

Connor runs this family, but when they meet like this, no one man is more powerful than the whole. They decide who lives and dies, who's in power, and when to take it away.

My eyes dart to the man on his knees as someone walks over and pulls the sack from his face.

"Pops," Roman breathes out heavily.

Tyler stares back at me, muzzled by thick silver duct tape.

Connor walks forward, placing his hand on my shoulder.

"This is how you show your loyalty. And it's also my gift to you. You want revenge for West. We want to know you're in. That you understand what you'll have to do from this moment on. Your father's death will be sanctioned by this Council so no punishment will ever fall on you."

My nostrils flare the longer I stare at my pops. Connor turns around to address the Council, and my head turns to Roman. He's shaking with every breath, just as murderous as I am.

Our eyes meet, and a promise is made between us. No matter what happens in this room, we tear that motherfucker apart.

"Gentlemen," Connor projects to the Council, "we're here to partake in our oldest and most valued tradition. The initiation of one of our own into this world."

I step forward, but Roman grabs my arm.

"You make him suffer. Don't you fucking dare make it quick."

I nod, walking past my uncle until I'm standing in front of my father.

The stories told to me about moments like this drift through my mind. Every man that joins this family pledges their loyalty, and then when the time's right, they're initiated.

But the Irish don't fuck around. Initiation is by blood.

You beat a man to death with your bare fucking hands. Because death should always feel uncontrolled and scary. And every Irishman should know how to wield it.

"Untie him. I want him to fight back."

Connor laughs, giving the nod as my pops stares up at me.

There are no bruises on his face or cuts. Nobody's touched him.

They've left it all for me to do.

Tyler's arms are released, tape ripped from around his mouth as he lets out a growl, shaking his hands. He stands, spitting to the side of him.

"I knew it would be you they brought."

The energy in the room crackles and vibrates as we walk around each other slowly. He cracks his neck as we stare at each other.

"What's the matter, Pops? Worried that I let you win all those times?"

He narrows his eyes as we stop, just standing in front of each other, chests heaving, anger growing.

"It's gonna take a better man than you to beat me."

I lift my fist, feeling the hunger. An insatiable evil winds through my veins, whispering for Tyler's head on a goddamn platter, hissing in my ear to take his life and to make sure I'm the last fucking face he remembers before he's sent to hell.

The first swing cracks his jaw, forcing him back as men close in, surrounding us.

I should feel pain, the crunch of my bones against his jaw, but I'm not in my body anymore. I'm a demon, fed by the shouts and curses calling for his death resounding through the shadows.

His head swings around, eyes coming back to mine as he wipes a hand down his jaw, bruising already blooming under his skin.

"That was for Roman."

Pops' eyes lift over my shoulder, seeing my brother behind me before he rushes me, lifting me off the ground and grunting as he does. All the wind is knocked from my body, ribs constricted by his hold as we crash down onto the cement floor.

"Come on, Pops," I bellow, hammering my hand down into his back.

His hand slaps to my face, fingers scraping, trying to gouge my eyes. I ram my hand into the back of his elbow, hearing a pop from his outstretched arm.

"Ahh," he screams, grabbing his arm to his side.

I flip him over, straddling him as I hurl fist after fist into his face.

"Fuck you."

My teeth grind, jaw hard as my fists squeeze with so much force it feels like my skin might pop.

All the rage I feel, the hate I have for my pops, and the guilt I feel about West pours out of me like a river.

"This is for West," I cry out, hammering into his face as it swings from side to side with each hit.

I grip Tyler's hair, jerking his head up before smashing it against the concrete. Every word falling from between my lips is mangled and unintelligible.

I'm so full of hate that I'm barely making sense. I'm gasping for air, breathless, fury leaking from my body as I groan, smashing his head over and over until I hear a crack.

"Die. Fuck. Die."

Blood splatters against the ground, wetness speckling my face, making my eyes blink. But even then, I don't stop. I push off him, scrambling to my feet, throwing kicks to his gut.

His body jerks as his arm lifts, but he's not fighting back.

He's begging me to stop.

"Look at me." Every kick elicits another groan as he gurgles on the blood in his mouth. "You fucking look at me. You remember who put you in the ground."

Tyler's head falls to the side. *No. Not yet. You haven't fucking suffered enough.* I haul back and kick him under the jaw.

Men jump back as teeth and blood fly their way. My breath is heaving, spit flying from my mouth as I lift my foot, bringing it down to his nose. The crunch makes a few men turn away. More blood gushes as the yells begin to silence.

"Fuck you," I shout. "You killed him. He was my brother, you piece of shit. My brother."

Empty thuds mixed with my dark grunts are the only sounds as I kick the sides of his body.

Calls for me to stop fall on deaf ears because Connor's standing, watching, living for the monster he helped create.

Roman rushes over to me, trying to grab me, but I throw him off, lunging for Pops' body again.

"It's not enough, Romes."

He wraps his arms around me in a bear hug, forcing me backward as I try to get at Tyler.

Roman whispers in my ear, past my heaving breaths and grunts.

"It's done, Calder. West is at peace, brother. It's done. You gotta walk away now before you're lost for good. You gotta keep some good for her. For her, C."

My arms are shaking, weak from use but also high from the adrenaline. I know what I've done is wrong, but it's also righteous. Because that motherfucker should burn in hell.

"He was a kid, Roman," I say on ragged breaths as my body begins to shake. "He was our brother."

"Yeah, C. You did good. It's okay."

My legs want to give, but Roman holds me up as I gather my strength. This shit isn't over. I hang my head, taking a breath before stepping out of his grip.

The faces of the Council stare back at me, fear along with respect reflected on them. They should be more focused on fear.

My face drops to my blood-soaked hands as I flip to my palms, eyes drifting over them and the spatters covering my clothes.

I knew what this day meant the moment I walked into this warehouse, but standing here, anointed in Tyler's blood, means I'm never going back.

This is who I am. And who I will remain.

My voice carries, filling the room as I walk back to the middle, wiping the blood from my cheek.

"You asked for loyalty. But what you got is my obligation."

I point up, high into the rafters, to a tiny red dot. "I'm not fucking stupid." I scoped that shit the minute we walked in.

Hushed voices hiss around the room, but I speak over them.

"We're all guilty, right? No man can turn on the other. But I just killed my father. A smart man might ask what I'd be willing to do to them without that obligation."

The men around the circle begin looking between each other as I turn, locking eyes with Connor.

"If you want fucking loyalty, you'll earn it. Not the other way around."

I stop in front of him, eye to eye, as I reach inside his jacket and pull out his gun. Clicks begin to echo behind me, death at my back, but Connor doesn't move.

My words are meant for my uncle, but everyone can hear them.

"You'll accept Roman as my brother. No different than blood. He's protected, initiated here, today. And you'll make sure Hunter heels."

He knows exactly what I mean. There's no fucking way I walk away from her wondering if she's in danger because I didn't kill him when I had the chance.

"This is me accepting my birthright, not cowering under your fucking coercion."

I turn around, walking past Pops' lifeless body until I'm standing in front of my brother.

My eyes dart down to the Glock, smeared in blood in my hand, before setting it in Roman's upturned palm. We're shoulder to shoulder as I turn around, staring back at the hardened faces of the men looking back.

"There's nothing left to fucking beat. Tyler Wolfe is dead. But that's not the point, is it, fellas? We good?"

The silence is fucking deafening as each man nods in my direction until it comes to Connor, who just grins.

I turn to Roman and blow out a hard breath, speaking so only he hears.

"I couldn't save West, but this is what I can do now."

I know every fucking thing he's thinking because that's what we do. He understands the gravity of what's just happened and what he's about to do.

The first man I've ever killed is my father.

There's no coming back from that.

Even if that motherfucker deserved it.

I'm all the bad shit people said I'd be, but it's the only way I protect the ones I love and get my girl back.

And now Roman's accepting the same fate.

He walks to the center of the room, staring down at Pops' body before spitting on him and lifting the gun.

The bang echoes as everyone stands silent.

Each of the men turns their back, folding back into the shadows at the edges of the room, leaving us alone in an empty warehouse.

One of Connor's guards walks forward with a sheet of plastic as Roman drops the gun on the ground. It clangs against the concrete before he looks back at me.

"You did good, Romes."

Connor looks over at his guard before he nods to us.

"Take the boys home to Southie. They're gonna need their family close now."

Year One

Chapter

fifteen

Sutton

Sutton

Tuesday—

My period started.

Of course it did. God. Why did I do this to myself? Like, hold on to this ridiculous idea that I had the tiniest piece of you—something left behind, a part of us growing inside of me.

I'm such an idiot. I just didn't want to feel like I really lost you. I knew it was a stupid idea, born from my irresponsibility. An idea soaked in desperation like a rag doused in gasoline, ready to light my life on fire.

Teen mom is exactly what I need right now. FML.

Jesus, I bet everyone could hear me in my room laughing at myself before it turned into fucking sobbing. It's like— Don't mind me, I'm just over here in the middle of another emotional breakdown. Wanna be friends?

Ugh. I can't even think about that right now.

How did I find myself here, willing to sit in this

fantasy, pretending I still had you because my reality sucks that bad.

I just want YOU. FUCKING YOU.

But sitting on a toilet, crying, bleeding all over the place, has a way of sobering a person up. Because I decided that it's time to grow up. Everything feels like it's moving forward, except for me. So I have to do what you said.

Survive today until tomorrow.

**reminder to rip this page out when I let him read this.

Basically, most of my month (October)—

"What is wrong with you? You're such a fucking psycho."

That's a direct fucking quote from the twat I checked with my lacrosse stick today. Her friends were less inventive. They threw out shit like "weirdo, slut, loser"—the holy trinity of mean girl slurs.

God, I fucking miss you today.

It's my birthday, but I don't think you know that about me—that it's in October. But, yep. I'm officially an adult and apparently starting an impromptu fight club.

Maybe Roman can join one day! ...he always looked like the type.

Anyway, I hit her, she fell, there was blood.

I've never hit anyone before. Like on purpose to hurt

them. There's an addictive release that happens. For a few glorious minutes, everything made sense. Nothing hurt. And the anger that's always inside was gone.

Until I was hauled to the headmistress's office, deposited in a chair, and yelled at. Now I'm pissed all over again and stuck in a week's worth of room isolation.

On top of that, it's been three months since I saw you. And I can't stop wanting to cry just thinking about that. But I don't. And that's why I hit her because all I wish is that you were here, taking me out to our field, with a pink cupcake from that bakery where you trapped me in the bathroom.

We'd sit out under the stars, and I'd blow out the candle knowing that everything I wished for would come true.

I'm so angry, Westley. Did you know you misspelled that when you put it in our phones? Lol. I watched the movie —well, I watch it...over and over.

I hate how unfair life is—I lose you, but I get to keep my shitty parents who, by the way, sent boxes of my things to me as a birthday gift.

I don't really care. It's not like I ever want to go home. But I haven't even opened the boxes. I just stare at them, wondering if what's inside will even feel like me anymore.

But I guess I'm surviving. Or maybe today, I'm slowly dying. I can't tell.

P.S. I think you'd be proud to know that I threw a mean right hook with that stick.

Thanksgiving—

So today was spent eating bland turkey with the cafeteria staff, alone, except for, like, ten other people that didn't go home. But I couldn't do it—go home.

The idea of sitting at the table and looking at my mother's face made me feel violent. And forget about the fact that any time I'm forced to speak to her, she always brings up Hunter.

It's disgusting.

She's really "keeping her fingers crossed" that our love affair's going to take off, and I'm over waiting for God to drop a piano on his fucking head.

I did do something stupid today, though. I turned on my phone.

God, I shouldn't have done it. Because I knew Aubs and Piper were probably freaking out, I also knew that my parents had PR'd that shit away. So burying my head in the sand didn't feel so cowardly.

I mean, it's not as if the world doesn't know where I am or my father's version of why.

Omg, I'm seriously fucking trying to justify being the WORST friend in a journal. Like I'll look back and be like, "Yep, wise beyond my years."

Fuck. I'm an asshole who's not ready to face them.

Because what do I say? I can't tell the truth.

How did you live like this when we were first together?

Half in, half out. How did you decide what you could tell me and what you couldn't?

It would've been great if, somewhere inside of this book, you'd left some helpful hints instead of a bunch of broody existential bullshit.

If you haven't figured it out, I'm really fucking mad at you today.

I've walked around the grounds of the school hating you, blaming you for everything. Because if we'd never met, I'd still just be another clueless girl, eating turkey with fancy silver off Tiffany plates, sneaking away with her friends to some party.

Yuck. I'm sorry I wrote that.

But today is hard. And that tiny red dot next to my group message is fucking haunting me.

I miss feeling like somebody fucking cares. Ya know?

I miss you. And kinda hate you. But mostly, I love you.

(K...I turned on the read receipts, so at least they know I'm reading all the really great and amazing and funny shit they keep sending me. Baby steps.)

Calder–December

R oman throws me a towel as I suck in heavy breaths, chest heaving. I catch it, wiping my face as my muscles burn, aching from the beating I just inflicted.

"You made Connor a ton of money tonight. He'll be happy."

There's nothing Connor loves more than taking the house at his own underground fights. He does these twice a month. All of Southie comes out to watch a bunch of wannabe fighters jump in a makeshift ring and try to kill each other. And I've been his ringer ever since we got here in Boston.

I throw the towel down on the wooden bench, trying to pick at the bloodstained tape that's wrapped around my knuckles. Roman jerks my hand to him, unwrapping it.

"But damn, C. I thought you were gonna knock that guy's head right off his shoulders."

The taste of metal in my mouth has me turning my head to spit on the floor as I say, "He wasn't shit."

"Exactly. He wasn't shit. So then why almost put him in a coma?"

I don't answer. Because what the fuck am I supposed to say?

That I can't help myself? Do I tell him that every time I do another one of these underground bullshit fights, all I do is picture Connor's face or my father's or Hunter's, until I'm lost to the comfort of my rage? Because that's easier than feeling helpless and fucking lost without...

Fuck. I inhale a harsh breath and drop my head, staring at the ground, feeling my fucking hands start to shake. I can't even think her name.

"C, man—"

I jerk my fist from his grip, lifting my face to his and cutting him off.

"We've been spinning our wheels for fucking months, Romes, trying to get this motherfucker to trust us. You think I'm gonna get his attention by being a Boy Scout? I gotta do whatever it takes."

Roman stares back at me, his eyes searching mine trying to read me as usual. My jaw sets before I bring my hand to my mouth, teeth gripping the tape, ripping it off enough to grab it with my other hand.

He gives a slight shake of his head but crosses his arms.

"Everything has a cost."

I throw my hand to my side, ready to go in, to tell him to shut the fuck up, but the locker room door opens with a bang and Connor walks through.

He's clapping his hands, flanked by two men.

"Merry fucking Christmas to me."

Connor grips the back of my neck just a little too hard as he stares into my eyes, making my fingers curl back into fists.

"You're a fucking animal. And I love it. Look at all that rage inside of you. Fuck."

He smacks my cheek, stepping back.

"You're unbeatable. That's what everyone's saying. What do you think? Are you unbeatable?" He tilts his head, eyes darting to Roman. "Leave us alone."

Roman looks at me, hesitating, but I don't nod because he should fucking know better.

I keep my eyes on Connor because that's respect.

He's the boss. So who the fuck am I? Other than another asshole who listens to directions. Roman shoves his hands into the front pocket of his hoodie, walking past us out the door, not saying anything.

Connor and I stand staring at each other, his eyes narrowed before he smirks. He waves the men away, his eyes never leaving mine.

The door opens and closes again, leaving us alone in the deafening silence. I won't speak first—not my place. So I stand there trying to mask my thoughts.

I could break your neck before anyone knew what happened.

"He's protective of you." Connor chuckles.

I smirk. "He's my brother. And old habits die hard."

He's quiet again, lost to whatever thought has him drawing his brows together. I swallow, feeling a chill spread over my body as the adrenaline from the fight begins to drop.

Connor nods like he's speaking to himself before his face morphs back into a stupid as fuck grin.

"You've been working hard for me. You're trying to prove yourself, and I see that. So next week, you can start doing just that. It's easy to win, nephew. Now you're gonna lose, just because I decide."

Sutton

Chapter sixteen

Happy New Year—

I snuck champagne. I might even be a little bit tipsy. The castaways, as I like to call them, aren't that bad here. We're like a band of misfits, left to roam these halls every holiday.

I can't believe practically half a year has gone by.

Time does not heal old wounds—people lied about that.

I'm still angry. And alone. (Maybe I'll take a leap and call Aubs and Piper tonight...liquid courage and all.)

Or maybe I'll do my new fave hobby and flip through the front of this journal until your face is all I can see. And your fingers are all I'll feel when I slip my own down between my legs until I'm so wet that I glide over my clit until I'm screaming your name under a pillow.

What a cruel world. I lost my virginity only to basically get revirginized, waiting for you to come and rescue me from this nightmare I call my life.

But what if you never come?

I thought that yesterday and started searching obituaries in New York and Boston. Because I don't know where you are. I don't know anything.

Except that I fucking love you.

Just as fucking much today as I did the night you said our not goodbye.

Life sucks. But at least I have champagne.

Calder—May

"**M**otherfucker," Connor thunders, tossing his glass across the room, shattering it on the wall.

Roman doesn't move because this is what Connor does. He's a fucking lunatic. Unbalanced. Moods shifting like the fucking wind.

It took five fucking months and a lot of broken ribs to appease whatever cruel ass kick Connor got off on watching me get my ass beat. But I did it because it got me in this room and one step closer to my hand around his throat.

I hang my head, sitting on the arm of the couch, and take a deep breath before looking up.

"You need me to take care of something, Uncle?"

It's not the first time I've made this offer, and it probably won't be the last. Connor runs his hand through his hair, shaking his head.

"No. No, this is street bullshit."

But as I crack my knuckles, he stares at me for a minute with a debate in his eyes. I know because I've gotten better at reading him. Not that I let on.

Connor leans back into his chair, reaching for his cigar only to smash it into the ashtray as his anger peaks again.

"I give these kids a shot, a way to better their lives. They come and work for me. Sell some product and make their lives better. They can give a little to their moms or take care of their girls." His fist hits the desk. "I do this for the neighborhood. And the fucking disrespect to not pay me on time."

I nod. "Of course. You care. You're a good man, Uncle."

The lies come so much easier now. I almost enjoy telling them.

Connor inhales harshly through his nose.

"Do you think anyone else has ever done things for these people the way I have? Their fucking bellies are fat because I created that shit they sling. I found the fucking Kellys."

He stabs his finger into the desk. "Me. I did that. And when that piece of shit Michael died, I am the one that made sure his sons had the majority vote. I turned a Forbes 500 company into my personal fucking distributor."

My entire body tenses as he says the Kelly name. He put Hunter and Tag in charge. *Motherfucker.*

I don't even notice that my fists are balled at my sides, squeezed so hard they're turning white around the edges, until Connor's eyes drop to my hands before meeting mine again. He narrows on me as he wipes spittle from the side of his mouth.

Fuck. *Get her out of your fucking head. Right fucking now, Calder.*

I let out a breath and shoot to my feet, trying to cover my tracks.

"It's the fucking disrespect," I bark. "They're stealing from you. Let me take care of this."

Roman comes to stand next to me, following my lead.

"Calder's right. Let us do this for you, Connor. You've done a lot for us over the last ten months. So let us take this off your plate."

Connor's staring between us as I put my palms on his desk.

"I'll get you your money, Uncle. Even if I have to sell someone's mother. But more importantly, I'll deliver a message that nobody fucks with this family."

Silence bleeds out as he stares back at me. I know he still doesn't trust me. I'm sure his gut tells him better...but I don't need to be his right-hand man. I just need him to put me on the streets.

His mouth slowly spreads into a smile as he slaps the desk again. *There it is.*

"You're a good boy, Calder. Loyal. You understand." His eyes pierce mine before he nods. "Okay. Pete will tell you where to go. But listen closely to my words—you bring me back something special. I want that animal I've watched on the mats. Make everyone see what'll happen when I send my angel of death."

My chest rises and falls as I say nothing, letting the last of what he said sink in—his angel of death. He wants me to bring him someone's life.

I knew it would come to this. But... *No. Focus.* I rap my knuckles on Connor's desk and give a tight nod before turning, locking eyes with Roman.

He's searching my face, digging, trying to read me. *I don't fucking have room for this, Roman.*

My jaw tenses as I walk past him because he's calling to shit inside of me that I can't let live here anymore.

Connor's so drunk on power that he just handed me the knife to place at his throat. This is what I need. What we've been working for.

Even saying that to myself, Roman's words still whisper in the back of my mind.

"Everything has a cost."

Fuck. My chest hollows as I walk out of Connor's office, with Roman on my heels, neither of us speaking until we slide into the car. He pulls out his phone to call Pete before looking at me.

His lips part to speak, but I do it first, staring out the front window.

"What I have to do today—the fucking horror that I'm about to inflict on someone I've never even met. Romes, it means that I give a little of my soul back to the devil. That's the fucking cost."

My eyes drop to my lap, looking at my hands, wishing I didn't feel her on them still as something that I heard that day at mass—the one when I waited for her up in the balcony—pulls to my mind. The priest said, *"For they eat the bread of wickedness, and drink the wine of violence."*

It's stuck with me since that day, it's why I almost left. I knew I was damned and that I would damn her too.

Because I was baptized in blood as my mother lay dying on the street, anointed in my father's blood as my hands beat the life out of him. Wickedness is my sustenance, and my thirst for violence will never end.

My face shifts to Roman.

"There isn't any fucking room inside me for *her* or the man that loves her. Not anymore. Not if I'm gonna keep her safe."

He doesn't say a word, just turns the engine over and puts it in drive as I close my eyes and welcome the numbness. Because I have to try to really let her go.

Sutton

It hasn't stopped raining—

I've been lying in bed all day, reading this journal because it's pouring outside. But I stopped to write this because I couldn't believe what I just read— YOU were not born bad. I don't care if some old lady told you that you were after you beat up her grandson.

But I want it on record that you were NOT and could NOT ever have been born bad.

I think the universe knew that you'd need to be strong enough to do what was required one day. And the only way you could be that strong was to lose a little bit of your soul. Not everyone in this world would be brave enough for that task.

And if that makes you bad, then so be it. Her grandson probably deserved it.

But you show me what it feels like to be someone's universe. And nobody all bad could do that. So, wherever you are, and whatever you're doing...tonight, someone is really fucking grateful that you know how to be "bad."

I love you, Calder. Make 'em all pay, baby. And fuck you to that old lady.

Soon.

Today sucks—
They stopped texting, Aubs and Piper.
It's for the best. But it doesn't feel like that.
I could really use some "better" right about now.

Calder-July

Chapter seventeen

S moke burns my lungs as I take another drag before flicking my
cigarette out the window.

I motion to an alley next to the dilapidated house deep in the
Southie neighborhood.

"Park over there," I grunt, staring out the window.

Roman pulls the Mustang between the houses, slowing to a stop. He
glances over at me, shaking his head as I pull my gun out.

"What?" I bark.

"Nothing."

For fuck's sake. I shove my door open, then slam it behind me, uninterested in this conversation. *Again.* Roman hasn't let up since that day in the
car before I shot the second person I've ever killed in my life.

I know he's worried. He reeks of it, but I've nothing to fucking say. And
all the looks and the *You goods*—I don't want to fucking hear it anymore.

I tap my gun against my leg, steps ahead of Roman. Not paying attention to what's in front of me because my mind is on the shit he said without
saying as I hear a gun cock.

Fuck.

My eyes lift, connecting with a beady-eyed motherfucker about ten feet
away.

"Whoa," I say, nice and slow. "Jackie, don't do something stupid. Your neighbors are watching. The whole fucking street knows I'm here."

His hands are shaking, making the metal clack. Fuck, I bet he's never even held a gun. Jack Baker is just a low-level drug dealer who slings to rich kids in the city.

This isn't fucking good.

"Hey, hey, hey. Let's just put the guns away." I slowly tuck mine against the small of my back, trying to ignore how fast my heart is beating. "We're cool. I'm just here to talk."

Where the fuck is Roman?

He straightens his arms, pointing closer to my face, making me draw back.

"Fuck. Easy, man."

The gun shakes harder in his hand, and I wince.

"How do I know you're not here to kill me? I know about you. The Wolfe. You tear people apart. That's what everyone says. But not this time. I'm gonna shoot first."

Sutton.

Oh fuck. My heart stops. Her name's nothing but a whisper in my mind. But it's as if I'm suddenly awake, aware of everything around me in vivid fucking color. Because the one fucking thing I've avoided, packed down deep inside me, is the only goddamn thing I can see.

Not this way.

He's sweating as he stares at me like someone who wants to run. That look makes him dangerous and me willing to beg.

"Jackie, I really don't want to die today. I promised someone I'd make it home. So I fucking swear, I'm only here to talk."

The adrenaline pumps so fast through my body that my fingertips tingle as he stares at me. *It wasn't enough time. I've got to make it back to her. Fuck.*

He's shaking his head like he doesn't believe me as my heart beats out of my fucking chest. He's going to shoot me and let me bleed out on this dirty fucking sidewalk, and there won't be any fucking cops or paramedics to help this time.

Because in this neighborhood, nobody sees or hears anything. Especially not to help me. I did what I came to do in Southie. I'm feared. And people don't help monsters.

He pushes the barrel at me again, making my hands come up in front of me.

"Come on, Jackie. Please."

We stare at each other for the longest time as my baby plays on a goddamn loop in my mind. Over and over like a song I can't forget, humming it when I don't even realize what I'm doing.

"I promise to die by your side when we're wrinkly and fucking gray. So that we'll never be apart again."

"And I promise to love you even after death."

"Only one of us gets to keep our promise," I whisper to myself, closing my eyes, ready to die.

"Oh fuck," Jackie exhales, springing my eyes back open.

Roman crept around the back of the house, jumped the rail, and has the barrel of his gun pressed to the back of that motherfucker's head.

"Shit," I say in a whoosh, head dropping to the ground to stare at the cracked cement.

I hear Roman take his gun, saying, "Jesus, Jackie, you could've killed Calder. Get in the fucking house, ya crackhead."

But I'm rooted in my place because I can't catch my breath. That was too close. I wasn't focused. I was thinking about... *Oh fuck. No.*

My head's shaking, trying to shove what I'm feeling away, needing to settle everything that feels like it's fucking shaking inside me, but I can't. Because she's here, weighing me down.

"I can't think about you. Just get out of my head," I say quietly, still looking down.

I lift my face, not knowing what to do, eyes blinking fast because I can't stop this fucking pain in my chest. But Roman's not looking at me as he grabs the back of Jack's shirt, yanking him inside.

My fists open and close, trying to pump the blood back into them before I wipe a hand down my face. *Get your shit together, Calder. Don't let them see you like this.*

I clear my throat, giving my head a shake as I walk up the steps.

The metal screen closes behind me just as Roman tosses the guy on the couch before surveying the dump.

Roman's face screws up as he looks over at me, but I keep my eyes on Jackie. He almost killed me. This motherfucker almost took me from... My fear of her name slowly curls in over itself, turning into hate for the dick sitting in front of me.

All I want to do right now is beat Jack to death. I want to feel his bones crack under my fists until I can't lift my arms.

"Tell me why I shouldn't kill you now?" I say under my breath so only Jackie hears.

He stares at the foul mess of a coffee table, not looking up at me.

"Damn. This place is fucking nasty. It smells like old Taco Bell and stale cigarettes." Roman chuckles, oblivious to my fucking headspace. "You need to open a window more often."

My breath is calm as I exhale, reaching behind my back for my gun.

Roman peeks his head into the kitchen as I say, "Anybody else here we need to know about, Jackie?"

"No," he answers, finally looking back at me, body fucking quaking because he knows he's about to die.

Roman's smirking as he turns back toward us, something sarcastic on his tongue, but his humor fades when his eyes land on me. I know because the room is silent.

The kind of silence that worry and fear produce. The kind only narrated by the quiet sniveling coming from that dirty fucking couch.

My gun cocks as Jackie begins to plead, but Roman's voice fills the room, booming.

"That ain't happening today. Yo, you hear me, C? Put it the fuck away."

I do hear him, but I'm not trying to listen. Because she's still fucking here. Like her perfume when it lingers over my skin. Jackie's going to die because I can't forget and he almost robbed me of time.

"Hey," Roman barks.

I swallow, turning my head, our eyes locking.

Jesus. So much passes between us. But this time it's nothing I haven't seen before. My brother looks afraid again. Just like he did in that hospital room when he told me about West. But this time, it's me that he's losing.

That's what his eyes say, and I'm fucking scared he's right.

Jackie takes the opportunity to start fucking rambling, trying to plead for his life. Still, Roman doesn't look away, and neither do I.

"Everything has a cost."

Jack lets out a whoosh of a breath, running his hand through his greasy hair before pulling a used-up cigarette from an already filled ashtray. He blows on it before putting the butt in his mouth.

"Calder. Look, I'm fucking sorry about all that. Please. You said you weren't gonna kill me. So please, I got a sick mom, and my grandma just passed—"

The lighter clicks as his knee bounces a mile a minute. He looks up, blowing smoke out along with his words.

"And I got information. Shit I heard about who's selling the same stuff as Connor but cheaper. I'll tell you everything you need to know. Just don't kill me."

I drop my eyes from Roman's, tucking my gun into my pants before closing my eyes for only a second, letting myself see her face one last time before I reopen them.

"It better be good, or I'm gonna put a bullet between your eyes."

"What the fuck was that, C?"

I shake my head, still off, not wanting to answer anything as he barrels down the road away from Jack's house.

"Fuck this." Roman swerves, yanking the car into park, throwing us forward as we hit the curb.

My hand hits the dash before I'm slinging the door open, needing air, feeling fucking violent and too confined.

"Calder," Roman thunders, but I'm on the move.

I'm stalking toward a chain-link fence, jumping it to walk across a beat-up basketball court that's probably seen everything from sweat to blood to drive-by shootings.

"What the fuck, man? Calder, fucking stop."

I spin around, my shoulders so tense it makes my jaw grind.

"Just shut the fuck up, Roman. What do you want from me?"

"You can't keep doing this, C."

I could break his neck. Beat the fuck out of him. I could because I want to right now. Fuck. I turn away from him, shaking my head, voice rising.

"Fuck you. Don't talk to me about what I can't do. I'm doing what I have to. You don't know shit."

He swings an arm through the air, shouting.

"The fuck I don't. I'm standing right behind you in the same goddamn place I've always been. But now, every time you turn around, I don't recognize my brother anymore."

A guttural yell rips through my body as I kick a half-deflated basketball across the pavement before my hands link behind my head.

"That's because he fucking died. With *her* on that floor and with *West* in that fucking basement."

My mouth hangs open, watching Roman's face drop before I turn, walking the fuck away, not even knowing where I'm going, but Roman follows.

"You can't shut them out, C, and become someone else. That's not what they need."

I spin, almost face-to-face with him as I grab his hoodie between my fists.

"Don't you fucking tell me what she needs. I know what she needs. It's to be safe and not have to fucking suffer because I pulled her into this goddamn world."

He doesn't push me away, just looks into my eyes.

"Naw, man. She knew what she was doing. She knows who you are, and she loves you anyway. So the cost can't be your soul, C."

I shove away from him, but he smacks my face, bringing me angrily back as he keeps speaking.

"Because if you keep doing this, shutting her out, shutting me out, not talking about West, then when you get her back, the man you've become won't even be close to the one she loves."

My hands raise as I stumble back away from him before I'm running them through my hair. I can't fucking feel this shit. I can't. It's too much.

I tilt my face to the sky filled with clouds as I say what I never do.

"I can't just be a man, Romes. I gotta be more than that. But every time I think about her, that's all I am—a fucking guy who's split wide fucking open with grief. Because every single day that I'm away from her is harder than the one before."

His voice is lower, calmer.

"C. Loving her is what makes you strong. You're taking down an entire fucking organization. For her. She's your purpose. You told me that once. If you take that away, then all you are is a fucking animal. No better than Connor or the other families."

My eyes fall to the ground, closing them and letting myself feel. Because, fuck, he's right, and I know it. But it still doesn't make anything easier.

The sound of a ball hitting the ground lifts my eyes. Roman passes it to me hard, checking my chest.

"Let's play, like old times. Until we can't anymore. Sometimes that is all you can do, C. Just keep shit moving so you don't fall. But if you do, I got you."

I nod, bringing the ball to my chest, feeling that tightness that's always there, before I pass the ball back, letting out a whoosh of air.

"Let's go," I say without another word as he bounces it off the concrete before rushing me, because we just keep it moving until we can't.

Three hours later, we're sliding back into the car, sweaty and grinning.

"You gonna make a call about what we found out today from Jackie?" Roman says, spinning the keys around his finger.

I nod but draw my brows together.

"But I wanna do something else first."

Roman shoves the keys into the car. "Name it. As long as it's not shooting someone or beating the shit out of poor Jackie." A grin spreads over his face. "His knee was fucking bouncing fast with you staring at him."

It's sick, but it makes me laugh for the first time in forever. This feels like old times, and I'm okay with that.

"You're not the funny one. West was. Stop trying to fill his shoes. You fucking suck at it. He's probably looking down, all kinds of disappointed."

Roman shoves my shoulder, smiling as he nods, before turning on the car and throwing it into drive. We're not good with feelings, so this is how we deal with shit that fucks us up. Dark humor and jokes...and sometimes guns.

"Hey," he says, not looking at me, "You wanna go tell him about today, huh?"

"Yeah." I nod, looking out the window as we tear down the street, not saying another word.

Because my brother and I just got back on the same damn page.

Twenty minutes later, Roman and I slide out of the car at the same time, walking the distance to a gray headstone that reads:

WESTLEY RICHARD WOLFE:
BROTHER, SON, FRIEND
AND THE FUNNY ONE IN THE FAMILY.

Year Two

Sutton

chapter
eighteen

Freedom—

I graduated today. Technically, I had to do summer school, but I did it. I can't believe it, but I actually did. Because pretty much the whole year feels like a blur.

I don't know if you know, but there was this whole terrible breakup thing I went through with this hot piece of ass. The D really went to my head. But I'm all good now.

Psych.

I did do well in one class, though. Greek mythology. I wonder why?

God. It was incredible. Like a tiny piece of you every day—a bright spot in an otherwise dreary fucking week.

It's safe to say my parents pulled a lot of strings to get me into any college.

Not going to lie—I thought about telling them to go fuck themselves. Like try to make it on my own.

Until I realized that I had no fucking idea what I was doing.

Don't take this the wrong way when you read this, but I think the universe has a plan...you know, way past all the burning in hell retribution stuff. But an even bigger one.

Like maybe to let me figure out how to stand on my own two feet.

When I lived that "padded walls life" for two weeks, all I did was wait for you to rescue me. Even this whole year, I just kept waiting for some kind of bat call that it was our time.

But I don't want to always be the one everyone needs to look after. I want to know that I can take care of myself.

Regardless of who I'm standing next to (you, always you...I can almost feel future you grumbling).

Okay, now that I've shared my plan to be badass, if you could just hurry up and rescue me, that would be great. JK. But only because I have to go downstairs and do a photo op with my parents. More specifically, with my mother. Who, by the way, wore head to toe black to my graduation.

Calder...if there was a hole dug, I'd have pushed her in. Since she was already dressed for a funeral. Bitch.

Anyway, I love you. I'm pretending you're wishing me luck.

Calder—September

"I can't stop thinking about that night Roman and I took you to the docks. When we made you sit in the car and threatened to put you in the trunk. Because your ass would've definitely been in the trunk last night for the meeting we had with the Italians."

I brush my hands over West's headstone, clearing some leaves from the top. This has become part of my week. I visit my brother, tell him about shit that's going right and the stuff that goes wrong too.

I don't know if he can fucking hear me, but there's something satisfying about telling him that I'm gonna make them pay for what happened to him.

Footsteps fall behind me, drawing my head over my shoulder.

Roman's grinning behind me, cigarette in one hand, beer in the other.

"You about done talking about a girl West called first?"

I laugh, looking back at the grave.

"The fuck he did."

Roman takes a drag of the cigarette, coming shoulder to shoulder with me.

"No, he did. When we walked around to the bathrooms the first day, we saw her and her friends. West called dibs on red."

I laugh harder because of course he did. My face turns to Roman's.

"Did I ever tell you he was the one that thought of the code names I put in the phone for Sutton and me? Because I liked that movie, *The Princess Bride*. I didn't even catch on to the sneaky shit he was doing until I went to add that fucking pirate's name into her phone and..."

I don't even have to finish because Roman's laughing.

"Motherfucker." He wheezes.

"Right." I laugh harder. "She would've been walking around with *his* fucking name in her phone. But I couldn't think of anything on the fly, so I just spelled it wrong and left the *T* out."

The two of us stand there, laughing our asses off and letting ourselves heal. Roman wipes tears from his eyes, smiling wide as we catch our breath until it's silent again.

"Fuck I miss him," I whisper as Roman nods.

"Me too, brother. Me too."

Calder-November

The hotel suite door closes with a thud behind Roman, but something feels off. We were told to meet Connor here, but nothing else.

And guilty people worry, so right now, I'm on edge.

Connor's security walks past, not bothering to pat us down, grunting for us to follow. We do as Roman's and my eyes meet again. He mouths, "The fuck?" with confusion on his brow.

But I shrug because they left our guns on us, so we're not dying tonight. Even though there's something definitely going on. I just don't know what.

As we enter the open area of the hotel suite, my uncle's seated in a black leather chair, eyes locked to mine, surrounded by his closest advisors.

I glance around at the other men spread throughout the room. All their faces are solemn, eyes fixed on us as the guard comes to a stop before turning around, leaving us in front of a low black coffee table.

Nobody speaks, all remaining in their places as Roman and I look at each other and back to Connor.

"What's going on, Uncle?"

"Do you know why you're here, Calder?"

No, you fucking dick, or I wouldn't have asked. I shake my head, glancing around again because of the grin growing on Connor's face.

"No, but I feel like you're about to tell me."

Connor's smile doubles over his face, big and wide, as laughter erupts around the room. He joins them, saying, "Can you believe this kid?"

Believe me for what?

His fat head swings back to my cautious face.

"Did you think I'd forget my only nephew's twenty-first birthday?"

Oh fuck.

The room goes nuts with cheers and revelry as my face swings to Roman, who's grinning. He holds up his hands.

"Don't look at me. I didn't say anything."

I don't celebrate my birthday. I haven't since West. It doesn't seem right to have them when he never will. So I've kept my mouth shut all week, and I thought I'd slipped under the radar. But I should've known better.

I smile, hanging my head and pretending to be happily surprised, smiling like he's a great fucking guy.

Connor walks toward us, clapping his hands as I lift my head.

"You shouldn't have, Uncle."

"Did you think you could hide from me? I know everything, Calder. And this is an occasion to celebrate."

The way that Connor said *"hide from me"* was with truthful intent, and it requires an answer, but my mouth doesn't open. *Because yes, Connor. I do think I can hide from you. I've been doing it for a minute, you piece of shit.*

Roman slaps a hand to my shoulder, filling in all the words I don't say.

"Damn. It looks like we're in for some trouble tonight, C. And here you thought you were gonna go low-key." Roman turns toward Connor, grinning like the devil. "He never wants to bring attention to himself. You know him, always thinking about business. Never wanting to be a burden. I told him, 'Connor would want to mark this moment.' But good luck making him listen."

All bullshit, all perfect.

Connor wags his eyebrows, coming in close. "Stubborn, just like your mother." He pats both our faces. "My boys, so good." His eyes connect with mine. "And so loyal. Time to reward that."

Connor stares into my eyes for a long moment before snapping his fingers. That look felt a lot like mistrust. Fuck.

The doors behind us swing open again, drawing my and Roman's heads over our shoulders. Connor steps in between, arms slung over us as women crowd the doorway.

Shouts and catcalls boom around the room as, one by one, girls dressed in the kind of shit that puts all the merchandise on display sway their asses inside. Some cozy up to men as the music begins playing as others climb onto the tops of tables and dance.

These aren't just strippers though—they're the kind of girls that know business better than most men because slinging your body on the streets isn't something that leaves you soft.

That's why we're here, instead of a club. Connor's throwing the kind of party where secrets are kept and wives never find out.

A blonde slides up next to Roman, saying, "Hey." He drops his face to hers, reaching down to grab her ass, making her squeal.

Connor laughs, stepping away, looking back at me.

"You deserve this night, nephew. And I'm going to make sure you get your fill. Because I got ya something special."

Connor steps out into the middle of the room, spreading his arms as his voice booms over the ruckus.

"Fellas, take your pick because tonight, these lovely ladies are on me. You can have anyone you like, except this one—she's special, just for my nephew."

The doors to the suite reopen as Connor's handed a drink. He lifts the scotch as hollers from the men become deafening.

"Happy Birthday, Calder," he thunders as I follow his line of sight.

Long red hair. That's all I fucking see.

Sutton walks through the door in sky-high heels, wearing nothing but black lace panties and a bra.

"Oh fuck," Roman whispers next to me, but I give my head a slight shake as the girl with green eyes licks her lips.

This was why Connor stared at me because he knew what he'd done. This is a test.

"C. You good?"

I nod, smile still in place because that's not my girl. She's just some redhead with green eyes, meant to dig the knife in deeper.

This motherfucker. One day, I'm going to look him in the eye and watch as his life fades out. I'll be there just like I was with my father because I want Connor to see the look on my face and understand I did it all for her.

The hooker saunters forward as sick enjoyment plays behind Connor's eyes. He doesn't even hide that he's enjoying his little game, sights on me, watching my every reaction.

But all I'm giving is interest. Like a guy who's about to stick his dick in some girl that likes to fuck. Even if what I'd rather do is pull my gun out and decorate the wall with his brains.

I lock eyes with his and wink, letting my deep voice carry as the chick stops in front of me.

"You're too generous, Uncle."

Connor walks toward me, reaching out and grabbing her tit roughly.

"I'm glad you like my gift, nephew. I know how partial you are to redheads. And this one I'll let you keep."

The depth of the brutality and violence I have to swallow makes me fucking sick because I can taste the bile that's creeping up my fucking throat. *He'll let me keep?*

Roman's eyes are on me because he knows I'm about to fucking explode. He's not wrong.

Connor grabs her hair, forcing her eyes to his, and something inside of me snaps. I don't give a fuck about this hooker, but I'll be damned if Connor flexes on me like this.

My voice is rough as I reach down, grabbing the black band of her panties over her hip, jerking her forward.

"You want him? Or you want me? Because I don't fuck hand-me-downs."

Connor laughs loudly, stepping away. The chick winds her fingers around the strings on my hoodie.

"Baby, you get as many wishes as you want tonight."

The sneer across my lip is real because her perfume is Sutton's. Connor did his research. Fucking bastard.

I grab her wrists, pulling her hands off my chest before I close a hand around her petite throat.

"Then tonight my wish is for you to do as you're told. No crying or saying no. Am I understood?"

She nods, fear in her eyes.

I walk her backward, leading her by the throat as she stares up at me, all the way back into the bedroom before the door closes behind me, my fingers twisting the lock.

I let her go, stepping back.

"I'm sorry." I run a hand through my hair. "Don't let him touch you. He gets off on cruelty, which is why I said that shit. You don't have to be scared."

She smiles, relieved as she nods.

I'm already peeling off hundreds from the stack that I just pulled from my pocket as she says, "I'm Krystal."

My face lifts as her fingers pull the strap of her bra down.

"Hey, hey," I whisper, reaching out, tugging it back up. "Let's just talk."

I hand her the money as she eyes me suspiciously.

"You just want to talk?"

I nod, peeling off another couple hundred as I say, "Yeah, but if anyone asks—"

"You're the best I ever had," she interjects, biting her lip. "It's cool. We'll hang for a minute." She looks me up and down. "Or maybe like an hour, and then when we walk out, I'll tell everyone you're a real fucking animal."

I almost laugh, but I wink instead, walking deeper into the room and looking over my shoulder.

"Smoke?"

She shrugs, following behind me. I slide the patio door open to the chill in the air. So I peel my hoodie over my head, handing it to her.

I chuckle because she looks confused.

"It's cold, Krystal. Put it on."

She takes it from my hands, draping it over her head and letting it fall to her thighs because she's swimming in it. I step outside, taking a deep breath before pulling my pack out of my back pocket and offering one to her. But she shakes her head, opting to sit in one of the patio chairs, drawing her knees under the hoodie.

I light my smoke, putting my forearms on the rail, and stare up at the sky.

Fuck. Everything about that navy sky, peppered with bright lights, makes me remember how Sutton looked that night I saw her on the beach, cursing at the damn moon.

Miss you, baby.

"Wanna talk about her?"

I chuckle, looking over at Krystal. "Who says there's a *her*?"

"A him?"

I grin, taking another drag of my smoke, but she doesn't let it go.

"In my experience, men don't look at the moon unless it's the pants-down kind."

I laugh as she continues. "And they certainly don't stare at the stars. So, baby boy, you got it bad."

I drop my head down, looking at my hands hanging over the rail, cigarette burning red, smiling.

"Yeah. I really fucking do."

We dragged our asses through the door at 4:00 a.m. equal amounts of buzzed and tired. The rest of the night was easy, smooth, mostly thanks to Krystal, who didn't leave my side.

She did what she said she'd do. And it was pretty fucking convincing.

It's fucking wild, but Krystal is the easiest moment I've had in the last sixteen months. Because the only thing I had to be responsible for was loving Sutton. There was no pretense or fucking second-guessing her interest. I just got to love my girl out loud again.

I didn't even realize how much I'd missed it until I caught myself looking for reasons to stay in that fucking room.

I wipe my hands down my face, scratching my beard, body warm from the liquor as I lie in my bed, one leg bent at the knee. The joint pinched in between my fingers burns bright as I suck in a drag, holding it for a minute before releasing a thick plume of smoke.

My bottom lip draws between my teeth, dragging out slowly as my head falls back against my headboard, enjoying the tingly feeling in my body as my muscular thigh falls open.

"Damn, I'm fucked-up," I say with a laugh before I drop my head back down, eyes catching on the chair in the corner. The hoodie I wore is tossed over it. The one I let that chick wear—the one that smelled like my baby.

I blink slowly, staring at it as the thought brewing takes a minute to stick in my mind.

I drape my legs over the side of my bed before I stand and walk across my room, ass on display, over to that fucking sweatshirt.

I pick it up, turning it inside out immediately hit with the sweetest smell of grapefruit and rosemary, almost knocking me down.

"Baby," I whisper.

I bring it to my nose, inhaling as my eyes close, letting out a quick exhale before doing it again.

"Oh fuck," I groan.

I'm like an animal, devouring her fucking scent. The veins in my forearms bulge as I grip the fabric tighter, my mind drifting to the image of Sutton's body. Thinking of all the fucking places I could smell that perfume on her.

"Fuck," I grunt as my cock twitches, bobbing heavily as it grows.

My stomach contracts, abs tightening as I bring it to my neck, head falling back as I rub the fabric over me, dragging it over my throat. Licking my lips as it slides down to my chest, wanting her fucking scent all over me.

"You smell like heaven," I whisper, slowly trailing the fabric down my abs as my eyes follow, thinking about my hand in her hair as she sucked me off.

I press my cock into the fabric, rubbing my hand up and down as a growl vibrates through my throat.

"Fuck. I want to be inside you."

I chuck the hoodie, breathing hard. My hand comes to my mouth as I drag my tongue flat and wide over my fucking palm before wrapping it around my cock.

A groan leaves my parted lips as I tug down my shaft and back up, staring at that fucking hoodie. My eyes close as I lean forward, my other hand slapping down onto the wall in front of me. I roll my hips, pushing into my hand, tugging down my dick again.

"Fuck me," I groan.

I want to be inside her so damn bad, fucking her tight little pussy, treating her like the bad girl she really is.

The memory of the last time I said that to her takes over my thoughts.

"Are you my bad girl, baby?"

She looks like she's going to explode as her answer comes out husky and needy.

"Yes."

I'm stroking my cock in front of her face. Fuck she looks beautiful like this. I slide my hand up my shaft slowly, before running it down, watching her lick her lips wanting to taste my cock.

"Lemme get it wet," she whispers, making me groan.

Sutton parts her lips as I guide the tip of my cock into her mouth. Her tongue swirls over the bead of cum that crowned before her mouth covered my length, moaning her pleasure.

I could come on the spot, drip down her fucking throat as she swallows everything I give her.

"Oh, baby. I love you bad."

My hand drops from feeding her my dick, coming to her head. She moans, gripping the side of my ass, pulling me deeper into her mouth.

"Oh fuck, take it," I breathe out remembering our sixty-nine.

I'm jerking my cock, breath ragged, fingers curling into the wall as I think about all the things I wanted to do that night but couldn't.

It's so fucking real in my mind that I lose myself, hanging my head, my teeth clamped together. I wanted to fuck her, then flip her over. Run my hand up her back as she lay on her stomach, legs spread, cum on her ass as I got hard again behind her.

I tuck my arm under her, yanking her hips up as my other hand grips the back of her neck, keeping her face on the ground as she arches her back.

"Yeah, baby. Put that ass on display for me." I breathe, seeing it all in my mind.

Fuck, my cock is so hard, it almost hurts as I jerk myself, gasping for air.

My hand drags across her stomach, rounding over her perfect ass, as I use my fingers and thumb to spread her cheeks before I drop my head, spitting on her tight puckered hole. She rolls her hips as I watch the spit roll down from her tailbone before I reach between her legs, sticking my fingers in her pussy.

I dart my tongue out, licking my lips, almost hearing her moan.

"Baby, you're so fucking wet. It's dripping from you, begging for my cock to do bad fucking things to this ass."

My hand glides faster and faster as I press my hips forward wanting inside her in my fantasy. But it's not enough, so I bring my hand up again and spit into it.

"Fuck, yeah," I groan, listening to the slapping sound of my cock getting off.

I gather her sweet sugar, letting her slickness coat my fingers, dragging it over her tight ass, feeling it contract. I do it again and again watching as she's writhing under my hold.

"Tell me what it feels like."

"It feels like I'm your bad girl."

Her ass is red under my hand as I squeeze, growling as I push my dick inside her pussy, pumping my hips viciously. Fucking her raw. She moans my name before I pull out, bringing the glistening tip over her asshole, rubbing it back and forth.

Her pelvis rocks as my thumb slips inside, fucking that beautiful ass, before stretching her with another finger.

"Yes," she cries in my mind as I do the same aloud, eyes springing open as I pump my cock with a single focus.

I'm chasing my fucking release, lost to the filthy images playing in my mind.

My fingers in her ass are replaced by my cock. It's covered in her pleasure, mixing with the spit as I crown her asshole, spreading her inch by fucking inch, as she opens for me. I push inside, feeling her locked around my shaft until I'm seated deep inside her.

"Fuck."

She reaches between her legs, rubbing her needy little clit as my hand grips her waist, fucking her tight little ass, letting my shaft drag in and out, feeling my cock strangled until I'm thrusting into her, my body doubled over her like an animal.

Grunts and heavy breaths fill the air as I fuck my own hand.

My release builds in my stomach as I scratch at the wall.

"Yes. Take it, baby."

I'm fucking her hard and fast, one hand covering her tit as the other pulls her hair, using it to bring her mouth to mine.

My body contracts as I bite her shoulder, coming inside her, hearing her scream my name.

"Fuck," I grunt, body tensing as warm cum shoots out onto the fucking hoodie and all over my hand.

I'm panting, body jerking as I come riding out my fucking release until I drop my head back, feeling my body growing limp.

The vision of me fucking Sutton's sweet ass fades as my eyes blink open slowly. I milk myself, hissing between my teeth, as I reach down with my other hand to grab the sweatshirt. I clean myself with it as I walk to my bathroom.

I turn on the sink faucet, looking into the basin, letting out a long breath before I grin.

"Soon. Can't come soon enough, baby."

Sutton

chapter
twenty

The day the sky fell—

Promise me that the day you read this that if Hunter isn't in the ground, you'll bury him. And my father for turning a blind eye.

Since that day, I haven't survived.

I've been swallowed whole, and I need you. Because all I want to do is disappear, even though I'm not seen.

January—

Same shit, different day since August. I go to class, I come back to my room. My roommate tells me I'm a fucking downer, and then I watch a bunch of television I can't remember.

I guess the silver lining is that I didn't disappear?

God, I don't want to write in this anymore. And I'm

fucking crying all over this stupid page. And I don't want to think about when you're coming OR be reminded that I'm a fucking idiot that can't take care of myself. I just want to watch TV.

I wish you were a different person. Someone from regular parents who could just love me without all the fight to get there.

Calder—July

Fireworks fill the sky. No matter which direction I turn, color explodes, lighting my face and Roman's in streaks of gold and purple before growing dark again.

"Fuck," I whisper to myself.

"You good?" Roman asks, leaning back against the hood of the GTO.

"Yeah." I nod.

He narrows his eyes on me, but I wave him off with a grin as my phone rings.

"What's up, Unc?"

"How's the shipment?" *Wrapped up hours ago.*

"Golden."

"Any problem at the docks?"

"Nah, we're heading back soon." My eyes land on my brother as I speak. "But you know Roman. We might hit a strip club or two before we're home."

Connor laughs before coughing.

"Okay, but not too much trouble though."

"Wouldn't dream of it."

The line disconnects as Roman stares at me, chuckling. "It's not a terrible idea. It's a long drive back to Boston."

I ignore him, turning around and walking out into the field. *Our field.*

Fuck me. Being back in St. Simeon is bittersweet because everything reminds me of her. She's all over me. But I like it.

Even the smell of the ocean reminds me of her. The way it was always on her skin, like the sunshine she loves so much.

Fuck. When Connor proposed Roman and I start making some trips down here to check up on shipments, it was the first time I was happy to take a job. Although, thank God I'm only here for the night, or I'd go fucking crazy. Probably throw away all the plans and set whole cities on fire, because damn if this feeling ain't fucking potent.

If someone bottled her, I'd be a fucking junkie. I smirk to myself, because I am though—completely and totally fucking addicted.

"It's been two years since we've been back here. Two fucking years," I level, shifting my head over my shoulder to Roman.

It feels like forever and also no time at all because I swear to everything that I love that fucking girl just as much as the first day I told her.

Roman laughs. "If this situation wasn't so goddamn serious, I'd make fun of you for being pussy-whipped. Because you know your ass is thinking about her."

I laugh too, because he's not wrong. I'm always thinking about her.

Roman walks over to me, staring at my profile with a grin.

"I don't want jinx shit, but are you in a good mood? For like the first time in our lives?"

I look up at the sky as I smile.

"I've been filling pebbles in a sack, one by one. Every goddamn day. But today feels like I've got a big enough sandbag to hold them all under. So yeah, I guess that's put me in a good mood because I'm a giant step closer to my girl."

He says nothing, looking up along with me.

"You think she'll like this?"

I smile. "I think we'll die here together one day."

We stand in silence again before he pats my shoulder, saying, "It's almost time."

I nod as a breeze carries over the grass, making me remember our last moments here. She was so fucking beautiful, gifting her body to me because I'd already stolen her heart.

All the sweetest moments pull to the forefront of my mind as my lips tug into a half smile. Damn, the look on her face when she laid her green eyes on me from the hood of that car.

"I got you. Fuck. Baby, I got you. Don't cry."

She draws her head back, hands planting on the sides of my face.

"I was so scared nobody would believe us. Or that you wouldn't come."

My lips find hers before saying, "Nothing could've kept me from you."

"It's still true, baby," I whisper.

Over the last two years, it's been a methodical, unwavering fucking attack on Connor and everyone who hurt her. I've made friends out of enemies. Become a name that invokes fear and respect. And it's all happened in the shadows.

Because nothing will fucking keep me from her. I believe it so deep that I'm here, on our field, planning our future.

I drop my eyes before turning around to stare at the taped-off outline of the house to be built.

"It's all for you, baby."

I bought it all, the whole fucking plot of property. And bribed quite a few people to keep it quiet. Nobody knows it's mine, and that's the way it'll stay until this shit is over. Because one day, we'll sit out on our porch, looking up at the same stars that we fell in love under, not being able to remember ever even being apart.

"C. They're here," Roman calls.

I let out a deep breath before walking over to the car to join him. Three black SUVs come tearing down the dirt road until they slow, stopping next to each other before four men dressed in expensive black dress suits exit the cars.

"Calder Wolfe."

Dante Sovrano, the head of the Italian Chicago mob, steps forward, extending a hand toward me as I do the same.

"Nice to see ya again, kid. I was happy you called. Now, tell me how I can help. Because word is, you're the one that really runs Boston. Not Connor O'Bannion."

Sutton

July—

Happy two-year anniversary.

I was actually kind of scared to open this journal today. Still, I have things to write, and don't worry, it's not all about the television I've watched. Although there's a lot.

Shit got dark. But I crawled out all by myself.

I'm proud of that part, and I know you are too reading this.

So, on to happier news. I ran into Aubrey last month. Like actually ran into her.

She was in the city, visiting some guy she's banging at NYU, and we collided as I was coming into the dorm that she was sneaking out of.

I'm not ashamed to admit that I immediately broke down in tears. She did too.

And then she hugged me, and I cried harder because I realized nobody I love had touched me in two years. TWO.

Honestly, that was the best fucking hug I've had in forever.

(Yours excluded. I'm rolling my eyes because I know you're hugging future me.)

We're having lunch today before she flies back to London... she went to Oxford. Of course, she did.

I guess that's all. I just kind of wanted there to be one journal entry that says, "I'm okay. And a helluva lot stronger than I give myself credit for."

You've helped me learn that.

Definitely a lesson less fun than the others. But I love you even more than yesterday, if that's possible. And I miss everything about you.

-Soon.

P.S. I almost scared myself at how good I was at telling just enough of the truth without revealing it fully. I was marveling at my double-life skills until Aubrey looked at me, patted my hand, and said, "One day, you can tell me the truth. Until then, we'll go with what you just said."

So I guess I'll keep working on it.

Year Three

Sutton-December

"Okay. All right. I swear, Piper. Christmas break is three days away. I have time to pack, then I promise I'll be there. Okay, bye."

I'm smiling, and it feels good, phone sandwiched between my ear and shoulder, bookbag barely staying in place over my jacket as I open my dorm room door.

My head pops up. *What the fuck?* My phone slides down my jacket as I reach for it, coming up short.

"Shit." I huff, squatting to pick it up off the floor.

"Hello to you too. Good to see your manners are still intact," my mother cuts, switching her legs, letting the other drape over.

She's seated on my bed, back as straight as a steel rod, next to my father, standing in his signature navy suit.

I place my backpack on the ground, a scowl on my face.

"What the fuck are you doing here? I thought we had a deal. I show up for the photo-ops and anything press-related, and you both stay far away from me."

"This *is* press-related," my mother snaps.

My eyes narrow. "Is it? Or should we revisit the definition?"

My father clears his throat.

"It seems as though the trouble that found Hunter during his senior year is rearing its ugly head again. The press has leaned into the narrative of 'rich kid with too much time on his hands.' Questions are being asked about his involvement with the company. There's even speculation about Michael Kelly's death. And we think—"

"Marianne thinks," I spit, anger coating my words. "Don't give yourselves more credit than you're due. But personally, I think for the first time, the reporting is spot-on. So, shouldn't you be in Tiffany Astor's room? Isn't that who he allegedly knocked up senior year? Or are you scared there's more to the story, Senator?"

The fucking nerve you have to be here.

"We think," he presses, "that it would be nice for you two to be seen out in public."

My heart stops beating as he speaks.

"The media loved when you two seemed like an item. And Hunter needs the positive press. We'd hoped to rekindle that a couple of years ago after your graduation, but—"

My hand shoots to my mouth as goosebumps pebble over my skin. I shake my head as he trails off, my stomach turning over as my body grows immediately cold. Like ice fucking cold. I stare into my father's eyes, standing silent, willing my body not to share my lunch with the floor.

They can't be serious. That day, two weeks after my graduation is the whole fucking reason we have this deal between us. The reason I almost disappeared into myself.

I know my life is not my own, but they can't actually be this indecent.

I close my eyes, remembering how they forced me to come back to St. Simeon, all to attend some "important fundraiser." And I went because as much as I hate them, they were still paying for the freedom I was desperate for. Even if it's just the scraps that life has to offer. *Something* in this hellhole of an existence felt better than *nothing*.

But I was wrong, because the fundraiser turned out to be Hunter's graduation party.

Marianne had anyone and everyone who would make Page Six in her back yard with a glass of champagne all lifted to toast the man of the hour.

But I never made it downstairs.

I wince, remembering how he smelled and how small I felt before blowing out a hard breath, opening my narrowed eyes on them.

"What's it like to be you? The kind of people who ask their only daughter to be seen with the boy who tried to rape her. Or did you conveniently forget walking into his bedroom, Senator?"

My eyes bore into his. "Did you forget seeing me struggling underneath him, crying out for you to do something? To help me." My voice rises, "Yelling, *Daddy, come back.*"

"Enough," my mother snaps, making my shoulders jump as she holds up a hand, but that only makes me want to bite it off.

I stab my finger at him, my words hurled with all the anger they deserve.

"You closed the door, you fucking bastard. I begged you for help, and you fucking closed the door."

My eyes begin to water, so I snap my jaw shut, running a hand through my hair. *I will never cry in front of them.*

I turn my face back toward theirs, and the indignant looks pull a laugh from my chest. Not in hysteria, but because the goddamn nerve they possess is unbelievable.

Did I ever even know them?

I throw my hands in the air, mainly talking to myself.

"I guess it doesn't really count in your mind since he couldn't get hard. I'm sure you know that part?" I pat my cheeks as I blow out another breath. "In the future, I should really invest some of my inheritance into whiskey stocks since they were the real heroes that night."

My father stands silent, staring down at the floor. God, he used to be such a presence. He always felt a little intimidating but also safe. Now he just looks like a coward.

The thought breaks my heart, but this is the last time that'll ever happen.

Because I know what it's like to be loved and protected. I have someone who would never close the fucking door. And I will fight, scratch, and claw my way back to him.

My mother stands, drawing my attention, as I cross my arms. She looks me in the eye, saying one of the worst things she's ever uttered to me.

"Your pussy wasn't discerning enough to keep you from a criminal, so then why would it care if Hunter fucked it."

I blink, mouth falling open, dumbstruck as she continues.

"I'm not making a request, Sutton. You will have dinner together, be photographed...together, and that's that. The public wants their Romeo and Juliet, and you'll help provide it. Despite your trauma."

My hands are pressed to my chest, pushing in, feeling my heart pounding against the palm of my hand.

"Jesus Christ. What does Marianne have on you that makes you so willing to sacrifice me with such little disregard?"

"It's *who* she has, Sutton. You brought that filth into our life, and he brought with him the whole Irish mob. We all work for Connor O'Bannion, remember? And he likes it when his dirty senator looks good, and nobody's asking questions about the Kelly pharmaceutical company. This time, Sutton, bad press is bad."

"You could've dressed a little sluttier. You know, make the world really believe I would fuck you."

Bile rises in my throat as flashes come from a camera. I keep my eyes on my menu, smiling as I speak like I'm gunning for an Oscar.

I am, though. I will never let Hunter know that he affects me in even the smallest of ways. Because I want to take *everything* from him. That's how much I hate him. But tonight, I'm just starting with his glib satisfaction.

"Well, you've already had one Macallan and Coke, disguised as only a

Coke, so I'd say the chance of you raping me is slim to none. I think we've come to learn that about you. Remember?"

Saying it out loud makes the inside of me shake. But Hunter can't see that, so it's okay.

My eyes lift to his as I shrug my shoulders like I'm flirting, batting my eyelashes.

"Hunter"—I bite my bottom lip leaning forward—"I'm a whole kind of bitch you aren't prepared for now. This version of me fights dirty. So be very careful, or I'll cut your dick off with the butter knife when nobody's looking."

"Noted." He winks, going along with the façade, but I see the worry in his eyes.

Oh, you should believe me, Hunter.

"Good, because I'd never lie to you about how much I despise you."

I giggle before looking back down at the menu.

His mother booked us a fucking table by the window at Bagatelle. A posh restaurant in the meatpacking district. I'm actually disappointed, it's just so obvious, and yet the cameras haven't stopped flashing.

Idiots.

Tomorrow, I'm sure we'll be all over the society section with this bull-shit. My mind wanders to Calder, momentarily wondering if he'll see these photos. Fuck. I hate this.

The waiter comes to the table to take our order, so I choose the first thing I see because, frankly, my stomach soured the minute I saw Hunter's fucking face.

He does the same, then lifts his glass, nodding to the waiter as I turn my head from the window ticking over the other diners. *People are everywhere. You're fine.*

He takes a deep breath before leaning sideways to pull his phone from his Armani slacks.

"Seriously? Nice manners. Eat fast, and then you can go and check your phone for whatever STD's texted you lately. In the meantime, can't you just play along?"

Every word is said with a smile. I pick up my water, taking a sip as Hunter stares at me.

"Yeah, Freckles, I can play along. Like a fucking champ. Let's see if you can too."

"Eww. Don't call me that."

He chuckles, but it's dark, off in some way. My brows draw together as my lips part, but he stops the words from coming out of my mouth.

He holds his phone out toward me, covering it from the glass, so nobody gets a photo, motioning with his head for me to lean in. The smile on his face says he's flirting, being cheeky, but the image in front of me is Piper.

She's standing on a sidewalk in a tank top.

Oh my God, this was taken in L.A., but she only just got there a week ago.

My eyes dart back to his.

"What is this? Why do you have a picture of Piper on your phone?"

"Smile, Sutton."

I do immediately, and he laughs, pulling his phone away, shoving it back into his trousers.

The waiter returns with Hunter's drink, and he doesn't hesitate to take a long swig before saying, "Think of it as a reminder that we're all just puppets in a show. We all have our parts to play, Sutton, and nobody is ever out of reach."

My heart stills. *This isn't happening again.*

"I am playing my part," I whisper, quietly taking a deep breath. "I'm here, aren't I? What more does *he* want?"

He laughs, and it's genuine, throwing me off.

"Do you think I'm talking about Connor O'Bannion?"

"Shhh," I hiss before he smiles again, rolling his eyes.

"Smile, Sutton."

I do as my fingers come to my fork, flipping it over slowly again and again. Hunter's hand brushes over the white tablecloth as he speaks casually.

"I guess, in a way, you're right. I am talking about *him*. But only because he doesn't have to give any orders; everyone's fear does the heavy work."

"What are you talking about? Spell it out," I whisper.

Hunter smirks, tapping a finger on the table before he speaks.

"Our mothers understand that *he* only cares about power and money. Your fucking criminal is the power. As long as he has Calder, that organization is his. Now, my family is the money. Because we make incredibly potent little white pills. You remember those, right?"

I swallow, reaching for my water to take a sip.

"*He's* nothing without either. I fucked up, made a mess that needs to be cleaned up, and because I'm the company's future, that threatens his money. And unlike your mother, mine wants me alive, hence this fucking dinner."

My mind is racing because I still don't get what this has to do with me. *Why show me Piper?*

"But I didn't do anything. I did what I was told. I walked away."

I hate how scared my voice sounds.

"Smile."

I do.

Hunter tilts his head, extending his arm, letting his fingers skim over mine. The action sends chills over my body, my throat suddenly feeling dry, but I don't pull away, staring straight into his eyes.

Fuck you, Cunter. I'm not ever running scared of you again.

"You're so naïve. It's always amazed me that someone like Calder saw anything other than stupidity behind those green eyes."

His fingers retreat, leaving me to take a quiet, relieved inhale as he speaks.

"Freckles, they only found assurance in your weakness. Then you had to go and start acting like your life was yours. Did you think you'd just jet off to L.A. with Piper or have long lunches with Aubrey? If they can't control you, then they don't trust you. And that's a direct threat to *his* power. And I'm certain you would rather die than see your beloved hurt."

I'm sitting silent because I'm not stupid. I know Connor is always somewhere watching. It's why I don't make waves. And I know this fight doesn't truly end until Calder finishes it, which is why I toe the line with my parents.

I just have to survive until we're together.

But I just got Aubs and Piper back in the smallest way. Fuck, I just got some of myself back. And the thought of losing it all again... The lump in my throat is swallowed down as I lift my eyes back to his.

"You know," he chuckles, "if you would've just died, we wouldn't be here. So really, we only have you to blame."

He lifts his drink to me, adding, "Cheers to that, right?" before he downs it.

My eyes grow wide as I let out a half laugh, uncaring about my face.

"I could say the same for you." I hold up my water like I'm toasting him back. "It's a real fucking shame you were such a good swimmer when you got tossed off that cliff."

He sneers.

"Smile," I say, all sing-songy, reveling in my dig as I watch him force a grin.

I tap my fingers on the table, shaking my head, noticing out of the corner of my eye how close the photographers begin to close in on the window.

"So what's the point of all this? I have to ignore my friends again. Fine, done. Am I to never leave my room? Okay, whatever. Do they want me to fail out of college? What?"

The grin on his face stays, growing into a smile.

"How you didn't turn out more like your mother, I'll never know. College is over, Freckles. You're officially withdrawn. They're not paying for it anymore. There are no decisions for you to make. They've decided how to get rid of both of our problematic existences."

I blink, lips parting as Hunter stands from the table, motioning between us. "Figuratively speaking, they've figured out how to kill two birds—"

He reaches into his pocket, pulling out a small blue box, eyes locked to mine.

"—with one stone."

The box flips open to a pear-shaped Tiffany diamond as he lowers down to one knee.

"We all have our parts to play. Yours is as my wife. Now say yes, because *he's* always watching."

Cameras flash like strobe lights next to me. And I see Hunter still speaking, but all I can hear is the quiet slowing of the breath inside my body. Like a countdown to my end.

I've held on for so long to the idea of *one day*. But I'm not sure anymore if there will be anything left of me when Calder comes.

The last time I write—

I can't keep doing this. Because one day, this part of my life will be a memory that I choose to forget. I refuse to honor its existence here for you to read. So just know that I have loved you, never wavering.

And I'm doing what I have to because of that fact.

I hope you find me and that I'm still whole.

Because I never anticipated that when I told you I was willing to wade through hell to be with you—that tonight, the Devil would call my bluff.

Aubrey: Why am I waking up in London and feeling like I'm in a parallel universe

I can't.

Since we've reconnected, I've told the same story: Calder and I broke up, things got out of hand—there was a robbery, and my parents thought it was best to send me to Madison. I did tell them about West, but only what was reported. That lie hurt the worst.

For the most part, I stuck with the truths I could say—ones that felt plausible enough and wouldn't garner too many questions.

Jesus, I've told her and Aubrey about the depression without giving the actual reasons, sometimes blaming the season. I sat quietly on phone calls pretending to have an off day when I was really missing Calder so much I couldn't get out of bed.

And other days, I blamed school or something else just as flimsy instead of saying that I couldn't stop the memories of Hunter violating me with parental approval.

I've cried in silence all this time, but for whatever beautiful miracle of a reason, they've stuck around, accepting my half-truths, even though we all silently acknowledge the lies.

But this time I don't trust myself, because this feels too big to carry alone anymore.

I place my phone down on my bed and look at the boxes delivered to my dorm room today. My life is being stolen from me again.

"Fuck you, Elizabeth."

I lie back on my bed and close my eyes, just wanting to sleep this nightmare away because I'm not going to visit Piper. The only packing I'm doing is taking me back to St. Simeon.

A few hours later, more texts come through.

> Aubrey: This has Baron and Elizabeth written all over it. It stinks of social politics. WTF is going on?
>
> Piper: Don't ghost, Sutton. And don't fucking marry Hunter.
>
> Aubrey: Yeah. Say the hard shit this time. We're here for it, bitch.
>
> Piper: I can't stand the idea that you are all alone with this.

I pull the blanket over me, all the lights off even though it's the middle of the day. I still haven't started packing, but I haven't gotten out of bed either. I'm just staring at my phone, the urge to say something, anything, building more and more.

I have been alone through all of this, and I'm tired. So fucking tired.

Butterflies go off in my stomach as my fingers hover over the keys.

God, what do I say? Because I want to tell the truth. It's burning on the tip of my tongue to escape. I blink, shoulders jumping because I'm so deep in thought that the vibration startles me.

> Piper: Okay. I can't believe I'm asking this. But just tell us if we're team Hunter or team Cunter? That's all we need to know. No other questions until you're ready to answer.

Say it. Do it, Sutton.

If I ignore them, I may never get them back again. Bubbles pop up right before Aubrey's message populates.

Aubrey: I don't give AF what team you say—I'm
always gonna be that fucking pirate's biggest fan.
And I don't care what you say about him either
because you stink of him every fucking time I see
you. If love had a scent, yours would be called
pining. And for the record, modern-day arranged
marriages are not it, bitch. That is not a trend
that's coming back. So stop leaving us on read
and remember we keep secrets. All the fucking
secrets. Dread Pirate Roberts for life...I like that
nickname way better than Wesley...or Westley...
whatever his fucking name is.

Tears. Immediate fucking tears. I love her. She said it so I wouldn't have to. Fuck this, they can make me marry Hunter, give up school, run my life, but I'm keeping these two.

Me: Definitely team Cunter. Arrggh.

Calder-January

"Look at you being a grown-ass man. Sitting at the table, drinking coffee. I guess you're a whole new you in the new year."

"Shut the fuck up." I laugh.

Roman and I have been in New York since yesterday, staying in Brooklyn at a spot used for anyone who needs to lay low.

Connor wanted us close to the streets, to keep our eyes and ears open, since we're here for him to meet with the Italians.

He's trying to strike a deal because they just keep taking more and more control of the drug running in Boston.

But if I had a crystal ball, I'd tell him all signs point to *"you're fucked."*

Then again, I don't really need one. *Guess who owns your streets now— me, ya' fucking prick.*

Roman pulls out the chair next to me at the kitchen table, smirking. "You should've come out last night, C. It was good to blow off steam."

"Nah, not my thing. And your hands were full, I'm sure."

"True, but what'd you do? Jerk off thinking about your girl, all alone, watching the ball drop on television? Loser."

"Fuck you," I chuckle.

I'll never admit how fucking accurate that shit is.

I lift my coffee mug, changing the subject. "That chick you brought back last night made some before she snuck out. It's in the kitchen."

He laughs, stretching his arms as he yawns his words out. "Katie might be a keeper..."

The smile on his face tells me he remembers something I don't want to fucking hear. But it makes me pause to look at him because that wasn't her name.

"Romes," I level, shaking my head, "you're not even close."

His mouth opens, a deep v forming between his eyebrows as his face lifts to the ceiling like he's thinking, and it makes my shoulders shake.

"Amanda?"

"Nope." I grin.

He crosses his arms, deeper in thought. "Jen? Jennifer?" He snaps his fingers, pointing at me. "Chrissy. It was Chrissy."

My hands cover my face as I laugh, wiping them down slowly.

"You're fucking kidding, right? Sunshine, you fucking dick. Her name was Sunshine."

He claps his hands together.

"Yes. Sunshine. I couldn't remember because I was fucking hypnotized by this thing that she could do with her leg behind her head. It was really convenient when we—"

"Stop talking," I grunt, cutting him off as I pick up my coffee and take the first swig, only to spit it back into the cup. "Damn, that's fucking dirt. Sounds like she fucked better than she barista'd."

He wags his brows, reaching for the paper that's on the table as I shovel a forkful of eggs into my mouth.

"What's on the agenda for today? What are we escorting Connor?" he muses, spreading the paper open, making it rustle. "Do people actually read these anymore?"

"You are. So I guess, yeah," I counter, swiping the messages on my phone. "The meeting's late this afternoon. Then we drive the fellas back while Connor flies."

Roman's eyes lift to mine.

"He's gonna be fucking out of control after that meeting. A real pain in the ass all the way back to Boston. I'm suddenly glad he's a dick and making us drive the cars back. He's so fucking paranoid. We could've checked the cars that were here before he rode in them."

I smirk because I've thought about blowing him up a hundred different ways from Sunday.

My phone buzzes so I look down as a message pops up, reading it before it's followed by a photo.

"Oh fuck."

I turn my phone around, smirking as Roman lifts his brows, looking at the text.

"Stripper Chick? Is that who I think it is?"

I nod.

"Yeah, Krystal's happy to make a little side money passing on information when she entertains our local politicians. Looks like she caught a big fish."

"You sure we can trust her?"

I get why Roman's skeptical, but I nod, grinning to myself because the message above reads: **I thought this might help true love conquer all. Now go get your girl.**

Roman pulls my phone toward him, tilting his head to see the photo better.

"Holy shit. That's a lot of leather. He's really getting served, isn't he? Hold up, is that a ball gag?"

I chuckle.

"So much for being the leader of Christian values. I guarantee this photo isn't going on the Franklin family Christmas card."

"What are you gonna do with it?"

I look up to Roman's grin and shrug.

"I'm not sure yet. I'm weighing my options. It has to be the right move. Because I'm not just destroying a kingdom. I'm building a fucking empire. And that shit wasn't done in a day."

I flip my phone over, cracking my neck. Letting the possibilities play out in my mind.

"Why not just leak that shit. Let Prescott take the heat for being so buddy-buddy with the Lord's kinky little freak."

I shake my head.

"If I've learned anything, it's that impulse is the enemy. It's not enough to ruin everything Connor constructed. We have to be the people with the only replacements for what we take away. So that everyone comes to us ready to be led."

Roman folds the paper, shaking his head at me.

"I gotta say, C, they don't fucking know what's coming. I meant what I said earlier—this version of my brother is a grown-ass man."

I push the nasty coffee toward him with a smirk.

"Maybe you could grow up too and fuck a girl that knows how to make coffee."

He tosses the paper at me as I laugh, catching it before slapping it down on the table. I'm grinning as my eyes drop, my body immediately freezing.

My face hangs, fixed on the photo in front of me, as everything inside slows to a scalding simmer.

"What...the fuck?" I growl, spreading the pages open.

Big, beautiful eyes stare back at me—it's her picture—and she's standing right next to Hunter fucking Kelly.

Roman stares at me as my jaw fucking grinds because I can't make any sense of the words on the goddamn page.

Engaged? What the fuck does that mean?

I lift my head, shaking it. "No. Un-uh." My finger stabs down hard. "Why the fuck does that say engaged? She wouldn't fucking touch him. What the fuck—"

The sound of my chair hitting the ground is the only thing that fills the space as I shoot up, exploding in anger. My fists are balled as I look at Roman.

"Why the fuck is my girl next to that motherfucker? I said he needed to heel. I made that deal with Connor."

I throw my fist down onto the table, making everything bounce off the surface as the salt and pepper shakers fall over.

"If Connor let him off the fucking leash...to do this. No. Roman...no."

The paper rips as I ball the article in my hand, grabbing my gun off the table.

"Connor's doing this shit on purpose. Maybe it's another one of his fucking tests, I don't fucking know. But I don't give a fuck either. I'm putting a bullet in his head, and then I'm gonna finish what I fucking started with Hunter."

Roman stands, blocking my way, hand on my chest to stop me.

"C. You ain't going anywhere. Think before you do something stupid. You just fucking said impulse is the enemy."

My voice is too calm. Because I'm in that comfortable place where I stand next to death as I speak.

"This isn't impulse. This is me...protecting what's mine. Because nobody hurts her. And I know they have. I made a deal with Connor; if that little bitch Hunter is marrying my girl, it's only something sanctioned by my uncle. That means he's willing to sacrifice Sutton for whatever cruel fucking reason he's made up in his head. And he ain't holding *nobody* back from doing the same. So move your hand because I won't tell you again. I love you, but I will kill you if you come between me and my fucking girl. Make no mistake. I will put a gun in your mouth and blow you away if you try to keep me from her."

He doesn't flinch or even look surprised. I think he's known that since that night we had it out about her that she's my only priority. It's her above all. And always will be.

He turns with a nod, grabbing the keys off a table and tossing them to me before grabbing his boots.

"You better hope she fucking forgives you for what you're about to do."

The car comes to a screeching halt in front of the fucking Lotte New York Palace. The article said the engagement party was being held at an exclusive club inside this fucking place.

"Calder, man, fucking look at me," Roman presses as I throw open my door.

Cars whisk by as horns honk, but I don't give a fuck. I'm singularly focused as I stalk around the front of the SUV.

A valet rushes forward, forehead wrinkled, pointing to my car.

"Excuse me, sir. You can't just leave your car here—"

"Watch me," I growl, cutting him off, and walk past him, hearing Roman say something. But I'm not listening because I don't give a fuck what Roman has to say.

She's marrying that little piece of shit. What the fuck did they do to her? There's no fucking way that she ever agreed to this.

I can feel myself disconnecting, tearing the fuck away from any part of me that gave hope to reason because my fists want to pound into something. I just want to hit someone until I feel better.

And today, that gets to be Hunter. Right before I blow him away.

My teeth grind so hard they could break as I inhale a rough breath through my flared nose.

If he fucking touched her...

My feet can't carry me fast enough as my head swings from side to side, looking for the fucking room or bar or whatever the hell it is. Some asshole rushes toward me with a shiny gold nameplate above the breast pocket of his beige suit.

"May I help you?"

I jerk to a stop, grabbing his cheap fucking suit by the lapel, bringing his face close to mine.

"What's the name of the members-only club here?"

He stutters, "Rarities," eyes darting around for security, but I shake my head.

"Just tell me where it is. Because trust me, they can't help you if you don't. I will leave you on this floor fucking bloody if you don't speak."

His arm raises, trembling finger pointed toward an inconspicuous door along the far wall.

I'm already past him, letting him scurry away to probably call someone as I close the distance to where he pointed. My hand darts out, grabbing the door's handle and twisting it before I slip inside.

It slams behind me as I stand at the top of a dark wood staircase, chest heaving as I stare down. I reach for my gun in the small of my back, pulling it out before the sound of it cocking bounces off the walls.

I don't even know if she's fucking here. But if I have to sit in this fucking room all goddamn day, I will. Tonight she comes with me, and anyone that gets in my way dies trying.

My feet are bounding down the stairs, heart racing, beating out of my fucking chest because I'm so filled with rage and sorrow that I can't tell the difference between them anymore.

A growl rumbles as I hit the bottom of the stairs, my finger brushing the trigger of my Glock.

But there's no one. The room's empty.

My head shifts around the room, walking inside. It's filled with chocolate leather club chairs and dark wood paneling, like a cigar room out of the 1940s.

This isn't Sutton.

The door I just came through slams as heavy steps fall behind me. It's Roman. I don't even turn around to know. He doesn't say anything as he comes to stand beside me, catching his breath.

We stand in silence, him trying to read me. And me going over exactly what I'm going to do to everyone—the hurt I'm going to inflict.

"She's not here, Calder. And honestly, this is fate working for you, brother. Turn around and leave because nothing good comes from this. Listen to me."

I lift my gun, pointing at nothing, sneering before letting it drop to my side.

"I'm not leaving without her."

He holds out his arms. "And then what? Huh? You're gonna kill everyone and run forever? That's not what you promised her. Walk the fuck away before everything was for nothing."

My head swings to his to say that I can't walk away. That I'm physically rooted to this goddamn spot.

"Then we fucking run, Roman," I shout. "Because I did this to her. I left her here."

A sharp gasp comes from behind Roman, spinning him around and drawing my eyes before my breath empties from my damn lungs. As if I'm being sucked into her orbit as all the oxygen is stolen from my body.

Time stands fucking still. There is no sound. No fucking existence past this moment.

Because it's her. Her—my sweet fucking girl.

Soulful emeralds stare back, locked on me. She's looking at me like she can't believe her own eyes. Fuck. Every piece of her calls to me.

I love you.

I want to say it, tell her, but I can't even open my mouth.

Her shoulders begin to shake as her lips part. She presses her palm against the frame of the door like she needs to hold herself up, before her eyes drop to my hand.

Sutton looks back, brows drawn together as her eyes begin to shine. She steps backward, shaking her head.

"Baby," I breathe.

I take a step forward before my eyes dart down too, realizing what she saw. The gun suddenly feels heavy in my hand, and I hate that it's so comfortable there that I don't feel it anymore.

Fuck. My head lifts as I tuck it back into my pants, eyes pleading with her to not be afraid. But she sucks in a breath, her hand immediately covering her mouth like she's refusing the sound. Not wanting to cry.

My heart's beating too fast because I can feel her panic. It's coming off her in waves, crashing into me, begging for me to make it better.

"Sutton."

But she shakes her head, taking another step back as she viciously shouts.

"No."

I exhale harshly like I've been punched in the fucking stomach. But before I can say anything, Sutton spins around and fucking runs.

Goddammit.

Moments crash into each other. The door she went through slams behind her as my hand shoves against Roman, who's trying to hold me in a bear hug.

Grunts and thwacks echo through the space as I reach around myself, throwing my fist into Roman's side. He loses his grip as I jerk away, shoving him off hard into a table.

"Fuck. Stop, Calder."

I tune everything out, hearing only the blood pumping inside my body as I weave around chairs and tables, throwing shit out of my way. Wood splinters and glass crashes down as my feet dig into the ground before I hurl the door against the wall, bouncing off it as I chase her.

"Sutton," I thunder.

Red hair flies recklessly down a short hall in front of me as I close the distance quickly, taking three steps to her one.

"No," she screams before I grab her arm, yanking her around, making us crash into the wall, her back slammed against it.

She sucks in a quick breath, closing her eyes as I grip her wrists, holding them up at her shoulders.

"Open your eyes," I breathe, feeling the roughness of my words.

She shakes her head, hair falling into her face as she fights against my hold. But it doesn't matter because I can feel it—all her pain, everything she's suffering. It's all over her. It's why she ran and why she won't open her eyes. She knows I'll see the pain behind her eyes because she's mine, and I'm hers.

"Open your fucking eyes."

Her chest shakes as her head hangs.

"I can't," she whispers.

I let out a shaky breath, bringing her fists to my lips, inhaling her scent as I lower my forehead to hers.

"Baby. What have they done? Tell me, and I'll take you away."

"I can't," she growls, cries beginning to fall from her lips as her hands struggle to slap my face, breaking my fucking heart.

I don't stop her, letting her wrists go as she hits me over and over, eyes on mine as she yells.

"I hate you. I hate you. I hate you." She slaps me harder. "How could you do this?"

She's weeping, her fists hitting my chest before trying to shove me backward, but I don't move. I deserve all of this and more. How could I leave her? I should've known better.

My fingertips brush her cheeks as she wails on me. I lean in, trying to kiss her, but she shoves my face away hard, shouting, "No."

I bunch my shirt in my hand over my heart, taking a step back.

God, forgive me for what I've done.

Our eyes connect, anger and love married. I reach for her, but she slaps my hand, hurling her words at me.

"Don't you dare fucking touch me. Not unless you can look me in the eyes and tell me it's all over."

Her eyes burn with rage as I wipe my hands down my face.

"Say we don't have to run or live in fear. Tell me you're here to give me what you promised. *Us* with all the magic, and forever. If you can't say that, then listen to Roman and leave."

My feet stumble backward, hands gripping the back of my neck, knocked silent. My back slams against the wall across from her as I open my mouth, but nothing comes out because I can't say any of that.

And she knows it.

She wipes the tears from her face roughly, staring back at me.

I could put my fist through every wall, scream until my voice gives, but nothing would ever strip this feeling from me. I'm hurting her.

The truth falls from my lips, in the way I can only ever share with her.

"All that keeps me going is knowing you're okay...but now you're here, and I know they're making you do this...and I keep thinking—at what cost?" My voice trails off, filled with too much anger. "Because I know the fucking cost. I've paid it."

I lift my eyes to hers, pushing off the wall.

"Don't ask me to walk away."

"Don't ask me to run," she cuts back.

I spin around throwing my fist into the wall, shouting, "Fuck," before I shove off of it, running my hands through my hair, staring at her, feeling my chest grow tight.

"Then tell me how to walk away. Go ahead, tell me how when I feel like this"—I motion between us—"it's like my soul tore from my body the minute I saw you because it was desperate to reunite with its other half. You're like a homecoming."

Her arms wrap around herself as tears stream down her face.

"How do I stop feeling that? I look at you and all I want to do is carry you the fuck out of here. Put you in the car and let you hold on to me as we fucking drive away. So tell me...how do I walk away, when everything inside of me says otherwise?"

Silence plays out between us as we stare deeply into each other's eyes, so connected that the world around us falls away and all that's left is me and this girl and the stars that measure our love.

"I love you," I breathe. "I fucking love you."

Sutton takes quick steps toward me, arms lifting as I bend down, wrapping mine around her waist and picking her up off the ground. Her lips press against my neck, arms engulfing me as we stay like that, breathing each other in, not saying a word. Because we don't have to.

We feel it all.

My fingers dig into her sides, squeezing her closer to me as I whisper against her skin,

"I won't condemn you to my hell. I'll kill them all. Your mom, your dad, Connor, Hunter. All of them. Today."

Her head rises as she brings her hands to my face, tugging it up so that we're staring at each other.

"I want you, Calder. But I also want picnics and movies and car rides in the rain. I want to hold your hand while we walk down the street. I want your last name as my own and one day to have your babies."

My eyes drop, because I can't house what I feel. It's so big that I can barely breathe. But she jerks my face, making me look at her again.

Pots clang in the background, coming from a prep kitchen, making us swing our heads to the side. As our eyes meet again, I see urgency is reflected in hers.

"None of that can happen if we leave today. You said it—we survive the best we can until we're together again. It doesn't matter what's happened or what will happen because I'm still fucking standing. And I'll be standing when you take your place. We don't run. Ever again."

Her hands brush over my beard as she glances to the side again. *Fuck.*

"Baby—"

She looks back, bringing her lips to mine gently before pulling back with the saddest fucking smile.

"I learned how to stand on my own two feet and how to be strong because of *you*. So that I can carry you too. And now is when you listen to *me*, Wesley."

I can't help the tiniest grief-stricken smile that matches hers as she uses that name.

"This part of our story isn't done yet."

Her voice cracks before she presses her salt-soaked lips to mine, letting them linger like it's our first kiss. I'm clinging to her, wrapped around her petite frame, trying to soak up every fucking last drop of her before I have to let go.

Because I'm going to. Again. She deserves forever and I'm going to give it to her. And I won't fail her again.

Her words are whispered into my ear, "Go and finish this, and then come home."

The way she says *home* almost breaks me because she means her. She's my home.

My face burrows into her neck again as she peppers kisses over my cheek. *Fuck. I want more time. I need more time.*

I inhale against her neck, wanting to take some of her with me. To breathe her in so I can carry just the smallest piece of her.

"Let me go, and walk away," she whispers again.

I know I should, but I can't let go yet.

"Whatever they break, baby, I'll spend our lifetime putting back together."

I press my lips to her neck, traveling up over her jaw and across her cheek, kissing away all her tears before I slow, letting them brush over her lips.

"I love you, Calder."

"I love you too, baby."

Our breath is shared as I lower her to the ground before I start to step back, almost unable to. But she shoots her hands out, grabbing my shirt, holding me in place. And for a minute I'm praying that she's going to tell me to take her with me. But I know better.

She's staring at my chest, not looking up as the plea in her voice almost brings me to my knees.

"Don't look back again. Promise me. It's too cruel to only give me bits and pieces of you."

I don't say anything, tipping my face to the ceiling, bottling my emotions. Shoving them down as deep as I can get them before lowering my head back down, kissing the top of her head.

"On my life."

I'll never forget this moment. This will eat at me until the day I come for her. And God help anyone that breaks even a hair on her fucking head.

My chest rises and falls in time with hers as I stare down, jaw tensed. She's clinging to me, my shirt bunched in her hands, and I know she can't let go either. So I reach out, peeling her fingers off my shirt as a sob bursts from her chest. But I give her what she needs. Exactly what I promised.

I turn around, walking back down the hall. Straight through the doorway. Closing it behind me, leaving my baby alone again.

Sutton

chapter
twenty-three

I'm seated on the floor, face buried in my hands, just breathing. I don't even know how long I've been here, but if I get up and try to put one foot in front of the other, I'm scared that all I'll do is run after him.

The pull is that strong.

God, so much time has passed, and even though Calder looks exactly the same to me, his presence feels even more dominant and that much more enslaving.

It wouldn't matter if today were ten years later. I am *his*.

The way his voice carried a deeper bass booming around the room melted me and woke up parts of me that felt dormant. It was all I could do not to run to him, throw myself into his arms, and let him take me away. But I knew before I listened to every word he said to Roman that he wasn't here because it was over.

Or he wouldn't have been holding a gun—no need.

I let out a breath, resting my forehead on my knees.

Calder was here to kill anyone that got in his way because he'd seen that fucking announcement in the papers. I think a part of me knew this would happen—as if I could feel his heartbreak. That's why I couldn't open my eyes. But it doesn't matter if I wanted to hide from him. I can't.

And I knew when he looked at me with that gun in his hand. The one that I have no doubt he's used before. It would just become an extension of the beautiful monster he is now.

Calder's traded his soul for me—for us. And I love him *more* for it.

It makes him all the goodness I'll ever want in the world.

And I'm greedy for more. A moment isn't enough. I want him and all the magic. And I don't care if that means that I'm damned too.

"Take it," I whisper. "Take my soul too."

My chin quivers as I try to calm my breathing.

God, when he used to say, "*If we only had tonight, would it be worth it?*" I always said yes, without hesitation. Because it was the truth. The idea of living a whole life, never knowing what it's like to be loved by him, even for the tiniest moment, seemed tragic.

Not a life worth living.

But there's a flip side to that. Now I know what it's like without him. What life feels like *because* I had him. And it's worse. If I'd never known what his lips felt like, I wouldn't beg God to let me forget. Or if I'd never felt what it was like to be safe in his arms, I wouldn't hate the feel of my own hands.

It's not that I only want him. I need him. Like the fucking air to breathe. But I need all of him, not just a piece, because that could never be enough.

The sound of footsteps lifts my head.

Shit. The staff must be showing up for today. I scramble up the wall, brushing my hair from my face, standing up straight before wiping my cheeks one last time.

But it's not a waiter I see as I smile toward where the sound is coming from.

"Hunter?"

What is he doing here?

Hunter strides up next to me, so I shift, making sure my back isn't against the wall.

"Well, well, well. Color me confused." He smirks with the kind of arrogance of someone that thinks they have the upper hand. "I thought you two were supposed to have said goodbye. None of that looked like a goodbye. I mean, I can't read lips...not that you were doing much talking."

My eyes narrow because this is a threat. Even if all Hunter saw was our goodbye.

But that's not what's beginning to settle over me like a match thrown on lighter fluid.

My eyes lock to his as my hands begin to shake.

He invaded our moment. Peeked around a corner like some kind of sick fucking voyeur enjoying our misery, again, because he's the fucking person that started it all.

Oh God, I feel violent, like everything inside of me is fucking vibrating, feeding off my hatred for him. I let out a shaky breath because I feel like I could kill him. Jesus Christ, like actually kill him.

Scratch his eyes out and wrap my hands around his throat.

How dare he stand here readied with whatever threat he thinks he's going to make.

Hunter steps in closer to me. "I bet if I were to tell Connor..."

Fuck you. Chills cover my body as I stare into his eyes.

"Or I could keep my mouth shut, and you could go about proving how much your criminal really means to you. You wouldn't want him in trouble, would you? Because I'm pretty sure they handle things way differently in that world."

I shake my head, forcing my breath to stay even as the hairs on the back of my neck stand on end. Hunter lifts his finger to my collarbone and trails over it as he licks his lips.

"What will you trade for my silence, Freckles?"

I grab his hand roughly, lifting it to my mouth, and cover my lips over his forefinger, sucking.

He groans, reaching down with his other hand, grabbing his dick.

"Oh fuck. He trained you well."

Hunter's eyes blink slowly as I smile against his finger before clamping down. Teeth slice into his skin as I bite so hard that a scream explodes from his mouth.

He shoves my face away with his other hand, sending me stumbling backward as he immediately covers his finger.

"You made me bleed, you bitch."

I spit on the floor, wiping my mouth as I laugh.

"The only thing I'll trade you is *my* silence for *yours*. Touch me again and I promise to make sure Calder knows. It would be worth all of us dying just to see him tear you the fuck apart."

I shove past him and walk in the other direction, hearing my own words in my head.

"We don't run. Ever again."

I lied—

I said I wouldn't write in here anymore but here goes because I couldn't not talk to you.

I slept on the floor of my room last night...yeah, I'm back at Elizabeth and Baron's house. No school and no money=no choices.

But it doesn't feel like home anymore except for my room. That feels like us.

I think it's why I slept on the floor last night. I literally dragged the blanket onto the floor to where you almost died. And lay there thinking about you.

Kind of morbid, right? But maybe this is my late-in-life emo phase?

Don't laugh too much at that because you really fucked us up, Calder, showing up, doing what you did today. Saying what you said.

I feel like I'd just figured out how to handle the pain.

How to deal with it. But now it's compounded. So I'm mad at you...still. Before I saw you today, I'd been looking around this room a lot, wondering what was going to happen to the people we used to be. Would we ever be them again? Maybe find bits of them once we're back together.

And then you showed up and suddenly I was me again because I was seen.

So even though I kind of hate you for the torture, I also love you so much.

And I need you to know that I wanted to run after you, but that I love you too much for that. I was keeping my vow to protect you, even from yourself.

*kiss me right now while you're reading this and say, "I'm so lucky to have such a smart and beautiful girl."

Anyway—now I'm crying because I can kind of still feel your lips. So...in conclusion, I love you more today. I want you to know that too. I love you MORE today, and I see you for everything you are.

And my favorite part of what I see is that you're mine.

-Sooner, please.

chapter
twenty-four

Calder

"**Y**ou good?" Roman breathes from my doorway.

My eyes lift from the chair where I'm seated, hidden by the shadows of my dimly lit room, as the beer in my hand dangles between my two fingers. It taps the side of the couch before I lift it, taking another swig.

"Am I good?" I breathe out with an empty chuckle at the end because, no, I'm not fucking good.

Roman starts to speak, but I hold up a hand, stopping him. Because there's something more important that needs to be said before I answer him.

"Romes, I should've said this shit earlier—but thank you. You tried to protect me from *me*, but more importantly, you tried to protect *her*. And I'm sorry I didn't see that sooner."

He nods, stepping inside my room as I run a hand through my hair.

"I want to kill him, Roman. Tear Connor apart for what he's done. For the way he treats people like fucking game pieces on some kind of board, just playing with them for his own fucking enjoyment. He gave her to him, Roman..."

My voice trails off as I shake my head because I have to stop talking. That's how much my blood boils. It makes me want to tear the fucking walls off this house, and I need to be clear right now because yesterday changed everything.

There's no way I'll make it another year, two, three more without her. I won't survive.

Fuck. I lean forward, elbows on my knees, holding the neck of the bottle with both my hands as I stare down at it.

"Do you know how hard it was to sit outside that meeting with the Italians and pretend I didn't want to gut him? Roman, the shit going on in my head about Connor and Sutton. Fuck. I can't stop thinking about her and what could happen, and it just makes me..."

I inhale harshly through my nose, blowing it out just as hard because I'm too volatile. I'm ready to explode, aggression readied at the surface like a bottle that's been shaken.

"What's the play, C?"

I suck some beer left behind on my bottom lip, not immediately answering because once I say it, there's no going back. And that's why I've been in here sitting in this dark room—

I've been trying to make peace between what I *should* do and what I'm *going* to do.

I should walk away, stick to the plan, not get anything messy. But that's not what I'm going to do. I lift my head, fingers picking at the label on my beer.

"When I was driving back in the other car, one of the boys said he's heard a rumor that other families were pushing for a Council meeting. He didn't want to tell Connor—scared, you know."

Roman raises his brows. "You think the other families know Connor's weak?"

I nod. "Maybe. If they do, then there's blood in the water. If they don't, I need to make the first kill the messiest so they come swarming."

I hesitate as Roman stares back at me for a minute.

"I have to hit Connor where it hurts most."

He lets out a heavy breath, laying his back against the wall before shoving his hands into his pockets.

There's no hiding from him. We don't have to speak to understand each other.

"Fuck, C. That's going all in."

I set my beer on the ground, rubbing my face as I sit back, feeling the weight of my world laid heavily on my shoulders.

"You know that you don't have to do this. You could keep your head down. It can all fall on me."

His face darts to mine as his hands fly from his pockets.

"Why are you doing all this? Taking Connor down, going after the Prescotts and the Kellys. Tell me why."

My brows draw together as I grip the arms of the chair, dragging down the length of them, feeling my teeth grind together. Because what the fuck kind of question is that?

"I'm doing it for her and for West. Are you fucking kidding right now?"

He pushes off the wall, face screwed up like he's pissed.

"Yeah, me too, but I'm also protecting you, dick." His jaw tenses as he runs his hand over his head. "And I'm fighting to have a say over my own life. You're not the only one held here by this last name. So don't ever say that shit to me again. I'm not keeping my head down like some pussy. We do this together."

All I can do is nod as he lets out a breath before turning away.

Fuck.

"All right. I'm sorry."

He waves me off before looking back at me.

"So like I said before, what's the play?"

"We're gonna need eyes on her, now. Because I'm about to incite a war and topple a dynasty. And at the end—it's either gonna be me or Connor six feet under." I pick up my beer and take the last swig. "Until then, just don't let me kill him."

Roman's silent for a minute before his face matches mine. "What if we just maim him a little? Fucking dirtbag."

My chest shakes as I look at him. Because fucking Roman. He gives me a nod before turning around and walking out, leaving me alone again with my thoughts.

But there's only one—her.

Sutton

The phone on my nightstand vibrates, so I pick it up, seeing Piper's name.

"Hi."

My voice is quiet as I lie on my bed, staring out my opened balcony doors.

"How'd the fake-love engagement party go?"

"I saw him."

She's silent because of the way I just said *him*...she knows exactly who I'm talking about. No explanation or context is needed.

"Holy shit. Are you okay? Can you talk about it?"

"No. And I'm not." My chin trembles, and my voice breaks.

"What can I do, Sut?"

I wipe my fingers over my cheeks. "Just sit with me on the phone. It's nice not to be alone."

"I hate your parents for doing this to you. Forcing you to marry Hunter, all for political gain. Try to tell me what you can. Maybe that would make you feel better?"

I close my eyes, focusing on my breathing, feeling it fill my chest and leave before my lips part.

"Imagine loving someone so much that you'd be willing to stand in the middle of hell and take on the devil just for a chance to be with them again. You'd do unimaginable things, Piper."

"Sut—"

"But it's something you'd have to do alone. Because it would be too dangerous for other people to help you. I'm in hell, Piper, so just sit with me, tell me something funny, make something up if you have to because it's just nice to hear what life can be like on the other side."

I hear her suck in a ragged breath, and I know she's crying, but she clears her throat.

"Okay, so...Aubrey had a threesome with her professor and his wife—she is now passing her International Laws of Business course. However, she's now failing her Women's Studies course. The one taught by said wife, because apparently the nutty professor only wanted to spread his butter on our honey Aubs."

I can't help it. Tears mix with laughter until all we have is laughter.

"I love you, Sut. Thank God Aubrey's a gorgeous little skank, or we'd have nothing to laugh about."

How I got so fucking lucky to have these friends, I'll never know.

"I'll have to send her pussy a thank-you card."

Piper screams, laughing, and for a minute, I'm happy.

Some of my favorite things—
I opened this journal today and just kept reading. Maybe because it's Valentine's Day. And getting out of bed to hang out with Elizabeth and Baron was a hard no.
So I've been holed up reading and rereading the entry you wrote after that night in the car when it was raining. The night we stayed cuddled in the back seat.
We never did finish that conversation, and it's made me

*think about all the other things I have that are unfinished.
Like College. And Us.*

*Jesus, we're sooo unfinished, and today that hurts a little
too much. So I'm going to start compiling questions you have
to answer like we did that night. All the ones you distracted
me from answering. This way, we can catch up on all the
things left unfinished.*

I love you. Soon.

The pen drops from my hand as I grin, lying back on my bed, letting my mind drift back to that night. Trying to remember all the questions we asked as we lay wrapped in each other under that blanket, rain hitting the roof of his Mustang as the windows fogged.

"You picked tonight on purpose, didn't you? Admit it."

His fingers trail up my arm, all the way to my shoulder, and back down.

"I plead the fifth. But are you complaining?"

I shake my head as he leans in to kiss me again.

"Me neither," he growls against my skin. "I think the rain might beat the stars."

I giggle as the vibration tickles my neck, a thought springing to mind.

"Would you rather be stuck in the rain or in the snow?"

Calder pulls back, staring down at me with that smirk on his face that makes me crazy.

"What?"

I raise my brows, but he just keeps looking at me.

"Oh my God," I laugh. "Which do you like better?" He shrugs as I stare at him. "Have you never played Would You Rather?"

He laughs, smooshing my face with his hand.

"No. Nobody plays that. You're making it up."

I shake free of his hand, laughing harder. "Lies. You totally look the type."

He darts his fingers out, tickling me, growling, "What type is that?" so I bite at his arm, saying, "A secret nerdy dreamer," but he leans in, grabbing my chin.

"I only dream about you. You're always my rather."

I smile as he brushes his lips to mine but hovers before saying, "Kiss me."

We press together, tongues dipping inside, gliding over each other's as he weaves his fingers through the hair at the nape of my neck. Kissing him always leaves me breathless.

He pulls away, looking down at me as I smile big and bright.

"Your childhood was stunted, Calder Wolfe. Everyone should have a solid list of rathers."

His face is so serious for a moment as he looks down at me.

"My choices aren't always my own. So I guess I try to never really think about what I'd want—until you. You make me want everything, Sutton."

The smile on my face feels permanent. In so many ways, we're the exact same, beholden to our names, locked in obligation. But he's been robbed of the simple pleasure of a dream.

I scoot in closer, hitching my bent leg higher over his hip. I'm going to give that back to him.

"So then, let's play." I grin. "I mean, you keep refusing to have sex in the back of this car, anyway, and it is raining. And you've already—" I bite my lip as he tilts his head, staring at me, eyes taunting me to say what he just did to me, but I'm not going to.

"Shut up with that look." He winks, and I feel more of the blush I know is already on my face creep up again. "Just answer the question, and then you can ask me one."

He shifts us, sitting up, forcing me to straddle his lap.

"Sorry. You're making me hard."

I bite my lip, feeling shy in the best way. He smirks, reaching out and tugging my lip from between my teeth, pulling me forward so that we're nose to nose, eyes closed.

"Baby, with your legs spread like that, and that fucking look on your face, my dick was begging to grind against your pussy, to get hard enough so I'd give in and fuck you in the back of this car. But you only get the first time once, and that deserves magic, Buttercup."

I let out a long breath as he releases me, and my body falls away from him.

Jesus, he's fucking hot.

Calder drapes the blanket we brought over my shoulders, cocooning us in and keeping me warm since I'm only in jeans and a bra. He brushes the back of his hand over the fabric covering my nipple, letting his fingers gently pinch the pebbled bud.

I suck in a breath, back arched, grabbing his shirt on either side of him at his waist as he speaks.

"Let's play differently. Our way. Every kiss you give me, I'll answer your questions."

He takes his finger away, making me lick my lips.

"And what will you give me for my answers?"

"The same. A kiss. But neither of us can kiss the same spot twice or repeat what the other did. I'll go first."

I giggle as he runs his fingers down my throat to the space between my breasts. Curling his finger over the wire of my bra, he jerks me forward, pressing a kiss between my cleavage.

"Fuck," I whisper before he says, "What's your favorite color?"

"Matte black. It makes me think of this car and what you did to me on the hood of it."

He grins. "Wanna redo? In the rain?"

Heat spreads over my core as I smile, leaning forward, kissing his right cheek sweetly.

"Favorite food?"

He buries his face into my neck as he bites and licks over my skin while he answers.

"That's easy. There's this place back home called the Yankee Lobster Company. And I could eat their lobster rolls every day for the rest of my life."

He groans, pulling my jeans up, making the fabric pinch between my legs in that way that makes me gasp as my hands lock around the back of his neck.

"That's not all I could eat every fucking day."

His hand dives under my ass, forcing me forward, as his fingers come up between my legs, pressing against my clit.

My head falls back. "You're cheating."

Fuck, that feels good.

He laughs quietly against my ear as his fingers rub in small circles.

"Nobody wins this game. There is no cheating."

I circle my hips, feeling my clit throb.

"But I can't concentrate."

"Favorite song?" he whispers, taking his hand away and gripping the front of my bra again. With his other hand, he presses against my stomach, laying me back between the two front seats as he trails his fingers down my body.

I lift my face, eyes locked to his. "You forgot to kiss me."

Calder licks his lips, yanking my pants open, unzipping them slowly until my bareness is exposed. He jerks them over my ass before gripping it, bringing my pussy to his face.

"You forgot to take off your fucking pants."

I suck in a breath, eyes rolling back into my head, breaking from the memory as I reach between my legs to rub myself. I'm soaked, so fucking wet, remembering how his tongue felt on my clit. How he ate me, back arched, pussy brought up to his mouth like he was feasting.

"Oh God."

My fingers work my clit, gliding over and over, but it's not enough. I miss the way he felt inside of me, the way he filled my cunt, making me beg for more.

I reach next to my bed, sliding open the nightstand drawer, and grab my toy before pressing the button. My legs spread as I push my vibrator inside.

"Oh fuck."

My hips rock forward as it nestles inside, humming against all the right places as my other hand moves faster and faster. I draw it out of me slowly, feverishly playing with myself, opening my legs further. My mouth opens, feeling the tension between my legs as the hardness drags in and out of me.

I lick my lips just as I'm hit with the image of me, down on my knees.

Calder's hands in my hair, filling my mouth with his rock-hard cock. Inching it in before pulling back, more each time until he says, *Swallow me, baby.*

It doesn't matter that I'm all alone because right now, Calder's everywhere. He's down my throat, hands on my clit, and inside my pussy. All fucking over me, possessing me, and fucking me raw.

"Oh God, yes," I pant, feeling myself tighten over the hard steel inside me. "Make me come."

My body contracts, knees drawing up as my slick, wet release gushes from me, and I moan, long and hard, doubled over before all the breath in my lungs releases, and my body becomes Jell-O. I lie on my bed, naked and still happily caught up in Calder until it fades, and I have to open my eyes again, taking a deep breath. As I do, a smile graces my face, and I lean over feeling around for the journal still on my bed, speaking the words aloud as I write them.

"God, I miss you in the most nonromantic, whorey way, Calder Wolfe. Today your dick is my rather."

Calder-March

"Hey," Roman says, looking down at his phone. "All the shit's in place. Invitations were made by Senator Franklin and accepted."

I nod, knowing what he's talking about, saying, "If this shit goes well, she won't have to do shit with that little prick," under my breath to him as I push the door open to Connor's office.

Connor's boom greets us as we walk through.

"What the fuck."

Shit spills out over his desk and onto the floor as he swipes a hand over it. He's raging again.

"Aww, I guess everything's going wrong for him," Roman whispers.

Let me just put you out of your misery and stick a gun in your mouth, Uncle.

"The Italians are undercutting me on my own streets. Those fucking greasy wops got a supplier in Chicago, making the same shit I'm making but at a cheaper fucking price. They're stealing all my business. Taking food right off my plate. And my own people are betraying me and selling for them."

Roman and I sit quietly on the couch, surrounded by other men, all watching Connor come undone.

"How'd they get by us? Huh?" he shouts.

Pete, his second in charge, stands up, glancing over at me before he does.

"We think one of the other families has cut a deal with them—to make a play for your position. That's why we're hearing rumblings about a Council meeting."

It was so fucking easy to plant that seed and watch it grow, but that doesn't mean I'm not on edge. Because all it would take is for Pete to point a finger in my direction, let Connor know I'm the little birdie that gave him that info. And bang. I'd be over before I got started.

I'd played it. Acted chill when I passed it along, pretending I didn't want to upset my uncle with neighborhood gossip. Acting like I didn't know who to go to. Letting Pete get greedy for that credit, to be held in the favor he's so desperate to have from Connor.

I knew who I was choosing; I needed a sacrificial lamb, and he couldn't be better.

Here's hoping I didn't get a little bitch too.

Connor throws an ashtray as men jump out of the way before ash lingers in the air and a thud dents the wall.

"If the Council meets, it'll be for my head. And then you'll all go fucking hungry. I need to know who the fuck's in bed with the Italians."

Fuck. The satisfaction I feel right now. I took his drugs. That was the first step.

Dante and I have been working over the last year to make him the main supplier. I obviously get a cut, and he's agreed to an equally beneficial deal for us regarding guns.

Now I'm taking all his power. Feeding his paranoia, turning his men against him without them knowing, like the one standing in front of Connor right now.

Connor paces behind his desk, breathing heavy, spit flying from his mouth like a lunatic as he mutters.

"Connor, with all due respect," Pete starts, then hesitates.

Roman turns his head, just barely lifting his hoodie, letting me see where his gun is in case I need it since mine is at my back.

Connor stops, looking straight at my patsy.

"Speak."

Pete cracks his neck—nervous habit, probably—before he begins again.

"You've put us at a disadvantage by not telling us what's been going on. If we lose control of the drugs in South Boston, we lose control of Boston. I know you know that, but you should have let me help with the renegotiation, Connor. Because now that it's fallen through, that's left us weak. So I think we need to try again. Call another meeting."

I swallow, almost seeing how it's going to play out before it does. My eyes fix on Connor, waiting, adrenaline coursing through me so fast that my heart feels like a goddamn hummingbird.

Nobody knew Connor tried to renegotiate. Only me and the Italians. And Pete, once I slipped that information in so fucking casually that he actually pretended to already know it.

Connor hangs his head, fingertips pressing into the wood like he's trying to scratch through it. His voice is low and sinister, his words said in almost a growl.

Fuck, I can feel his anger. It's like my own, just under the surface, always ready. We're alike, my uncle and I, except what he does for power, I do for love.

"You don't need to tell me what I already know. You think I'm scared of having a knife at my throat?" Connor's eyes lift, connecting with mine. "That's always the position of the king. And when it presses down, you flip it and stab your enemy in the throat."

Connor's body lifts quickly, his gun coming from the holster as a bang reverberates around the room. Shouts ring out as everyone ducks, knocking shit off tables before they hit the ground.

But I don't move. I'm sitting in my spot, staring directly at Connor as Pete collapses to the floor. This is the Connor I knew I'd get.

My uncle's lips pull into a sneer as he hurls his words out to the room, looking straight at me.

"Pete Gallagher betrayed me. Nobody knew I'd had another meeting with the Italians. Find out what family he was working with. I want to know fucking yesterday. Do you understand me?"

His voice booms through the room as everyone nods.

"Go."

Men scatter, looking over their shoulders as they hurry out of the room, but Roman and I stand, letting them all go before us.

Connor's eyes narrow on me.

"You bring me heads. Do you understand? Or I'll take yours."

I give a half smile and nod.

"Absolutely, Uncle."

He lowers down back into his chair, running his hand through his hair before he says, "And send someone to take care of the body."

Roman and I walk out side by side, silent until we hit the street.

My face shifts to his. "Gather the fellas. We're gonna remember Pete right. He died for a bigger cause."

To start a war that will burn down this family tree.

Roman nods, opening the driver's-side door before we both slip into the car. I roll down the window, putting a cigarette between my lips.

"Where's my girl?"

"The island. Back at her bitch-ass parents' house."

I nod. "We need to find the right time and send her the thing."

Roman smirks before he makes a right.

"I'm signing it from me because you ain't stealing my thunder on that shit."

I laugh before taking a drag and letting it drift from my lips.

"All right. Fair."

Sutton

"Jesus Christ," I breathe out.

My mother and Marianne are engrossed in some wedding magazine, talking about flower arrangements as I stare down at my phone.

This has become the norm over the last month of April—they dream up a wedding that I battle, and we stand off with no winner. But I know I can only do this for so long until it comes down to actually choosing dates. And actually marrying Hunter Kelly.

> Me: Meeting number 1,785,927 in the great wedding debate is about to commence. Wish me luck. I'm proposing minimalism—example, no groom.

The bubbles jump to the screen immediately.

> Piper: Read me clearly: If they force the whole big wedding, we all wear black. Marrying Cunter deserves funeral attire. God I hate him.

A string of mad emojis pops up from Aubrey before her message comes through.

> Aubrey: Fuck them. Like all of them, equally and without lube. Piper—Sut's not having bridesmaids. Because I will not stand there. I'll fucking object. I'll say I've been pegging that little fucker behind her back for years.

I bite my lip to stop the chuckle that wants to spring out, suddenly picturing Aubrey really giving it to Hunter. My eyes lift to him, seeing him staring down at his phone before another message comes through.

> Piper: But seriously, I wish I was there and not all the way on the other damn coast because I love you so much. Also—here's a good point to make. Nobody gets married before they're twenty-one anymore.
>
> Aubrey: Dude—if there was ever a wedding where booze was needed.

I blow out a quiet breath, flicking my eyes to Hunter again because I'd rather he was as sober as possible. Not that I think alcohol is to blame for his vileness. But the veil he exists behind seemed to slip so easily when he was drunk that I'm pretty sure every fucking "Coke" would just guarantee his cruelty.

> Me: K. Keep compiling the list. I'll text soon. I've got a fight to have.

I pocket my phone, looking up as my mother's eyes lock to mine. I felt her staring at me.

"Is there a reason you look chipper, Sutton? Not that I'm complaining. It's a nice change from your usual personality. But I'd like to prepare myself for your mess if there is one."

My lips press together before I speak. *God, she's such a bitch.*

"I was texting with my friends. Nothing for anyone to worry about."

I grip the back of the couch, trying to calm my temper because it's already ready to charge at her.

"Well—" she starts, but I interrupt her, quickly changing my mind about staying calm.

"Before you say that I'm not allowed to have friends—*again*—remember what I told you. I'm keeping them. They aren't a threat, obviously, because I'm here, agreeing to marry this dick."

Marianne bristles as I motion toward Hunter.

"So there's no mess to clean up, Elizabeth...other than this shitshow of a wedding you want to throw."

My mother slaps the magazine in her hand down on the table as Marianne glares at me.

"I spoke too soon. Seems you're back to your regular self. Let's try to be less of that when you and Hunter meet with Father Michael tomorrow."

"Meet with? Not happening. I've been clear the last four hundred times that I've said this. It's either the justice of the peace or nothing."

Marianne huffs, turning her body toward me. It's rare she even addresses me, but I've never underestimated her hatred.

"I don't like empty threats, Sutton. They aren't intimidating. I prefer to be straightforward."

"Do you like the truth, Marianne? Really?" I say it dripping in sarcasm with *"Your son's a rapist"* sitting on the edge of my tongue.

I glance at Hunter, who's staring at me with malice behind his eyes as he sips his drink before smirking as he says, "Just tell it to her, Freckles, or aren't you brave enough? Where's all that bite?"

The room is silent, all eyes on him as he stares back at me. *You prick.* He's talking about Calder and his little discovery. But I know he won't tell because it's bad for both of us.

Marianne stands, drawing my eyes back.

"Yes. Why are you in such opposition to this wedding, Sutton? Tell us the truth."

I huff a laugh before I answer with one of the thousand reasons I hate this wedding.

"Because I refuse to sit through some elaborate political spectacle. One where you all pretend to cry while telling everyone a story about high school sweethearts turned into a forever kind of love." My voice lowers to a patronizing tone. "Because all this is, is a cleanup job so that Hunter doesn't end up like his father."

She swallows, crossing her arms. I'll never believe she cares about her dead husband. She's as motivated by greed and power as Connor is. That's why she wants the spectacle.

"But you're right, Marianne. I have to be there. I'm under Connor's thumb as much as any of us. I just don't give a fuck about your side agenda. So like I said, justice of the peace or nothing."

If looks could kill. She's scowling at me, matching the glare coming from my mother. I can't believe I was scared of her because she just feels pathetic now.

"Thank you for your honesty." Marianne sneers.

I nod back, going for the full bitch effect.

Because what they don't need to know is what Hunter already suspects. That the most important reason for opposing this tragedy in the making is Calder.

I won't twist the knife with photos of us kissing in front of an altar plastered on every news outlet and paper on the East Coast.

It's the only thing I can do for him, so they'll have to drug and prop me up to get me to do what they want.

"Jesus," my mother snaps, avoiding my eyes. "Someone just negotiate terms with the little bitch because the sooner they marry, the better."

I huff a laugh, looking up at the ceiling before bringing my eyes back to Marianne's.

My father stands, offering, "Sutton—"

Go to hell, Baron. My face darts to his.

"I think you should leave this one to the grown-ups. If you're confused, the kids' table's over there."

I point to where Hunter's sitting as I stare my father down. He says nothing, retaking his chair, scowling as he does.

Marianne walks toward me, clearly trying to be some kind of voice of reason, but I'm so ready for a fight.

"Sutton, sweetheart. I know this situation is impossible. It's not ideal for my precious boy either. He had different plans for his life. Dreams that have been ruined too."

I wish I had a better response, but all I manage is "Eww."

But she keeps talking.

"The whole point of this union is to draw attention away from the things we don't want the press to talk about. So far, it's been working, so yes, I admit that a big summer wedding is beneficial to all of us. And we've thought about how that can positively affect our futures."

"An announcement after the justice of the peace would do the same," I counter.

Marianne narrows her eyes, bringing her hand to her hip as she tilts her head. *Read me, Marianne. I'm not stupid or intimidated. Your dream isn't happening.*

"A small private church wedding...keeping with the narrative of two Catholic political dynasties. And you get to re-enroll in school for the fall."

My eyebrows rise, hearing my mother scoff. Wow, we really are negotiating. I hate that my happiness plays out on my face. But the idea of getting something back, even the smallest thing, makes me want to smile.

All right, let's do this, bitch.

"Done. But not a church in St. Simeon. And in the off-season—preferably December. With no bridesmaids or groomsmen."

I will not marry anyone but him in our church, where he first kissed me. No fucking way.

Marianne crosses her arms, taking a deep breath like she's thinking over her options.

"With exclusive photos from the church for specific media outlets and candids taken from your newly leased pied-à-terre."

What the fuck? My eyes grow wide, shooting my head toward my mother.

"Apartment? Tell me you haven't already leased it? Are you fucking kidding? What is wrong with you?"

"You didn't tell her?" Marianne says, eyes darting to my mother, then back to me. "You're moving in together next week."

I look around. I feel shaky, turned inside out.

"You knew," I rush out, drawing out the words as I volley between my parents, "and you're shutting the door again? I mean, I shouldn't be surprised. But I am. I actually am."

My mother screams her frustration before slapping the table and standing.

"Where did you think you'd live once you got married?"

I push off the couch, ready to meet her where she is.

"Forgive me, Mother, but I thought we were all in on the joke. That this marriage was a farce, just for looks, so we'd have separate places just like half of the other Upper East Side marriages."

She crosses her arms, turning away as my eyes shift, landing on Hunter, who's grinning as he drinks.

"Fuck you," I spit.

And without hesitation, he mouths, "With pleasure."

I can't breathe. Because all I smell is whiskey. His face feels soaked in his intention as I stare back at the harsh angles of his jaw and the way he licks his lips.

Oh my God.

It's as if he's thinking of all the things that could happen behind a locked door.

My feet start in his direction before I even know what I'm doing. But I blink, catching up as my palms begin to sweat. All those disgusting memories begin to lay themselves in front of me as I close the distance.

I drop my eyes to his hand, watching as he circles the bottom of the glass on the table, making the ice clink together. All I can think about is how much I'd like to break that glass and stick him with a piece of it.

My arms wrap around me as I stop in front of him, chills covering my body and bile coating my throat.

You filthy piece of shit. I can't wait until he makes you pay.

Hunter winks as he lifts the cup to his mouth, pausing with it against his lips for a moment.

"You're so beautiful on your back."

A hard whoosh of air tears from my body before I violently slap his fucking drink out of his hand. Whiskey splashes everywhere as the rocks glass thuds to the carpet. Someone behind me gasps, but I don't react.

I just stand there looking down at Hunter as he stares down at his shirt. His chest rises up and down heavily as he wipes the liquid from his face. Not a sound is made as I glower at him. He licks his lips, brushing the liquor that's beaded on his blue polo with his fingers.

My voice is quiet, but it's not just for him.

"If you think I would ever share a bed or a place with you after what you did, you're more of a drunk than I thought. There is no flipping this bitch. I will not back down."

His eyes lift to mine, and they're cold. So damn cold. Hunter hates me just as much as I do him. He sucks his bottom lip between his teeth, letting it drag out roughly as he stands, forcing me back a step.

But I stay rooted in my place, our eyes locked as he hovers over me until he lifts his face to his mother.

"Justice of the peace. One photo. She can have the apartment."

I blink, completely caught off guard.

He walks past me, but I've already spun around, watching him walk to the bar and blatantly make himself another drink, hearing his mother say, "Done."

What the fuck?

I don't know what to think, but the room is silent, eerily so as ice cubes fill his glass, before the sound of liquid sloshes, so I clear my throat, preparing for whatever the next fight is.

"Did we settle on a month?" I whisper, still eyeing Hunter.

He walks back, taking a large gulp of his drink, and I realize Marianne hasn't answered, so I press, voice rising, "Marianne, did you hear me?"

The first slap stings, sending a hot flash over my cheek as my head's thrown to the side. The second one knocks me to the floor.

I suck in deep breaths, not able to grab onto a thought, eyes searching the ground. My hand presses to my cheek, and it feels hot and numb. Oh my God. I'm not crying, but I can feel it welling inside. I look up as Hunter glares down at me, his bottom lip wet from the last drink he took.

"The first one was for spilling my fucking drink. And the second was to remind you of your place. I'd back down now if I were you."

Hunter steps over me, walking back to his chair as I look around the room. Nobody moves a damn muscle. My father turns his head away, wiping a hand over his jaw as Marianne looks right through me like I'm a pane of glass.

But it's my mother who takes the cake. Because she's smiling from where she's seated, as if to say, *You got what you deserve.*

I press my palm into the ground, pushing myself back to standing. My back is ramrod straight as I smooth my hair, face red from his handprint. I turn around the room, looking each person in the eye until I land back on Hunter.

"Are you done, precious boy? Because I'd like to get back to the negotiations now."

The hits keep on coming—
The title is enough said. I'm grateful that I am loved by a man who would never hurt me but possesses the strength to hurt those who do.
**take this out, don't make him live with this.

chapter
twenty-eight

Sutton

"**M**iss Prescott, there's a **delivery for you**. Would you like me to bring it to your room **since you**'re turning in for the night?"

"Call me Sutton. **And yes, please** bring it back."

The housekeeper nods, shutting **my bedroom** door behind her as I look back at myself in the vanity mirror. *Jesus Christ.* I blow out a breath, looking around the room filled with **boxes, all labeled** "Bedroom," reaching for the bottom of my hair as I stare at **them**.

How did I get here?

Sometimes that question feels **heavier than other** times. Because sometimes my life feels too surreal, as if **I've lived ten** lifetimes in a couple of years.

I moved into this apartment on May **1**. And as negotiated, I'm alone. Well, almost because I've been gifted a **live-in housekeeper**. One that I'm pretty sure answers to my mother—so **basically a fucking babysitter**.

There's a knock on my door before I say, "**Come in**."

The housekeeper walks back inside, handing me a small rectangular box wrapped in black paper. I look at **her**, brows drawn as I weigh it between my hands.

"Did it have a card?"

She shakes her head before my **eyes drop** down to it. I flip it over, searching the wrapping for a name. She starts to leave, but I turn my chin toward my shoulder.

"Hey, you can be off the clock for the rest of the night. I'm good here. If I need anything, I'll handle it on my own, okay?"

She nods her head as I try to smile, failing as she walks out and closes the door behind her.

I stand before walking over to turn the lock, eyes still inspecting the mystery gift. I look up, eyeing my phone on my bed, and pad over, hopping up.

> Me: Out with it, who sent me the housewarming gift?

> Aubs: Not it.

> Piper: No, ma'am.

Nobody else knows I'm here. This is weird.

"Who sent you?" I whisper to myself.

My fingernail picks at the corner of the wrapping as another text dings.

> Aubrey: Take a pic and send it to us. I'm curious now. What does it look like? How big?

I laugh, ignoring her text as I push my finger in past the paper and tear it open. Pieces of wrapping fall around my legs as I lift the box, freeing it from the rest of the paper before brushing it all to the floor.

It's a small dark wooden box with a hinged lid, so I flip the top open, and a folded white note comes into view. I'm grinning because it feels all mysterious as I pick up the paper, revealing what's underneath.

Oh. My. God.

A gold switchblade with an antique wooden handle is nestled on a bed of black silk fabric.

What the hell?

I can't help but chuckle as I pull it out, feeling something on the other side of the handle, so I flip it over, and my mouth falls open.

True Love is embossed onto the wooden handle in Shakespearean letters.

A full laugh bursts from my chest as I pluck at the fabric, ensuring nothing else is inside before my eyes dart to the note.

HERE'S TO TRUE LOVE, MAMA
AND SLICING ANYONE'S THROAT THAT COMES BETWEEN IT.

Mama.

I gasp as I drop the note, covering my mouth.

Roman. You amazing, incredible man.

I love him almost as much as Calder because he did this for my beautiful monster. My eyes begin to tear as I squeeze my hand around the knife's handle, using my fingertips to pull the blade open, feeling its weight and its intention.

It shines like a deadly treasure, making me smile even bigger until a bigger realization hits.

He knows where I am. Oh my God. My Romeo knows where his Juliet is.

Suddenly and all at once, this place feels like home. Because Calder's with me.

I lean over, grab my phone, and snap a picture of the blade before sending it to Aubrey and Piper.

> Me: Someone sent me True Love.

Aubrey responds immediately.

> Aubrey: Arrrgggh motherfucking arrrgggh.

I let out a laugh, scooting back into bed, and put my phone on the nightstand before I crawl under my blanket. I'm snuggling, lying on my side as I tuck the covers up under my chin and stare at my present.

"I love you forever. Until we're dust and bones and even after that."

My eyes close, and for the first time in a long time, I'm not scared. Because Calder is out there, and he's coming for me.

Calder

chapter
twenty-nine

"Senator."

Sutton's father stares at me from the back seat of the police car, hands cuffed, fear behind his eyes.

"God help me."

My head tilts as I look at him, fingers coming to my beard scratching my skin.

"Why do men like you always try to pray at the end? You hope for mercy."

He swallows hard, not speaking, leaning back as much as he can in the car. So I squat down in front of the door, eyes locked to his. "God isn't here, Baron, and I have no mercy to give you."

I stand, jaw tensed as I look between the two crooked cops I paid to bring me Baron, and motion my head to the side. One of them reaches inside the car, grabbing Baron by the collar, but he struggles, shuffling his feet and fighting being pulled out. His protest almost makes me laugh.

"No. Please. What are you doing?"

I smile, taking a step back as they pull him out, tossing him back against the car, letting his body bounce off.

He's breathing heavy, sweat already beading on his brow as he stands

470   *sinning like hell*

hunched over, leaning to the side. The cops turn back, giving me a nod before they walk away.

"Do you know why I'm here, Baron?"

He doesn't speak but judging by the way he's already fucking shaking, he knows exactly why I'm here.

"You know, I made a special trip to New York for this very moment."

His face shifts to the cops, then back to mine. I chuckle, running a thumb over my bottom lip before I turn my head and watch them walk, knowing they're going to turn a blind eye to whatever I do.

We stand silent while Baron drowns in fear, breathing quickly, the further they get down to the end of the alley. My mouth tugs into a grin as I speak calmly, eyes still on them.

"They can't help, you dumb motherfucker. Tonight, they're going to deliver you to a holding cell, and then some friends of mine are going to string you up and let you hang."

My face turns back to him, inhaling, almost immediately fucking drunk off his fear. *This is for you, baby. For the fear you felt when they locked you up in that fucking hospital.*

I take a step toward him as he cringes.

"The interesting thing about hanging, Baron, is that it's a slow death. The life is wrung out of you, but your body never stops fighting to try to free itself."

I take another step closer, feeling the always simmering rage begin to boil over like lava cresting the mouth of a volcano. Violent intent oozes through my veins, pumping inside of me like blood as my chest rises and falls.

"I imagine it's a lot like what my baby felt like in that fucking hospital." My voice grows louder, hand darting out, gripping his throat, squeezing hard.

He sputters, body jerking, but his hands are cuffed as I squeeze harder, feeling the muscles in his neck constrict as I speak.

"She had to fight to survive the hell you stuck her in, against the lies you fucking told her."

My teeth grind, veins bulging on my forearm with force as I crush his trachea. I dig my fingers in hard, closing my eyes, listening to the squeaks of air desperate to fill his lungs as I lean in closer to his face. My cheek almost to his.

"There's a peace born from the brutality of righteousness. I've waited years for this moment—to kill you in *her* name. And on the day I meet my maker, I won't pray. I won't ask for forgiveness. Because this is what you fucking deserve."

I release him, stepping back, sucking in a deep breath as he does the same. He bends forward, coughing, spit falling from his lips as he gasps for more air.

"Fuck," I bellow as I stare back with the cruel hint of a smile.

"I have money," he snivels as he begins to weep.

My feet rush back to him again as I grab him by the hair, jerking him forward so I can whisper in his ear. My words are ground out with the evilness I feel.

"You made her pray, you motherfucker. You forced her down on her fucking knees in front of that worthless piece of shit and had photos taken. Fuck the money, your life is the price you'll pay for that."

I yank his head back roughly as he squeals like the fucking pig he is. Tremors, guided by hate, ripple through my body. The rage can't be contained anymore because I don't want it to be.

He put her on her knees. So I'll do the same to him.

The fingers I have weaved in his hair squeeze as I growl, pulling the strands as hard as I can, watching tears stream down his face before I thrust him down.

Baron cries out in pain as I look down at him. He starts to mutter a prayer, and it makes me laugh.

"You have to be sorry to receive forgiveness. Beg me. Confess your sins, say what you've done to her."

His body shudders, sobs rolling over him.

"Please, Calder. Please don't kill me. Elizabeth made me do everything."

I can feel my heart racing as I stare at him. His head hangs as I let it go.

He hunches over, ass falling onto his feet as I stand there looking down on him in that dirty alley.

"Confess," I whisper, eyes hooded, feeling my nature begin to lead.

His face tips up. "Please let me live. I'll tell you anything you want to know."

I step back from him, eyes narrowed, feeling possessed with the need to draw his fucking blood.

His shoulders shake uncontrollably as he begins to speak, "I'm sorry. I'm so sorry."

I draw in a breath and spit on him, listening as his cries grow.

"What are you sorry for?"

I want to hear it. Hear the fucking words from his mouth because I want them to make me cruel.

He's pleading incoherently, rocking in place, so I step forward, smacking the side of his head, watching as he falls over onto the asphalt. My boot presses down on his face, grinding his cheek into the rough concrete as the gravel in my voice echoes.

"Make your peace with me, you motherfucker."

His words come out from under my boot.

"Okay. Okay. Please."

I step back, fists balled as he cries his words out.

"I turned my back on my daughter. She needed me, cried out for me to help her, but I shut the door because I was scared of what Marianne Kelly would do. Scared of Connor O'Bannion. I was a coward, so I shut the door and let Hunter..."

Shut the door... Let Hunter...

I'm shaking, vibrating. Numb to time and the world around me. Because in my mind, I'm back in hell, gathering that black smoke, letting it wind around me. The same way my hand wraps around a piece of rusted scrap metal next to a trash bin.

His sobs grow louder as my face tips to the night sky. A guttural sound, almost demonic, rips from my lungs because everything inside of me breaks, shatters into a thousand pieces fracturing my soul.

He let him hurt her. I felt it on her that day at the hotel—the sorrow.

This is what she wouldn't tell me. My brave, beautiful girl.

"Baby," I whisper, sucking in a breath as I stumble back.

He let that filthy cocksucker put his hands on her.

My feet carry me forward as my mind replays his words over and over until I hear *heaven or hell, heaven or hell* hissed deep inside the recesses of my mind again.

"Hell," I grit as I throw myself down, shoving the metal into Baron's side. It slides into his flesh as I blink from the splatters hitting my face. Drawing the scrap metal back out and shoving it in again and again, faster each time until I'm stabbing and grunting as blood blooms over his white dress shirt. He's gurgling on his own blood, drowning in it as I watch.

My face leans down close to his ear so that I make sure he hears me past his choking.

"You failed her. Now go and get a place ready for your wife. Because I'm gonna gut that fucking bitch for what she's done."

He coughs, blood spattering over his lips, but I draw back slowly, kneeling next to him, staring as his pupils begin to grow and the gurgling grows silent. I wait there until his lifeless eyes stare up at the sky, then I reach out and close them.

"You don't deserve to see her stars."

Sutton

The sound of glass shattering yanks me from sleep, making me kick my legs, scurrying up to sitting as a shriek leaves my lungs. I'm shaking, blinking a mile a minute, pointing True Love at my bedroom door.

My chest rises and falls quickly as I search the space, but nobody's here. *What the fuck?* I lower my hand, running my other one through my hair, glancing at the clock to see it's eleven p.m., just as a crash echoes again.

Holy shit. It's from the living room.

Before I think twice, I hurry out of my bed toward my bedroom door, unlocking it as I swing it open.

"Greta?" I call out for the housekeeper. "What's going on? Is everything okay?"

I'm halfway down the hall as my eyes land on her. She's standing in a bathrobe, arms wrapped around herself, looking back at me with red-rimmed eyes.

"What's going on—" I whisper, confused, but I'm met by a different voice.

One that has my feet slowing their pace as my head swings to the side.

Hunter's voice thunders as he charges toward me.

"This is your fault, you fucking bitch."

"What are you doing here?" I yell.

My feet stumble backward as I thrust the knife up, eyes wide, panic welling. He slaps it from my hand, hard, as I scream before he grabs the back of my neck.

He forces me down, bent over, my eyes to the ground. Glass shards cover the floor, scattered everywhere as he guides me down the hall like I'm on a leash, and his hand is the collar.

"What are you doing?" I cry, gripping his wrist for support as I stumble over my feet.

My shoulders lift as he tightens his grip, his fingers digging into my skin. He forces my bare feet over broken glass toward the television, pulling me to a stop, breathing hot, heavy breaths into my ear as he grits out his words.

"Listen."

I'm standing in front of the television, body trembling, blinking through the tears pouring from my face.

"Hunter—"

He grabs my arm, jerking me still.

"Stop fucking crying and listen, Sutton."

I wince, feet stinging, but I hold my breath to try to stay quiet as I shake. Hunter walks to the television, turning it up as the news anchor's voice fills the room.

Breaking News: Senator Baron Prescott of New York has been found dead along with two NYPD officers in what police are calling an assassination. Possibly associated with the O'Bannion crime family in which he'd had a long history of legislating against. This was following his surprising arrest during a sting operation conducted by the NYPD. Senator Prescott was arrested with Senator Thomas Franklin of Maine and other prominent figures. Charges were issued, including soliciting an act of prostitution and distributing drugs for sex. No official statement has been released by Senator Prescott's office or family as of yet.

My hands press to my chest as everything feels like it's going in slow motion. "My father's dead," I whisper, unbelieving of my own words. I wait for them to taste bitter on my tongue, for the humanity I should feel to kick in. But I feel nothing.

That's not true. I feel relief because this was Calder. I know it like I know my own name. This was his first move, the single domino that starts the topple of the others.

"Miss," I hear behind me.

My head swings to see Greta, hand lowering from her mouth as shock plays over her face.

But I don't say anything. Because there's nothing to say. Calder took his life for me, but I still hate him. So all I can do is take his legacy. I'll never speak his name again. I won't grieve him or say kind words, especially out of obligation.

He may be dead, but now I'll make it so he never lived.

"Get the fuck out. And keep your mouth shut or I'll find you," Hunter yells at Greta as he comes from my room, tossing a bag at my feet. I didn't even see him leave.

I stare at him as he stalks toward me again, glass crunching under his shoes, but I don't move. Hunter stares down at me, taking heaving breaths of air as my lips tug into a smile.

"He's coming, Hunter. And you should be afraid."

"No. Sutton, *you* should be. Because I promise there won't be anything left for him when I'm finished with you."

Calder

My fingers tap on the gun in my lap as I stare at my uncle asleep in his hotel bed. I've been here, sitting in this chair watching him for the last twenty minutes.

And it's taken a lot of fucking self-control not to just pull the damn trigger.

I could blow his brains out of the back of his fucking head before he even woke up. But that's not the plan, and it's also too generous.

Plus, I already went off course with the way I killed one man tonight. *Fuck you, Baron.* So I need to keep my head because Connor needs to stay alive.

But I can't trust that he'll just show up to the Council meeting, or that he won't do something stupid, not after he hears about Baron.

I'm going to have to take him.

But son of a bitch, if the tap of my finger on the side of this goddamn Glock doesn't sound like the ticking of a clock. Like the countdown to the end of his worthless life.

The shit you will suffer, you filthy prick. Angels will weep watching my cruelty.

"Connor," I whisper, before barking louder, "Connor."

His hand's already reaching under his pillow before his eyes open.

"Uh-oh." I grin, holding up *his* gun that's in my lap. "You looking for this?"

The darkness always on his face seems to multiply as he slides his hand back, sitting up slowly. I'm watching the look in his eyes volley between confusion and suspicion.

"Calder," he breathes calmly, furrowing his brow. "What the fuck do you think you're doing? Why are you in New York?"

Goddamn, it feels like I've waited forever for this moment, so I take a minute before answering to really look into his eyes, searching them, because I don't ever want to forget the look in them as I answer.

"Betraying you, Uncle."

The silence fucking bleeds out, down the fucking walls and over the floor. It banks the room in unease and fury. I can almost taste it. Our chests rise and fall together, eyes locked like two fucking lions challenging for dominance.

"You came here to meet with the Italians again, except that's not what's happening. I just needed you in the fucking city. So my friends helped."

"You," he grits out. "It was you. All this time...running my drugs," he snarls, eyes narrowing on me. "It was never another family."

I was always right under your nose.

I grin, eyes locked to his, breathing faster but not answering. The evil inside me is being fed by the contempt in his eyes because now I can finally hate him back, right in the open.

He shakes his head, so many expressions crossing his face as he begins piecing it all together. In all fairness, it wasn't hard to see. He just had to look. But that's where our genius lied—we fed him lies for what he craved.

His invincibility.

"You told Pete about the meeting so I'd believe a war was happening. You knew I'd lose it—"

I tilt my head, smirking.

"Anger is predictable. So is greed. You have both afflictions in spades. So sacrifices were made. You always said that one day I'd do what was needed for this family. Guess you were right."

His eyes shoot to his bedroom door as my grin grows.

"Nobody's coming, you piece of shit. They don't work for you anymore. Haven't for a minute now."

His face swings back to mine, mouth hanging open as he stands slowly from his bed. He's staring at me the way I'm looking at him—with predatory fucking intent.

I draw my bottom lip between my teeth, dragging it out roughly as I push slowly from the chair, digging my fingers into the fabric of the arms.

Fuck, I feel so animalistic that I could bite down on his fucking throat and rip it from his body. That's how much I want to kill him right now.

"This was always going to happen, Connor." I take a step forward. "You took her from me." My teeth grit as I repeat his words back to him. "Kept her close. Isn't that what you fucking said?"

He's walking toward me as well, our stares never breaking.

"You don't know what you're doing, boy. The mess you're making."

We stand only a few feet apart, tension rippling off us, jaws tense, chests rising and falling in sync. His eyes search my face, drifting down to my hands, which are still stained red with Baron's blood as I narrow my eyes.

"I killed Baron Prescott. Stabbed him to death in an alley and linked it to you. Because she's mine. Just like your fucking throne."

Red begins to crawl up his neck as his fists ball at his sides. But I'm not done.

"Don't worry. I won't let you go to jail because I plan on sending you to hell."

He's fucking snarling, looking at me like he could rip me apart with his bare hands.

I breathe out a whoosh of air, feeding off his energy as I tip my face to the ceiling.

"Fuck I wish you'd try," I say aloud to my own thought before lowering my face to his again.

He takes a step back, then another as if I can't see he's walking toward the door. *Oh, run, Connor. The boys will have so much fun chasing you down.* He stabs a finger at me, reaching for the handle behind him.

"The Council will never approve my death, Calder. And when they don't, I'll have your fucking head. Mark my words."

I smirk. "Guess we'll just have to find out"—I raise my phone to show the time—"in less than forty-eight hours. The Council was more than happy to meet sooner. In fact, I think the Irish are already here from Dublin." My words rush out. "You or me. Me or you."

I can't help myself. I close the distance between us, standing almost chest to chest, backing him up against the door.

"It was for her. Always. Remember that when Roman's cutting you open. He's gonna take his time, keep you alive. I want you to feel every cut you made to her heart."

He says nothing as I put the gun under his chin.

"You don't get to walk this earth while she's on it."

I use the gun, digging it into his chin as I step back and guide him away from the door. My other hand reaches for the knob, opening it and letting Roman walk inside.

He grins as he lays eyes on Connor.

"Hey, Connor. You can go easy, or I can have some fun taking you outta here. I'd really like for you to pick the second option because I wanna make you bleed before I get to slice you up."

Sutton

chapter
thirty-one

"**W**hat the fuck did you do to her?"

Tag's voice carries past the bathroom door, the one I'm hiding behind at the Kelly house in St. Simeon because Hunter forced me from the apartment barefoot and in my nightgown after he attacked me.

God, his hands were everywhere, pulling on my skin, ripping at my nightgown.

He was trying to tear it off my body and do God knows what, and the only thing that stopped him was his mother, who walked into the apartment.

I begged them to leave me, even saying my mother would need me. But Hunter just kept insisting, saying this was my fault and I had to pay the consequence.

My shoulders shake as I try to push the memory out of my head, cleaning the scratch marks marring my cheeks, reddened over my freckles.

I stare into the mirror, looking back at red-rimmed eyes and his hand-print along my jaw where he slapped me. My hands drop to my chest, and I pull the fabric back in place from the rip in my nightgown.

The stinging on my cheek smarts, so I turn my head to the side. Jesus, he drew blood. The red gashes are scrawled over my cheek from just below my eyes to my nose. He looked at me as if all he could think was to hurt me in the cruelest ways possible.

Not just hurt me—make me stop *being*. He tore at me like he was trying to rid himself of my existence as if I were a piece of paper with a story he couldn't read anymore. Something that needed to be destroyed, burned... Hunter wanted to make me disappear.

A bang on the door makes me jump.

"Sutton. Get out here. Now," Hunter shouts.

I take a deep breath, staring at myself in the mirror. They're afraid, scared to death that Connor's coming for them too. Like they think he came for my father. But I know better.

This was Calder.

"Just survive tonight," I whisper to myself.

I just have to make it through tonight. Calder has someone watching because he sent me the knife. *He'll find you, Sutton.*

Tears stream down my face as I stare in the mirror because the reality of my situation lies heavily on me. No matter how much I tell myself that Calder will come, I don't really know if he will. But the thing I *do* really know is that given enough time, Hunter will kill me.

The salt from my tears stings my cheeks, but I wipe my face, shaking my head, and take another deep breath.

No. I survive. That's the only outcome I choose.

There's another bang before the door crashes open into the wall as Hunter charges in. I scream, ducking as my hands cover my head, but he grabs my hair, yanking me out.

"I said to get the fuck out here."

"Hunter," Marianne yells, but this time he ignores her.

My shoulder bounces off the doorjamb as Tag steps in front, yanking Hunter's hand from me, pulling strands of hair with him. I'm staring down at the ground, trying to stop my body from shaking, but I can't because I'm so fucking scared.

"What the fuck are you doing, Hunter? If you make her any fucking uglier, how are we supposed to travel? She's a walking red flag. Jesus, little

Kelly. For once, think before you act. I don't even know why you still want her anyway."

I glance up as Hunter's jaw tenses, so I take a step back because my breath is coming out too fast. He's beyond angry.

The others are worried about Connor, game-planning how they evade his wrath if this is what's happening, but every piece of me sees that Hunter couldn't care less. This is about him and Calder, and using me to level the playing field.

"Why wouldn't I want her. She's the queen. The players protect the queen, and I have a feeling, Tag, that Connor may be willing to trade me something for her—like my life." Hunter's face twists to me. "But that doesn't mean I can't have my fun first."

Tag looks at me and frowns.

"Sutton, just go upstairs and stay out of the way until we figure out what to do or what's going on. Got it? You're making my brother crazy."

I nod, taking quick steps backward, jumping on this opportunity to get as far away as possible, but as I turn, chills creep over me because Hunter says, "Go to my room. Nobody else's. I mean it, *Freckles*."

My stomach tries to turn over as I look back over my shoulder, swallowing every bit of hatred I have, and nod, but Hunter's tongue darts out over his bottom lip.

"Come here."

Oh God. I turn back around slowly, trying not to wince as I walk back, stopping in front of him.

He's looking down at me, saying nothing as my heart beats out of my chest.

"Are you afraid of me?"

I don't lie as I stare at his chest.

"Yes." His fingers trail up my arm to my shoulder, then over the tops of my breasts until he lifts them to my face. He brushes my hair behind my ear as he leans in so close that his breath warms the lobe.

"You should be afraid. I'm not done making you hurt, but if you promise not to scream, I'll be nicer tomorrow."

A soundless sob wracks my body as my lips part for me to suck in air because he's pressed a kiss to the cheek marked by his fingernails before turning his back to me.

I'm standing there, frozen by fear, body so rigid that I'm not even shaking anymore as he casually looks over his shoulder and says, "Go to bed, Freckles."

I turn, body so cold, heart beating so hard it may explode as I take step after painful step up the stairs and into Hunter's room. He's going to come up here. And this time, he will finish what he started.

The panic inside me is screaming to be heard. *What do I do? What do I do?* The rest of me is trying to go numb and prepare myself to not feel so that none of it will hurt. But as I close the door behind me, there's a louder voice. The one I've grown and nurtured.

The survivor.

My head shifts around, eyes pausing on his closet...shoes?

"No, too big," I answer myself because there are too many thoughts, too many fears in my head that I need to say everything out loud, or I won't even hear it.

I look to the other side of the room, sucking in a breath as I see a window. But really, all I see is a tree outside that window.

"Go."

The carpet's softer on my feet, so I hurry toward it, face shooting to the door as I think I hear someone coming up the stairs.

"Fuck."

Adrenaline pumps through me as I run smack into his window, unlocking it before I lift it open. My hands shove the screen, jutting it out enough so that I can grab it and pull it inside.

I glance over my shoulder again, feeling my entire body break out in chills from the ocean breeze that drifts through the gaping space. My head peeks out, and I look down to the ground then back to the tree, swallowing hard.

Dammit, it's close, but I'll have to drop to the branch. I'm on the second story, and if I fall, there's no way I'll be able to run.

Not on a broken leg or ankle. But if I stay here...

So before I second-guess myself, I hitch my leg over the frame before doing the same with the other so that I'm sitting.

I'm almost panting as I look out into the night.

"It's okay. I've got this. It's okay."

My hands grip the wood as I roll over to balance on my stomach, as I strain to let my foot feel for the branch closest to me.

My toes just barely touch bark before I let my stomach scrape the windowsill until I can almost feel the balls of my feet resting against the oak. So I drop. I let go, hitting the branch so hard the wind is knocked out of me.

But I hold on, gritting my teeth so that I don't make a sound.

The breath inside of my lungs burns as it releases, but it doesn't matter because I can't stop. Hunter, Tag, Marianne...any of them could find me at any time.

My legs burn, muscles aching as I begin to climb down and out of view, balancing and weaving under branches until I get to the lowest one, which is still high off the ground.

But I don't hesitate to drop down, feeling the sharp pain reverberate through my legs, making me clamp my hand over my mouth so that nobody hears me as I fall to the ground.

I press my palm into the grass, taking deep breaths as my fingers dig into the dirt below, but I push myself to stand. Everything hurts, so I take careful steps, limping as the pain fades. Until I grow stronger and stronger, carrying me into the shadows away from that fucking house and everyone in it.

"Where do I go?" I whisper. "God, where do I go?"

My words keep coming as I run down streets I know like the back of my hand, but somehow, nothing looks familiar. I look around the darkness, feet stinging, eyes thick with tears, feeling so lost. I stumble, knocking my battered body into a fence just as I hear bells.

Stuttered cries fall from my lips because I know that sound. My face lifts in the direction they're coming from as I run faster and faster toward the only place I know I'll be safe.

I'm running over the concrete, across the paved street, until my feet rush up steps.

There is no pain anymore. All I can feel is hope.

I slow, grabbing the sides of my nightgown as I stare up at the stained-glass angels in front of the church. *Our church.*

"Calder," I breathe as I reach for the door, eyes darting to a gold plaque affixed to the wall next to the door that's never been there before.

I can endure all these things through the power of the one who gives me strength.
—Philippians 4:13

It's as if reading this was an answer to his name.

The door creaks as I open it and slip inside, feeling warmth envelop me. Until now, I didn't even realize how cold I was, but my skin is like ice, goose bumps pebbling my arms.

I walk inside, staring up at the rafters. God, it's exactly how I remember it. My head shifts around, looking from place to place, almost seeing us again.

"Lamb, are you okay?"

I jump, startled, eyes wide as I turn around scared, but a woman, petite with the kindest blue eyes, stares back at me. Still, my first instinct is to run, so I stumble back toward the doors, but her words rush out.

"You're safe now, sweet girl." Her eyes lower to my outfit, taking me in as she looks back to my face. "You've endured so much."

She holds her arms open, and I don't know why, but I rush into them, letting her wrap me in her warmth. My shoulders shake as she soothes me, running her hand down my hair.

"Shh, now. Shh."

The sound of a door opening from inside the church makes my head lift, but the woman cradles my cheeks, whispering, "Go now. Upstairs, to the confessional. Hide there. Everything will be okay. You can endure all things through the power of the one who gives you strength."

I nod, staring at her, repeating the words from the plaque in my head as

I turn. My feet carry me quickly as I make my way to the familiar stairs, hurrying up as my white nightgown sways against my legs.

The moment I'm at the top and slipping into the confessional, it feels as if I can finally breathe because I'm back in the room I remember in my dreams.

Calder

"You gonna stay awake all night? It's 2:00 in the morning. Go home. I'll keep him here."

Roman means back to the field house because we're standing outside my old room in Tyler's place on the island. We needed to keep Connor someplace nobody would come looking, just in case.

"Hey, did you check in on my girl?"

Even though I ask, I know he would've told me if something was wrong.

"Yeah, earlier. Before Baron. The housekeeper said she was already turning in for the night. No Hunter around. We're good until the Council meeting."

I blow out a breath, tired and worn down from the day, as I look back at my brother. Everything I've done in the last two, almost three years feels like it's finally catching up with me.

Because tomorrow, I'll be judged. I'll stand before the Council and make my case—my life, my allegiance, in exchange for Connor's life. I can't help but wonder if between Connor and me...if either of us would really be more deserving of life than the other.

Except I know I want her, so whether I'm worthy or not, I'd do it all again. My eyes close for a moment before I look past Roman, feeling stripped down to the barest bones of the truth.

"Tomorrow decides if I live or die. But if I *die*, then promise me—"

He shakes his head, holding up a hand for me to stop. "No. Quit that shit. You'll take care of your own girl."

"Roman."

His jaw tenses as he looks back at me. We stand there staring at each other because he doesn't want to lose another brother, and I don't want to leave my girl. But we both know that's what could happen. It's why I'm waiting to get her. I need it all in place so she doesn't have to spend even one fucking day in hell.

He gives a tight nod before looking away.

"If I protect you, then I protect her. I remember our deal, and that shit counts even in death, brother."

I bring my hand down to his shoulder, patting it.

"Call and check up on her later, when normal people are awake, will you?"

"I got you."

I let out a long breath before I turn my back and head out. Because there's nothing more to say. Roman knows what to do. We hold Connor until the Council meeting. If I walk out, then we go get Sutton. If Connor walks out, he gets Sutton.

It's that simple. But tonight, at least, she'll have peace.

I cross the lawn, heading to my Mustang, then pull open the door and slide in. The engine growls as I turn the key before I pull out and slow at the end of the driveway.

My head swings to the left, the way that takes me to the field house, but I don't move. I sit, letting the car idle as I look to the right.

I can see the tracks off in the distance, the ones I cross into downtown St. Simeon, and something about it keeps calling me.

I need to make my peace.

The tires turn right, taking me down the street. I grip the steering wheel almost on autopilot because the call is so fucking loud. I need to fucking make my peace with God. Not for myself, but for her.

I need to know that if I'm going to die that he'll have her back.

My mind begins to drift between all the sweetest fucking moments with my girl.

I let them wash over me as I pass by familiar places, smiling as I drive past the basketball courts, remembering how nervous she looked when I walked around the corner or the way she stared at me when we played basketball.

I'll never forget that. I'd had plenty of girls look at me, but the way Sutton stared like she could feel my thoughts...it was different because I could feel hers too.

I slow to a stop before turning the engine off, staring up at the Gothic-looking church. My hand wraps around the handle, pushing open the car door before I slide my head out and stand.

"Fuck," I whisper, feeling her everywhere.

The keys bounce in my hand before I shove them into my pocket and walk across the grass, thinking about when I snuck back just to fucking kiss her that day.

I follow that same path, walking around the side of the church, reaching for that same handle I twisted to sneak in the first time.

It opens, making me hesitate for a moment before I slip inside. The familiar smell of frankincense and myrrh waft in the rafters as I look to my sides, seeing an empty church.

I walk through the hall that connects to the church's main room, letting my hand drag over the pews as I pass between them to the center aisle.

Fuck. I stand staring at the crucifix above the altar.

"I'm not sure I even believe in you anymore, but she does. So tell me how to make peace with you because I need you and every good thing in the world on her fucking side if I go."

A throat clears behind me, making me spin around and reach to the small of my back. But the priest staring back at me just smiles.

"Father," I offer, relaxing.

"Calder Wolfe. It's been a while."

My eyes narrow. "How the fuck do you know who I am, priest?"

He frowns before answering, probably because of my language.

"I met your father once or twice. And you, but I saw you up there." He turns and points to the balcony. "I remember because I lost an outstanding communion volunteer that day."

My lips tug into a grin as I chuckle before I change the subject.

"Why is your church open in the middle of the night, Father? Or do you lead mass in your pajamas now?"

"Our doors are always open for any lost soul. But currently, I'm here because the bells rang. Probably just some kids messing around."

He puts his hands behind his back before smiling. "Take the time you need with God, Calder Wolfe. But come and visit me tomorrow for confession. For now, I'm going back to bed."

I smirk as he walks past me, the doors clanging behind him as he leaves.

"The Devil and God in the same room," I whisper, eyes landing back on the balcony.

I walk back out to the hall, wanting to see it all again, even if it's only a memory. I take those familiar steps, eyes catching on that basin of holy water as I ramp it up, taking two stairs at a time until I land on our balcony.

It's completely the same, untouched, from the bookcases to the goblets and stored containers of oils.

And there's still that damn confessional. I close my eyes, wanting to see her face as I say, "Baby."

chapter
thirty-two

Sutton

"Baby."

My knees are drawn up as I hug them, pressing my face down as I hold my breath because I'm hearing things. Goose bumps grow wild over my skin, but I'm warm. I'm so still like I'm trying to be invisible, waiting for the footsteps to retreat. But then I hear the voice again.

"I miss you."

I gasp, my body rocketing toward the confessional door. My fingers scramble, throwing it open before I burst from my hiding place.

My hand clamps down over my mouth because I don't want to scream or cry. Because if this is a dream, I don't want to wake up.

"Sutton?"

Calder steps toward me, brows drawn together deeply as he shakes his head, his hand already reaching for me. But I run. I launch myself into his arms, wrapping mine around his neck.

"Baby. Oh my God. How are you here?"

He's engulfing me, holding me off the ground as we hug, wrapped tightly around each other so there is no start or end point between us.

"You're here. I can't believe you're here."

"Let me see you. Are you okay?" He tries to pull back, but I won't let him go. "Okay. It's okay. I've got you, baby. Let me make it better."

I wrap my legs around him, needing him close, never wanting to let go.

"I prayed for you," I whisper, kissing his neck, feeling the smooth warmth of his skin on my lips. "In the confessional. I prayed you'd come for me."

He holds me there, one hand under me, the other around my back, swaying back and forth.

I don't even know how long we stay like that, but his hand runs down my hair as he kisses the side of my head, saying nothing, just loving me.

"Sutton. You need to look at me now."

I shake my head against the crook of his neck because a part of me still doesn't believe this is real. Maybe I've died, and he has too, and this is someplace we get to meet.

"Baby, look at me. I promise I won't disappear."

I blink before I pull my head back. Our eyes lock, but the instant sorrow on his face makes me hate myself. I should've been stronger because this is breaking him.

His fingers brush over the marks on my cheeks so gently that I barely feel them.

Soft kisses rain down over each mark as he catalogs the bruises and rips on my nightgown. He brushes my hair from my face, trailing his fingers over darker bruises down toward the back of my neck.

His hand lowers over my arm, reaching behind him to my calf before feeling my bare foot locked at the ankle behind his back.

"Baby," he exhales as if weeping on the inside as his face tilts to the ceiling.

But as he looks back to me, the muscles in his jaw ripple, his eyes shining.

Calder looks deeply into my soul, voice so low that my breath stops.

"Who did this to you?"

My tongue darts out, tasting the salt left behind from my dried tears.

"They all did this to me. You're the only one that protects me."

Calder's eyes grow cold. There's so much anger behind them, but I can't help but think how beautiful it is because it's fueled by his love.

"Tell me it's over," I rush out, already knowing what he'll say.

"I can't."

I crush my lips against him, needing to feel his kiss. To taste him.

His tongue slips inside my mouth as I pull him closer, curling an arm around his neck as he turns us and begins to walk.

"What are you doing?" I breathe, pulling away.

Calder looks at me with so much love that it knocks the breath out of me.

"I'm stealing you back."

I can't help how my chest shakes as my hands come to his cheeks.

"This isn't the plan."

His feet stop as he holds me up and takes one of my hands, bringing the palm to his lips.

"I will never leave you alone and unprotected ever again. *You* are coming home."

All the emotion I've held on to, everything that I've pretended not to feel. All the sadness, the rage, all the goddamn grief—it explodes from me, exorcised from my body as I cling to him.

I weep as he holds me tightly to him, letting me feel for the first time in almost three years. It's as if I've been turned off, the lights dimmed so as to never be seen. And now he's here, and I can't hide, but really, I don't want to because he's the only one that can make it all better.

With just his arms wrapped around me and his lips against my hair.

Because he's my home.

I bury my face into his neck as I'm carried down the steps. He whispers about stars and magic, love and forever to me as I cry, never breaking his stride as he walks through the entrance of the church.

His lips press to my head as he speaks.

"I love you. You are so strong and brave, and I'm so proud of you, baby. But let me take care of you now. Let me make it better, my sweet girl."

As he says the last part, my head lifts, tears still in my eyes as I look around, searching for the woman.

"Wait, there was a woman here. She helped me, and I need to thank her."

Calder slows, looking around before he rubs his hand over my back.

"No, baby. There's nobody here except for the priest and me."

His arms hold me close as he walks us out to his car, but I suddenly cling tighter. I don't want him to let me go. I can't be away from him.

"Baby, what's wrong, what's wrong, what's wrong?"

My head shakes against his neck.

"Please don't let me go."

I feel him release a whoosh of breath as he hugs me tighter.

Calder walks over to the driver's side and turns sideways after opening his door before saying, "Just unhook your legs."

He lowers us, my feet only touching the ground for a second before I'm pulled inside the car, straddling him, arms still firmly around his neck.

It's the way we were so many years ago the first time I was in this car.

I feel him lean to the side, but I don't move, hungry for more of the peace he brings me. The sound of ringing fills the car seconds before a deep voice answers.

"What up, C?"

Calder's voice vibrates through his body as he speaks.

"Send a couple of the guys over to the Kellys'. Tell him to hold everyone there until I arrive." His hand strokes my hair as he whispers into it, "Is your mother there?"

I shake my head, closing my eyes as he says, "Sutton's mother is missing from that crew. Send someone to grab that bitch. I want them all there together."

"Done. But you want to tell me what the fuck is going on?"

A kiss is pressed to my head as the engine turns over.

"I found Sutton at the church, Roman. Something went south with our contact. I'm taking her home."

There's silence before he says, "I got you. Give our little mama a hello."

The line disconnects as Calder puts the car in drive and pulls out, keeping one hand on me and the other on the steering wheel.

"Better now, baby?"

I nod into his neck, feeling his hand stroking me from my head to my back.

"Only until we get to the highway," he breathes out as the feeling of déjà vu washes over me.

But my eyes stay closed, our hearts beating in sync as we drive. Until I finally connect the dots. I lift my head as the car slows to a stop. Goose bumps spread over me as I look into his eyes.

"Time to buckle up now, Buttercup."

I feel like I can't catch my breath as I ask, "Where's home?"

He leans in, brushing a tender kiss to my lips before saying, "The only place it should be."

Sutton

thirty-three

The minute we pulled up, I **barely waited** for the car to slow before I threw off my seat belt and **scrambled** out into the middle of our field.

Deep, gasping breaths fill my lungs **as I stare up** at the stars.

Even though the dark blue sky **is getting lighter**, they're still looking down, twinkling like they didn't want **to miss out on** seeing me either.

God, this is more than a sky or **stars. This** is our magic. The place where I dreamed of a love that would **last forever** and he promised all those damn stars in the sky.

This is our forever.

"The house is the other way," he **whispers, coming** up behind me.

I spin around, staring up at him.

"I'm..." There are so many endings to that sentence—broken, battered, scared, exhausted—but the only one **that matters** is the one I say, "...yours. Forever."

Calder cradles my face, staring down at me as the universe finds its place again.

"I'm yours too, baby."

He lowers his face, lips pressing **to mine as** we linger until I lift to my toes, dipping my tongue inside his mouth. His fingers weave into my hair,

496   *sinning like hell*

holding my head as our tongues dance over each other's, tasting and teasing, getting reacquainted, effortlessly falling back into rhythm. I was made for kissing this man.

My head changes positions as our kiss deepens, my hands gripping the front of his shirt as I arch toward him.

His hand comes to the small of my back, his fingers bunching the fabric of my nightgown before he pulls back breathless, the wind knocked out of him just like me as our foreheads touch.

I have so many questions to ask him, but right now, I just want to be loved, to feel him everywhere until nothing else exists but him.

"Take me inside," I whisper.

Calder sweeps me off the ground, tucking his hand under my knees and cradling me. He walks toward the house as I stare, lips parted.

It's so beautiful and warm. It feels like a place where love would grow. I can see us sitting on the porch, having picnics on the field, making a family. He built me everything I've ever wanted—a place meant just for us.

"You built us a home," I whisper.

"I did."

My chin trembles. "How do I even begin to say thank you?" I don't mean to say it aloud, but it comes out without permission. He stops at the door staring down at me as a grin begins to grace his face.

"You don't." He hugs me closer, leaning down to kiss my lips. "You don't ever say thank you for getting everything you fucking deserve. You are owed beauty and magic. And, baby, you better demand it from me every goddamn day for the rest of our lives."

He opens the door carrying me across the threshold as I all but climb him, sealing my mouth over his. Calder shifts me so that I can wrap my legs around him as the door closes behind us.

We're moving—he's carrying me, but I'm lost in this kiss. Our lips glide, dipping in between each other, and dragging away as his hand splays against my back. His right hand is on my ass, fingers kneading as he growls into my mouth.

I jostle against him as he climbs the staircase, pulling myself closer, wrapping my arm around him. My other hand stays on his cheek, wanting the feel of his skin under my fingertips.

Our heads tilt and turn, tongues rolling over sloppily as we devour each other.

Calder's hand runs up my back and into my hair pulling it, so that our kiss breaks, forcing my chin up just as his mouth assaults my neck. I moan as his lips drag over my throat.

"Yes."

We walk through a doorway as he guides my face back to his using my hair.

"This is our bedroom."

"I love the décor," I breathe out, voice husky, only looking at him.

He laughs, deep and rumbling as I'm placed to the ground. But our eyes don't part because right now, he's all I want to see.

I draw my bottom lip between my teeth, and the longer we stare, the faster my heart beats and butterflies unleash from their cages inside of me. I'm nervous.

I'm not the same girl I was the last time we found ourselves in this place. So much has happened, and I'm scared of everything and nothing all at once. I think that I'm afraid to let myself feel because what if it's ripped away again and I'm left with a huge gaping hole that only he fills.

A piece of me knows that I can't survive that anymore.

I know that all of my thoughts play out on my face because his brows furrow as he steps in so close that our bodies are almost flush. I'm dwarfed by him, leaning forward to place my forehead on his chest.

His voice is quiet as he strokes my hair.

"It ends tomorrow, baby." I smile even though he can't see me because I never say anything. He always just knows, even after years. He knows what I'm feeling because he's feeling it too.

Calder takes a deep breath before I feel his lips press to the top of my head.

"I tried to give you peace—"

"I can only find that with you," I say, cutting him off. "That's why fate intervened."

An empty chuckle shakes his chest like he believes what I'm saying. As if he feels the truth like I do. Tonight brought us together because we needed something only the other could give.

I step back to look up at him, but his fingers lift, tracing over the scratches on my face. He's searching my eyes with an equal amount of rage and love as his brows draw together deeply.

"Show me the way you need me to love you, baby," he whispers.

My heart stops. He knows what Hunter's done. I can see it in his face, feel it in the tenderness of his touch. I stare back in awe of everything he is before I grab his hand, pressing it to my face, then to my chest.

"You know how to love me. Fuck me, kiss me, make love to me. I want everything you give, Calder Wolfe. Because there is and will only ever be *you* and *me*."

His eyes meet mine, and so much passes between us. One day I will tell him everything, but that shit doesn't get to exist here. Not in this room. Or in this moment.

Calder lifts my hand to his lips, kissing it before he steps past me, making me turn as he leads me to a door at the far side of the room.

He opens it to a large bathroom, turning on the lights but leaving them dim. I'm standing, staring around the room, taken by all the details. The beauty in just a bathroom, from the white-gray marble to the matte black fixtures that accentuate the floor-to-ceiling double shower.

But the sound of water draws my eyes to the corner. Calder's sitting on the edge of a clawfoot tub, his hand testing the water as it runs.

I take a hesitant step onto the tile, feeling warmth, but he's already walking back to me, hands coming to my waist.

"Let me look at you now."

I blink up as he bunches the fabric of my nightgown, raising it over my body before slipping it over my head, exposing my bare frame.

If I were broken or battered, I'd never know because the way Calder's staring at me only reflects beauty.

His hand comes to his mouth, wiping over his beard as his eyes drift over me.

"You have never been more beautiful." His blue eyes lift to mine. "My strong, brave girl."

He leans in, kissing my chest, bending lower to my stomach, pressing more kisses as his arm hugs me in. My head tilts before dropping down, bringing my face to the top of his head.

Calder's lips move from bruise to bruise, ones I don't even feel but are speckled over my body until he falls to his knees in front of me.

His hands hold my hips as his cheek lays against my stomach, letting me feel the ragged breaths he draws in.

"Never again, baby."

His ass lowers to my feet as his face sweeps over the small tuft of hair on my pussy.

"Oh." I gasp, hands on his shoulders as he presses a kiss right to my center.

The feeling almost knocks me over. Makes me feel greedy for more.

"Again," I breathe out, fingers weaving into his hair.

It's been so long since I've felt his mouth on me that I'm instantly overwhelmed as Calder's tongue cuts through my hair, licking up my wet center, gliding over my clit.

"Oh my God."

My stomach contracts, but my body begins pulling back because it's all so sensitive. The counter hits my ass as I lean back, but he chases me, tugging me back by my hips to his face with a growl.

"More."

The sound of water filling the tub bounces off the walls as I'm pinned between Calder and the counter. My legs are nudged open by his broad shoulders, already shaking as he licks and eats the most sensitive part of me like an animal.

His mouth feels everywhere as his tongue rolls over my clit, flicking and sucking, pressing his face in harder as my hips circle. My leg is yanked over his shoulder as his palms splay over my stomach.

Calder's holding me right where he wants me.

"Calder. Oh God."

He moans, vibrating against my clit as he sucks the swollen bud, letting it go with a pop as he looks up at me, his face glistening with my desire.

"Look at me, Sutton. Watch."

My eyes lock to his as he presses two fingers inside of me, hitching my breath.

"Fuck," he groans. "My fingers fucking missed you."

He juts them in and out, switching between quick thrusts before slowing again. We stare at each other so fucking lost to this feeling that everything could be on fire and we'd never know.

"Fuck me," I whisper, combing my fingers through his hair.

My stomach contracts as he pulls out, suddenly standing. He's breathing hard, staring down at me as he trails the wet fingers over my lips before his mouth crashes down to mine again. He grabs my jaw, tilting my head as his tongue swipes over my bottom lip, making him groan.

"Fuck."

He draws back, eyes narrowed on me.

"Put your fingers on that wet pussy and show me what you learned to do without me."

Calder takes a step back, then another as I stare into his eyes. My hand lifts, but I can't help it—I feel shy. The way he looks at me like he sees all the places I hide. I'm wholly exposed past my naked body.

His head tilts as the gravel in his voice stirs everything inside of me.

"Are you my good girl or my bad one tonight?"

He reaches down, eyes still on mine, turning off the tub as he gives me a wink.

Oh fuck. My eyes close as I step open wider, bringing my fingers to my lips, pushing them all the way inside my mouth, and suck.

"Mmm," he rumbles as my eyes reopen.

He reaches behind him, dragging his shirt over his head.

"Baby, you keep sucking those fingers like that, and I'm gonna feed you my cock to let you remember what it feels like to swallow me back."

My hand drops past my stomach, through my folds, emboldened. Wanting him to see. My fingers flank my clit as I begin rubbing in small circles, pressing my hips forward. My tongue darts out over my lips watching his hands run over his abs.

God, he's so fucking primal. The way his head lowers, eyes narrowing as he watches me, lips parting with his focus.

"Spread yourself open for me."

I part my fingers, letting him see my swollen clit as he licks his lips before I tip my head back and play with myself.

The sound of Calder kicking off his boots and socks fills the room before my body starts to feel warm. I close my eyes, wanting more of the feeling, coaxing it to grow bigger as I hear his belt buckle.

My fingers rub faster and faster, back arching as whimpers fall from my lips. I'm gripping the edge of the counter, digging my nails into the marble as my core begins to tighten.

"Eyes," he growls.

Without hesitation, they spring open just as Calder grabs my wrist, stopping my movement.

"*I* make you come."

My chest rises and falls as I pant. He leans in, kissing my cheek, then my nose before pressing his lips to mine.

"This is *my* reunion with her. Hands off now, Buttercup."

He dips down, picking me up and spinning us around, walking to the tub.

The water's hot against my skin as he lowers us down, stinging before it soothes my feet and body. I'm straddling him, feeling his hard cock between us as he reaches to the ledge next to the tub, grabbing a washcloth. He dips it in the water, soaping it up.

I can't stop looking into his eyes because the love reflected is so powerful that I have to keep catching my breath.

Neither of us speak as he begins slowly washing my body.

"I love you," I whisper, staring into his eyes after a moment.

Water cascades down my chest as he runs the cloth over my skin and down my shoulder. He dips it into the water again, running it down my leg and over my calf, before gently cleaning my feet. It doesn't hurt. Nothing ever hurts with him.

He repeats the same thing on my other leg before dropping the damn rag outside the tub and pulling me close. My arms wrap around him, bodies flush as he buries his face into my neck. We stay there just breathing as his fingers urge me closer as if we can't be close enough.

Calder's palm is against my spine as his other hand holds the back of my head. I feel the warmth of his breath against my flesh as he peppers kisses to my neck, traveling over my jaw until we're face-to-face. His ocean blue eyes bore into mine as I cling to him.

"I love you, Sutton."

His voice is barely above a whisper, but he doesn't even have to say it because I feel it. It's washed over me like the fucking water bathing my body.

He loves me. It's all the life I ever want to live.

I reach down between us, lifting myself up, seating the head of his cock at the rim of my pussy. We're locked on each other. Never breaking eye contact as I lower down slowly, feeling the inside of my pussy drag over the thickness of his cock.

"Fuck, baby," he groans, hands running up my waist.

Calder's hands grip me tightly, stopping me in place before he locks eyes with me, controlling the movement. Taking it achingly slow.

I could come right here, right fucking now, all because of the look on his face. His jaw is so tense the muscles in his neck are strained as heavy breaths come from his nose. He's fucking wrecked by the feel of being inside of me, forcing himself to hold back because he's savoring it.

It makes me want to shove his hands away and ride him fast and hard until he's coming undone.

"You feel so fucking good. Let me feel that pussy on me nice and slow."

His mouth falls open, breath wisping against my nipple, as he leans forward, taking it between his lips before tugging me down farther.

I gasp, completely filled by his thick cock, swallowing hard. Water sloshes as my hands press against his shoulders, rising up before rocking down again.

"Oh, fuck." He grunts, pressing into me each time I lower.

We're moving faster, craving the closeness as his cock slides in and out. Our mouths taste every fucking spot we can reach, as his hands slide up my waist to caress my tits.

I moan, pushing them into his hands as he runs his thumb over my nipple.

"Yes."

Slickness builds inside of me making Calder groan. His hands drop to my waist, holding me still, as he fucks me harder from the bottom, rocketing water from the tub.

I lean down, gripping his hair, pulling his head to the side, sucking his neck. I bite it and lick, wanting to leave marks all over him.

The sound of his foot squeaking against the basin accompanies a low, "Out."

Jesus, he all but growls it, lifting us in one big motion from the tub, spilling water all over.

His cock falls from me, but it doesn't matter because I wrap my legs around him, writhing against him. Calder steps out, stalking from the bathroom taking us straight to the bed.

As my back touches the mattress, he's over me, having never let go before his body lifts.

"Oh my God." I gasp.

I'm struck by the picture in front of me.

Calder's kneeling between my legs, his dick rock hard above my pussy. He's holding one of my legs open from behind my knee as my other is draped over his hip. We're beautiful.

"This is your last lesson." He grins.

His tongue glides over his bottom lip as he looks down between us and back to my face.

"This pussy is mine to do with as I please. I will fuck it until it cries for me, and then I'll kiss it better. Because, baby, *I* was made to fucking worship you."

He crowns my entrance before thrusting inside deeply.

I suck in a breath, gasping his name. "Calder."

His hips rock, pounding inside of me, ass indenting at the sides with each movement. He's powerful and dominant, bathed in tattoos and graced with the bluest eyes that are so connected to mine as he fucks me raw.

"I'm so fucking wet for you, Calder."

My hips meet his movement as I drag my hands over my tits, feeling the slick warmth grow in my center.

"Aw fuck, baby. Drip for me."

The smell of sex is thick in the air as our wet bodies slap against each other. Calder throws my leg over, so I'm flipped to my side before he comes behind me, pushing back inside of me. Our bodies are flush, my back to his front as he draws my knee toward my body, fucking me deeper. His dick strums all the right places, hitting deep in my belly with every thrust.

His beard scratches my neck as he whispers in my ear, "I fucked myself picturing your pussy. How it would taste, feel on my fingers again. I fucked every part of you in my mind."

I'm moaning as he pushes inside, over and over, rocking our bodies together. His hand covers my breast, pinching the nipple between his fingers, rolling it as my body aches for more. My hand holds his wrist, pulling his fingers to my mouth, rolling my tongue around them before I suck, hollowing my cheeks.

"There's my girl. You want me everywhere. In your mouth, your pretty little cunt, and that ass. Don't you?"

My mouth drops open so fucking turned on as my body undulates.

"Fuck. Calder. I want to come."

My hand lowers between my legs, but he grabs my wrist, quickly sliding my arm out, forcing me onto my stomach. My legs are shoved open, feeling his tongue hit my clit.

"Oh my God," I scream, feeling my body shudder.

His arms are hooked under my legs, keeping them open as he eats my pussy from behind. I'm breathing so hard, I feel like I might pass out, but his face tears away as his dick hammers back inside.

He reaches around my throat gently, pulling me upright as I'm fucked hard, bouncing forward.

"*I* make you come," he growls.

I can barely catch my breath. I'm panting, needy, wanting all of him.

Calder reaches around me, his fingers pushing through my tuft, rubbing my clit. It's not slow or easy. It's demanding. I'm treated exactly the way I want, like his.

He isn't just fucking me or making love to me. He's laying his claim.

My hand closes over his, around my throat, chin tilted up, as he brings my mouth to his. I'm filled, building while he strokes my swollen clit.

Everything begins to curl up inside of me, compounding, rising as my stomach tightens.

Oh God, I'm covered by Calder, his tongue in my mouth, his cock gliding through my slickness. It's thrusting, pounding in and out of me, over and over as his fingers rub.

"Oh... I... Calder... Please..."

I'm begging as my eyes roll back, and my body is gifted what it's praying for.

"Oh my God," I scream against his mouth before my breath is held.

My body explodes as my eyes squeeze shut, shaking and tense.

Calder engulfs me, ramming his cock inside me as I come harder and harder. My body is rocketed into the heavens, his name launched from my lips.

The crest is so high that my entire body slumps as it leaves me, a long breath whooshing past my lips.

"You're mine," he growls, pulling out of me, rolling me over on my back as he jerks his cock.

Calder shoves my legs open, spreading me wide as he stares at my pussy coated in my own release. He tugs viciously on his cock before releasing thick white ropes onto my clit.

"Oh fuck," he grits out, tensing, marking me as his.

His jaw is tight as his chest rises and falls quickly. I lick my lips, breath slowing as I lift my head, looking down to see his release on me.

Calder groans as he milks himself before lowering his hand. He drags his thumb between my folds as I let out a breath. Gathering the cum he hooks his thumb inside me to push it in. His other fingers spread cum over my clit, and through my folds, breathing heavily as he does it.

His eyes meet mine again, and I'm hollowed by his possession. My palms press to the bed as I push myself to sit, bringing my face to his, capturing his bottom lip between mine before letting it drag out slowly.

"Now I'm baptized in you."

Calder

We've fucked too many times and too many ways to count. The sun's already up but I can't get enough of her.

I reach for her, never wanting her too far away again, so I drag her naked body closer. Our legs intertwine as we lie there, staring at each other, bodies slick with sweat, married together in our release.

I grab her hand, bringing her fingers to my lips, taking one between my teeth.

"Animal." She grins, but I growl, making her giggle.

It's the most heavenly fucking sound. I let her finger fall from my mouth as she begins playing with my beard.

"What happens today?" she whispers, leaning in to kiss my chest. "You said it all ends tomorrow."

I inhale deeply, humming the exhale before I answer.

"I have to go before something called the Council. Think of them as a jury. They decide the life and death sentences of this family. So they'll decide between Connor and me."

My head is lowered, watching the thoughts cross over her face before she looks up.

"And if they choose Connor?"

I open my mouth to answer her, but I hesitate because I don't want to tell her the truth. I can't. Fuck.

Her hand brushes over my chest as she leans in, kissing it again.

"Your heart's beating so fast."

"I'm scared."

It's so honest it hurts to say.

She blinks a few times, not looking at me before she lifts her chin.

"Of the Council?"

I shake my head.

"Of leaving you."

She says nothing, just stretches her arm across my chest, holding me closer. My fingers trail up and down her arm as we sit in silence, just listening to each other breathe, drowning in the bittersweet moments. Fuck, I just got her back.

Minutes tick by, weighing us down deeper until she takes a breath.

"We won't leave each other. You promised me that we'd die together, remember? So no matter what happens tomorrow, I'm following you everywhere you go, Calder Wolfe. So let's have right now, for us, until we know what today will bring."

My chin drops as I look down at her. "I'm gonna marry you."

"Yeah, ya are."

I tuck my hands under her armpits, dragging her up my body, growling as I kiss her again.

"I love you. But if I'm celebrating my possible last night on this planet, then I should get a last meal."

She laughs, leaning in to kiss my lips. "And what would you like to eat?"

"Your pussy."

I roll her onto her back as she squeals, but a clang from a box I had on the nightstand makes her jump.

"Oh shit." I chuckle. "It's okay."

She smiles, relaxing as I lean over, surveying the mess.

"What was that?"

I'm half off the bed as she laughs, anchoring me with her legs wrapped around my waist. But I press a palm to the floor before I pick up the box, muscling myself back into bed.

I shift around so that she can sit as I lie on my side, placing the container between us.

"This is something special. These are all the things I have left to remember my mother. Some are random trinkets. Others are things she specifically left me. The only thing missing is the coin."

I watch her as she smiles, but it's sad.

"You're lucky," she whispers. "I know that sounds weird, but..."

My brow furrows. "Do you want me to let her live?"

Sutton's eyes cut to mine as she stares back into my eyes because she knows I'm speaking about her mother, but she just shakes her head as she looks back down, sorting through the belongings.

I won't push her to tell me what they did when we were apart, and I'll never let on to some things I already know. Because they're hers to tell when she's ready.

But goddamn if I wouldn't move heaven and earth for this girl.

She's pulling things out to look at them closer, the sadness in her eyes fading as they flick to mine. She holds up a postcard that says Memphis.

"She always wanted to go to Graceland. Obsessed with Elvis."

Sutton grins, putting it back inside, reaching for something else before she looks up at me.

"What makes you think the Council will choose you over Connor?"

I run my finger down the slope of her nose and over her freckles as she blinks back at me.

"Because I did everything he did without taking from people. We're alike in so many ways. But this life is about family. We do wicked things, but in the end, we're supposed to protect our own. I remembered that because of you. Connor looked after himself alone. So I took everything away from him—the drugs, the money, the power—and I made it better. People respect me as much as they fear me."

She grins. "Like an Irish Robin Hood, huh?"

I chuckle, looking inside the box too. "Not exactly, but I like it." My eyes drop, seeing a folded picture. I pull it out and open it, staring down at the old faded photo, smiling before I hand it to Sutton.

"It's so faded, but people always said that we had the same eyes."

She's grinning as she looks down at the photo before her fingers come to her lips.

"Baby?"

She pales, blinking quickly, eyes darting to mine before she shakes her head and whispers, "Holy shit." She laughs as tears spring to her eyes.

"Whoa. Hey. What's wrong?"

I'm already sitting up, pulling her into my arms, but the smile on her face feels like it arrested my heart. Her hands come to my face as she straddles me, fingers brushing over my beard.

"You wouldn't believe me if I told you."

My head tilts as I lock eyes with her. "Try me."

Her eyes search mine before she leans forward, brushing her nose against mine.

"I just think destiny works in amazing ways. And if you ask me, your eyes are identical."

My brows draw together, but she kisses me deeply, and she doesn't stop until I've forgotten what the fuck I was going to say.

My eyes dart to the clock, hating this fucking moment because of how she looks—hair wild and laid out over the pillow, body covered in one of my T-shirts because she got cold last night. Fuck, she's perfect. This is perfect.

I take a deep breath, letting my chin lift before I step back from the bed.

"It's almost over."

The butt of my palms wipes my eyes as I turn, walking away, but the minute I touch the handle, I look back, staring at my girl. My beautiful girl, with emerald eyes and hair like fire who landed in my life like a goddamn earthquake, shaking it up and leaving me destroyed. I wouldn't have it any other way.

Because what she tore down, she rebuilt.

"I love you, baby. And I'll kill every motherfucker there if they try to keep me away."

I pull the door open, eyes locking to Roman's, who's already standing guard outside the door.

He gives me a nod as I pass him, but I stop and look at him.

"Did you have her things brought home?"

"I did. And I thought you could use this later. For Hunter."

He hands me the knife we had made for her. This is his way of saying I better make it out.

All I can do is nod before leaving my brother in that fucking hallway, looking after my heart.

Calder

The room is dark and ripe with the scent of death. Because the call for it is oozing off the men standing around us. This is it. What it's all come to. The Council will decide who leads this family. And who dies.

"On your knees."

Connor and I drop directly across from each other, eyes locked as a gun presses to each of our temples. My teeth grind as I look at him because I want to grab the fucking gun at my temple and shoot him with it.

But I won't. Because even if I die, Roman's going to make sure Connor does too.

The head of the Irish Chicago family—the MacGregors—walks to the center of the room, standing between us.

"Only one of you will leave here alive." Connor's eyes lock to mine as the man continues. "Now's the time when you convince us of which."

This is tradition. These ten men stand in the shadows, all silent until they vote, and then bang, one of us goes down.

"Answer this, Calder Wolfe...why should this family"—MacGregor looks around—"these men, why should we follow you?"

Fuck. Time feels like it stands still. All I ever heard growing up was shit about my birthright into violent delights, to a family that did wicked things with sometimes dire consequences. I hated it. I ran from it.

I ran to her.

And somehow, deep in the vastness of finding love, I also made peace with the devil inside of me.

Birthright meant nothing to me. Even as I walked in this door, it's always just been a means to an end. But as I look around this room, at the faces of the men who stare back, I'm suddenly struck with the enormity of what my life means.

This family will protect her and the babies I fill her belly with. It will leave a mark, take lives, and better others. And it should only be led by me.

I reach up, bringing my hand to the gun at my head, lowering it as I stand. Unease sweeps the room as I look at each man inside this warehouse.

"I don't expect anyone to be led. I expect that we'll walk together. Side by side like brothers in arms." I step toward Connor, jaw tensed before I speak, "Because what I took from him, I'll give to you."

The men around the room exchange glances, because he keeps them hungry so they obey. But I'll keep them fed so they're loyal. I take another step feeling anger begin to course through my veins, pulling my fists closed tight as my voice is gritted between my teeth.

"I own his streets—the ones he abandoned and turned into ghettos." My head shifts to MacGregor. "I run his fucking drugs, but I'll make sure that everyone gets a piece. Because that's what this family was built on. Our violent loyalty and understanding that no man is ever above being Irish."

Connor's inhaling through his nose like a bull, face red as he glares back at me. I crack my neck as I look back.

"Get off your fucking knees and face me like a man."

Tension bounds through the walls as the gun held to his head is lowered. Connor stands, his chest heaving, snarling as he stalks toward me.

But I'm fucking ready. It feels like I've waited my entire life, building, culminating to this moment. It's right in front of me, mine for the taking.

We stand toe to toe, ready to kill as his hand darts out, gripping my throat.

"You think these men will turn on me? After all I've done for them? I know what's right. I am King, you little prick."

My fist swings down across his face, knocking him to the ground as I hover over him. The sound of guns cocking echoes through the silence.

But I won't be stopped. My words are growled, bellowed from within me.

"You've only done for you." I heave out breaths as I lower my voice, body stilling as the comfort of killing wraps itself around me.

Connor's staring up at me, fear in his eyes as he wipes the blood from his mouth.

"There is no longer a king. Because my family will be a fucking army. And Uncle, I will take my place by any means necessary."

My eyes are narrowed on Connor. I could kill him right here. I take a step just as my head is pushed sideways by the cold hard steel of a barrel to my temple. MacGregor steps into view, sneering.

"The only means are the ones we give." He presses the gun harder as my heart pounds. "We decide who lives and who dies. Who's in power and who's starved."

Connor is yanked, forcing his back straighter as his lips tug into a grin, before a heavy hand pushes on my shoulder.

"Get on your knees, Calder."

I drop, glimpses of Sutton flashing through my mind because I'm either going to be anointed or annihilated.

chapter thirty-six

Sutton

My eyes drift open slowly as my hand slides over the bed, reaching for Calder. But I already know it's empty. There's only the sunlight shining through the window, hitting the sheet and leaving a streak of brightness to spotlight his absence.

I just lie there, staring at the crumpled white sheet, scooting closer to smell it.

My eyes close again, picturing him lying next to me, a smirk on his face as I trace my finger over the tattoos on his chest.

"Please come back," I whisper.

A knock on the door shoots me to sitting, eyes wide open. My heart's beating too quickly as I drop my eyes, seeing that I'm still wearing Calder's T-shirt.

Another knock brings Roman's voice. "It's just me, Sutton. Roman."

I let out a breath, running my hand through my hair.

"Come in," I say quietly, hating that I'm so unnerved.

Roman peeks his head around the door, meeting my eyes.

"Hey, Mama."

He must see the look on my face because he shakes his head. "Hey. Hey. Hey," he says as he walks inside, beelining to me.

Roman is scary and intimidating, but at this moment, the way he holds my face in his hand—it's everything I need. I'm gripping onto his wrist, staring up at him, just needing the anchor he's giving because...

"I'm so afraid I'll lose him," I whisper, finishing my thought.

He shakes his head.

"C fought death for you. You really think a few gangsters are gonna get in his way? This is what he knows, baby girl, and if shit doesn't go his way, then I got you. Because you ain't alone anymore. You are a part of him, and that makes you my family."

I smile up at him, letting him pull me into a bear hug.

"I would trade my life for his," I say on a ragged breath.

"Me too."

I hug him tighter for what feels like forever until he lets me go, giving me one of those Roman nods I remember. They say so much without saying anything at all.

He clears his throat. "I'll check on you later."

I nod, sinking back into the bed, and pull the sheet up before I close my eyes again and pray.

I don't know how long I've been asleep, but the sun's lower in the sky, shadows cast across the walls in our room. I roll to his space, still empty, so I close my eyes again, but a knock on the door reopens my eyes as I sit up.

"Haven't we already done this?" I tease quietly as Roman walks inside, holding a bottle of water in one hand and something in a bowl—maybe soup.

"You need to eat and stop grieving. He'll be pissed when he comes back and you're all hungry and sad."

I run my hands through my hair before smacking down on the blanket a little too hard.

"Don't do that."

His face swings to mine as he puts the bowl on the nightstand.

"Do what?"

"Act like he went to the store. Like he'll be right back. Don't do that, Roman."

He looks down at the food, placing my water next to it before he gives a quiet growl. God, it reminds me of Calder, so I scoot back into the bed and roll over so my back is to Roman.

But I'm nudged, and I only move because I feel him sit down on the bed.

"Can I tell you something?"

My brows furrow, but he can't see that, so I shrug as I stare at the wall.

"Every year while you've been apart, I went to see that old witch."

My chin meets my shoulder, eyes fixing on his.

"Why?"

He crosses his arms, leaning back against me as he stretches his legs in front of him.

"I don't know. At first, I thought maybe she'd cursed us." He pauses, giving a sad chuckle. "Because of West dying and all."

My teeth find my bottom lip before I whisper, "I'm so sorry about West, Roman."

He doesn't look at me, just gives my shoulder a gentle tap of his fist before he continues.

"The thing is, she always said the same thing. It was stupid. But everything felt pretty out of control, so I figured fuck it, what's the harm? I thought maybe I'd go one day, and she'd say you were over him."

I poke his back, scowling, but he grins, still speaking. "Then I could tell him you'd moved on, and maybe he wouldn't be so fucking lost without you."

His face shifts to mine. "Because he was lost. My brother hasn't looked like himself since this morning when he left. You breathed life back into him."

I shift, roll over, and push to sit up again.

"Or, fuck, I kept thinking best-case she'd use her hoodoo voodoo to tell me something we could use against Connor. But it was always the fucking same. Until it wasn't."

I grab my water, twisting the top before taking a sip.

"What did she say the last time?"

He motions to the soup, so I pick up the warm bowl and take a bite.

"She told me that men were like fish—the great ones devour the small. But that Calder was the ocean, and he'd swallow everyone whole. She said death wasn't waiting for him. It was listening for his instruction."

The spoon slides out from between my lips as I frown.

"What does that mean?"

He chuckles, and he looks out the window. "I have no fucking clue, but I do know what's important about it."

"What?" I answer weakly.

"She never said he'd lose, Sutton."

The sun's gone down. The house is dark.

And I'm standing in front of the window, drawing the curtains, because I can't bear to see the stars.

There are none anymore, not without him.

The bedroom door creaks open as I turn to look over my shoulder.

"Is he dead?"

"We haven't heard anything yet."

My chin trembles as my arms wrap around me as I almost double over. Roman rushes to me, but I hold out my hand, stopping him as I stand back up.

"No. Just leave me alone. Please. Let me do this part alone."

Roman reaches for me, but I step away, so he drops his hand.

"There's no way to prepare for this." My voice is so shaky as I look back at him.

Roman nods, taking a step backward as I turn around and stare at the fucking curtains. My eyes search over the fabric, thinking about the spot I can see on the other side of them. The place on the field where he made love to me, took my innocence, gave me his heart.

The door closes as my shoulders fall, letting my head hang.

Silence crashes around me as I stand there, my fears fighting hope, our love threatening death. I don't even know how long I've been there, but it's long enough that I'm cold. Even though I don't feel it because goose bumps spread over my arms, and my chest feels hollow.

Calder.

The sound of the door opening again makes my chest shake. Because Roman's not speaking behind me. And there's only one reason for everything to feel and be so quiet.

"He's gone," I whisper.

Tears drop to the floor, but the sound of heavy footsteps lifts my head just as Calder rushes past me, tearing back the curtains.

"They're gone. I'm right fucking here, baby."

I gasp so loud that my hands shoot to my chest. He grabs my wrist, yanking me into him as his mouth crashes down on mine. I'm sobbing, kissing him back with the same fierceness, arms crawling over his shoulders and wrapping around his neck as he picks me up.

He pulls back, breathless, drops of blood splattered on his face, body infused with the smell of gasoline as he stares at me.

"It's over, Sutton."

It's over. The words don't come out. They linger inside, flicking switches, igniting sparks as I begin to shake, gripping his shirt in my hands. Calder looks out of the window as I follow his line of sight, immediately knocked still.

From our window, a fire burns like the fucking sun, set against a backdrop of stars on top of that black glass of the bay. Oranges and reds color the sky, reflecting off the water.

"Oh my God," I rush out.

I'm breathing quickly, watching the fire rise and grow, flickering in my pupils. I can't look away. It's as if everything taken from me is being reborn from the ashes of that fire. I can feel it inside of me like I'm coming back to life.

"It's over," I breathe out, breath doubling in speed until I'm almost panting. My skin tingles as Calder bends, placing me back to the ground, whispering against my skin, lips touching my neck.

"Yes, baby."

His face touches my cheek as I **watch the fire**, and my ragged breaths turn to cries.

"Thank you." I shift to bring my lips to his. "I love you so much."

His hands cradle the sides of my **head as he** kisses my face. The blood on his hands is on me now, but I don't **care, because** I want to share this with him.

No part of Calder isn't also a part **of me.**

Our lips touch as I say, "Connor?"

He tips my chin up to look into his **eyes.**

"I promised his life to Roman. And **he's gone to** take it."

We stare at each other so deeply **because, at** this moment, I feel free. My lips part, wanting to say something, ask questions, but I can't find the words. But I don't have to because Calder **always** knows what I need.

He licks his lips before his thumb **brushes my** cheek.

"I faced death today but then I **wielded it. Because** everything I do, I do in your name."

My eyes close, feeling the peace **before he gifts** it to me.

"I tied them to chairs."

I suck in a breath because I want **to know. I** want to know it all. I need to know that they suffered because I **did for as long** as I can remember.

Kisses are pressed to my skin, hands **weaving** into my hair.

"I put them around the dining table **and made** them watch..."

My T-shirt is lifted over my head as **I stare** up at him. His lips meet mine before he draws back, lowering **his head** to my neck, kissing the bruises left by Hunter.

"I castrated him. I cut him over **and over and** then fed him the filthiest fucking piece of him."

My shoulders shake as Calder **brings his mouth** to mine again, almost feeding me the air I need. I'm gripping **his shirt**, back arching toward him, wanting more of him as our eyes lock.

"I made him eat his cock until **he choked**, shaking from the fucking shock. Then I took his hands for laying **them on you.**"

Air fills my lungs as I inhale harshly, **reaching** for his face. He takes my wrists, kissing my palms, smearing the blood from his cheeks to my hands. His forehead lowers to mine as I close my eyes, listening to the love in his voice.

"I threw him on the table and taped all their fucking mouths shut because they never listened to your cries." His words grind out between his teeth. "So nobody got to hear theirs."

Calder's lips press to mine before pulling away but staying so close that they brush mine as they speak.

"I burned them alive, baby. Nobody will ever hurt you again."

I lift to my toes, kissing him so profoundly, pouring my love, gratitude, and life into this one solitary moment before my eyes open. I look into his— ones bluer than the ocean and the sky—as I say the only thing that matters anymore for the rest of my life.

"I am yours. And you are mine. Forever."

Calder—One Year Later

S he's been walking around the field for an hour, picking flowers, staring up at the clouds, pretending not to watch me as I sit on this porch reading. But I can't keep my eyes off my girl.

But that's nothing new.

I look up again, staring at her red hair that's hanging wild and free down her back, just the way I like it.

She tucks some behind her ear, glancing over at me, then looks away as her hand comes to the slit in her long baby blue dress. It's the kind with skinny straps that hugs her body in all the right places, falling all the way down to her ankles.

Fuck, it makes me want to do bad damn things.

I look down again, having lost my place for the three hundredth time before I chuckle, not lifting my head as I shout.

"Stop tempting me and let me read."

I hear her laugh, and it stirs everything inside of me.

Because that's what she always does—reminds me I'm alive.

I close the journal, *our journal,* and put my eyes on her again. She gave this to me today as an anniversary gift. But I know it's making her nervous for me to read it because my girl hasn't stopped playing with the ends of her hair or biting her perfect bottom lip.

"How much more do you have to read?" she shouts back, still standing too far away.

My head shifts to the side, to the guards that are always watching. They make her feel better, and that's all that matters because I'm still the scariest fucking thing here.

"Hey, get inside, go make yourself a sandwich. We're fine."

"Okay, boss." One of them stops and grins over at me. "Should we shut the curtains?"

I smirk as I stand, giving him a nod, my eyes staying locked on my baby. The journal drops to my chair with a thud just as the door closes.

She's already smiling, with her hands clasped behind her back, just waiting for me as I take the steps down to the grass, making my way toward her.

"You sent the guys inside."

"I did."

I stop in front of her, bringing my hand to cradle her face as my thumb brushes her bottom lip.

"So I read that you popped some chick in the face with a lacrosse stick, huh? Who knew my girl was such a fucking bruiser. I should put ya in the ring."

She laughs, holding my wrist, leaning her cheek into it.

"I mean...full disclosure: I'd think twice before messing with me." She tries her hand at a Boston accent. "Imma ringah."

My laugh cracks my chest because I taught her that word when I told her about the fights I did for Connor. I tuck my hands under her armpits, lifting her to my eye level.

"You wanna tell me what's got you so nervous. Because you were all excited an hour ago for me to read."

Her hands are on my shoulders as her brows draw together. Damn, she's fucking cute when she's thinking.

"Wrap," I growl.

She reaches down, hiking up her dress, and hooks her legs around my waist. My arms close in around her as I walk us farther out into the field, just letting her hug me.

It only takes seconds before she takes a deep breath and whispers, "Better."

I shift my face, kissing the side of her head, nudging her with my shoulder, so she looks up at me.

"If you carry it, then so do I. You get me?"

She nods. I know she understands. Sutton and I don't know how to not be full fucking disclosure.

"And baby, there is nothing in there I don't already know."

She's staring at me, so thoughtful as her fingertip traces the constellation on my neck.

After the Kelly housefire, the world turned upside down. But it all stood back a comfortable distance because my girl was with me. And nobody was crossing the line to try to get to her. Not reporters, not lawyers, nobody. Not even the cops.

It gave her the room she needed to find peace. And with that peace came all her truth. I listened, never interrupting. I kissed her when she needed it and let her scream when she couldn't hold it in.

That beautiful girl bared her soul to me, and it was a fucking gift.

She takes a deep breath before giving me a little frown.

"I know. But—"

I say nothing, letting her find the words she wants to say. Because I can see them sitting back there behind emerald eyes that speak to me before she does.

"A part of me wants to forget it all. To burn the book like none of it ever happened. I just want to fill all the pages with this"—she motions around with a hand—"with our magic. And our dreams. I needed that journal because I didn't have you. But now I do."

I lean in, rubbing my nose over hers.

"And you don't want it to follow you here."

Her eyes lock to mine as she blinks, so fucking stripped down and honest.

"Exactly. I don't want it anymore. I just want to let it go, and I didn't realize that until you were reading it. Because you reading it makes it all that much more real."

I pat her ass, lowering her to the ground, and take her hand.

"Then, baby, let's rewrite history."

I've turned, making my way across the grass as I tug her behind, listening to her laughter like it's my favorite fucking song.

"Hey," I bellow toward the front door, seeing one of my guys come out quickly. "We're going downtown."

"Choose."

Sutton's got a journal in each hand, eyes volleying between them as we stand in the tiny bookstore in downtown St. Simeon. She told me once that this was the store she was standing near the first time she saw me driving down the street.

Fuck me. The way her eyes lit up made me realize I couldn't take her from here. She loves it, so Roman stays in Boston, and I'm here for all the New York shit.

"I can't pick."

She scowls before grinning, weighing them between her hands. So I grab them from her, wagging my brows.

"Then we'll get both. One for me, and one for you."

She hurries up behind me as I walk toward the counter, setting them down to pay. Her arm wraps around my waist as mine rests over her shoulders.

"Will you let me read yours?" she whispers absentmindedly, playing with some trinkets.

I chuckle. "Of course, I will. But only if you write about me in yours at least once a day."

She pokes my side, shaking her head, humor crossing her face.

"Deal. But you're going to have to try harder to be interesting. Because you're really just a completely uneventful person with no life. It's all broody—who am I? What's my destiny? Blah, blah, blah."

I laugh as I turn in toward her, tickling her stomach, but she squeals, sealing her body to mine in a bear hug.

"I'm gonna put you in a headlock with that smart mouth."

I've got her tucked against me, hugging her as she laughs, but I've stopped because my eyes are staring out of the large shop window. Because looking back at me is that old woman—the one that told Sutton her fortune, and me about my destiny.

Eyes I remember as cold now stare back with kindness. Her eyes drop to Sutton as my arms tighten, and I press a kiss to the top of her head.

A small smile comes to the woman's face before she cranes her neck as if she's looking at the display on the table. It's one we didn't check. The books are neatly stacked, arranged for people passing by.

Her finger points to a book in the front, but I can't make out what the design is. But as a v forms between my eyes, she gives me a nod and walks away.

"Your heart is beating fast," Sutton whispers, kissing my chest before resting her chin on it to look up at me.

I'm still staring out of the window at nothing as Sutton chuckles.

"Hey, are you okay?"

I nod.

"Yeah, but do me a favor? Go check out that table, just in case you see another journal you like. I have a feeling there's something there for you."

I point to where the old lady did before Sutton furrows her brow, a smile playing on her face.

"You have a feeling, huh?"

She saunters off as I throw some money on the counter because the cashier's already bagging up our purchase.

My eyes are on my girl, watching her peruse the books until pure fucking joy lights her up. Her eyes are wide open, teeth showing from her smile as she holds up a thick black leather journal.

She hurries, flipping it over and back.

"Oh my God. Look at this one."

I take it from her hands, shaking my head. Son of a bitch, that fucking witch.

On one side, there's a sun engraved in gold and on the back a moon. I open it thumbing through the pages.

"Oh my God, there are tiny stars on the bottom of the pages," she whispers like it's the best thing she's ever seen. "And we can both use it because it's double-sided."

I put it on the counter as the salesperson picks it up, looking at Sutton.

"These are the best."

The girl opens it, then flips it over and opens the other side—like two books in one.

I grin, taking the bag, lacing my fingers through my girl's hand, watching her marvel over the journal. I couldn't have been led to anything more perfect.

My mind starts thinking of all the notes I'll leave her. The moments I'll replay for her to read. Fuck, I need to buy a hundred of these.

She opens the front cover as we begin walking out back toward the car, squeezing my hand.

"Oh wow, it's inscribed."

She holds it up to me as my face turns down to hers.

"Write about a love that defies the stars. Write about yours."

"It's as if it was meant to be. Like fate," she whispers, leaning into me.

The car door is opened for her, but as she gets in, I tug her back. "It's not fate, baby. Or destiny. We're bigger than all that shit."

Her eyes close like she's letting my words soak into her skin before I lean in closer.

"But when we get home, I wanna show you something that is your destiny."

She laughs before leaning forward, pressing her lips to mine.

"And what exactly would that be?"

"The back seat of the Mustang."

Sutton bites her lip, so I reach up and tug it free before grabbing it between my fingers and pulling her into another kiss.

She's breathless the minute I draw back as her husky voice breathes, "I thought back seats were for bad girls."

Goddamn. The way she's looking up at me—she looks just like heaven and I can't fucking wait to show her how fun sinning like hell is. I suck my bottom lip between my teeth, letting it slide out slowly before I answer.

"They are."

Sutton

"**M**arry me."

I roll my head to the side, staring at him because we've been lying in this bed all day, wrapped up in each other, celebrating our five-year anniversary.

"When?"

His hand reaches between my legs, cupping my pussy as I draw my bottom lip between my teeth. God, he's good with his hands. Two fingers slip inside me as his other hand grips the inside of my thigh, easing it open as he tilts his head to watch.

"Fuck, your pussy is pretty."

I exhale heavily, lifting my hips, gasping as he leans down, pulls his fingers out, and licks them before closing his mouth over me.

"Fuck, Calder."

His tongue makes a slow figure eight around my clit, teasing before he gently flicks his tongue up and down, making me shudder.

"Marry me."

It's hummed onto my pussy, lifting my head, my hooded eyes on him. "When?"

He growls, making me chuckle before he crawls up my body, his cock sandwiched between us. I smirk, but he just stares at me.

I'm not giving in. We do this all the time. He asks, and I say, *"When?"* and then he never gives me a date. When our nightmare ended, he'd asked me to marry him, and I'd said yes immediately—but once life calmed down, and I found my footing.

I wanted to be his wife, but I also wanted to stand on my own two feet. So I went back to school and graduated early this year and started a nonprofit for women in abusive situations. I did it with my inheritance— seemed like a fitting end to their money.

I became a woman that could take care of herself and still had a fucking lion at her back.

Two, actually. Roman's my family too.

Because it was never going to be enough for me to just rely on Calder's empire. Not if I was going to stand next to him. Because it *is* an empire. There is no doubt that Calder was born for this, because he is the Irish mob and all that it implies.

But he deserved a queen. And I deserved to become one.

"Just tell me when," I whisper, lifting my lips to kiss his beard.

He shakes his head, so I reach down and grab his ass, making him smirk as he presses his cock against me.

"Baby, I'm not choosing for you. That's not something that happens ever again. *You* tell *me.* Until then, I'm gonna fuck you until you're sticky and sweet, and then I'm gonna lick you fucking clean."

Not something that ever happens again. That part hits me so hard that my eyes bore into his. He's still always giving me what I need. My whole life before him was decided for me, but he sees me. Everything is on my terms now.

I blink up at him, remembering our moment last night. He was chasing me outside, promising dirty rewards when he caught me, but once he did, he tugged my face to his and told me he was proud of the woman I've become. It will forever be one of the greatest moments of my life.

Because Calder never says anything he doesn't mean.

"Ask me again," I rush out.

His hands trail up my naked body, stopping between my breasts as he locks eyes with me.

"Marry me, Buttercup."

I'm already nodding.

"Yes." I lift, kissing his lips. "Now."

He smiles, drawing back, searching my eyes.

"Now?"

I nod faster as he brings his hand to my throat, leaning in to kiss me again, growling his words into my lips.

"I've been waiting for you to say that for too fucking long."

I chuckle, wanting a deeper kiss from him, but he leans over me, grabbing his phone and letting me go. I'm staring at him, confused but laughing as he peppers kisses over my face, his weight almost crushing me.

"What are you doing?"

He ignores me, speaking into his phone.

"She finally said yes. But it's tonight. We'll see you in an hour."

I'm blinking, staring back at him, shaking my head.

"What are you doing?"

Calder wags his eyebrows and rolls out of bed, walking his gorgeous bare ass to the closet before he comes out with a slinky white gown. It's spaghetti-strapped and almost backless. And honestly, everything I've ever wanted.

"Where the hell did you hide that?"

"Baby." He winks. "I'm a fucking criminal."

My hand covers my mouth as I laugh, trying to process what's happening.

"Get dressed. Don't ask questions. And don't peek." His eyes dart to the window. "You've got an hour. Then I'm hauling you out over my shoulder. Because you said yes."

"Wait." I'm laughing, naked in the bed, but he's already got basketball shorts on and is walking out of our bedroom.

"Calder," I yell after him.

But he just bellows, "Get your pretty ass dressed, baby."

Oh my God. I scramble out of bed, wanting to look outside, but the moment my toes touch the floor, he's shouting again.

"Don't fucking peek, baby."

I bite my lip, grab my dress, and behave like the good girl he wants as I walk into the bathroom and get ready.

Almost to the minute, there's a knock on my door. So I check myself out in the mirror, beaming because I've never felt so beautiful. I kept my hair down, and I'm barefoot because that's what I've always wanted.

I don't have to peek to know he's planned this in our field. The only place it should be.

I walk to the door and open it, still smiling as Roman extends his arm.

"Well, look at you, in a suit."

"No tie," he counters with all the broody grumpiness that never leaves him.

"Still, you look very handsome."

He leans in and kisses my cheek. "Thank you. And if you wouldn't mind, I'd like to give you away."

My heart almost explodes because he can't even look at me. After all, Roman and feelings don't mix, but I could hug him to death.

He clears his throat. "I always wanted a sister, and you've been...you know. I'd like to be the one that walks you down the aisle if that's okay?"

My eyes are already glistening.

"I love you too, Roman. And I'd really love for you to do that."

I take his arm, following his lead as we walk down the stairs, but I almost scream when we hit the bottom because Aubrey and Piper are staring back at me.

"Oh my God."

Piper grabs my hand, pulling me away from Roman.

"I can't believe this is happening. It's kismet. What are the chances we'd all be in the same place, at the same time?"

Aubrey hands me some wildflowers as I smile, hugging her.

"The chances are good, Pipes. Considering their anniversary is in July and we always spend it here on the island."

"Whatever," Piper counters, rolling her eyes. "I'm just saying it's all fate and destiny."

She hugs me too, my smile planted on my face. Piper starts talking to Roman, and Aubrey takes my hand, staring at me.

After everything happened, she's who I told everything to. I always felt like a third wheel with her and Piper when we were young, but I realized that none of us worked without the others. But Aubrey is the friend that can shoulder the kind of story I lived.

She pulls me in for another hug, tears in her eyes before she reaches up and tugs my hair.

"You look amazing. And bitch, this was all most definitely your damn destiny."

Piper snaps her fingers. "Wait, we have to do the thing, Aubs."

"Oh yeah," she breathes.

Piper reaches inside her purse. "So, your something new is the dress. This is your something old." She hands me Calder's mother's rosary, wrapping it around my wrist like a bracelet, letting the cross hang down over my middle finger.

Aubrey wipes her eye as Piper looks at her. "Did you just shed a tear, Miss Cold Dead Heart?"

"Allergies." She winks before taking off her diamond drop earrings. "Now, if Piper would shut up, I'd be able to tell you this is your something borrowed."

I take them, laughing as I put them in my ears, hearing music start playing from outside.

Piper looks at us, eyes growing wide. "Shit, we forgot something blue."

Aubrey snaps her fingers like she's trying to think, but I reach out, grabbing their hands.

"I got it. Hold on."

They're staring at me like I'm crazy as I hurry back up the stairs and grab the one thing I can think of before I rush back down.

"Okay," I whisper, laughing and breathless.

Roman walks back to where I'm standing, eyes dropping to Aubrey's for a moment before he offers me his arm again.

The girls walk ahead as we follow out to the porch and straight to Calder. There are no frills, with the exception of a framed photo of West on the railing of our porch. And candles, so many candles lit everywhere, illuminating the dark field, making everything glow amber.

Calder is standing next to Father Paul.

His blue eyes shine against his all-black dress shirt and slacks. God, he's so fucking gorgeous that I almost can't breathe. I lick my lips as he wipes his eyes.

So strong until he sees me.

We walk step after step until Roman slows us because I'm not even paying attention. The moment my beautiful man put his eyes on me, I was lost—tethered to my other half, where the outside world becomes only a myth.

Roman takes my hand from his arm, giving it to Calder.

Our hands join, eyes locked on each other as a breeze blows up from the water. It's a gust, rippling my dress, sending pieces of my flowers up into the air as the candles blow out.

We exhale simultaneously, tipping our faces to the sky, because without the candles, Calder and I are surrounded by a blanket of stars.

"I understand you have your own vows," Father Paul whispers.

The smile grows on my face as our eyes meet again and petals drift downward.

Calder's hands are shaking, chest vibrating, overtaken with emotion.

"I vow to always love you above all others. No matter what."

My eyes close, remembering where we started as I repeat what he's said.

"I vow to always love *you* above all others. No matter what."

He brings my hands to his lips, kissing them over and over before saying, "I will always protect you, even with my life."

God, we came so close to that, and we've made it through all the bad parts, scratching and clawing our way past destiny and fate, to this—to us. We're stronger than any of that. We're indestructible.

"And I will always protect you, even against yourself."

I'm crying, tears falling down my cheeks as he lets go of my hand, stepping in closer as he wipes them from my face.

"Baby, I promise to die by your side when we're wrinkly and fucking gray. So that we'll never be apart again."

My hands cradle his face.

"And I promise to love you even after death."

He's silent, staring down at me, so deeply connected that I'm not sure if he's speaking or it's his soul making promises to mine.

"Not even death does us part."

"Forever," I answer as he leans in and grabs my face before kissing me like it's the first and last thing he'll ever do.

A throat clears, pulling my lips into a grin against Calder's. We don't separate, staring into each other's eyes as Father Paul whispers to us.

"You have to wait for me to declare it."

Calder growls, making me laugh.

"I'm not good with impulse control when it comes to my girl, so declare it already."

He's already lifting me off my feet as the priest pronounces us man and wife. Calder's mouth crashes down on mine as yelps and howls echo in the background.

He pulls away, arms wrapped around me.

"Can I get you pregnant now?"

I laugh loudly, nodding, reaching inside my bra and pulling out my small, round birth control case.

"I needed something blue, and it was the first thing I thought of."

He attacks my neck, taking a bite as I squeal before popping me up, right over his shoulder, as he turns, stalking back toward the house and grunting, "Right now. We're doing it now."

I never thought in my wildest dreams that I'd marry a man that would not only make my dreams come true but that he'd redefine the idea of them altogether. He carries me up the stairs, placing me to my feet as he closes the door behind him.

My hands fall on his face, and I swear the entire glimpse of our lives passes before me.

Our happiness, children, joy, pain…a lifetime. But no matter what I see, through it all, he's by my side. And I'm by his. It took us five years after we parted to get to this moment, and I wouldn't do it any differently.

He kisses me softly, brushing my hair from my face as I look up at him...
my husband.

"You are mine, Calder Wolfe. And I am yours. Promise it again."

"Forever and ever and ever, baby."

chapter thirty-nine

Calder Thirty Years Old

"Look at you," I whisper, not really sure if the words have come out. My face lifts to Sutton's. "She's beautiful. Look at all her hair."

My wife is smiling from ear to ear, exhausted after laboring with our daughter for too many hours. It's moments like this that make me feel small, holding this tiny little life after witnessing my beautiful girl birth a miracle from her body.

I have nothing to offer that could even compare to what they've brought to my life.

So I just keep protecting them with mine and my whole fucking army.

A nurse asks Sutton if she should get the boisterous crew in the hallway, making me chuckle.

"Yes." She smiles.

I stand, carrying another piece of my heart to my wife as I sit down next to her. The tiny little life in my hands suckles as she lies peacefully sleeping.

"Are you crying?" Sutton breathes.

"I do every time."

She inhales deeply. "Well, I don't care how Catholic you like to pretend we are. This uterus is officially off-limits."

I grumble, rubbing my nose over the tiny one in front of me. "Did you hear that, Saoirse?"

Sutton laughs, hitting my arm. "We are not naming her Saoirse."

I hold her up, facing Sutton.

"Come on. She looks like one."

"She looks like someone who nobody can pronounce? It's not happening. Unless you're moving us all to Ireland."

I lift my brows.

"Don't even think about it."

We're laughing as the door swings open, and my boys come running in, along with Aubs and Piper behind them, Roman trailing behind with a grin.

"West," Sutton warns as our oldest jumps up on the bed, smiling like the devil.

The room fills with giggles and excitement because all three of Saoirse's brothers have prayed nightly for a sister. Roman helps the other two up as I give them a look to be careful of their mother.

"Fellas, this is your sister. And your job is to protect her for your whole entire lives."

West reaches a finger out, and she grips it with her tiny little hands, making his little eyes shoot to mine.

"I promise, Dad. Forever."

My jaw tenses, holding back my emotion as I look to Sutton, whose emerald eyes stare back into mine as she mouths, *Forever.*

I don't deserve this kind of happiness, or maybe I do, because I was willing to fight for it, no matter the consequence. All I know is that I love this goddamn girl, and nobody will ever take her from me.

And I will keep building this empire for my children so that one day she and I will look down from the stars and watch our legacy thrive as they stare up at us and tell our story.

Sutton—Fifty years old

God, he's so handsome. I laugh to myself because I'm not sure I'll ever stop thinking that. He's aged in all the most perfect ways, like a damn fine wine. The man is just as much of a presence as he was when we were young.

Calder runs his hand through his hair, tattoos a little more worn, his smile just as bright as he sits outside with two of our grandkids, letting them look through the telescope.

"Grandma, Grandpa said he brought you here when you were younger and made you see stars."

My mouth pops open as Calder's booming laugh fills our sky.

"This one's a filthy liar, baby. You can't trust him. I said I brought you here to see *the* stars."

"No, you didn't..." rings in unison behind him.

They both giggle as he grabs them, tickling their sides. I lean a hip against the doorframe, smiling, just marveling at our life well lived.

My husband is a dangerous man, a fallen angel, but still, he came from heaven. And that's exactly what my life has felt like.

I've never felt alone. Always been loved, worshipped even.

And from that, we have a legacy, not of hate or violence, but one from love.

A few years back, I stopped into that tea shop, the one where I had the tarot reading when I was a kid, because I saw a flyer just like before.

At first glance, it looked like the woman hadn't aged, but I came to find out it was her daughter. She told me her mother used to tell her the story of our love. How it was so powerful that it punched a hole into the world of the living, letting Calder walk in both because not even the devil could keep him from me.

We laughed, treating it as a story told by an old woman with magic in her veins and too much age to tell the difference between what's real and what's not.

But as I walked away, I looked over my shoulder just like when I was seventeen, feeling that indescribable pull to him. Because my life tells me her story is real.

Our love has always been too big to contain.

"Hey," he whispers, making me blink up into his blue eyes. "You thinking about me again?"

"Absolutely."

"Then kiss me."

I smile before I push to my tiptoes, pressing my lips to his as he picks me up and places me on his boots, and we dance to music only we can hear.

Calder—Eighty years old

Her gentle face lies next to mine, pillow caressing her head. She's so fucking tired. My baby held on for so long, waiting until every one of *her* babies made it home to say goodbye.

Always my brave girl.

She's always been the strong one our entire lives together. And last year, when the doctor told her she had six months, she smiled at me, smoothing tears over my wrinkles, saying, "Don't you be sad. It's better this way. Now I can make sure they let you into heaven."

But I'd sell my soul for one more second with her. Just one more. One lifetime isn't enough.

"Baby," I whisper as I stare at her peaceful face.

Sutton left me only a moment ago, body stilling as she released her last sweet breath like she was giving me her soul to keep.

"Dad."

My name comes from behind me, but I'm not leaving my girl. I'm going to lie here until God takes me too.

"Just leave him. Let him grieve, West," Saoirse says.

The door quietly shuts as I run my shaky hand down her long hair that used to be red, now silver. My eyes close as I lean in, kissing her lips one last time.

"I promised you all those years ago that we'd go together so we'd never be apart."

My chest shakes as I take her still-warm hand in mine, doing the thing I swore I'd never do again. I pray.

"Our Father, who art in heaven. Hallowed be thy name."

I see her in my mind, smiling, running through the field as I chase her. So beautiful, so alive, and so filled with love.

"Thy kingdom come. Thy will be done. On Earth as it is in heaven—"

A pain shoots through my chest as my mouth opens. I gasp feebly for air, tears falling from the creases of my eyes.

My eyes close, body sinking into the mattress as I exhale.

Sutton.

Her name is all I can feel. But I can't open my eyes. Everything inside of me pulls to a surface I can't see, but I dig my heels in, fighting it like I'm holding myself down.

"He's not breathing," I hear somewhere in the distance, but I turn my back.

Baby.

Suddenly, warmth fills my body as my eyes finally blink open.

Sutton looks up at me, eyes so green, red hair blowing in the wind. She looks exactly how she did the day I first kissed her. I look around as she laces her hands through mine, bringing them to her lips, pressing kisses to the palms before she looks up at me.

We're in our field.

My eyes drop to hers as the edges around us blur, and she smiles.

"You're here."

I cradle her face, bringing my lips to hers, feeling warmth on her lips, almost tasting the sun.

"Not even in death, baby."

The *never* End to a kind of love story we all deserve.

Acknowledgments

Gretchen Eddy. Jennifer Mirabelli. Katie Friend. Amanda Kay Anderson. Erica Russikoff.

Those are my acknowledgements. When I tell you that the process of writing is hard, it's grueling. It humbles in ways most could not handle—me included. But these women held me up, reminded me I was badass, sometimes told me "You're better than that." Because, Yeah I am. They pushed me to write the best possible story.

I love you guys forever.

Also thanks to Sandra from One Love and Ellie McLove , Sarah Plocher, and Rumi Khan for the countless hours and dropping everything they were doing to edit because I decided to change the whole end of the book. You legit held me down.

Thank you to everyone that read this story, bloggers, crew, readers...and whether you loved it or not, it means something to me that you took the time to pick up something I created.

Xoxo —T

About the Author

#1 Amazon and USA TODAY Bestselling Author, Trilina Pucci, loves cupcakes and bourbon.

When she isn't writing steamy love stories, she can be found devouring Netflix with her husband, Anthony, and their three kiddos. Pucci's journey into writing started impulsively. She wanted to check off a box on her bucket list, but what began as wish fulfillment has become incredibly fulfilling. Now she can't see her life without her characters, her readers, and this community.

She's known for being a trope-defier, writing outside of the box and creating fictional worlds her readers never want to leave. With every book and each character, she's committed to writing rebellious romance with heart.

Connect with Trilina and stay up to date.

just like heaven/sinning like hell

2021 © Trilina Pucci Books LLC

Cover Design: Ashes and Vellichor

Editing/Proofing: One Love Editing, Erica's Edits, My Brother's Editor, All-Encompassing, Rumi Khan

Ingram Content Group UK Ltd.
Milton Keynes UK
UKHW020359210623
423783UK00006B/63

9 781960 842022